The Summer Daughter

Books by Colleen French

THE SUMMER I FOUND MYSELF

THE SUMMER DAUGHTER

Published by Kensington Publishing Corp.

The Summer Daughter

COLLEEN FRENCH

KENSINGTON
PUBLISHING CORP.

www.kensingtonbooks.com

KENSINGTON BOOKS are published by
Kensington Publishing Corp.
119 West 40th Street
New York, NY 10018

All Kensington titles, imprints, and distributed lines are available at special quantity discounts for bulk purchases for sales promotion, premiums, fund-raising, educational, or institutional use.

This book is a work of fiction. Names, characters, businesses, organizations, places, events, and incidents either are the product of the author's imagination or are used fictitiously. Any resemblance to actual persons, living or dead, events, or locales is entirely coincidental.

To the extent that the image or images on the cover of this book depict a person or persons, such person or persons are merely models, and are not intended to portray any character or characters featured in the book.

Special book excerpts or customized printings can also be created to fit specific needs. For details, write or phone the office of the Kensington Sales Manager: Kensington Publishing Corp., 119 West 40th Street, New York, NY 10018. Attn. Sales Department. Phone: 1-800-221-2647.

The K logo is a trademark of Kensington Publishing Corp.

ISBN: 978-1-4967-2965-1 (ebook)

ISBN: 978-1-4967-2964-4

First Kensington Trade Paperback Printing: June 2022

10 9 8 7 6 5 4 3 2 1

Printed in the United States of America

CHAPTER 1

Her uterus?

Natalie stood on the sidewalk, trying to get her bearings as she shoved on her sunglasses so no one would see she was tearing up. Her gynecologist wanted *her uterus?*

When Dr. Larson gave Natalie the news, she was as blasé in her delivery as she would have been predicting the weather. Sunny today, with a high of seventy-nine and a chance of a hysterectomy. By nothing short of an act of God, Natalie managed not to embarrass herself in the doctor's office by melting onto the floor in a puddle of blubbering tears. She stopped at the front desk, made her next appointment, and walked out of the building without anyone knowing how devastated she was by the news.

But now that she was outside, her vision was so blurry that she couldn't see her car. Realizing her sunglasses were dirty, she pushed them onto her head, saw where she'd parked, and made a beeline for her Subaru wagon.

She couldn't have a hysterectomy.

She was only thirty-eight. Only old women had hysterectomies, old, shriveled-up women who no longer enjoyed sex. She wasn't old. Not yet. And she certainly still enjoyed sex.

At the car, she fumbled for her keys in the outside pocket of her handbag where she always put them so she wouldn't have to look for them. At least she always had good intentions of putting them there.

No keys.

She groaned and dug into the cavernous main compartment that desperately needed an intervention. She found her wallet, a sunglass case, a bottle of Advil. *No keys.* She dug deeper into the abyss: a bottle of nail polish, a receipt, a nest of lip balms and lipsticks, and what felt like a single peanut butter cheese cracker. Minus the wrapper.

She had a loose cracker in her bag, but no keys?

Her mascara was beginning to sting her eyes. The keys had to be there. How else would she have driven to the appointment?

Then, just when she was about to dump the whole bag onto the pavement, her finger touched something hard and rectangular. Her key fob, at last.

The funny, not so funny, part about the missing keys was that this wasn't even the first time she'd had to search for them that day. She'd spent ten minutes looking for them at home, making her late for the appointment. *After* she'd walked around the block twice, looking for the family dog that had some sort of canine ESP.

Winston always knew when she was in a hurry and didn't have time to chase him. That was when he managed to dig under the fence or, as in this case, squeeze out the front door as she opened it to grab a package on the front porch. When she hadn't been able to find Winston, she'd said a silent prayer to the Virgin Mary—not sure who the patron saint of naughty dogs was—and left for the doctor's office. After she found her keys under a pile of mail. With any luck, the corgi would be in the backyard waiting for her to let him in when she got home. When he escaped and no one could find him, he always managed to find his way back into the yard when his junket was complete.

Her eyes still stinging, Natalie hit a button on her key fob to unlock the car. The Subaru beeped twice, locking the locked car. *Wrong button.* She tried again. This time the doors unlocked and she climbed into the front seat.

Her tears began to flow in earnest as she started the engine and set the air conditioner on high, redirecting the vents so cold air blasted her sweaty face. It was the last weekend of May and only seventy-nine degrees, according to the dashboard. It felt like it was a hundred and seven.

She reached into her bag again and came up with her cell on the third try. She plugged it in because it was down to seven percent battery and hit a button on her steering wheel. "Call Laney," she said, sliding her fingerprint-ridden Ray-Bans back on her face.

"Calling Kip Blaney," the car responded in the Australia accent her ten-year-old had programmed. She hated that accent. Not because she had an issue with Australian pronunciation, but because it was a fake one and poorly done at that. She'd meant to ask him to change it.

"No! Cancel! Not Kip Blaney! Cancel!" Natalie shouted, tapping the steering wheel to terminate the call. She tried it again. "Call Laney!" she enunciated. "My sister, not the GD school principal!" she added under her breath so the car wouldn't hear her.

Thankfully, the call to her son's elementary school did not go through. Her sister picked up on the second ring.

"Hey, Nat. How'd the appointment go?" They had talked about Natalie's enormous fibroids and the possible solutions the night before. For the hundredth time, at least.

Natalie sniffed and searched for a pack of tissues in the console. "You with a client?"

"Nope. Slow day. It's a good thing we went to summer

hours because I'm not going to be able to afford to keep the lights on, it's so dead here. As soon as the weather gets warm, pets apparently don't get sick or need immunizations. My next appointment isn't for half an hour. What did Pixie Patty say?"

That's what they called their gynecologist, who had such perfect bone structure that at sixty years old she still looked amazing in an ultra-short haircut. Laney had assigned the nickname. She had cute names for everyone.

Natalie wiped her nose with a linty tissue. "She says I need a hysterectomy."

Laney took a moment to respond. She sounded like she was eating. "I've been saying that for two years." Her mouth was definitely full.

"But you're not a gynecologist," Natalie countered. "You're not even a people doctor."

"Meh. There's a lot more crossover than you think. Especially if you're a pig."

No matter how dark the sky was, Laney was always positive. It was one of the zillion reasons why Natalie's sister had been her best friend in the world since she was three and Laney was six.

"She said I was a pig, too." Natalie grimaced, listened to her sister chew. *"What are you eating?"*

"She called you a pig? That doesn't sound like Pixie Patty." Laney took another bite. "Yogurt with chia seeds and peanut butter granola," she said, her mouth full.

Natalie leaned back, shifting in the seat. She'd worn a short denim skirt instead of cropped pants. As if the short skirt would make her younger, her uterus any less fibrous. Big mistake, the cute skirt. Her sweaty thighs were sticking to the leather of the car seat. "You eat chia seeds in yogurt? Ew."

"Not again I won't. I feel like they're stuck in my teeth. Sexy Sam's bringing Chichi in this afternoon for an ear check," Laney said. "He's not going to ask me to marry him if I have black seeds that look like bugs between my teeth."

"You said you're never getting married and I don't think he's divorced from his last wife yet, Lane."

"So maybe he'll just ask me to have hot sex for hours with him. He's definitely separated. I saw his ex, or soon-to-be, on the boardwalk holding hands with Toothy Tim. Remember I told you I ran into him at The Frog Pond? He's an attorney. Just joined Button, Button, and Boob."

The legal firm was Button, Button, and *Boon*, but Natalie didn't correct her. Instead, she adjusted her sunglasses that had slid down her sweaty nose again and looped the conversation back to her current crisis. "Pixie Patty said I need a hysterectomy, *and* I need to lose fifteen pounds. *At least* fifteen."

"Nat, *are you crying*?" her sister asked in disbelief.

"I can't have a hysterectomy," Natalie blubbered. "Who will I be, then?"

"Who will you *be*?" Laney repeated, though with an entirely different tone. One of mystification. She thought Natalie was being ridiculous. Which had felt like a common theme lately.

"If . . . if I don't have a uterus, how can I be a wife?" Natalie tried to choke back her tears. She *was* being ridiculous. She knew that, but she couldn't help herself. "How can I be a mother?" she whispered.

"Oh, sweetie." Laney's voice softened. "You don't need a uterus to be a mother or a wife. You have two amazing children. What do you need a uterus for?"

"Easy for you to say. You still have yours."

"Nat, I'm confused. You and Conor decided you weren't having any more children after Mason was born. Conor got fixed years ago, didn't he?"

Natalie leaned forward, pressing her sweaty forehead to the steering wheel. "A vasectomy can be reversed."

"What did you say? Sorry, honey. I didn't catch that last bit."

Natalie lifted her head from the steering wheel so her voice wasn't muffled. As she did it, she caught a glimpse of the time on the dashboard. "Oh, GD! I'm late."

"Late for what? I wish you'd learn to swear properly." From the sounds she was making, Laney was sipping from her water bottle now. Probably to get the chia seeds/bugs out of her teeth.

Natalie grabbed the snotty, linty tissue and wiped her nose again. "To pick up Lady Voldemort." Her nickname for her daughter, not Laney's. Laney hadn't read the first three books in the Harry Potter series aloud to a son too young to read them on his own. Laney had never read the books. Only seen the movies.

"That's right. Her first day at the new job. I hope she had a good one." Laney took another swig of water. "You better get off the phone. If you have a fender bender, you'll be even later."

"When have I ever had a fender bender?" Natalie fastened her seat belt.

"That time you backed out at the market into the mayor's husband's new pickup."

"That was his fault." Natalie sniffed, forcing herself to focus on backing out without hitting anyone. "He was driving too fast for a parking lot. Hey, can you check on Nana on your way home? I'm not sure I'm up to it today and I already skipped yesterday."

"I can, but Mom said we didn't need to go every day. I don't know if Nana cares when we come or not. Half the time, she thinks it's 1941 and Pearl Harbor has just been bombed."

"I know," Natalie said. "But I still feel bad about putting her in that place. The least I can do is go see her a couple of times a week."

Two years ago their mother had put her then ninety-six-year-old stepmother in an assisted living facility, but a few months ago the staff had recommended that Nana transfer to a nursing home with a memory care unit. She'd just moved to the new facility three months earlier and was still resisting the change. And with their parents living in Arizona, it was up to Laney and Natalie to facilitate their grandmother's care and visit her. Their mother flew east every three months or so to visit. She had always had a complicated relationship with her stepmother because her father had married her three months after his first wife's death, but Natalie and Laney had never held that against Nana. She was the only grandmother they had ever known. And lucky for them, their mother had never tried to impose her own feelings on her daughters.

Natalie heard Laney speak, but her voice was muted. It sounded like she was talking to someone in her office. Something about a dislocated hip. She was back on the phone a moment later. "I gotta run. I've told the Cartwrights they can't let Ludwig jump off the couch anymore. He's too old and too fat. Apparently, they didn't heed my warning because they're on their way in for an emergency appointment. Call me later. And don't worry, Nat," she added, upbeat. "You don't need your uterus to be a mother to the kids nor a wife to Conor. More importantly, you don't need it to be who you are. The little sister I love and adore."

Natalie smiled. "Love you, too. Talk later." She ended the call and pulled out of the parking lot and onto Route 1. As she maneuvered around minivans and SUVs with out-of-state plates, the first vacationers of the summer season to their little beach town, she contemplated how she would tell Conor about the hysterectomy. Did she address the subject matter-of-factly, Pixie Patty–style, or did she throw her arms around him and have a good cry, Natalie-style?

Either way, she knew her smart, handsome husband, who was wicked at competitive darts, would accept either approach with his usual good-humored, kindhearted words of soothing encouragement. But what would he think later when they were through the details and had moved on to whether Mason was going to space camp in August and what they were having for dinner because nothing had been thawed out? Conor would *say* the right things, but later would he lament the loss of a wife able to bear him children? Would he wish he'd married a woman ten years his junior instead of three? How would he take the finality that once she had the surgery, there would be no more children?

Tears slipped down Natalie's cheeks, and she blinked, breathing deeply as she turned off the highway, onto Albany Avenue, the main drag through town. During the winter months Albany Beach was home to around sixteen hundred people, barely enough to keep the Irish pub she and Conor and his brothers had recently bought going, to more than twenty-five thousand in the summer. There wouldn't be an available parking spot on the avenue until September, and the lines in the grocery stores would be out the door on Saturday afternoons. Living in a resort community was an interesting dichotomy. Locals like her family needed the revenue the tourists brought in to feed their families and pay for hysterectomies, but every summer it felt like a foreign invasion.

For a moment, Natalie's mind had led her away from her medical crisis, but here she was again. Back to the hysterectomy. She pressed the brake and rolled to a stop behind a pickup truck with a hot-pink kayak in the bed and a bumper sticker that read:

> Love Is Love
> Science Is Real
> Black Lives Matter

That was one of the good things about being overrun by tourists every summer; the onslaught brought a wide range of people to their little town. In the summers, Albany Beach became a place where the political right and left and everyone in between ate pizza together. Their beaches were invaded by folks of every race, religion, and sexual orientation. Natalie and Conor liked living in a small town, but each summer they had the opportunity to expose their kids to the world as it was. At least the world they wanted their son and daughter to know.

Natalie gripped the steering wheel hard enough that her

hands cramped. She couldn't have a hysterectomy. If she had a hysterectomy, she would never have another child. Two would be it. She would never have the third child she had secretly longed for.

The child who would actually have been her fourth.

CHAPTER 2

Fifteen minutes later, Natalie was two blocks from the designated pickup spot off the boardwalk, but she hadn't moved more than ten car lengths in the last five minutes. She stared at the red light ahead, inching closer to the red Mustang convertible in front of her, hoping she'd make the next light.

It was Friday of Memorial Day weekend. She should have known she'd never be able to get across town by the time McKenzie got off work. She should have asked Conor to pick up their daughter, or better yet, she should have suggested to McKenzie that she walk the ten blocks home. But that would have turned into a whole thing with the teen protesting loudly as if she had been asked to trek across Siberia in below-zero temperatures rather than a few blocks on a warm, sunny day at the beach.

As Natalie waited for the light to change again, she grabbed another tissue and blotted her eyes, blew her nose. She didn't want McKenzie to know she'd been crying. Like most teenage girls, McKenzie could spot her mother's weaknesses from across a room and she knew how to take advantage of them. The girl was like a heat-seeking missile on autopilot—seek and destroy was always her mission when it came to Natalie. Or at least it had seemed like it the last two years. It had been the strangest, quickest transformation Natalie had ever seen in a human being. One night her sweet, relatively obedient, braces-wearing daughter had gone to bed with a smile on her face, and the next morning she woke with her head spinning, spewing negativity and anything that was remotely associated with added sugars.

Well . . . maybe it hadn't been quite that bad, but days like today it seemed like it. And Natalie wasn't up to sparring. Right now, all she wanted to do was go home and put on some elastic-waist gym shorts and one of Conor's big T-shirts, and pour herself a twenty-four-ounce tumbler of Pinot Grigio with a side of honey sriracha potato chips. The kids could scavenge for their own dinner. Conor had already said he wouldn't be home until nine or ten and would grab something at the pub.

The light turned green and Natalie hovered her foot over the gas pedal. "Come on, come on," she muttered. "Green is not sit behind the wheel and scroll through your Facebook page. Green is go."

The cars in front of her began to inch forward and she managed to make it through that light, passing the new family business on the right. O'Sullivan's wasn't actually new. Her husband's family had owned the pub for more than thirty years. But it was new to Natalie and Conor because they and his two brothers had recently purchased and taken over the operation of the bar/restaurant. Conor's parents had gone on a thirty-day cruise and settled into a life of leisure in Florida.

As Natalie approached the boardwalk that separated the street from the Atlantic Ocean, she scanned for an empty parking space. Which she knew she wouldn't be able to find. When she passed the designated pickup spot and didn't see McKenzie, she circled the block twice and then, in frustration, double-parked. Something she never did.

Fortunately, before Meter Peter, one of the two *meter maids* the city employed and the grumpier one, spotted her, McKenzie appeared.

Natalie watched as her daughter walked toward the car, long, wavy blond hair blowing in the sea breeze. She was dressed like every other teen in Albany Beach that day: too-short jean shorts, a T-shirt, flip-flops, and sunglasses. But she was prettier than the other girls in town, prettier and smarter. Maybe that wasn't true, but it was a mother's prerogative to think so. When McKenzie wasn't busy being a thorn in her mother's side, she was an A student and volunteered at the local animal shelter.

Reaching the car, McKenzie pulled on the door handle. It was locked. "Mom!" She rapped her knuckles on the glass.

Natalie hit the unlock button, and her daughter climbed in.

"You're double-parked," McKenzie observed.

"Not for long." Natalie signaled and nudged her way into the traffic, thankful the teen hadn't said anything about her Uber ride being late. Natalie hadn't told her she was going to the gynecologist. "Big day today. First day of your first real job. How did it go?" she asked, trying to sound upbeat.

McKenzie tugged on her seat belt, uncharacteristically animated. "It was amazing! I couldn't believe four hours went by so fast. It felt like I'd just clocked in and it was time to clock out."

Her daughter's enthusiasm took Natalie by surprise. McKenzie hadn't been all that excited about the idea of getting a summer job. It was Natalie and Conor who had decided that their about-to-turn-sixteen-year-old needed to start working, earning money of her own, and learning responsibility. They were hoping she might take the responsibility part more seriously from someone other than her parents, who made everything in her small world so perfect.

"It was?" Natalie asked, trying not to sound too pleased because expressing emotion of any kind was one of the things that could set her daughter off. McKenzie was allowed to laugh and cry in the same sentence, but she expected her parents, and Natalie in particular, to always remain stoic. There was no room at the kitchen table for anyone's emotions but McKenzie's.

"I worked with this girl, Isabella. She's new, too, but she's been working at Burke Brothers weekends for weeks. She's *trill*," McKenzie told her mother, clearly in awe.

"*Trill?*" Natalie repeated the word as she moved into the turn lane to get off the main street and out of the traffic. "I don't know what that means."

McKenzie exhaled loudly. "Trill. You know, true, real. She's so real, Mom. She's like smart and funny and so gorgeous. I feel like a troll standing next to her."

Pleased that McKenzie was talking to her in such a civil tone, Natalie decided not to ask why she would compare herself to a troll. Instead, she just listened.

"And Bella is so good with customers. And she knows how to do everything in the store. She showed me how to catch a hermit crab even when it doesn't want to be caught. And she can use the electric air pump to pump up rafts way better than Mr. Burke."

As they crossed Albany Avenue, Natalie spotted Conor and his youngest brother, Shay, on the sidewalk in front of the pub, staring up at the new O'Sullivan's sign that had been installed a week ago. Even though their father had Americanized their surname to Sullivan when he immigrated to the US, he'd named the pub in Albany Beach O'Sullivan's because it was good marketing. Customers, he had explained, expected an Irish name.

Natalie could tell they were still arguing over the sign's placement. Shay thought the gazillion dollar investment, made to look as if it were carved from a piece of wood, was crooked. Conor disagreed. The argument had been going on since the installment. They were too far away to hear her if she beeped the horn. Besides, Albany Beach wasn't the kind of place you used your horn unless it was absolutely necessary. They were too laid-back, too cool, possibly too *trill*, for beeping horns and cursing out the window at traffic offenders.

"Old Mr. Burke or young Mr. Burke?" Natalie asked. There were two generations of Burkes in the family business. The young Burkes lived one street over from them, and Mrs. Burke the Younger served on the library board with Natalie. She was the one who had offered to give McKenzie a summer job.

McKenzie made a face. "They're both old." She shook her head and went on. "Bella's blond just like me. That's what she told me to call her. Bella. Isn't that the best name? Why didn't you name me Isabella?" Fortunately for Natalie, the question was rhetorical. "Bella was wearing this green top that I have to have, Mom. She said she got it at the outlets. Do you think we can go tonight?"

"I thought you have to wear a Burke's T-shirt at work." She indicated the new yellow T-shirt advertising the five-and-dime she was wearing.

McKenzie rolled her eyes. "She wore her own shirt to work and then changed. Anyways. She got these leather flip-flops there, too. I have some money, but I might need to borrow a few dollars. Bella says the Burkes pay every Friday, so I could pay you back then. The Burkes don't care what we wear as long we're not showing butt cheeks or boobs. She said . . ."

As they made their way home, McKenzie went on extolling the virtues of her co-worker and Natalie contemplated what it would mean to be barren and to know she would never be able to replace the child she gave away.

CHAPTER 3

Natalie woke the following day to the sound of her son's voice. "Mom?" Not ready to start her day yet, she kept her eyes closed behind her silk eye mask. There was background noise, a buzzing she couldn't identify. If she didn't move, maybe Mason would think she was asleep and give her another five minutes.

"Dad, I think she's dead."

The buzzing stopped and Natalie heard her husband's voice. "She's not dead."

Natalie felt Mason lean over, breathing his ten-year-old morning breath on her. "Nah, she's definitely dead. Should I do CPR?"

The ten-year-old had recently declared his intended career—a doctor. He was trying to decide between a pediatrician, cardiologist, and ENT, of all things. Consequently, he was obsessed with anything related to medicine. He'd been disappointed when Natalie had been unable to sign him up for a CPR class because he wasn't twelve yet, but not to be discouraged, he learned on YouTube and had been hoping for weeks that someone would need CPR so he could practice.

"Probably not a good idea first thing in the morning, buddy," Conor said.

The buzzing began again. Stopped. Buzzed again. Natalie knew the sound, but still groggy, she couldn't quite place it. She had always been slow to wake, unlike Conor and Mason, who bounced out of bed, balls of energy.

Natalie had stayed up too late the previous night waiting for Conor to come home so she could tell him about the hysterectomy. Worrying about the surgery, about what it would mean to the family. What it meant to her. She'd also had too much wine, at least too much to go with her dinner of a bag of microwave popcorn and a Peppermint Patty she found in the freezer left over from Halloween. Twice Conor had texted to say he was about to leave the pub, then texted again to say it was a false alarm. She was asleep when he finally crawled into bed.

"You sure she's not dead, Dad?"

"I'm not dead." Natalie groaned and pushed the purple face mask onto her forehead.

"Tide's low. You said you'd take me skimboarding," Mason said eagerly.

Conor came out of the bathroom, bare-chested, in red boxer briefs, and she couldn't help but smile. He looked pretty good for a forty-one-year-old dad. He had his beard trimmer in his hand. The sound she had heard.

"Hey, sleepyhead." Conor leaned over and kissed her on the mouth. His breath was minty fresh.

"Mmm," she murmured. "Can I have more of that?"

"Sure." Conor leaned down for another kiss.

"Ga-ross," Mason moaned, heading for the door.

"Okay, skimboarding!" Natalie called after their son. She glanced at her phone in its charger on the bedside table. It was 7:45. "Give me like . . . half an hour?"

"N'kay. Dad made waffles for breakfast. I'm going to finish mine." Mason walked out.

"Let the dog out!" Natalie told him. As it turned out, Winston had not been run over by a car the previous day. He'd been waiting for her on the porch when she and McKenzie arrived home.

"How much will you pay me?" Mason hollered from the hallway.

"Just let the dog out!" Conor's two cents.

"And ask your sister if she wants to go with us," Natalie added as an afterthought.

"She's probably still asleep!" Mason, still hollering.

"Ask her anyway!" Natalie called. She knew McKenzie wouldn't go. She avoided any kind of family activities, especially when they were public. Likely fearing someone would embarrass her in some way.

Natalie listened to the sound of Mason's footsteps on the stairs and sat up, pushing hair from her face. "You made breakfast?" she asked Conor.

"Yup. Waffles and sausage. We're out of flour."

He stepped back into the master bath.

"You made them out-and-out? Not out of the box?"

"We were out of the mix."

Her first impulse was to ask him if he'd added either to the grocery list, but she already knew the answer. Months ago, she had set up a system throughout the house that would allow anyone to add items to the grocery list by a simple voice command. Only she and Mason used it and the only things he ever added to the shopping list were Maserati cars and baseball bats that cost in excess of two hundred dollars.

Natalie held her tongue on the grocery list. It was too early in the morning for petty bickering.

The beard trimmer hummed again; then she heard him turn it off and put it into a drawer. He was out of the bathroom a second later.

She watched him as he dressed, enjoying the reverse strip show. "What time did you get up?" she asked. "It was after one when you came to bed."

"Sorry about that. Got up at six. I had some documents to look over. Thinking about changing distributors for our microbrews. And we want to deal directly with Dogfish Head, which no one is happy about except our buddies at Dogfish."

He stepped into a pair of khaki cargo shorts, the kind that came to his knees and had lots of pockets. He added a new aqua-colored T-shirt that advertised O'Sullivan's. The color scheme had been a contentious topic of conversation for weeks. Not so much with the two of them, but with Conor and his brothers and her sister-in-law. Green and white were the obvious choices, but Beth had insisted that even if they used green and white in the pub and for advertising, the staff should wear beach colors in the summer. Their merchandise should be beach colors as well. She insisted they would sell far more that way. Beth was pregnant and cranky, so they all eventually acquiesced to her on the T-shirt colors. The aqua looked good with Conor's suntanned skin, dark hair, and blue eyes.

As Conor slid on his belt, he walked over to the side of the bed. "I'm probably going to be late tonight again. The new menu is wreaking havoc in the kitchen, bills are coming due and I want to look them over before you pay them, and—" He shook his head. "And I think we'll be busy, being Memorial Day weekend. It was sure as hell busy last night."

Natalie pushed off the sheet and drew her knees up, hugging them to her. She'd slept in one of his old T-shirts from a fun run in Rehoboth Beach years ago. "I was hoping we'd get some time to talk." She glanced at her bare toes. She needed a pedicure. "Something I wanted to talk to you about."

He dropped down on the bed, but she didn't look at him.

"Can it wait?" he asked.

She glanced up to see him checking his watch.

"It's just that I told Shay I'd help him stack the booze in the storeroom better," he explained. "Right now, you can hardly get in the door. I don't know what the hell Rory was thinking. He's supposed to be in charge of all of that. He knows how it's done. He worked for Dad for years. I don't know why he suddenly feels the need to reinvent the wheel."

Natalie pressed her lips together. She didn't want to get into a conversation this morning over Rory. Rory was the middle Sullivan brother between Conor and the youngest, Shay, but Rory was only fourteen months younger than Conor. She had always thought the youngest child in a family was the black sheep, but it was Rory in their case. In the time she had known him, he'd landed and lost more good jobs than she could count. He was constantly having money trouble and wanted to borrow from Conor, money he always swore he would pay back, though he rarely did. He was in the middle of a second ugly divorce and he had four children by three different women. Baby Mama Two had been the one to cause the first divorce and had become wife number two, soon-to-be Ex Two. Rory was currently dating Baby Mama Three, but word in the family was that she had just moved out of his condo. And taken his son with her.

When Natalie and Conor had decided to buy into the family business with his brothers, it was Rory she had been worried about. She and Conor had their entire savings and a big, take-your-breath-away loan riding on the pub continuing to be successful. They couldn't afford to have Rory ruin it. The problem was that despite the black sheep's questionable work ethic and personal relationship disasters, he was an amazing publican and front man for the bar. Whether he was bartending, carrying a plate of loaded fries to a table, or just greeting customers at the door when there was a waitlist, he was the kind of guy who brought the people in night after night, just to talk to him, to laugh with him. Everybody loved the guy. Except for his ex-wives and ex-girlfriends, and she couldn't help wondering how his sons and daughter would feel about him someday. He wasn't exactly an involved father. Didn't he realize what a precious gift a child was?

A lump rose in her throat and she had to fight not to tear up.

Rory was running around town making babies he didn't really want, and she would never have another child. How was that fair?

The only thing that makes life unfair is the delusion that it should be fair. One of her father's pithy sayings.

Conor took Natalie's hand in his. "You want me to stay home this morning, babe?"

She closed her eyes for a moment and then opened them, forcing a smile. The pub's success was so important to him. He'd given up his partnership in a CPA firm to make this life change. She wanted to be as supportive as she could and that meant not distracting him on one of the biggest weekends of the year. "Nope. Absolutely not. It's Memorial Day weekend. Game on." She threw her legs over the side of the bed and sat up beside him. "Go to work. Stay as long as you need to."

He looked into her eyes. He had the most gorgeous blue eyes of any man she had ever known. "Maybe date night Monday or Tuesday?" he asked.

She nodded firmly. "Absolutely."

"Kids okay?" He frowned. She could see the wheels of his brain turning as he tried to figure out what she wanted to talk about. "McKenzie's first day at work go all right?"

"Kids are fine. She had a great first day. So great that she offered to take someone else's shift tonight." She bumped her shoulder to his. "Go on. Go. Don't keep Shay waiting."

He pressed his hands to his legs to stand. "Kiss?"

She kissed him, and he rose, obviously eager to go. "I'll try to call you later. See you tonight," he said as he crossed the bedroom.

"See you tonight," she echoed.

Half an hour later, slathered in sunscreen with one cup of coffee down and another in a to-go cup, Natalie walked out onto the front porch of their turn-of-the-century two-story bungalow, her beach bag on her shoulder. Mason was waiting on the sidewalk singing some ridiculous song he'd learned on TikTok. McKenzie sat on the front steps wearing jean shorts and a teeny-tiny yellow bikini top that Natalie knew full well she hadn't purchased for her daughter. The triangles barely covered her nipples. Natalie wanted to order McKenzie to go back into the house and "put on something decent," as her mother used to say. Instead, she bit back the words, pleased McKenzie was going to grace them with her presence.

"All ready to go," Mason said, flipping his skateboard out of the flower bed. He wore a knee-length swimsuit, a neon-yellow rash guard, and one of his dad's old floppy bucket hats. She could see a smear of syrup on his sleeve, but she didn't say anything about it. He had a habit of using his clothing as a napkin. "I got your chair." He pointed to the beach chair leaning against the bottom step. "And the cooler bag has water and grapes."

Natalie glanced at McKenzie, who was busy texting. "He's certainly the organized one this morning."

"Father's child," McKenzie responded without looking up.

"Dog?" Natalie asked, sliding her sunglasses on.

"Fed, watered. Poop scooped in the yard." Mason saluted her.

"Where on earth did I ever find you?" Natalie asked, putting her arm around him.

He ducked his head, embarrassed, and slung his boogie board over his shoulder as he stepped onto the skateboard. "Want me to carry your chair?"

"I've got it. Thanks, sweetie. Your sister can carry my bag." She dropped it at McKenzie's feet. "But no skateboard today, Mason. It's a holiday weekend. People will be driving crazy, not paying attention to what they're doing, texting and such."

"And this weekend is different how?" McKenzie asked. She'd taken driver's ed and in a little over a month she'd have her graduated license, and suddenly she had a lot of opinions on how other people drove.

"I'm with you, Mom. No one's going to run me over," Mason complained. But as he argued with her, he returned the skateboard to its place under the azalea bush.

"Thank you." Natalie slung one strap of the backpack-style chair over her shoulder and took a sip of her coffee. She wrinkled her nose. In response to Pixie Patty's comment about her weight, she'd made her coffee black this morning the way Conor drank it. No half-and-half, no caramel-flavored syrup. It was disgusting, but she needed to learn to drink it this way because she had to have her caffeine fix in the morning.

Mason led the way down the sidewalk with Natalie behind him. McKenzie trailed, carrying the bag. It was only two blocks to the beach, and when they crossed the sand dunes Natalie had to stop and take in the view of the fine, white sand beach that stretched to the edge of the water.

It was a calm morning, and the blue-green waves lapped the shore more than crashed onto it. Even though there was no lifeguard on duty yet, the beach was already dotted with early-morning sunbathers. An equal number of unoccupied towels, blankets, chairs, and colorful umbrellas peppered the sand like multicolored sprinkles on ice cream. People staking their claims. Folks came out early in the morning after the sand machines had done their business, chose their spots for the day, set out their place cards, and then went back to their rental condos or off to find coffee. It was always amusing when visitors didn't check the tide chart and left their belongings in the path of the incoming tide. Towels, flip-flops, and sand toys, along with the occasional brand-spanking-new beach chair, were always being swept out to sea.

Because the tide was about to reverse and start coming in, they chose a spot in the dry sand, not the wet that would become wet again. Natalie set up her beach chair, McKenzie plopped down on a towel beside her, and Mason headed for the water.

"Hat!" Natalie called after him as she lowered herself into the chair that only sat a few inches off the sand.

He ran back, sailed his hat on the sand at her feet, and took off again.

Natalie slid her coffee cup into the drink holder and relaxed in her chair, digging her toes into the warm sand. She tried to relax for a moment and appreciate the beauty of the morning, her children's good health, and the fact that she really did have an amazing family life, an amazing life. She took a couple of deep, cleansing breaths and glanced at her daughter. Having McKenzie join them had been such a surprise; she didn't want to waste the few precious minutes she might have with the teen before she headed back to the house.

"Who you texting?" Natalie asked, knowing she was taking her chances asking such a question. Any question of her daughter, really. It was kind of like sticking her head into the lion's open mouth; she had a good chance of being bit.

McKenzie stretched out on her towel on her stomach and propped herself up on her elbows, her phone in her hand. She had removed her cutoff shorts to reveal a minuscule bikini bottom to match the minuscule top. Of course, she looked like a million bucks—she was fifteen-going-on-sixteen. She was tan and lithe with curves in all the right places. Beautiful too. And smart. She'd just been inducted into the National Honor Society, though she never studied, always procrastinated. McKenzie didn't know how to start a paper before 11:00 pm the night before it was due.

"Not texting."

As Natalie adjusted her wide-brimmed straw hat, she eyed the phone in her daughter's hand. She hadn't worn a bathing suit, just a pair of comfy gym shorts and a tank top because she didn't intend to go swimming. Not that she never swam in the ocean; she did. But not until July at the earliest. The water was too cold for her this early in the season. Wearing shorts instead of a bathing suit also meant Natalie hadn't had to shave her bikini line that morning. A big plus.

"Not texting?" Natalie echoed. "You *look* like you're texting."

McKenzie sighed. How a teen could sigh with such angst, Natalie didn't know.

"Mom." She drew out the word. "Snapchat."

"Mm." Natalie glanced up, scanning the expanse of blue for Mason. He was easy to spot in his neon-yellow rash guard. She watched him ride a wave in. He leaped up and waved, hollering something to her, but she couldn't make out what he was saying between the crash of the waves and the country music someone nearby was playing on the radio. Natalie smiled and waved as if she had heard him. It was a lesson she had learned from her mother: it wasn't necessary to hear every word your darling children uttered.

Natalie returned her attention to her daughter. "Okay, so who are you Snapchatting with?"

"Mom." McKenzie turned her head to look at her mother. She was wearing large orange sunglasses Natalie didn't recognize. "You don't *Snapchat with* people." She frowned and looked down at her phone again. "Bella is working the five-to-ten shift tonight, too. She said she could pick me up. We were going to go early and get Thrasher's fries before we start our shift. *She* has a car."

They'd been talking about cars for months. At least McKenzie had been talking about them. She spent hours looking at used vehicles on craigslist and Facebook Marketplace, as well as the local newspaper. She hadn't been able to decide if she wanted a Mustang convertible or a Jeep. Neither of which she was getting, of course.

Conor was of the mind to buy her an old clunker just to shut her up, but Natalie was holding firm. Their daughter didn't need a car until she was fully licensed. A car right now wouldn't do her any good anyway. Where was she going to park it, except in their driveway? Her graduated license would only allow her to drive with an adult in the car for the first six months, so she couldn't drive to work. And even if she *could* drive and *could* find a parking spot downtown, she'd have to feed the meter. And it was faster to walk.

Natalie stretched out her legs, checking on Mason again. He was out in the water, looking for the next decent wave. She looked down at McKenzie on the beach towel. "We've talked about this, Mac. I don't how I feel about you riding with someone I don't know."

"You said you didn't want me riding with sixteen-year-old boys you didn't know. Bella's not a boy, and she's eighteen!"

Eighteen? Natalie's first thought was why would an eighteen-year-old girl want to hang out with a fifteen-year-old? They were at an age that even a year made a big difference. "She still in high school?"

"Graduated. Well, done. Graduation is next weekend, but she's not walking. She says she's over high school." McKenzie's fingers were flying. The speed at which she could type on her phone was mind-boggling. "She's going to college in the fall. Well . . . maybe. Her parents want her to go, but she's thinking about a gap year. She's sick of school, you know?"

Natalie frowned. "I thought Snapchat limited the number of characters you could use. You're typing a lot."

"Now we're texting. Bella can pick me up right at four." McKenzie looked. "Please, Mom? She's a good driver, I promise."

"How do you know she's a good driver? You haven't been in a car with her, and you've known her less than twenty-four hours." Natalie glanced at the shoreline and felt a flutter of panic when she didn't see Mason. Where was he? He'd been right in front of them a minute ago. How far could he get in that amount of time—in a neon-yellow rash guard?

A second later she spotted him. He'd drifted south. She stood up, waiting for him to see her. When he hit the sand on his boogie board, she waved him over. He knew the rule. He had to stay in front of her. That way, they would know where to start looking for his body; that was what Conor always told him. The two of them always thought that was hysterical. Male humor.

Mason picked up his board and trotted back to where he'd originally entered the water, and Natalie sat down in her chair again.

"Please, Mom?" McKenzie asked, pulling her sunglasses off to look up at her. "I really want to ride to work with Bella. Mom, she is so nice. Do you know how hard it is to find someone my age who isn't a bitch or a loser?"

Natalie ignored the curse word. She rarely cursed. Not that she had a problem with it; it had just never been something she did. She didn't like her children cursing, but it was Conor's opinion that their kids would do it more if they got too worked up over it. Right now, Mason was enamored of the word "shit." Except that he always spelled it rather than said it outright, which Conor found hilarious. Her, not so much. But she and Conor were a team, and they parented together. This was an issue she was willing to bend on.

"Mom, you'd like Bella," McKenzie went on. "She's smart and funny and sooo gorgeous. She highlights her hair. What do you think?" She turned her head one way and then the other, posing. "Wouldn't I look good with highlights? Her hair's almost the same color as mine. I think mine would look good with highlights, don't you? Did I tell you that some lady buying a hermit crab for her grandson yesterday thought we were twins?" She laughed. "Twins! But if I highlighted my hair, I'd look more like her. Bella did it herself, so it wouldn't cost much. Like twenty bucks. And Bella says she'll help me do it. Bella does her own manicures, too. And I'm talking gel, not nail polish that chips off in an hour. She's got one of those light things that bake it on."

"We can talk about the highlights," Natalie said, pleasantly surprised that McKenzie was still talking to her. The teen didn't share much about her life or what was going in it. When she wasn't in school, she was with her friends or in her bedroom. Conor insisted it was the way teenage girls were supposed to behave and that he'd be more worried if she didn't hide from them.

"Can I tell Bella she can pick me up? Please, Mom? She's waiting for my answer."

Natalie was confused by a lot of aspects of social media. She didn't do social media except for Facebook and she rarely went on there. Her circle of friends and family was small, and she preferred to talk with them or see them in person. "She's waiting for your answer on Snapchat?"

McKenzie rolled her eyes. "*Text*, Mom. She's *texting*. Please . . . ?" She drew out that word. "Things suck at home for Bella. She's adopted. Did I tell you that? An only child. They adopted her when she was born. Can you imagine giving a baby away? The thing is, all her parents do is work. No one ever pays attention to her and she needs a friend right now. Please?? I told her . . ."

Natalie looked away, barely hearing McKenzie as she chattered on about her new friend. The word "adopted" had caught her off guard, and tears welled suddenly in her eyes. Once she had the hysterectomy, she'd never have another child. She'd never be able to replace the baby she had given up for adoption more than eighteen years ago. Not that she could *replace* the daughter she lost, but somehow, in her head, the idea that she *could* have another baby had made the loss bearable.

Natalie stared straight ahead, unseeing, as McKenzie went on exalting the virtues of her new friend, Bella.

McKenzie didn't know she'd given up a baby for adoption. Mason, either. The number of people who knew, Natalie could count on one hand: Conor, her parents, and her sister. No one else knew in the world . . . except the adoption agency and the adoptive parents, of course. But it had been a closed adoption. McKenzie never knew who took her baby, and the parents would never know who their daughter's birth mother had been.

Her precious baby that she'd only seen for a moment after seventeen hours of labor had been the result of a one-night stand in Paris. It had been her sophomore year at the University of Delaware. She hadn't been particularly promiscuous, not like some of her friends. It had only been the second time she ever had sex. She'd been young and foolish, that age when you still felt invincible. She met Sébastien at the café where he worked her second night in Paris. The café was just around the corner from the hotel where she stayed for winter term and he had been so sweet, his English as poor as her French. During the day, she attended a class on French literature, fortunately for her taught in English. But evenings she spent with Sébastien.

It was a whirlwind romance with neither having any notion of the relationship going beyond the three weeks she would be there. They walked for miles in Paris, taking in the local sights: the Eiffel Tower, the cathedral at Notre Dame, and the Arc de Triomphe. They walked the Pont Neuf bridge that crossed the Seine River, connecting the Right Bank to the Île de la Cité, and gazed out at the city from Belleville Park in the middle of the night. But they didn't just hit the touristy places. He took her to off-the-beaten-track bars and cafés and to the place where Louis XVI, Marie Antoinette, and Robespierre had been executed by guillotine. They laughed and talked about their greatest hopes and their worst fears. The handsome Sébastien, a struggling artist, was such a dreamy free spirit and so different from her that it only seemed natural she would be so enamored. Looking back, it was predictable that she'd end up in bed with him her last night in Paris.

What had not been predictable was that she would become pregnant while on birth control pills. A month after returning to her dorm in Delaware, she stood in the bathroom crying, a positive pregnancy test in her hand. How could she be pregnant? She never missed a pill. She wanted to be a CPA, for heaven's sake; she never played the odds. Laney, the first person she told, had been so kind to her but also realistic. No birth control was foolproof. It happened.

Natalie's parents had been surprisingly supportive through the entire nightmare. Not once had they chastised her for having premarital sex, even though they'd never had sex with anyone but each other. "They'd done the deed at least twice," Laney always joked. But from day one, they had gently steered Natalie in the direction of adoption. They knew, probably better than Natalie had at the time, that there was no way she was ready to become a parent. She remained at school until the end of the semester without anyone there knowing she had gotten knocked up by a seventh-generation Parisian. She took the first semester of her junior year off, and when she returned to the university the following January no one there knew she'd had a baby girl the month before and given her away. A month after she returned to a dorm room, she met Conor.

"Okay," Natalie heard herself say as she reached into her beach bag for the book she was reading.

McKenzie was still talking. "I promise we'll go straight to the boardwalk. Bella knows a secret place to park that—"

"I said okay," Natalie repeated, interrupting her daughter. "You can ride to work with Bella."

"I can?" McKenzie stared at her.

Natalie flipped through the paperback, looking for where she'd left off. "But no drive-by. I want to meet this paragon called Bella before you go anywhere with her."

CHAPTER 4

At 3:55 that afternoon, McKenzie squealed and leaped off a stool at the kitchen island. "She's here! Red RAV4!" She grabbed her phone and raced, barefoot, out of the kitchen. "We've got to go so we have time to park and have fries and get to work on time. If you want to meet her, you have to come now!" she hollered over her shoulder as she ran.

Natalie pulled off the hot-pink kitchen gloves the kids had given her as a joke the previous Mother's Day and tossed them on the counter. She'd been trying to clean her cast-iron Dutch oven that Mason had burned popcorn in. She had no idea why he thought using the most expensive pot in the house was a good idea. She probably should have made him clean it, but she was afraid he would only make it worse, scratching the finish, scrubbing it with steel wool or something worse.

"Mom!" McKenzie yelled from the front of the house. "Have you seen my green flip-flops? They were right here by the front door!"

Natalie walked out of the kitchen. "You look in the shoe bins?" She pointed as she entered the front hall. A few weeks ago, she'd bought a cool turn-of-the-century coatrack that had a bench to sit on. Beneath it had been room for two storage cubes. The kids were supposed to put their shoes in the cubes rather than leaving them piled by the door. "Your cube?"

McKenzie groaned and yanked out her cube. Sure enough, she came up with said green flip-flops. "I didn't put them in there."

"Probably not," Natalie said dryly.

Sliding into the sandals, McKenzie yanked open the front door. Before she stepped out on the porch, she whipped around. "No interrogation, please, Mom?" she begged.

Natalie drew her head back. "What do you mean, 'interrogation'?"

"You can't ask Bella where her parents went to undergrad or what she wants to major in or anything nosy like that."

Natalie opened her arms. "I can't ask what she wants to major in? That's supposed to be something you ask high school graduates."

McKenzie gave her a look, the kind that could potentially shoot laser beams at her mother. "Please. I really like her and I don't want to scare her off."

Natalie started walking, and McKenzie cut in front of her to keep her from reaching the car idling on the street before she did.

"Please, Mom," the teen begged under her breath.

"Wait. Let me be sure I'm clear on this. I can't ask the first day of her last menstrual period?" Natalie deadpanned. Her theory was that, once in a while, you had to have a little fun with your kids at their expense. Otherwise, you'd abandon them at a rest stop on I-95 before they reached adulthood.

McKenzie whipped around again. "Mom, *please.*"

It was a tortured whisper this time, and Natalie took pity on her. "Fine. I'll save my interrogation for another day."

At the car, McKenzie opened the passenger side door. "Hey!" she said, as sweet and pleasant as she had ever been in her life. She dropped into the leather seat. It was a nice car and looked brand-new. Not the Maserati McKenzie and Mason discussed when they were actually speaking to each other, but a darned nice car for a high school graduate.

"Bella, my mom." McKenzie pointed at her friend behind the wheel. "Bella. Happy now?" she directed to Natalie. "We have to go, or we're not going to have time to eat."

Natalie leaned down to get a better look at the teenager and froze. For a moment, she lost her equilibrium and reached out to rest her hand on the car to steady herself.

At first glance, Bella could have been McKenzie's doppelgänger.

"Let me shut the door, Mom." McKenzie's hand was on the door handle.

"Hi, Mac's mom." Bella lowered her head to look up at Natalie. "Thanks for letting her ride with me. I swear I'm a good driver. Not a single speeding ticket or accident. Well, some ding-head backed into my old car with his pickup in the school parking lot, but that doesn't count, right? I was in Calculus taking an exam when it happened." She grinned. "Got an A, but I got two wrong. Chain rule for derivatives."

Natalie stepped out of the way to let McKenzie close the door as she tried to think of something to say to Bella.

Isabella had the same thick, slightly wavy blond hair as McKenzie, just lighter because of the highlights. She had the same jawline, the same cheekbones, and she moved like McKenzie. Natalie couldn't tell what color eyes she had because she was wearing big sunglasses that looked just like the pair McKenzie was now wearing, only Bella's frames were clear.

"It's . . . nice to meet you," Natalie heard herself say. By all indications from her daughter, she was acting normal enough. But nothing felt normal here. She felt the way Alice must have when she fell down the rabbit hole. Suddenly her world had tilted, and she had come face-to-face with inexplicable unknowns.

Natalie wondered what color eyes Bella had. Were they

green like hers and McKenzie's? She wanted to ask her to take her glasses off, but of course she didn't dare. "It's nice of you to give McKenzie a ride," she said as she did the math. Bella was eighteen years old with a December birthday. McKenzie had said that Bella turned eighteen in December. Eighteen years ago, this past December, Natalie had given up her newborn baby.

Was Isabella her long-lost daughter?

"Summer hours now. We close at ten," McKenzie said, fastening her seat belt. "Bella will bring me home, so you or Dad don't have to come for me."

"Okay," Natalie mumbled. She forced a smile. "See you tonight."

"Nice to meet you, Mrs. Sullivan," Bella said cheerfully as she shifted the car into drive.

Natalie stood there hugging herself as the girls pulled away from the curb. She watched until they came to a full stop at the stop sign at the end of the block and turned right out of sight.

Natalie walked back to the front door and opened it. Out of the corner of her eye, she spotted Winston as she pulled her cell from her pocket and chose her sister's name from her favorites. The phone rang, and she got Laney's voice mail.

Natalie didn't leave a lengthy message. All she said was, "Can you walk?" As she disconnected, the dog slipped out the door and raced across the lawn. She didn't bother calling him. He wouldn't come to her, not once he got a taste of freedom. He'd run through the neighbors' yards, chase squirrels until he ready to go home, and he wouldn't be back a moment sooner. Instead, she sat down on the top step and waited for Laney and the dog to come to her.

CHAPTER 5

Less than an hour later, Natalie and Laney were walking side by side on a jogging path in the local park. They preferred walking on the beach, but on a holiday weekend it would be too crowded. They'd spend their entire hour circumnavigating people and ducking wayward Frisbees.

"I thought we weren't walking until after the holiday weekend," Laney said. They had talked a second time the day before, rehashing Natalie's impending hysterectomy. During the conversation, Natalie had asked if they could go back to walking every day. She had to lose that weight somehow.

Laney looked cute, as usual. She was wearing a pair of tangerine nothing-left-to-the-imagination yoga shorts and a matching tank top. Sans bra. She had never breastfed a baby or had children. Didn't want them. So, naturally, her breasts were still as perky as they had been when she was sixteen. She wore blue sneakers that had an orange stripe the same color as her shorts. Natalie wore an old pair of shorts made from sweat-shirt material and a baggy T-shirt. Her sneakers were splattered the same color as the master bath she had painted the winter before. She wasn't cute, but at least she was comfortable.

The tight workout tanks Laney wore all the time didn't look comfortable.

"I needed to talk to you. McKenzie made a new friend at work. Isabella. *Bella*. She picked McKenzie up a little while ago. They were going for Thrasher's fries and then to work the evening shift."

"That's nice." Laney pumped her arms as she walked. "Nice name, Bella. Some guy I once dated had a cat named Bella." She worked her mouth thoughtfully. "A big, fluffy, gray cat. His name was Fred, I think. No . . . Maybe that was Hugo."

Natalie would have asked her if Fred was the cat or the guy in ordinary circumstances, but she didn't want the conversation to go off on a tangent. They both tended to do that. It made Conor crazy. He'd ask if Natalie and Laney wanted grilled burgers or chicken for dinner, and they'd end up talking about the best Birkenstock styles. And not having answered the question.

"Lane, Bella looks just like McKenzie. And I know what you're going to say. It's my imagination. But McKenzie said someone at the store thought they were twins. Almost the same color hair. Same height, same weight. Same cheekbones," she said, a little out of breath. Her sister liked to walk at a grueling pace.

"I'm glad she made a new friend. Summer jobs are always more fun when you have someone to talk to and make fun of the other employees with."

A nice-looking guy in his forties jogged past them, going in the opposite direction, and Laney slowed down. "He's cute," she said, watching him pass them.

Natalie grabbed her sister's arm, propelling her forward. "Probably only here for the weekend."

Laney looked over her shoulder. "I can live with that."

Natalie exhaled and walked faster. "Lane, Bella is eighteen."

"You think McKenzie's too young to have a friend who's eighteen? Nat, I know you don't think so, but your daughter is mature for her age." She tilted her head to one side and then the other. "Most of the time. And this girl is just a work friend, not a *friend* friend, right?"

Two joggers passed them from behind. They were both very tanned and wore matching lavender running shorts. Natalie waited until they were ahead of them before she spoke again. "Did you hear what I just said?" Suddenly out of breath and feeling a little dizzy, she stopped and rested her hands on her hips, leaning forward. "Laney. She's eighteen years old. *Eighteen in December.*"

A bicyclist with a dog on a leash rang his bell, and Laney grabbed the hem of Natalie's T-shirt and pulled her off the jogging path, halting. "So?"

Natalie stood up, nose-to-nose with her sister. Laney was an inch taller and two sizes smaller. "She turned eighteen in December, and she looks like McKenzie." She pulled off her sunglasses and opened her eyes wide, frustrated her sister was too busy ogling men to follow the conversation.

Laney shrugged. "And again, *so?* Come on, we haven't even done a mile yet. You said you wanted to walk three miles a day." She tried to move back on the path again, but Natalie grabbed her forearm.

"What if it's her?" Natalie asked, her voice cracking.

Laney shook her head, looking at Natalie like she was nuts. "What if she's *who*?"

Natalie shoved her glasses back onto her face, frustrated. Was Laney teasing? Because if she was, it wasn't funny. Or did she still really not get it? "The baby. My baby."

Laney started to laugh, then froze, staring at Natalie. "You're kidding, right?" She hesitated. "Oh shitty-shitty bang-bang. You're not."

Natalie pressed her lips together, willing herself not to cry. "Laney," she breathed. "She looks *just like* McKenzie. They could be twins if Bella weren't two years older."

"Sweetie." Laney threw her arms around her sister and hugged her. "That's not possible. They just look similar. All girls that age look similar. She can't be the baby. It would be too big a coincidence. Monumental."

Natalie clung to her. "I know. I know. I keep telling myself that, but you didn't see her."

Laney leaned back, looking into her face, her arms still around her. "The baby's adoptive parents were out-of-state, right?"

"I think the agency told me that. Or Mom, maybe. I don't remember. But what if they just said that to keep me from looking for her in every grocery store in Delaware?"

Laney let go of her and sighed. "Come on. Let's walk. You want to walk?"

Natalie blew out her breath and nodded.

They started on the path again, walking past the duck pond with a fountain in the middle. Everywhere around Natalie, people seemed happy. And what wasn't there to be happy about? They were on vacation. Sunburned couples walked hand in hand, laughing. A father was throwing a Frisbee to two kids while Mom set up a picnic under a big maple tree. A woman passed them, going in the opposite direction, pushing a double stroller. Twin babies, maybe six months old, slept in the stroller as if they didn't have a care in the world. Everything in the park seemed so normal, so idyllic. Neither of which Natalie felt.

"Okay," Laney said after they were quiet for a couple of minutes. "Let's think about this logically. It's too big of a coincidence to be true—McKenzie winding up selling hermit crabs in Albany Beach with her adopted-at-birth half sister. That's even too crazy for an episode of *Dr. Phil*." Natalie's sister had a weird affinity for reality shows. She watched reruns of *Dr. Phil* and regularly streamed *Hoarders* and whatever version of *Big Brother* was on MTV these days.

"It happens. Crazy coincidences happen," Natalie insisted. "What, what about the woman who survived the sinking of the *Britannic and* the *Titanic*? And, and then she was on the *Olympic* when it ran into a warship!"

Laney said nothing.

"And John Wilkes Booth's brother saved Lincoln's son from getting hit by a train." Natalie lengthened her stride to remain beside her sister. "And that sailor that was cannibalized had the same name as the character in Edgar Allan Poe's *The Narrative of Arthur Gordon Pym of Nantucket*. Who was cannibalized."

"How the hell do you know these things?" Laney picked up the pace, forcing Natalie to walk faster. "You were an accounting major, for Christ's sake. You read Amish romances. No one is being eaten on Amish farms."

"I Googled crazy coincidences. And my major was business admin; I had a minor in accounting."

Laney said nothing as they crossed the one-mile mark of their walk, indicated by a signpost.

"Think about it, Lane. What if Bella is my daughter?" Natalie said. She kept her voice down because . . . she didn't know why. In case someone knew her secret? A ridiculous idea. No one knew. Maybe it was a sign of reverence. Like when you spoke inside a church. Not that she spent a lot of time in church. She was a lapsed Catholic. She went to Mass with Conor when he asked her to, but his attendance had always been sporadic. When he went, it was mostly because his mother guilted him into it. And they never went in the summer. The local church was too crowded.

"Exactly," Laney said loudly. "What if she is?"

"*What?*" Suddenly Natalie was annoyed. Laney was her sister, her best friend in the world. Her confidante, her confessor. She was her emotional lifeline. She expected Laney, of all people, to be supportive. Or, at the very least, hear her out.

"Okay, let's just say, for the sake of argument, that Bella *is* the baby you put up for adoption?" Laney gestured with one hand. "So what, Nat?"

Natalie made a conscious effort not to shout. "*So what?*" she asked.

"Yes. Why would you want to know? Why are you even thinking about this? What are you going to do with the information?" Laney walked faster, pumping her arms. "It was a closed adoption, Nat. The baby you gave up for adoption at birth is not your child. And it was your idea to have a closed adoption for just this reason. You didn't want to know where she went or who she became."

Hurt by Laney's response, tears stung Natalie's eyes. This was the reaction she would expect from Conor. Not her sister. Which was why she had called Laney and not him.

"Why would you want to know?" Laney continued. "How will the information add anything to your life?"

"I'd know where she is. That she's okay. That she's happy," Natalie managed.

"And that's all you'd want?" She glanced at Natalie. "This is a slippery slope, you know. First you just want to know she's okay, next you want to talk to her, then meet her— you can't do any of those things, because she's not your child."

"I think you've already made it clear you believe that," Natalie murmured.

Laney ignored her. "That baby was no longer yours when she was the size of a button mushroom in your uterus and you made the decision to put her up for adoption. Which was the right decision then, and it's *still* the right decision. And all of that means you don't have a right to know."

"Don't lecture me." Tears welled in Natalie's eyes again.

"I'm not lecturing you, sweetie." Laney looked over at her; their pace had slowed again. "I'm trying to protect you. As well as the eighteen-year-old somewhere in the world you put up for adoption," she added. "Have you thought about that? About her? About Bella. And I'm not saying she is the child you gave for adoption. There's no way she is. I don't care who didn't go down on the *Titanic*. But McKenzie's friend is not her half sister. But what if she was? How would her parents feel about you knowing you were her birth parent? Living in the same town?"

"They're new to Albany Beach, I think."

"So now they have to move?" Laney demanded.

Natalie didn't reply.

"Nat," Laney went on, toning down her indignation. "They sought a closed adoption for the same reason you did. They didn't want to know who gave birth to their daughter, and they *didn't want her ever to know who her birth parents were.*"

Laney's last words hit Natalie hard, and she grew quiet, trying to focus on her stride and her breath that was coming hard again. A seagull flew overhead, squawking. It was a perfect June evening. The temperature was hovering at seventy-five, and there was the slightest breeze coming off the ocean. Even six blocks from the shore, she could smell the briny sea. "Can we slow down?" she asked.

"Nope. Sorry. This was your idea. Walking every day to get some exercise. We're committed, kid." Laney glanced at her, and her sweaty face softened. "You know I'm not trying to upset you, right?"

Natalie didn't say anything.

"I'm trying to protect you. And that teenage girl out there somewhere who's leading a happy, healthy life, who deserves to be protected not just by her adopted parents but by her birth mother as well. She's not yours anymore, Nat, but you still have to protect her. From yourself."

"You're right," Natalie said, shaking her head as if she could shake some sense into it. "Logically, I know you're right. And I know Conor would say the same thing."

"You didn't tell him? WTF?"

"Of course not. I always bounce my crazy off you first. You know that."

Laney turned and began to walk backward, facing Natalie. "What do you think this is all about? You haven't mentioned the baby, even in passing, in years. I can't even remember the last time we talked about her. You think this has to do with the hysterectomy? That, in your mind, this means you won't have any more children?"

"That is a fact, Lane. If . . . when I have this hysterectomy, that *will* be the end of my childbearing."

"But . . . you and Conor didn't want any more children. You said that after Mason was born, and you never wavered."

"Conor didn't want any more and I went along with it. But there have been times when I wish I hadn't. When I wished we had had just one more."

Laney turned around, falling back into step with Natalie. "What does Conor say about the surgery?"

Natalie exhaled. She was hot and sweaty and tired. All she wanted to do was go home, open a cold beer, and float around in the pool in the backyard and think about nothing. "I haven't talked to him about it. I tried to stay up last night to tell him about my doctor's appointment, but I fell asleep. He didn't get home until one. Then this morning, I didn't want to bother him. He's got enough on his mind right now with the official opening of the pub. Tonight he's got a radio station broadcasting from the outside deck."

"You need to talk to him about the hysterectomy." Two Rollerblading teens in short shorts flew by them. "I think you'll feel better after you do," Laney said. "And I think you'll feel better physically once you have the surgery. No more fibroids. No more heavy bleeding. No more iron infusions." When Natalie didn't respond, Laney went on. "It's time you started taking better care of yourself, physically and emotionally. You have a hunky, amazing husband who loves you and two bright, sweet kids. I know some days it might not seem like it, but they love you and they need you, Nat."

She was probably right. Natalie knew that. About everything. But that didn't make any of it any easier. She cut her eyes at her sister. "Want to jog a bit?"

Laney hesitated, and then when she realized the conservation was over she forced a smile, "Race you to that next marker." She pointed and then took off.

"Hey!" Natalie hollered, running after her. "Nobody said anything about racing!"

on, we talked about this, right? It's one of the things that makes us something different on the avenue. No reservations." He did a Groucho Marx thing with his eyebrows. "Lively waitstaff, a kick-ass menu, and good beer on tap and in the cooler. To enjoy back at the condo or take home to friends and family." He said it as if he were auditioning for a commercial.

Natalie laughed and they walked through the cool, low-lit main dining room that featured a huge polished walnut bar that ran twenty-five feet in length. Behind the bar was the standard enormous Guinness mirror and signs advertising Smithwick's beer and Jameson and Bushmills whiskey. The Bushmills was for the Protestants, the Sullivan boys liked to joke, because Jameson was distilled in county Cork and Bushmills in Northern Ireland. The whole idea of Catholic and Protestant whiskey was kind of silly and not an Irish thing, but more of an American Irish thing.

Several TVs were going, all playing Irish Rugby matches. The rugby playing twenty-four/seven had been Shay's idea. At first, Conor had thought it was cheesy, especially since the rugby season didn't even extend into the summer. But he had soon admitted that this brother had been right. The pub's patrons didn't seem to care if the games were reruns, even from years ago. They still hooted and hollered at the TV and ordered more beer.

"Our window seat?" Conor asked. "Or you want to sit at the bar?"

Natalie spotted Rory pushing through the half door that kept customers out from behind the bar. He was wearing an authentic Munster rugby jersey. "Window seat," she told Conor.

It wasn't that she didn't like Rory. She loved him like the brother she never had. He was a lovable guy, despite the hot mess of a personal life and finances, but he liked to be the center of every conversation. If she and Conor sat at the bar, she'd be sharing her uterine news with Rory and he'd have an opinion. He had an opinion about everything.

Rory spotted her as they walked by. "Nat!" he hollered, throwing up a hand in salute. "Nat the Brat!" *Shades of Laney.* She gave him a closed-mouth smile. She didn't like the nickname, but it was better than "Nat the Rat," which he also used on occasion.

Natalie slid onto the bench seat, making room for Conor next to her. They always sat next to each other when they went out. It was a habit they'd begun when they met at the University of Delaware, and they had agreed no matter how many kids they had, no matter how old and wrinkly they got, they would always sit beside each other. She was glad they had made that commitment so long ago because it made their now-infrequent date nights more intimate.

Conor slid in beside her and pushed a cardboard tented sign to the far side of the table. It read *Comhartha in áirithe* with the translation *Reserved* printed below it. Someone, likely Rory, had scrawled beneath it in red Sharpie: *4 sullivans only!!!!!*

"Beer? Wine? A froufrou martini?" Conor asked. "I think there's a clementine martini special this weekend." Their father had grown up in the family pub at a crossroads outside the city of Cork where Gaelic was still spoken in the home. That O'Sullivan's had never served much beyond beer and Irish whiskey, but once his sons took over his pub in the United States they had added a full bar menu to reach a broader customer base.

"Name your poison. I'll get it. Looks like the waitstaff is swamped." The place was packed, and the relief evident on his face as he looked around.

"A light beer?" she asked. She didn't like light beer, but the fifteen pounds wasn't going to come off on its own.

Conor made a face. "You're kidding, right?" The Sullivan brothers had only added Coors Light under duress. Their distributor had insisted they needed at least one light beer, telling them them sales numbers didn't lie.

She groaned. "Fine. An O'Hara's wheat. Tap," she added.

He rose. "Holy *shite*, I would hope so." He leaned over to kiss her, and they smacked lips. "Back in a sec."

"A small one!" she called after him, competing with the sounds of the TVs and the young couple sitting behind her arguing about who ate the last waffle that morning.

Natalie watched Conor walk away, letting her thoughts drift as she checked out the place, taking note of the changes Conor and his brothers had made to the family pub. The upgrade to hardwood floors and the fresh paint had been well-spent money, moving the pub from quaint to hip. Their father, Darrah, had always made a decent living running the pub, but his sons had agreed they would have to up their game to make the place profitable enough to support three families. And at the rate Rory was knocking up women, Shay had commented, they were going to have to make a hell of a lot of money just so he could keep up his child support payments.

The moment Conor reached the bar, Rory engaged him in conversation. Natalie hoped Conor wouldn't be too long. She had never been jealous, per se, of her husband's relationship with his brothers, but she had worked hard at that and never hesitated to speak up if she felt she was being kicked unfairly to the end of the line. And Conor was also good at making her a priority and being willing to talk about it when she—when either one of them—felt like their relationship was off-kilter. Conor's ability to express his emotions and talk about hard stuff was one of the things that had attracted her to him to begin with.

The fact that her nana had liked him had been what had pushed Natalie over the edge. Nana had never liked any of Natalie's boyfriends, nor had her father, come to think of it. Earlier in the day, Natalie had gone to visit her grandmother. Cora Lawson no longer always knew her granddaughters' names, but she remembered the boyfriend who was killed at Pearl Harbor and she talked often of the dates they went on in Baltimore when he was home on leave. Oddly, Nana didn't remember her husband, Natalie's grandfather. Edwin seemed to have been erased from her memory. Today Natalie and her nana had enjoyed iced tea in the gazebo on the nursing home property and talked about whether President Roosevelt intended to deal with the Japanese or the Nazis first. But then they'd also talked about her grandmother's medication and the elder woman had known exactly what she was taking and why. It was funny how the human mind worked, and what was lost and what remained when it didn't.

Out of the corner of her eye, Natalie spotted one of the waitstaff, green apron around her waist, wearing a white O'Sullivan's tee, approaching. She didn't recognize her, so she must have been one of the people they'd hired in the last two weeks.

"Sorry, but this table is reserved," the stranger said. Her tone was polite, but it was clear she meant business. "The owners."

Natalie smiled. "I'm Natalie. That Sullivan belongs to me." She pointed in the direction of the bar.

"Rory's girlfriend?" she asked, her voice going up at the end of the sentence.

"Other Sullivan. I'm Conor's wife. Natalie Sullivan. And technically, I'm also an owner. And an employee. I'm the comptroller. I work from home. Too much confusion here for me to run numbers. "

"Oh, sorry." She winced. "I didn't know. I'm Margot." She was pretty. Early thirties, maybe. Natalie's height, with a head of dark hair and nice cheekbones. She looked to have Native American in her family tree.

"It's okay." Natalie laughed. "How could you know?"

"Except that you were sitting at the Sullivan table," Margot said, pulling the sign off the table and setting it on one of the empty chairs. "You should fire me. I knew I wasn't going to be good at this."

"No one is going to fire you," Natalie said with a chuckle. "Unless, of course, you steal from the till or get drunk while you're on the clock."

Margot laughed. "You're funny like Conor. A funny family."

"Oh, he can be funny all right." She glanced in the direction of the bar. He had one beer in front of him, a tall stout, and it looked like Rory was pulling hers from the tap.

"Excuse me!" someone called from behind Margot. "Excuse me, miss. Can we get two more beers?"

Margot glanced over her shoulder, seeming torn as to what to do: chat up the boss's wife or see to the boss's livelihood.

"Miss?" the customer Natalie couldn't see called out again.

"Go," Natalie told her with a wave. "The guy needs a beer."

"You want me to get you something?" Margot asked.

"Conor's got it taken care of."

"Okay, well, it was nice to meet you."

"Nice to meet you, too. Have a good evening."

As Margot walked away from the table, Conor walked toward it.

"I just met Margot," she said.

"I see that." He set their beers down and slid onto the bench. "She seems nice. One of the new hires, I assume?"

"Yup. And this one has a head on her shoulders. She's been here a week and I already wish she was interested in a permanent position." He picked up his beer. "But this is just a summer gig for her. Recently divorced. No children. She's going back to school in September. Studying to be a physician's assistant. *Sláinte is táinte,*" he said—"health and wealth." He touched his glass to hers.

"*Sláinte,*" Natalie echoed.

They both took a sip of beer, and she reached over to wipe the foam from his mustache. He met her gaze. "You always take such good care of me," he told her.

His love for her was easy to see in his gorgeous blue eyes, and Natalie felt herself relax. Laney had insisted Conor was going to be fine about the hysterectomy, and she was right. Natalie knew that.

They ordered an appetizer, Guinness cheese pretzel bites

that were new on the menu. Then they talked for a couple of minutes about whether there should be different specials for each night in various categories like appetizer and main, or if they should change some specials nightly and some weekly. Natalie appreciated that he wanted her opinion, outside of his brothers', and, as always, she told him exactly what she thought, even when she wasn't in agreement with him.

When Margot brought over the pretzel bites and another beer for Conor, even though he hadn't asked for one, "How about you?" Margot asked Natalie, pointing to the half of a beer in front of her. "Ready for another?"

"No thanks." She smiled back at the waitress, impressed by her own determination to lose weight. She just wondered how long it would last.

"You want to order something else to eat?" Margot asked Conor.

"Nope. We've got dinner reservations. Checking out our competitors," he told her. He seemed very friendly with her, but Natalie paid it no mind. He was always like that—it was part of his personality. And as he had often reminded her, no matter how much fun he might have chatting with someone else, he always came home with her.

"Okay, give me a holler if you need something."

When she walked away, Conor sat back in the booth, casually resting his hand on Natalie's thigh. "Enough about work. You wanted to talk to me about something?"

Suddenly Natalie felt nervous. Which was ridiculous because Conor was the easiest person to talk to, even when what she had to say was a little nutty. It was his good luck that tonight she had nothing nutty to talk about. She certainly wasn't going to say anything about McKenzie's friend. Not yet, at least.

"My doctor's appointment." She shifted forward on the faux leather bench, wrapping her hands around her frosty glass. "Pixie Patty says it's time."

He shook his head. "Pixie Patty?"

"Dr. Larson. The hysterectomy." She looked at him. "I need to have surgery."

"Oh, sweetie. Come 'ere." Conor set down his beer and wrapped his arm around her. "Tell me what she said."

The sounds of the pub faded as Natalie talked. She told him about her worsening symptoms, not sparing him any of the gory details and how the surgery would resolve them, and why her gynecologist thought it was time. Conor listened, asking questions but letting her do most of the talking. He agreed with Pixie Patty and Laney that she needed to be proactive with her health. She held it together until he asked her why she was even hesitating, and then she began to cry. Not big, ugly cause-a-scene tears, just the kind that slid slowly down her cheeks. Tears of sadness.

Conor held her hand as she admitted she wasn't ready to go into menopause. That she wasn't ready to no longer be of childbearing age.

Conor kissed her cheek ever so sweetly. "But hon, we weren't going to have any more children anyway. We've got our girl and our boy. Perfect human specimens. We didn't want to press our luck. And we wanted to sleep in once in a while. I got a vasectomy to prove it."

She took a shuddering breath and glanced around, relieved to see that no one seemed to be paying them any attention. "I know, but—" She sniffed and sat up, reaching for his beer. She'd finished her own. "Logically, I know you're right. You're right. Pixie Patty is right. Laney is right." She threw up her free hand. "Laney is always right. But it's just the idea of it, you know?" She met his gaze, relieved they had finally had the opportunity to talk about this. "It's the fact that I won't quite . . . be a woman anymore. Does that make sense?"

"Sweetie, there's no way I can understand because I don't have any lady parts, but from my perspective, you're still going to be every bit of a woman without that uterus. You're my

Natalie, the woman I've loved, been in love with, since . . . forever. The woman who's the center of my life. And the idea that you won't be bleeding half to death every month? I'm totally on board."

She slid his mug onto the table, debating whether to order herself another beer. But then she'd have to add it to the calorie counter on her phone. And a second beer wasn't in the plan. She'd stayed up late the night before while Conor was here at the bar sorting through a mistake in an order one of the Sullivan boys had placed. No one would admit to it, so their guess was Rory. But instead of getting the milk, cheese, sour cream, and butter their chef had ordered, they received cases of pancake syrup, assorted jams, and rice wine vinegar. So while Conor was doing his magic, she was in bed researching diet tips and apps. Everyone said planning was key, especially when eating out. Planning what you're going to eat and then following through was imperative, according to nutritionists.

But did that count when you had to have surgery?

She didn't think so.

"You sure you don't want another?" Conor pointed at her empty glass. "We've got plenty," he teased.

She smiled, appreciating that he was trying to cheer her up, even if it was in his goofy guy way. "Nope. I'm going with a ginormous margarita on the rocks at Banditos."

"That's my girl." He grabbed his beer. "Anyway, about this surgery. I think you should have it, but this is your body we're talking about, Nat, not mine. So whatever your decision is, I'm on board."

She gave a sigh of relief, realizing that was all she needed to hear. That he supported her. Because she knew Pixie Patty and everyone else were right. It was time. "Thank you," she said.

He made a face. "For what?"

"I don't know. Not making fun of me. I know we decided we don't want more children. I don't really want another baby.

I'm way past that point in my life. I just . . . I guess I don't want to be old."

He laughed, but not unkindly. "I've got news for you, *mo grá*." He leaned toward her until his nose nearly touched hers and he took her hand in his big, warm one. "We're going to get old. I hope we get very old together, because the alternative?" He tilted his head, grimacing.

She stroked his cheek. She loved it when he used Gaelic words of endearment. Irish words—that's what his family called them. His mother and father had both grown up speaking Irish and neither had learned to speak English until they went to school. All three of their sons had been born in Delaware, but they had grown up bilingual, something unusual in Irish American families. And the Sullivans were proud of that. They all were.

"You know what?" she asked.

He grinned at her. "What, my beautiful, sexy wife?"

"I'm hungry." She grabbed her jean jacket. "And it's almost eight. If we don't get over there, someone else will get our table and my margarita. So down the hatch." She pointed to what was left of his beer and then shrugged. "Or leave it."

He cringed as if in horror. "That would be alcohol abuse."

"Then drink up." She eyed the bar, looking for her brother-in-law. "And let's roll, because if Rory comes over here the two of you will start talking and I'll still be sitting here at midnight."

"Drinking up," he told her, grabbing his beer. He looked over the rim of the mug as he chugged it.

She smiled at him, thinking how nearly perfect her life was. Then, she remembered Bella and McKenzie in the front seat of Bella's car. The similarities in their looks. *Was* it just a coincidence?

"Uh-oh. You better hurry," Conor intoned. "Because here he comes."

Natalie looked up to see Rory trying to get their attention. "Be there in a sec!" he hollered over the roar of the crowd on TV as Ireland scored over England. "Yes!" he screamed, pumping his fist, then banging on the bar top with the palm of his hand.

Conor met Natalie's gaze, and they both agreed without having to speak. He grabbed her hand, and they made a run for the use-only-in-case-of-emergency back door.

CHAPTER 7

The sound of Mason squealing with glee brought the column of numbers on Natalie's desktop monitor out of focus. She sighed, realizing she would have to go back over the entire page, and shifted her gaze to the view of the pool in the backyard. There, Mason, his cousin Patrick, and a boy from down the street were taking turns leaping off the diving board into a brightly colored inner tube. After attempting to catch a Frisbee midflight.

Seeing her nephew Patrick, Shay and Beth's son, looking so happy and healthy made her smile. Patrick had been diagnosed with a form of childhood leukemia three years before and had been a pretty sick kid before going into remission. Through the entire endeavor, Mason had stuck by his cousin's side, and now they were better friends than they had been before Patrick's illness.

Smiling to herself, Natalie shifted her gaze to her computer monitor again. The payroll numbers in front of her still seemed blurry and she reached for the diet soda. She'd been struggling to concentrate all afternoon, but instead of doing the payroll and studying the pub's overhead numbers, she kept thinking about Bella. Thoughts of the teenager drifted in her head like the flotsam washing onto the beach on the incoming tide.

Laney's question posed to Natale kept going through her head, like a ticker tape. It was often grayed out, but it was there whether she was brushing her teeth or fixing her nana's hair as she prepared for her date with her boyfriend who had died at the age of nineteen in 1941.

Did she want to know if Bella was her child?

She vacillated with the answer the way she did when trying to decide which pair of too-tight jean shorts she wanted to wear.

How could she not know if she wanted the truth?

Because as much as she hated to admit it, Laney was right. At least on some level. What *would* she do with the information? Of course, she would tell Conor. But would she tell Bella? Her children? The adoptive parents? Would she tell anyone? *Ever?*

She stared out the French doors that opened onto the patio. When they'd built the addition to the one-hundred-plus-year-old cottage four years ago, they'd designed it so they could easily keep an eye on the children while they were swimming. McKenzie had been safe to leave in the pool when they put it in, though they had a rule that no one could be on the deck without an adult home. However, this was the first summer that Mason was allowed in the water without an adult outside with him. After he had been swimming all winter on the swim team, Conor had declared their son could swim better than he could. In celebration, he had made a ceremony of tying a piece of plastic around Mason's wrist, signaling that the boy was old enough to swim semi-unsupervised, much the way the lifeguard did at their local YMCA. Mason had been so proud of the "bracelet" that he had worn the piece of trash for days until Natalie had insisted it was time to toss it.

Natalie watched Mason, who was tall for his age, run off the end of the diving board, pull his knees to his chest, and hit the surface of the water with an enormous splash. The neighbor boy immediately followed him. They had grown bored with the jump-through-the inner-tube game and were having a cannonball contest.

Natalie looked at the framed photo on her desk of McKenzie at six, holding newborn Mason in her arms on a couch, surrounded by pillows. Mason had looked so much like McKenzie when he was born that Natalie sometimes had to use cues from what else was in the photo to figure whether a baby was McKenzie or Mason.

Had McKenzie and Mason looked like her first little girl? Did her first baby look like her half brother and half sister?

Natalie had no memory of the baby other than the vague idea that the doctor had held her up so she could see her, before she was whisked away to the nursery. It had been Natalie's mother's idea that Natalie shouldn't hold the baby, who would be going home from the hospital with her adoptive parents. It had made complete sense at the time, even to Natalie, whose hormones were raging. Why hold a baby who would never be hers? It wasn't until Natalie held McKenzie for the first time and she felt that fierce, instantaneous love for the infant that Natalie fully understood her mother's advice. Had she held her first daughter in her arms, allowing the oxytocin to kick in, she doubted she could have let the baby go, even if she was only twenty and had no way to care for her.

Natalie had not held the newborn, but her mother had.

Before she thought better of the idea, she picked up her cell.

Her mother answered before it rang on Natalie's end. "Cora die? I'm on the eleventh hole and I'm shooting two over."

It crossed Natalie's mind to say, "Sorry, wrong number," and hang up. Of course, her mother would recognize her voice, and the caller ID had identified her number. The gesture would only be to make a point. The point being, that was no way to answer a phone when your child calls, even if she is in her thirties. And how awful that her first thought was that her stepmother was dead. But Natalie wanted something from her mother, so doing that didn't make any sense.

Instead, she said cheerfully, "Sorry. I didn't realize you played golf on Thursday afternoons."

Her father, a urologist, had retired, sold the family home in northern Delaware where Natalie and Laney had grown up, and moved to Sun City, Arizona. There, it rarely rained and he could play golf as many days a week as he pleased. Her mother, a retired high school calculus teacher, had never taken up golf but had gotten the bug, because now she played more times a week than Natalie's father.

"I don't play on Thursdays," Natalie's mother responded. "Thursday is laundry and grocery shopping day. Today is Friday. I play Monday, Wednesday, Friday, and Saturday with the girls. Your dad and I play couples on Sundays."

Natalie pressed the heel of her hand to her forehead. "Of course it's Friday. I know that. Knew that," she said. "Mason's graduation is today."

Her mother gave a snort, and Natalie imagined her, petite and slender, standing near her custom golf cart, wearing a white skirt, sleeveless polo, and visor. In her hand, she held a number-something club. Natalie knew nothing about golf. Conor didn't play and wasn't all that interested in sports. He was a darts man, though he did run to prevent a beer belly.

"Graduating from fourth grade and they need a ceremony," her mother said.

She didn't say it unkindly. It was more matter-of-fact. Henry, short for "Henrietta," was a practical, no-nonsense kind of woman. Always the cool head in the room. Natalie's whole life she had considered her mother's candid, no-gray-areas personality a double-edged sword. Henry was sometimes so frank that she was hurtful, but she was who Natalie wanted on her side in an emergency. Not her father, who would kill her with kindness but never meet a problem head on if he could help it.

"I know, it's silly," Natalie agreed, watching Mason's friend try to pour pool water on their dog's head. Luckily, Winston was smart enough to run for cover under one of the chaise lounges. "But Mason is excited. And the whole ceremony will be quick, so we won't have lost too many hours of our life we'll never get back. We're going out for dinner and ice cream after."

"Natalie?" Her mother's tone changed. "Are you all right? You don't sound like it. Laney told me about the hysterectomy. You're getting yourself all fired up about nothing. I had mine at forty. Same problem as you. I say good riddance."

"Laney told you?" Natalie was annoyed. It wasn't her sister's place to talk about her medical issue with their mother. With anyone. "It wasn't her place to tell."

"You wanted privacy? You should have been born to another family," her mother responded unapologetically. Then, without lowering her cell, she yelled, "Play through! I'll catch you on the next hole."

Natalie cringed and pulled the phone away from her ear.

"Natalie? You there?"

Natalie brought the phone back. "I'm here. I didn't call you about the hysterectomy. We can talk about that when you're not on the fourteenth hole."

"Eleventh."

Natalie took a deep breath. "Mom, I called because . . . I've been thinking about the baby."

"What baby?" Her mother paused for barely a beat and then said, "Oh, *that* baby. What about her?"

"I was wondering." Natalie could feel her heart rate increasing, her blood pressure rising. Was this a mistake, calling her mother? Would this one step take her from simply wondering about Bella to something else? Something she couldn't turn back from?

"Did she look like McKenzie?" Natalie blurted. Then she added, "And Mason?" because she didn't want to give her mother any hint as to why she was asking. She had to be careful with Henry. She had always had the uncanny ability to suss Natalie out. More so than with Laney, who always had, despite Natalie's unwed-mother boo-boo, been the bad girl. And the one, unlike Natalie, who was good at lying.

Her mother was quiet on the other end of the phone, but Natalie knew she was still there because she could hear the faint sound of other women's voices. Someone was calling to her mother. Henry was quiet because she was thinking. She liked to take the measure of her thoughts before she voiced them. "Why do you ask?"

Natalie gripped her phone tightly. "Mom, you were the only one who saw her." Her father had refused, instead waiting for Natalie in her hospital room with tears in his eyes and a big bouquet of red and white roses in his arms. "The only one who *really* saw her. I was too drugged up with that sedative Dad insisted I have." She fought to keep her emotions in check. "But *you* held her in the nursery. What color was her hair? Her eyes?"

"All babies are born with blue eyes."

Natalie watched out the window as the three soon-to-be fourth-grade graduates tore into a ginormous bag of corn chips she'd left on a table for them, along with salsa and bottles of water. They were dipping the chips into a bowl of salsa and cramming them into their mouths, as ravenous as elementary-age boys could be.

"What's all of this about?" her mother said. "You never said a thing about this back in December on the birthday. You haven't mentioned it in years."

"You mean I haven't mentioned *her*? My baby?" It came out harsher than Natalie intended, and she was immediately contrite. Her mother had been so good through the whole unwanted pregnancy and in the dark days that followed. Henry had been her rock—not her best friend sister, not her father, whom she considered herself to be closer to. It was her pragmatic mother who had gotten her through that awful time. And Natalie was convinced it was because of her mother that she was able to heal enough to go back to university and to meet Conor and fall in love with him eventually.

Her mother took a breath. "Natalie, I don't remember, probably because she was never ours. We knew she wasn't going to be ours six months before you had her. When I think of my grandchildren, I think of McKenzie and Mason, of what they looked like. I'm sorry. I know that's not what you want to—"

The door to the office flew open from the hallway, startling Natalie, and she looked up.

It was McKenzie, dressed in a pair of board shorts and a bright yellow O'Sullivan's T-shirt.

"Is it okay if I work five to close tonight?" McKenzie asked.

"I need to go," Natalie said into the phone. "McKenzie's here. I'll call you tomorrow. Get back to your game."

Her mother sighed. "Too late now. I'm out of my groove. Tell Mason we said congratulations. I sent a card. I wanted to put money in his education fund; your father wanted to hire a stripper for him." Her delivery was unexpressive and spot-on. It always was. "We agreed on a gift card for those video games he likes to play. You know how it is; marriage is all about compromise."

Natalie smiled at the stripper comment. "Talk to you tomorrow." She disconnected and looked up at McKenzie, who was waiting impatiently. "No, you may not take the evening shift at work. We are going to your brother's graduation."

"Who ever heard of a fourth-grade graduation?"

Natalie laughed. "Two peas in a pod. Your grandmother just said the same thing."

McKenzie held her phone in her hand. "Grandma Henry?"

"Well, it sure wasn't Grandma Imogen." Conor's mother was a sweet old lady. Sweet, but dull and never, ever sassy. Natalie studied McKenzie, thinking how she had suddenly moved from that gangly, awkward teenager to looking like a woman. When had that happened? "Why are you asking if you can work tonight? I thought you asked Bella to take your shift so you could go to Mason's graduation."

McKenzie scowled. "I did. But T-Rex called out already. He told Mr. Burke he was sick, but Bella and I know he's lying. Tide's going to be right for surfing at Indian River tonight."

T-Rex was a boy she went to school with. Trevor. Like her aunt, McKenzie sometimes took to giving people crazy nicknames. "You tell Mr. Burke you thought he wasn't being honest?"

McKenzie got a look on her face that reflected such horror that it was a wonder the teen didn't recoil. "I don't rat people out. What kind of a person do you think I am?"

Natalie took the stance that the question was rhetorical. "You cannot work tonight, Mac. We all agreed we would go to your brother's graduation and then out to eat. Aunt Laney is meeting us for dinner afterward."

"Oh, so I have to go to the stupid graduation and Laney doesn't?"

"I don't like it when you call her by her first name."

McKenzie met her mother's gaze, head on. "She said I could call her Laney. That I was getting too old for '*Aunt Laney*.'" She added a mocking, childish tone to the name.

"I'll talk to your *aunt* Laney about that. No, you may not work tonight. Final Answer." Natalie returned her attention to her computer monitor. She needed to get through these numbers and then get a shower and do something with her hair. If Conor arrived home to pick them up and she wasn't ready, he'd be annoyed.

In her peripheral vision, Natalie saw McKenzie stand there a moment, looking poised for a catfight, and then the teen whipped around and marched out of the office, slamming the door behind her.

Natalie shook her head, wondering why on earth she was even contemplating finding out if Bella was her daughter. Why would she want another teenage girl? There were days when she barely wanted the one she had.

CHAPTER 8

A few days after Mason's graduation, McKenzie wandered into the kitchen, surprising Natalie when she plopped down on a stool on the opposite side of the island. *Without a summons.* Natalie had been listening to an audiobook while making dinner, in the hopes Conor would be home to eat with them. He promised he'd be home in time, but she was trying not to get her hopes up. Under all the stress with the new business, she didn't want to add to it by being the whining wife.

Natalie hit pause on her watch, wondering what her daughter wanted. She wanted something. Why else would she be there voluntarily?

The moment the thought went through her head, Natalie silently chastised herself. She needed to give the teen the benefit of the doubt. The night before, Natalie had gone to McKenzie's doorway to say good night. She ended up sitting on her daughter's bed, telling her about the hysterectomy, and they'd had a good conversation. Almost as if they were both adults, which McKenzie nearly was, Laney pointed out, whether Natalie wanted to admit it or not. The ten minutes they had spent together had made Natalie hopeful that someday she and her daughter could have a real relationship again. They had been closer—or what Natalie perceived as close—through middle school, and then something she couldn't identify had happened the day McKenzie had walked through the doors of her new high school. And nothing had been the same between them again. Every conversation was tense with accusations and genuine discontent with the other. *On both sides.*

Natalie continued working on the salad dressing she was making, playing it cool to not spook her teen. Maybe the hysterectomy conversation had been a turning point and McKenzie was going to go back to being the cheerful, pleasant daughter Natalie yearned for. "How was work today?"

"Good." McKenzie spun her cell on the counter. It had a new case on it with glitter pressed between the plastic sides to give it a snow globe effect. "Busy." Her somber face became animated for just a second. "We sold like a hundred of these weird whirligigs that look like tongues. Oh, and some kid barfed in front of the hermit crab cages. Of course, it had to be my area of the store. He'd eaten a lot of blue cotton candy, I guess. It was ga-ross."

Natalie glanced up from chopping the fresh oregano she'd picked from her herb garden in a flower bed in the backyard. "You had to clean it up?"

McKenzie made a face. "Ew. No. I figured Mr. Burke should. He's the one making billions selling cheap beach chairs that end up in a landfill in three months. Cleaning up barf was not in my job description. Not for minimum wage it wasn't."

Natalie eyed her. "I highly doubt he's making billions."

"Crazy thing was," McKenzie went on, "Mr. Burke had me put some orange cones out to keep people from walking in the barf. Can you believe people barf, or worse, often enough in the store that he has *cones*?" She went on without waiting for a response. "Mr. Burke said he'd take care of it when he got off the phone, but then Bella, she just—" She lifted her hand and let it fall to the smooth granite countertop. "She got a dustpan and scooped it up with paper towels, and then she finished with a mop." She shook her head in apparent awe. "Like she knew what to do."

"Not exactly rocket science. Maybe she's had to clean up after a brother or a sister before," Natalie dared.

Natalie hadn't decided if she wanted to know if Bella was hers or not. What she *had* decided was that she needed more information. Preferably proof that Bella was not her daughter. Couldn't be. The problem was that the best way to get intel was from McKenzie. McKenzie, who hated being questioned about her friends. Hated being questioned at all about anything.

Natalie had already taken the plunge, so she went on. "Bella have brothers or sisters?"

"I told you. She's adopted." McKenzie picked up her phone and began to message someone. Likely Bella. She was obsessed with her new friend and hadn't mentioned anyone else since she started her summer job. All she did was talk about the paragon, Bella.

Satisfied with the amount of oregano she'd added to the bowl, Natalie rolled a lemon and cut it in half on a cutting board. "A person can be adopted and still have siblings."

"Mom, people adopt because they can't have a baby of their own."

"Exactly. And sometimes they adopt more than one child." She squeezed one half of the lemon, and a seed dropped into the bowl. She groaned. "But some people don't have infertility issues; they adopt for altruistic reasons. Growing up, I had a friend who was a birth child and she had two younger adopted sisters. Her parents adopted because they wanted to give a home to children already born into this world who didn't have parents."

"Can you imagine giving up your baby?" McKenzie asked, her tone heavy with disdain. "I mean, how could you have a baby and just give her away?"

Natalie cringed. Luckily, McKenzie never looked up from her texting.

"I mean, someone gave away *Bella*?" McKenzie shook her head, and the long braids she and Bella had plaited all over her head swung with the motion. "If I got knocked up today, I wouldn't put my baby up for adoption."

"Wait." Natalie dropped her hands to the counter, leaning toward her daughter. "Are you having sex?"

McKenzie looked up, making a face. "What? With *who*?"

Not an answer.

"I don't know," Natalie said. She and Conor obviously didn't want their daughter having sex at fifteen, but they also weren't prudes. If their Mac was having sex, the first thing she needed to do was to confirm she was protected. They'd deal with other factors later. "You were sort of seeing Matthew Landon before school got out."

"Am I *having sex* with Matthew Landon?" The teen scrunched up her face. "Is that what you're asking me, Mom?"

Natalie wasn't sure what to say. It wasn't as if she had never discussed sex with her daughter. She had. Did. But more in a someday kind of way. She wasn't sure she was ready to talk about McKenzie's sex life. Not when she could still remember the feel of her in her arms after she was born. The sweet baby scent of her.

"No, I'm not having sex with Matthew Landon. Eww *and* gross. He's got hair growing out of his nose."

Natalie almost laughed with relief. And her daughter's rationale. The things that fifteen-year-olds thought of. She wanted to explain that most men had hair that would grow out of their nose if they didn't keep it groomed, but she decided to keep that to herself. The subject might make McKenzie bolt. Instead, she steered the conversation back to the topic of adoption, because what if Bella *was* her daughter? The story would come out as to why Natalie put her first baby up for adoption. McKenzie needed to understand that people who gave up their babies weren't monsters. Natalie certainly hadn't been one.

Mac needed to know that keeping a baby a woman wasn't ready to raise could result in ruining the life of the child as well as the mother.

Natalie tried to fish the lemon seed out of her dressing with her finger. "Giving a baby up for adoption is complicated, Mac. Women do it for a lot of reasons: maybe they're too young to be a mother; maybe they can't afford to care for a child; maybe they already have children and can barely provide for the ones they already have. Sometimes putting a baby up for adoption is the best thing for the baby. It's an amazing gift to someone else, to someone who will never be able to give birth to their own. Once you have a child, you'll understand."

McKenzie was looking at her phone again. "No way I'm having a baby. *Ever.* Push a bowling ball out of my V? No freakin' way."

Natalie did laugh this time. She couldn't help herself. "Put like that, it doesn't sound all that appealing, does it?" At last, she nabbed the seed in the salad dressing and retrieved a whisk from a drawer in the island. "But think about it this way. It can't be all that bad, or women wouldn't continue having babies."

McKenzie held up her hand, palm to her mother. "Pass." She looked up from her phone again. "Bella wants to know if I can spend the night tomorrow. We both work until four."

"Mm, I don't know." The question took Natalie by surprise and she covered herself by concentrating on whisking the salad dressing. What if Bella and McKenzie were half sisters? Wouldn't it be wrong to let them have a sleepover, not knowing that?

Talk about faulty rationale.

That made no sense. Natalie knew that. That didn't mean she was going to agree to let her go. Even if McKenzie was almost sixteen, Natalie still had a responsibility to keep her safe. To help her learn how to be safe herself. "We don't know Bella."

"I know her, Mom, and since when did you have to know

one of my friends to let them come here or me go to their place? I'll be sixteen next month. Old enough to have a baby," she threw in.

"As long as it's not with Matthew Landon." Natalie pointed at her with the whisk. "I don't want a grandbaby that has hair growing out of its nose."

McKenzie groaned. "Mom, I'm being serious, here. Please? I really want to stay overnight with Bella." She gripped her hands together. "I really, really want to go."

"I don't know her parents." Satisfied with the viscosity of the dressing and the taste, Natalie poured it into a jelly jar and added a lid. "What if they're serial killers, and they lure their daughter's friends into the house to chop them up, put them in sandwich bags, and pop them in the freezer?"

"Okay, so that could be a possibility."

Natalie looked up, confused. "You think her parents are serial killers?"

McKenzie shrugged. "They're arseholes," she said, pronouncing the word the way her father did. "I know that much. They treat her terrible."

Natalie's hackles immediately went up. *Someone was abusing her daughter?*

Okay, a girl who *could* be her daughter.

Natalie was carrying stuff to the sink and turned around, whisk in one hand, mixing bowl in the other. "They mistreat her?"

"Maybe not to the point where anyone can call Child Protective Services, but her mom and dad are mean to her. And they're never around. She practically raised herself. Have you not been listening to me? All they do is work and go to cocktail parties and stuff. They leave Bella home alone all the time. She has to make her own dinner, and they won't let her order takeout."

Natalie narrowed her gaze and turned back to deposit the dirty dishes in the sink. "Not being allowed to order takeout isn't exactly abuse, especially with an eighteen-year-old. Do they hit her? Is she sexually abused?"

"We talked a lot about domestic abuse in health class. It can manifest in a lot of ways. Mr. Angelo said it's not always sexual or physical."

"She's not physically abused in any way? You're sure?" Natalie asked, wanting to be clear. Because no matter whose daughter Bella was, she had a responsibility to report abuse of a child. Or, in the case of an eighteen-year-old, help her report herself, she supposed.

McKenzie groaned. "No one is hitting her or diddling her, Mom. Can I spend the night? Her parents are going to some fundraiser in Dover. They won't be home until really late. Bella and I were going to make pizza and do a movie marathon. Her dad has one of the rooms like a theater in their basement. She loves horror movies, too, so we just need to decide which franchise—*Saw* or *The Conjuring*."

"Why don't you invite her here?" Natalie shrugged. "We don't have a movie theater on the premises, but you could swim in the pool, go for a walk on the beach. You said they live on the other side of Route 1. She'd probably like going for a walk on the beach at night."

"You don't like me going for walks at night. You're worried about pervs and serial killers." McKenzie twisted her mouth one way and then the other. "You really need to expand your reading list. All those serial killer books are making you paranoid."

Natalie dried her hands on a dish towel, deciding not to remind McKenzie that like mother, like daughter. All of the horror movies Mac watched were about serial killers, too. Instead, she said, "I need to meet Bella if I'm going to let you stay overnight with her."

"You already met her!"

It was all Natalie could do not to shout back. "Please don't speak that way to me," she said calmly, instead. "You know what I mean. We exchanged half a dozen words. How do I know she's not a serial killer?"

"The profile is all wrong, Mom. Women rarely murder strangers. They kill their husbands and kids. Sometimes an old mother, if she's rich or mean."

Natalie was impressed with her daughter's parry. But not enough to give in. Especially when she had ulterior motives. "Would you rather I called her mother and chatted with her?"

"I'm not in elementary school anymore. And Bella's eighteen. She's old enough to vote! I'd die of embarrassment if you called her mother. Bella would probably die of secondhand embarrassment."

Natalie shrugged, feeling guilty about what she was doing but not guilty enough not to. "So what you're saying is that it would make sense for you to just bring her over here. Let me get to know her a little bit and then"—she shrugged—"if her background check comes back okay, maybe you can stay some night at her house."

"Very funny." McKenzie grabbed her phone, getting off the stool. "I cannot believe you're doing this," she flung. "I've finally made a good friend, someone who understands me, who's like me, and you won't let me be with her?"

"I didn't say—"

"Mom!" Mason burst into the kitchen. "Mom! Can you take me to the game store? Patrick just told me they got new Pokémon cards in."

McKenzie looked at her little brother. "Can you not see that we're having a serious conversation here? And you've got something all over your mouth. Chocolate."

Mason wiped his mouth slowly on his sleeve, keeping eye contact with his sister, and then returned his attention to Natalie. "Please can you take me? I have money to pay for them."

"Sorry. We're not going into town tonight." Natalie glanced at her watch. "Your dad is supposed to be home in twenty minutes, and we're having family dinner. I made chicken parm."

Mason stood in the middle of the kitchen in an obvious quandary as to whether to protest, because he loved chicken parm. He had also been missing his father, and earlier in the day had been excited that he would be home for dinner. Mason and Conor had big plans to play Mario Kart after they ate. "Can I go get the cards myself?" he asked. "If I go on my skateboard, I'll be back in half an hour."

"Oh, fine," McKenzie groused. "So you're going to let perv bait here"—she hooked her thumb in his direction—"take his skateboard to the boardwalk, but I can't spend the night with my best friend? Who's legally an adult. Really, Mom?"

Mac was bordering on belligerence now and was one click away from smackdown mode, as Conor called it when he disciplined the children. "I am not letting him go alone to the boardwalk," Natalie said. She looked to Mason. "Sorry, buddy. You can't go alone. You know that."

"Can I go if Patrick goes?" he asked, hopefully.

"There is no way Aunt Beth is letting Patrick go alone downtown. And Patrick couldn't go anyway. They're headed to Annapolis to have dinner with his grandparents."

Mason let his head drop until his chin touched his chest in an adorable sulk.

"How about if I take you in the morning?" Natalie suggested.

He stood his arms akimbo, looking utterly pathetic. He was dressed in camo shorts and a Cuphead T-shirt her mom had sent him from Arizona. Which now had a smear of chocolate across the sleeve. "I have swim team practice in the morning. Then baseball camp that lasts until three."

Natalie closed her eyes for a minute. She'd completely forgotten that baseball camp was starting. She'd registered him, and paid for it, but it hadn't made its way onto her calendar. The following day she had half a dozen errands to run, including stopping to see Nana, and had made an appointment for a pedicure for two-thirty. Which she would have to reschedule. Times like this, she couldn't wait until McKenzie could drive on her own. Then she could help with ferrying her little brother around.

"Just let him go," McKenzie said, looking her brother up and down. "Anyone kidnaps him, they won't keep the nerd long."

"Butt wipe," Mason responded.

"Mason." Natalie walked around the island. "Inappropriate. Apologize." She pointed to his sister.

"Sorry," he mumbled without a hint of remorse in his voice and walked out of the kitchen.

"I'll pick you up at baseball camp, and we'll go right to the game store. And then maybe we can stop at the pub and see your dad. Okay?" Natalie called after him as he went down the hall.

"Okay!" he hollered back.

Sensing that McKenzie was about to flee as well, Natalie turned around, and the teen almost bumped into her trying to make her getaway. "Your choice. I can call and chat with Bella's mom, or you can invite Bella over." She shrugged. "Or you can just wait until you've known her longer."

"Fine," McKenzie said, obviously displeased. She circumnavigated her mother.

"Fine what?" Natalie asked her daughter's back.

"I'll think about it, okay?"

Okay, then," Natalie murmured to the empty room.

CHAPTER 9

After Natalie picked Mason up from baseball camp, she dutifully drove around and around trying to find a parking space downtown so he could buy his beloved Pokémon cards. She had suggested they go home and walk back to the avenue, but he had looked so crestfallen when she said it that she had given in and headed straight downtown. There were no open parking spots on the avenue or on any side streets, as she predicted. Traffic was moving slowly, and there were jaywalking tourists everywhere, which always made her nervous. Her mother had a credo when Natalie and Laney were kids: *We don't want to make the evening news.* And Natalie didn't want to make the evening news by hitting someone with her car on Albany Avenue.

"I don't know, buddy," she said, glancing at him in the rearview mirror. "Maybe we *should* park at home and walk back."

"Please, Mom?" he begged. "Patrick gave me money to get him some cards, too. What if they run out before we get back?" He clutched his blue nylon wallet in both hands. "Can we park in the alley behind the pub?"

"You know we can't. There are only two teeny, tiny spaces.

With your dad and your uncles having to be there every day, all day, we can't take up one of them, not even for Pokémon cards. Why do you think your dad takes his bike most days?"

Driving bumper to bumper now, she let her foot up off the gas and slowly crept forward. It was so easy for someone to hit their brake unexpectedly, and the next thing you knew you were in a six-car pileup. Well, maybe it wouldn't be a pileup, but there would be a bunch of crumpled bumpers. "Mace—"

Out of the corner of her eye, Natalie caught a flash of movement, and she hit her brake hard. "Holy Hades!" she hollered as the car rocked in response to the sudden stop.

"I agree with Aunt Laney. You need some better swears," her ten-year-old piped up from the back seat.

Ignoring her son, Natalie watched as a woman in a bikini pushed a jogging stroller across the street, a quarter of a block from the closest crosswalk. She was looking straight ahead as if there weren't a car in sight. Horns sounded behind Natalie. Obviously, the drivers couldn't see the woman. "Am I supposed to run them down? Is that what they want?" she asked aloud.

When the jogger with a wish to simultaneously commit infanticide and suicide safely reached the median strip, Natalie breathed a sigh of relief and proceeded forward cautiously. "Mace, I don't think we're going to find a spot. This is the third time we've been around. How about if we go home and walk back?" *Like I suggested half an hour ago*, she thought but didn't say. He could have been at the cash register by now with a hoard of Pokémon cards.

"Can't you let me out and I'll go straight to the game store and straight home." His tone was bordering on a wail now. "I swear. I'll run too fast for the pervs."

"Absolutely not." She signaled to try another side street. "You get kidnapped, we'll have to call the police," she said, feigning boredom. "There will be interviews, paperwork to file. The FBI will want a current photo of you to put on all of the milk cartons and, if you recall"—she eyed him in the mirror again—"I didn't get your school picture for the first time since Pre-K because *someone* was sticking their tongue out in the photo."

"My picture on a milk carton? What are you *talking* about? Wait! There! There's one." He beat on the back of her seat with his hand. "That van has its backup lights on! The blue one!"

Natalie signaled, and then with the experience borne of a local, she crept up as close as she could without blocking the person's ability to back out, without giving another car room to zip in front of her.

The van with New Jersey plates backed out and she eased the car into the spot, noting that the oil light was flashing on her ten-year-old Subaru again. It wasn't on. It was just flashing. She sighed as she slipped her key fob into her shorts pocket. The last time it did this, she took the car to the shop and, of course, it had stopped flashing. And there was nothing wrong. Or so they said. Two days later, it was low on oil and Conor started talking about getting a new car. An electric car. Which was not in their budget, and she oversaw their household finances, so she got the final word. Sort of.

On foot, Natalie and Mason wove through the throngs of people on the sidewalk as they made their way toward the game store. As she walked, she tried to ignore the trash in the gutter and blowing past her. She understood that kids sometimes dropped their rainbow snow cones. You could do nothing about the frozen, sticky mess, but why couldn't parents pick up the paper cone?

When they reached the avenue, the heavenly scent of Thrasher's French fries filled her nostrils and her stomach grumbled. The hardboiled egg and banana she'd had for breakfast had long been digested. She'd intended to make herself a salad after picking Mason and Patrick up from swim practice and taking them to baseball camp, but then her manicurist had called. There was a cancellation and Natalie could have the appointment if she hustled. She'd hurried her grandmother to an early lunch in the communal dining room and made a quick escape. Now she was sporting pink toenails and fingernails.

They crossed the street, in the crosswalk, and on the far side of the avenue they walked up to the door of Mason's favorite store, where he bought most of his video games. While a lot of his friends just downloaded games, he and his cousin Patrick bought them and then shared them, which had been their idea and clever.

Mason halted at the door that was covered with posters advertising Cuphead and Fortnite games. He looked up at her. "Mom, you're not coming in, are you?"

She looked down at him and realized he'd had another growth spurt. It wouldn't be long before he was as tall as she was. McKenzie was already taller than she was.

"Mom," Mason groaned. "Mr. Jenkins isn't a perv. He goes to our church. He comes to you and Dad's Christmas parties."

She crossed her arms over her chest. "You don't want me to come in?" The thought of it made her a little sad. Her little boy was growing up too fast. It seemed like last week he'd begged her to stay with him in his kindergarten class.

"Can I meet you up on the boardwalk?" he asked hopefully. "Like in . . . half an hour?"

She hesitated.

"Please? There's too many people around for kidnapping anyone. And Mr. Jenkins got in this cool Japanese game, and only kids he likes get to play it." He looked up at her with his father's big, gorgeous blue eyes. "Half an hour," he repeated.

She glanced at the boardwalk a block away, then back at him. "Our usual place?" They always met in front of their favorite frozen custard stand. Kohr Brothers had been there since Natalie was a kid coming to Albany Beach with her parents.

"Yes! Thanks!" Mason bounced in his sneakers as he pulled open the heavy glass door.

"Half an hour." She looked at her watch. "That's four-fifteen!" she called after him.

The door closed and she stood for a moment trying to decide what to do for half an hour. What to do to avoid the Thrasher's French fry line. She looked up the sidewalk and down, stepping under the awning to keep from being trampled by tourists smelling of suntan lotion in a hurry to get to wherever they were going.

She considered ducking into the pub. She could get an unsweetened iced tea and say hi to Conor. He'd come home early the night before, as promised, but after dinner and video games with Mason, when he'd met her on the back deck for a glass of wine, he'd fallen asleep after only one sip. Not only had there been no stimulating conversation, but there had been no hot sex, either. And then he'd been up and out of the house before she was out of bed.

But she wasn't even sure he was there. Just before he fell asleep in his wineglass the night before he'd rattled off his schedule for the day, and it had involved time out of the office for various reasons. Besides, if she went into the pub, she wouldn't be able to resist ordering some delicious, fatty high-caloric appetizer, and she was trying to save her calories for dinner.

Natalie began to walk, and once she hit the boardwalk she naturally turned north. Burke Brothers was on the north end of the boardwalk. She hadn't planned to go to the variety store where McKenzie was working. It just sort of . . . happened.

As she strode, enjoying the feel of the sun on her face and the scent of the briny ocean, she told herself she wouldn't go inside. That would embarrass McKenzie. Mortify her. But there was no reason she couldn't walk by as long as her daughter didn't see her. Was there? It was a free country and all that. She was killing time until she would meet Mason.

And she just might catch a glimpse of Bella.

Natalie didn't know if Bella was spending the night at their place. McKenzie hadn't said another word about it and Natalie had been afraid to stick her head into the lion's mouth that morning at breakfast.

She slowed her pace as she passed a new pizza place and then a small arcade. Burke's was the next store. She kept to the ocean side of the boardwalk, studying the storefront. Colorful blow-up rafts and beach balls swung from ropes overhead. Tubs of beach toys, stacks of beach chairs, and tables of every sun product known to man crowded the apron of the store. One of McKenzie's tasks, when it was her turn to close, she had told her father, was to carry all the merchandise inside the store. And then, if she opened the next day, she had to drag it all out again. A few nights before, Mac had gone on about how tedious the task was and Conor had explained profit margins until the teen had voluntarily offered to do the dishes, just to get away from her father. *A smart move on his part.*

Natalie slowed further and people began to walk around her. She didn't see McKenzie, though there was a towheaded teenage boy in an employee shirt helping a customer pick out a beach chair. Natalie was almost past the store when she spotted Bella and her heart skipped a beat. The teen wore jean shorts and an employee T-shirt in pale yellow. Her hair was pulled back in a high ponytail and looked even blonder than the other day. Had she been in the sun? Her lean, lithe body was tanned and Natalie wondered if her mother had conversations about the importance of wearing sun block every day. Was her mother too busy to cook for her child and take the time for subjects like skin cancer?

Natalie stared at the girl.

Bella looked so much like McKenzie. Could she really be her lost daughter?

Natalie walked half a block past the store and, this time, to get a closer look, crossed the boardwalk so she was on the store side, headed south. A seagull squawked overhead, catching her attention, and she watched it dive-bomb a bench, snatching up an abandoned French fry.

When Natalie shifted her gaze to the store again, she saw Bella digging through a basket of water pistols, chatting to a woman with twin boys who looked to be around six. Bella didn't see Natalie. She was too busy digging looking for something, for a particular color, probably. That was how Mason had been at these boys' age. He'd been fixated on the color orange and had wanted everything in orange. He'd even asked if they could paint his bedroom a tangerine color. She bought the orange shorts, orange T-shirt, orange sneakers even, but the orange walls had been a hard no. Which was a good choice, because three months later his favorite color had changed to blue.

At the end of the store, Natalie stopped next to a rack of leashes that were supposed to look like you were walking an invisible dog. She fingered the brightly colored faux leather and glanced over her shoulder.

Bella was gorgeous. And she seemed so outgoing, so gregarious. She laughed with the customer, teasing the boys as she showed them some Super Soaker water cannons. A born salesperson. The mother already had two water pistols in her hands, one blue, one red, and a mesh bag of squishy balls.

Natalie felt a tightness in her chest as she watched Bella. A yearning. And she wondered for the hundredth time that day if she wanted to know if Bella was hers. Was it the right thing to do? To dig up the past? She would be naïve to think that it would just affect her. As Laney had said, it wasn't just about Natalie's family. She had to think about Bella and her parents.

But if her adoptive parents were bad ones, didn't she owe it to the teenager to find out? Because Natalie certainly wasn't perfect, but she was a good mom.

Laney kept saying Natalie needed to talk to Conor. But she wasn't ready. Not yet. She wasn't sure how he would react to—

"Mom!" a voice hissed from behind the rack of dog leashes, startling Natalie.

McKenzie popped out. "What are you doing here?" she demanded, keeping her voice low.

Natalie's first thought was to joke that she was looking for a new dog and grab one of the leashes. Winston had escaped that morning again. Mason had managed to find him in the neighbor's yard digging up a rhododendron. However, the look on the teen's face suggested this wasn't the time for jokes.

"I . . . Mason is buying Pokémon cards at the game store and"—Natalie took on a defensive tone—"and I was getting my steps in. Ten thousand a day. I told you—"

"Mom, you can't be here!" McKenzie whisper-shouted.

"I can't take a walk on the boardwalk, now?" she asked, taking a tone.

"You weren't just *taking a walk*," the teen accused. "You were spying on me!"

So McKenzie thought this was about her. *No surprise.* In Mac's mind, everything was about her. In this case, her narcissism served Natalie well. Natalie had already decided that she would not tell her kids if she chose to investigate her adopted daughter's identity. Not until she knew. And knew what she was going to do about it.

She did have to tell Conor. She knew that. And she intended to—if she decided to pursue this.

"Mom," McKenzie prodded. "Please leave before someone sees—"

"Mrs. Sullivan!" Bella called.

Natalie looked up to see her walking toward them.

"It's so nice to see you again." Bella looked at McKenzie. "You didn't tell me your mom was here." She looked to Natalie. "That's so nice of her. This is the fourth summer I've worked downtown and never once has my mom stopped to say hello." She threw her arms around Natalie.

The gesture was so unexpected that, for a split second, Natalie didn't know what to do. She couldn't remember the last time McKenzie hugged her. She slowly wrapped her arms around the teen and breathed in, wondering if she would know if Bella was her daughter merely by the scent of her. She had read about a study once where blindfolded women could identify their babies just by their smell.

Natalie took a deep breath. Bella smelled of coconut shampoo and some fruity teenage girl perfume. She didn't associate the scents with her baby, or any baby, so that was no help. Still, she was disappointed when Bella released her and stepped back. Her hug had felt good. She missed McKenzie's hugs.

"Did Mac tell you I'm spending the night tonight?" Bella asked.

Natalie glanced at McKenzie, keeping her instant excitement to herself. "She didn't. But I'm glad you can come," she said, looking back at Bella.

"It's so nice of you to invite me," Bella gushed, adjusting her sunglasses. "I don't really have any friends to hang out with anymore. My best friend Shanice moved to California the day after finals and the rest of my friends from high school"—she shrugged—"we're sort of drifting apart. You know?"

Natalie nodded. "It happens. Interests change. Everyone goes their separate ways after they graduate. I can barely remember the people I was friends with in high school and they were my whole world for those years." She glanced at McKenzie, who was standing there with her arms crossed over her chest, making it obvious she wasn't pleased that her mother was talking with her new best friend. Natalie ignored her. "Sometimes it happens sooner. McKenzie had a bit of a breakup this year with a friend she'd had since elementary school. Didn't you?" She looked to her daughter.

"We should get back to work." McKenzie's tone was flat. "If we leave the hermit crabs unattended, some kid will be stuffing his pockets with them."

Natalie laughed.

"Actually, it happened, didn't it, Mac?" Bella covered her mouth with her hand as if stifling her amusement. "Mr. Burke caught this like twelve-year-old with seven hermit crabs in his pockets. Mr. Burke called the police, he was so mad, because one didn't even have a shell. The kid didn't get arrested, but his dad had to come get him and he was in big trouble. We heard the guy hollering at the kid all the way down the boardwalk."

"We'll see you after work, Mom." McKenzie backed away, slipping her arm through Bella's. "We get off at six."

"Kind of random shifts, aren't they?" Natalie asked.

"Overhead," Bella explained. "The Burkes don't like to pay for any more employee hours than they have to. I get it."

"Right. Of course." Natalie put her hands together, pleased she'd just gotten a manicure and had worn something other than gym shorts. If Bella turned out to be her daughter, she didn't want the teen's first impressions to be of a mother with chipped nails and no style. "So dinner what, six-thirty?" If Bella was there for dinner and stayed the night, maybe she'd get enough information from her that she could determine the girl was not the baby she gave away and the issue would resolve itself. "It's burrito night. Is that okay, Bella? I already made the guac this morning. You like Tex-Mex food? If you don't, I can make something else."

"Actually . . ." McKenzie dragged out the word. "I thought we'd go to the pub and eat there. Dad will be there. He told me last night that he'd be home late."

"That's so amazing that you guys own the best restaurant in town," Bella said, her face as animated as McKenzie's was not. "I love the loaded waffle fries. But we can go another night, right, Mac?" Arms still linked, she pulled McKenzie closer. "Your mom's already made the guac, and I *l-o-v-e*"—she spelled out the word—"*love* homemade guac. Spicy, right?"

"Of course," Natalie responded.

"Oh, good." Bella clapped her hands together excitedly.

"The only kind I ever get is the packaged stuff from the grocery store. We can go to O'Sullivan's another time."

McKenzie exhaled loudly.

"Come on, Mac," Bella encouraged. "It'll be fun. Right? Just us girls. Your brother might spend the night with his cousin, right?"

At the mention of Mason, Natalie looked at her watch. "Oh, fudge," she muttered. "I'm late to meet him." She turned to go. "See you both later."

"See you later. And thanks again for the invitation!" Bella called after her, waving.

McKenzie said nothing.

CHAPTER 10

"Laney, you can't believe what an amazing young woman Bella is," Natalie told her sister. "She's so smart and funny and quick-witted. And she knows how to laugh. Unlike another teenage girl I know."

"Come on. Give Mac a break," Laney said on the other end of the line. "She's sixteen. Almost. Don't you remember how full of angst you were at that age? There's a big difference between the maturity of a sixteen-year-old and an eighteen-year-old. You get any intel out of Bella?"

"Some. I had to be careful so it didn't sound like I was interrogating her. Born in Delaware. Adopted at birth. Closed adoption."

"You ask her when her birthday is?"

Natalie hesitated. "No."

"Why not?" Laney asked impatiently. "You'd have your answer then."

"I told you. I didn't want it to seem like an interrogation. Bella didn't mind my questions, but I was ticking McKenzie off."

"Ask Mac. Or Bella. Rip the Band-Aid off," Laney insisted.

Natalie ignored her and went on. "Bella even helped me do the dishes after we ate. Did I tell you that?"

"You did. And she told you what a great cook you were, and I think you said she said she liked your hair in a ponytail. That it was youthful. Sounds to me like she was sucking up."

Natalie ignored the last comment. Laney was always suspicious of people. "Putting you on speaker." She set the phone on the sink and flushed.

"Are you in the *bathroom*?" Laney demanded.

Natalie washed her hands. "I didn't want the girls to hear me," she said.

"I ended my date early so I could talk to you while you pee?"

"Oh, please. Remember when we were little, and we would try to share the toilet at the same time?" Natalie turned off the water and reached for the fresh guest towel she'd put out before the girls arrived home. She'd scrubbed the toilet and the sink and added a new air freshener. She'd also managed to change the sheets on McKenzie's bed. Ordinarily, both of her kids changed their own sheets. But who knew how long it had been since her daughter had done it, and who knew how many cheese puffs were in her bed?

Laney laughed. "I completely forgot about that! Do you remember how pissed Mom was when she found out and how she sneaked around the house trying to catch us doing it just so she could punish us?"

Natalie laughed with her sister. "Which made us do it more." She flipped the seat down, sat, turned the speaker off, and brought the phone to her ear. "Sorry about the date. I'm just so excited, and you're the only person I could tell."

"Meh, I'm just giving you shit because it's what big sisters do. It was a lousy date. A drug rep who comes into the office occasionally. He showed up in a giant, diesel-guzzling pickup. Mistake number one. Then I offered to drive my Tesla because it will fit in a parking spot, and he started in about electric cars being a gateway drug to socialism."

Natalie cringed. "Two strikes before you left the driveway."

"He was on strike seven when you called. I went out the back door."

"You didn't," Natalie breathed, fascinated and horrified at the same time by her sister's dating adventures. And thankful she was married. At least once a month, she made Conor swear he wouldn't divorce her or die. There was no way she could put herself out in the dating world now. Not at her age. Certainly not as chubby as Pixie Patty thought she was.

"Sneaked right out the back through the kitchen. But I found the server and paid my tab first. Not big-truck-small-peen guy's, though." Laney laughed. "Oh, speaking of the Tesla. Conor asked me about that code I can give him so when he buys the car we can both get some free electrons. I found it. I'll send it to you."

Natalie heard Bella's and McKenzie's voices faintly in the hall, but she couldn't make out what they were saying. "When he buys *what* car?"

"The Model Three?" Laney asked with an *uh-oh* tone. She paused. "He didn't tell you. Christ on a crutch. I'd like to get through just one day without putting my size ten foot in my mouth."

"Conor is *not* buying himself a new car," Natalie said firmly. "We had that conversation. Several times. It's not in the budget right now. We already owe the bank enough money to keep me up at night. And what's he thinking? A Tesla? He needs his pickup for hauling things. It was invaluable when we were sprucing up the pub before the reopening."

"I think the Tesla is supposed to be for you, Nat."

"Me?" Natalie stretched out her bare feet, admiring her freshly polished toenails. "I don't need a car. I have a car."

"You have a car that's ten years old that's leaking oil."

"It is not—" Natalie caught herself. "Sorry. I shouldn't be giving you a hard time about this. I'll talk to Conor."

"Please don't tell him I tattled again, Nat. He'll never tell me anything again."

"Knowing him, he probably said something about it to you so you would say something to me and soften the blow."

"Aw, sweetie. I think you got the best man alive. He loves you, and he wants you to be safe and well taken care of. And he wants you to be happy."

"Remind me of that again when I tell him about Bella."

"You're serious about this?" Suddenly all the fun was gone from Laney's voice. "You're going to pursue this?"

Natalie was quiet for a moment. She could still hear the girls' voices down the hall. They were in the downstairs closet looking for hangers and a spare storage tub or two. They had talked about going for a walk on the beach but were working on a closet makeover for McKenzie, which she suspected would result in a list of clothing demands.

"Nat?" Laney pressed.

"She doesn't just remind me of McKenzie," Natalie said at last, her voice quivering. "She reminds me of Sébastien. She has his brown eyes."

It was the first time she'd spoken his name out loud in seventeen years. Once she'd told Conor the whole story about her unplanned pregnancy, she'd didn't know that she'd ever spoken of her Parisian lover again. "Something about her gestures. And she's such a romantic. A few months ago, she broke up with her boyfriend of two years because she said she wasn't her best with him, and she said she believed a relationship should make you a better person. A happier person. Oh! And she's an artist, too. Artistic, at least. Watercolors."

Laney was quiet on the end of the phone.

"You still there?" Natalie asked.

"Don't do this, Nat. Please don't do this," Laney begged. "Nothing good can come of it. And a lot of bad. Think about it. Your curiosity could destroy two families."

Natalie gripped the phone. "How can I not?" Her voice cracked on the last word.

"Mom?" McKenzie called from the hall. "Mom?" she hollered louder. "Where are you? Do we still have some of those plastic shoe boxes?"

"I gotta go," Natalie said into the phone.

"Want to walk?" Laney asked. "I can come over. We can get two or three miles in and talk some more about this. Plus, you wanted some help planning the menu for the Father's Day gig Sunday. I bumped into Beth at the coffee shop this morning, and she said you were supposed to let her know yesterday what you wanted her to bring."

Natalie closed her eyes for a moment. Conor had suggested they skip the Hallmark holiday, as he called it, this year, but she'd insisted a simple cookout in the backyard wouldn't be all that much work. They'd mentioned it to the family and to a few friends, but she'd been so busy that she'd done nothing to prepare for it. Now she wished she'd gone with his idea. Natalie still had to plan the menu, text everyone as to what they could bring, clean the house, weed the flower beds, vacuum the pool, and look like she wasn't stressed when everyone arrived.

"I think I'll just stay around the house," Natalie told her sister. "In case the girls need something. I can walk tomorrow morning before work if you want. I know you'd rather walk early when it's cool."

"And you'll actually get up?" Laney pressed, making it sound as if Natalie slept in until noon every day. It seemed like that to her sister, but only because she got up at 5:15 every morning, weekday or weekend.

"I'll be on the front porch. Six-thirty," Natalie said, studying the baseboard directly across from the toilet. It would need to be wiped down before Sunday. She wondered if she could enlist McKenzie's help getting ready, but Mason would probably be more reliable.

"Six-fifteen," Laney said.

"Six-fifteen," Natalie agreed. "We'll set the menu then, and I'll send out an email to everyone when we get back. Beth can wait until tomorrow for me to tell her what to bring. Which won't matter because she never brings what she says she's going to bring anyway. Or what I ask her to bring." She liked her sister-in-law, loved her, but they were very different people.

"Sounds good," Laney said. "Now, promise me you'll talk to Conor. Before you do something or say something you can't take back." She hesitated and then went on. "Nat, I'm serious. You *have* to talk to him. I feel like this is one of those genie-in-a-bottle situations. It can't be undone once it's done. You have to discuss this with your husband."

"Okay."

"Okay, yes, you'll talk to him before you go off the deep end?" Laney asked using her best big-sister "I'm warning you" tone. "Or okay as in okay you'll say anything to get off the phone right now?"

"Both," Natalie said.

"Mom!" McKenzie called from right outside the bathroom door. "Are you in there?"

"Talk to you tomorrow," Natalie said, and opened the door, a smile on her face.

CHAPTER 11

The following morning, Bella and McKenzie were up when Natalie returned from her walk with Laney. Bella had to get home to do chores before she went to work, but she agreed to stay long enough for Natalie to make a breakfast of blueberry pancakes and sausage. While McKenzie sat at the kitchen table, mostly picking at her food, Bella ate enthusiastically, impressed that pancakes could be made without a box mix and that fresh blueberries could be dropped onto the pancakes on the griddle. After they ate, Bella offered to help do the dishes again.

"I can take care of them," Natalie said, getting up from the table with her plate. She'd only had one pancake and no sausage, banking her calories for a beer or two with Conor that night. The previous night as she ate dinner with Bella she realized that she was ready to talk to Conor about the teenager. So that morning, she got up the same time he did and asked if they could get together for a beer that night. He wasn't sure if it would work, but if not tonight, then tomorrow night, he told her. They were going to touch base later in the day and make a solid plan.

"We can take care of them, can't we?" Natalie asked, glancing at her daughter.

"Sure." McKenzie rose from the table, at half speed, with most of her breakfast still on her plate. "I love doing dishes." Her tone left nothing to the imagination. She did not love doing dishes.

"I'm not leaving dirty dishes on your table, Mrs. S. Come on, Mac. We'll do them together," Bella said cheerfully. "We just have to rinse them and pop them in the dishwasher."

Sometime in the last twelve hours, Natalie had gone from "Mrs. Sullivan" to "Mrs. S." Natalie wanted to tell Bella to call her by her first name. Bella was, after all, legally an adult. The formality of "Mrs." seemed silly to her, but she wasn't sure how to broach the subject, especially with Mac giving her the stink eye every time she opened her mouth. So she let it go.

"I'll rinse. You load, Mac," Bella said cheerfully.

This morning Bella was wearing a white men's V-neck T-shirt and white jean shorts, her hair piled on top of her head in a messy bun, the way McKenzie often wore hers. The funny thing was that Natalie had played with piling her hair up that morning in front of the mirror. She had kind of liked it. But then, feeling self-conscious, she'd put it up in her normal ponytail, worried it might seem as if she were trying to look like a teenage girl.

"McKenzie says you're thinking about taking a gap year before you go to college?" Natalie asked Bella as she set her plate in the sink.

"Thinking about it. But my mom and dad want me to go this fall. Mom says if I don't go now, I won't go at all. That I'll be standing over a hermit crab cage for the rest of my life." She lifted one shoulder and let it fall as she began to rinse off the plates in the sink and pass them to McKenzie. "But I feel like I could use a break, you know? I want to become a nurse or maybe even a nurse practitioner." She used a brush to scrub syrup off a plate. "But I'm not a great student. I mean, I'm no dummy, but I had to work hard for my good grades. I think a year off might make sense before I commit to four to six tough years."

Natalie set the griddle next to the sink and gathered the mixing bowl, measuring cups, and such from the island. "What do your parents think about your possible career choices?"

Bella pursed her lips. "My mother doesn't think I should declare a major yet. She thinks I should take some classes and see what I'm interested in. And what I'm good at."

"And your dad?"

Bella shrugged as she handed the eating utensils to McKenzie. "Who knows? He doesn't say much; otherwise, my mother flips out on him."

"So, if you don't go this year, when— Where did you get accepted?" Natalie asked.

"University of Maryland, main campus."

"So if you don't go to Maryland this school year, what will you do?"

"I thought about joining the Peace Corps or something like that."

McKenzie rolled her eyes. "I told her you have to apply to do that. And that you can't apply in June if you want to go in September. There's like a process."

Natalie was thinking the same thing and wondered why Bella's parents hadn't told her that.

"Or, I don't know," Bella went on. "I'll just get a job. Maybe here. Or maybe I'll go to New Mexico. I've always wanted to see New Mexico."

Natalie grabbed a dishcloth, reaching around Bella to wet it. "So . . . did you delay your freshman year or not?"

"Not yet."

"You think they'll let you delay a year at this point? Or will you lose your spot?"

McKenzie shook her head. "I tried to tell her that, too."

Bella grinned. "I'm sure that if I delay a year, I can talk to someone at the university. I won't lose my spot. And if I delay, then Mac would only be a year behind me. Right, Mac?"

Natalie glanced at her daughter as she wiped down the

stovetop. "So, thinking about the University of Maryland, are you?" she asked McKenzie. She would be a junior in high school in the fall and Natalie didn't know how it had happened, but it was time for McKenzie to start thinking about SAT scores and where she wanted to go.

"I don't know. Maybe," McKenzie said. She looked to Natalie. "I was telling Bella that the University of Delaware is such a good deal money-wise. I feel like it's dumb to pay more for an undergrad degree somewhere when Delaware has so many majors. And a huge study abroad program. I could go to Paris like you did, Mom. Or maybe somewhere like Costa Rica or Argentina."

Bella began to rinse out the now-empty sink. "Miss Know-It-All here." She cut her eyes at Natalie. *"Kids today."*

Natalie saw hurt in McKenzie's eyes. They made eye contact, and Mac looked away.

"Well. All done here," Natalie announced cheerfully. "Thank you, ladies. I appreciate your help. I've got work to do, and I'm picking Mason and Patrick up after swim team practice."

"Aunt Beth took them but can't pick them up?"

"Doctor's appointment."

"I need to go, too. Otherwise, my mother will lose her crap." Bella grabbed her backpack from one of the stools at the island and all three of them walked to the front door.

On the porch, Bella slung her backpack over her shoulder and hugged Natalie. "Thank you so much, Mrs. S, for having me over. And for the delicious tacos and pancakes. I want your pancake recipe. Can you text it to me?"

"Um . . . Sure," Natalie said.

"Got your phone?" Bella slid her sunglasses on. "I can airdrop my number."

Natalie glanced at McKenzie. As she suspected, her daughter didn't seem pleased that Natalie would have her new best friend's phone number. "Got it." Natalie slipped it out of her back pocket.

Bella studied her screen for a moment and then swiped and tapped. "There you go. You just have to hit accept. Text me and I'll have your number, too." She turned to McKenzie. "See you at work?"

"See you at work," McKenzie repeated.

Bella skipped down the porch steps. "Thanks again, Mrs. S."

"You're so welcome," Natalie said. "Come anytime. You're welcome anytime you want to come. Overnight, just for dinner, whatever. Door's always open."

"Can I come for blueberry pancakes next time you make them?" Bella teased.

Natalie nodded, clutching her phone, feeling as if she'd been gifted something in the exchange of phone numbers. Because what if Bella *was* her daughter? She would have her lost daughter's phone number now. "Absolutely," she said with a smile. "In fact, we're having a cookout on Sunday. Join us if you're not busy."

Bella stood on the bottom porch step, looking up at McKenzie. "You're having a cookout Sunday? And you didn't tell me?"

"It's for Father's Day," McKenzie mumbled. "No big deal. My dad thinks the whole holiday is silly."

Bella looked to Natalie. "She didn't invite me. Maybe she doesn't want me to come."

McKenzie groaned. "Of course you can come. I just figured you wouldn't want to. It'll be mostly family. Hamburgers, hot dogs. Uncle Rory will bring some bimbo we don't know and get drunk and throw people in the pool."

"Your hot uncle Rory is coming?" Bella asked. "I'm in. What can I bring?" She smiled up at Natalie. "I can't cook a lot of things, but I can make a really good charcuterie board."

"You don't have to bring anything," Natalie said, delighted the teen had agreed to come. "But that would be great. One o'clockish."

"I'll be here." Bella headed for her car.

"And bring your parents!" Natalie added, calling after her.

"I'm sure they'll be too busy," the teen responded.

Natalie drew back. "On Father's Day? Your dad doesn't want to be with you on Father's Day?"

"It's complicated," Bella said, and waved good-bye over her head.

Natalie and McKenzie stood on the porch and watched Bella walk to her car parked out front on the street. Bella waved again as she climbed in and pulled out a moment later.

"Come over anytime?" McKenzie demanded, turning to her mother angrily. "Come to our family cookout? Thanks a lot, Mom!" She spun around and stomped into the house.

Natalie followed, taken completely off guard by her daughter's response. "You're angry with me."

"Yes, I'm angry with you," McKenzie spat, going up the stairs to the second floor where her bedroom was.

"But why?" Natalie asked, following her. She didn't understand why her daughter was so angry. "What's wrong with telling your friend she's welcome in our home? You said she's home alone all the time. I thought she might enjoy the cookout." At the top of the stairs, she stopped. "I'm confused, Mac. Isn't Bella your friend? Don't you want her to come over?"

McKenzie whipped around, her eyes red and teary. "Yes, Mom. I do want Bella to come over. But I don't want *you* asking her!" She turned around and made a beeline for her bedroom door, slamming it hard behind her.

"Well." Natalie glanced at the dog that had followed them up the steps. "I think that went well. What do you think?" she asked the chubby corgi.

Not unexpectedly, Winston did not reply.

CHAPTER 12

The next evening, Natalie walked out of the house at nine to meet Conor, leaving McKenzie to keep an eye on Mason. Or maybe the other way around; some days it was hard to tell. As she walked toward the pub, on first her quiet street and then the bustling main avenue with its crowds, she went over in her head how she would bring up the subject of Bella.

As she got closer, her anxiety increased, which made no sense to her. How could she be nervous about talking to Conor—about anything? He was the easiest person she'd ever known to talk to. Even easier than her sister, because if he had any snarky thoughts he kept them to himself. He had always been a good listener. It was one of the many reasons why she had fallen in love with him all those years ago. Why she loved him more with each passing year.

Natalie stood on the sidewalk at the crosswalk on Albany Avenue, waiting for the light to change. Ahead, she could see O'Sullivan's new, brightly lit sign. She wondered if her hesitancy meant that, subconsciously, she agreed with Laney. Did she, somewhere in the back of her mind, think it was wrong to dredge up the past? Or was she afraid because this was too personal a subject to share with someone else, even with the man she had been sharing a bed with for nearly two decades? She had always believed she could tell Conor everything, share anything, but was this the one thing she didn't want to share with him?

When Natalie reached the pub door, she hesitated. *Was this a bad idea?* She'd already gotten Laney all worked up, and Natalie had been fretting nonstop since she met Bella. Was there any reason to worry Conor until she'd decided what she wanted to do? What if she chose not to pursue it? Then she would have gotten Conor upset for nothing. And he was under so much stress already, did it make sense to—

Someone pushed the door from the inside, and Natalie stepped out of the way just in time to avoid being hit by the heavy glass.

"Whoa!" A young man came out of the pub, followed by a blonde with a short, cute bob. His date, probably. "Sorry about that."

Natalie smiled, holding up her hand. "No problem. My fault. I wasn't paying attention."

The guy, in his early-to-mid-twenties, held the door open for the young woman, who Natalie now saw was pregnant. At least six months.

"You gotta try the loaded fries; right, Callie?" he said to his date.

"They were to die for," she told Natalie, bubbly with excitement. "And the brisket sandwich? Wow. We're coming back tomorrow night, right, sweetie?" She looped her arm through his. "My husband." She giggled, resting her head against his arm. She was wearing a cute, fluttery skirt and tank top that only a twentysomething pregnant woman could pull off. "We're on our honeymoon. I can't believe I'm married!" She looked up at him, grinning. "I can't believe I married you!"

He laughed with her, gazing into her eyes. "Neither could my mom, right?"

"Congratulations," Natalie said. "And I glad you enjoyed your meal. This is my place, ours; my husband and I and his family own it. I'm curious. How did you wind up here, if you don't mind me asking?"

"Oh!" the young woman said. "The guy at the front desk at the hotel where we are staying recommended it. We're staying at the Surf and Sand on the boardwalk. He told us you guys had just remodeled and changed up the menu and he thought it was the best food in town. He even gave us a copy of the menu."

Natalie made a mental note to send a thank-you to the manager at the Surf & Sand and maybe offer to send lunch to him and his staff in the fall as a thank-you. Conor would be glad to hear that all his hard work was paying off and that word was getting around. They'd set quite a bit of money aside for advertising in the local newspapers and even paid for air advertising, something Conor's father had never agreed to. A couple of times a week, a small plane was flying along the coast pulling a banner that advertised Albany Beach's only authentic Irish pub. But Conor and his brothers had also gone to all the hotels in the area and dropped off menus that included a coupon.

"Well, congratulations again, on the wedding and—" She indicated the woman's baby belly. As she looked at the attractive young couple, she couldn't help but think about her and Conor as newlyweds. She'd been pregnant when they married, too. Though not quite showing yet. It had been the *second* time birth control failed her. But Conor had been so happy about the pregnancy and had insisted it was the best thing that had ever happened to him because now Natalie had to marry him. Her heart still swelled with love for him when she thought about it, glad the memory hadn't faded.

The woman rested her hand on her belly. "I know, it's like magic, right? We got married Saturday, and look, already expecting."

They all laughed, and the man held open the door for Natalie. "We'll let you get to it. Nice to meet you."

"You too. And thanks for coming in." Natalie watched them walk away, arm in arm, and then went into the pub.

Thankfully, the place was packed with customers, with authentic Irish music blasting from hidden speakers and all the TVs playing rugby matches, the sound off. The pub smelled faintly of suntan lotion, new paint, and French fries. She heard the chatter of voices, laughter, and a toddler fussing, and exhaled with relief. These were the sounds of a successful restaurant. She circled the people gathered at the door waiting for a table and entered the main dining room. A crowd gathered around the bar, and every table was occupied except for a six-top that one of their new hires was busy cleaning off.

"Natalie, there you are," a voice called from behind her.

Natalie spun around to see the new waitress, Margot, whom she'd met the week before. The one who was studying to be a PA. She was carrying a tray of meals that seemed impossibly big for her small frame.

"Oh, hey." Natalie frowned. "You want help with that?" she asked, nodding at the tray.

She wasn't exactly sure how she would help, but it seemed like the right thing to say.

She'd helped her father-in-law out in the pub occasionally over the years, but usually she took orders and made Conor or one of his brothers carry the food from the kitchen to the table. Not out of laziness but caution. She was such a klutz sometimes. She could barely move her own plate from the counter to the table in her kitchen without dropping it.

"Nope, got it," Margot responded as she passed her. "Conor asked me to tell you, if I saw you, that he's in the back, but he'll be right out." She wrinkled her pert little nose. "I think he's ready to get out of here for the night."

Natalie felt her shoulders sag. "Having a bad night, is he? What's up?"

"One word," Margot said over her shoulder. "'Rory.'"

"No surprise there. Thanks for letting me know!" Natalie

called after her. Natalie then wove her way through the men and women gathered at the bar and headed down the hall where the office was. Halfway there, the door opened and Conor walked out.

"Hey, you." Natalie smiled at the sight of him. Tonight he was wearing his usual cargo shorts but sporting a black O'Sullivan's tee.

"Hey," he said, turning the knob to be sure it had locked. He looked tired. "Let's get out of here, *mo grá*," he said, grabbing her hand.

"Bad day?" she asked.

He didn't look at her. "Wait until we get outside."

Natalie nodded and squeezed his hand, looking up at him, but he didn't make eye contact. As they passed the bar on the way out, he called out, "Got this, Keith?"

The forty-something, ponytailed bartender who'd worked there for several years raised his free hand while pouring a shot of whiskey with the other. "I got this, Boss. Enjoy your evening."

They passed Margot, who had served the meals she'd been carrying and was now wiping down another table.

"Need anything, Margot?" Conor asked as they walked by her.

Margot shook her head. "I'm good. See you tomorrow."

Conor led Natalie out of the bar and onto the sidewalk. As the door closed, the sound of Soda Blonde, a contemporary Irish band out of Dublin, faded. "I hope you don't mind that we're not staying for a beer," he said, stopping under their new green and white awning.

"Not at all. Want just to grab your bike and go home? We can sit out by the pool and have a beer." She rubbed his shoulder, which was tight. "Or we can just go to bed. You look beat."

He thought for a moment, pressing his thumb and forefinger to his temples. "Let's go home by way of the beach. We haven't taken a walk on the beach together all week. I'll leave the bike here and walk over in the morning. Or you can drop me off if that works for you. I don't even know what you're doing tomorrow. I've been here so much, I don't know what's going on at home these days."

Which is maybe a blessing, Natalie thought to herself. "I can run you over. I have to take Mason to swim practice at nine."

They started walking in the direction of the boardwalk that ran for six blocks along the shore. "Sorry about rushing you out the door. I had to get out of there. Did you want to go somewhere else for a drink?" he asked. The crowds were beginning to thin out, and there were fewer families on the sidewalks, fewer minivans and more convertibles parked on the street than earlier in the day. Albany Beach's nightlife was now in full swing.

"I don't need a beer. Let's just go home," she told him. They walked the next block in silence, hand in hand, and only when they were taking the stairs down onto the beach did Natalie say, "So, sounds like you didn't have a great day. Want to talk about it?"

"That *fecking* brother of mine—" Conor grunted.

"Rory."

"Who else?"

They walked past a couple of teens sitting on beach towels smoking cigarettes. Had Conor not been upset, Natalie might have said something to the kids about their mothers and the dangers of smoking, but because her husband hated it when she offered unsolicited advice to strangers she kept it to herself. *At least for tonight.*

"I heard. Rory." She stopped to step out of her flip-flops. She'd worn her leather ones, not realizing they were going to walk home this way, and she didn't want to ruin the flip-flops by getting them wet.

He frowned, his hands on his hips. "How'd you hear about it? The Beth telegraph?"

"I didn't hear what he did, just that there had been a problem today. And not from Beth. Shay may not have told her. She's been having some issues with the pregnancy. She's petrified she's going to have to go on bed rest. I heard it from the new waitress," she explained.

"Ah, Margot. Great waitress. Nice gal. And never any drama. Not with customers and not with the staff. And she's had a hard go of it this year. The ex-husband is a complete buffoon. Anyway, I wish I had twenty of her."

Natalie looked up at him. By the moonlight reflected off the water, she could clearly see his face. He looked tired and thoroughly disgusted. "So . . . Rory get into it with Keith again?" At the water's edge, they turned south for home.

"No, but probably only because he didn't have the opportunity. It's better than that. Much better. No, he got served. *In our pub.*"

"*Served?*" Natalie asked, confused, thinking he meant served food. But that didn't make sense.

"You know, *served*. A subpoena. Evidently, he hasn't been paying child support, so Elaine is taking him to court. And do you think my brother just accepted the papers and let the grunt serving them walk out? Oh, no." Conor pulled his hand from hers so he could gesture. "My brother has to make a scene in the middle of the seven o'clock dinner hour. In front of customers!" he shouted. And Conor rarely raised his voice.

She groaned. Elaine was Rory's ex-wife. "I'm sorry, hon." As they walked, cool water lapped at her bare feet and tickled her toes.

"I was so pissed that I told him to go the hell home. Made him leave, causing a mini scene of my own. I tended bar with the new guy until Keith could get in. Of course, you know that's not my thing. I don't know how to make an orange crush or a . . . a purple *haze*. I hate making mixed drinks. The new bartender training ended up making them while I pulled beers and ran the register and credit card machine. Which is on the fritz again." He balled his hands into fists. "I cannot believe he's already up to his nonsense. Rory *swore* he had his *shite* together. That was the agreement before Shay and I cut him in."

The fact that Conor and Shay had included their brother in the family business without any financial commitment was still a sore spot with her. She understood why Conor did it; his dad pressed him and Shay hard to include Rory because he'd always had a weak spot for his middle son. But she didn't dredge up any of that. Instead, she said, "And where was Shay during all of this?"

Conor took a deep breath. "It was his turn to have the night off."

"But he would have come in."

"I know. But he needed the evening off. He's worried about Beth and wanted to be home and—" He shrugged. "It's not that I couldn't handle things. I just . . . I guess I'm disappointed that nothing has changed with Rory. That he hasn't changed."

"Back to Beth," Natalie said, concerned. "Anything I should know?" They walked around a family of four splashing in the surf. "Anything she's not telling us?"

"Nah. I think she was just tired." He took her hand again. "She painted the nursery by herself because Shay's been at work fourteen hours a day. And, of course, he feels guilty about that now that the doctor is talking about bed rest for Beth, making me feel guilty."

"I wish she'd asked me to help her paint the room. She's got to be exhausted. I can't fathom what it would be like to be pregnant at my age."

As she spoke the words, the truth of them sank in. She'd been so upset about the hysterectomy, but why? She didn't want to be pregnant again. She didn't want the heartburn and the stretch marks, and she didn't want to get up three or four times a night to try to breastfeed a fussy baby. She'd done it, and she was over it.

So maybe it was time to let that go. Time to call Pixie Patty's office and set a date for the hysterectomy once the kids went back to school in the fall and business slowed down at the pub.

"Anyway, let's not talk about Rory. I'm not going to change him. At least not tonight." Conor slid his arm around her shoulders. "And I'm walking on the beach with my gorgeous, sexy, smart wife. I don't want to think about my derelict brother anymore. I want to be with you, Nat. I miss you. I miss being with you. Talking with you."

She felt a warmth spread across her cheeks. He'd been complimenting her like that since the night they met, and she liked it, but at the same time, it made her uncomfortable. As if she didn't deserve the praise. Maybe because she hadn't grown up in a household where there were compliments. "I miss you, too," she said. "But we're fine. We knew this summer was going to be crazy, and we're fine. Everybody's fine."

Conor squeezed her in a hug and then dropped his arm so he could take her hand again as they walked. He knew his praise made her feel self-conscious, but he'd told her that she would just have to get used to it a long time ago. The fact that she hadn't didn't deter him. "Enough of my *shite*. How was your day? Oh, before I forget, housekeeping. We set for Sunday? I told everyone one o'clock."

"All set," Natalie said. Which wasn't true, but it would be Sunday at noon. She'd already decided to skip weeding the flower beds. And she'd offered Mason money to mow the lawn and clean the pool.

"Of course you're set. You've always been great at hosting things. You make it look so easy, even though I know very well it's not." He pointed at her. "And did you order Mason's baseball uniforms? Wait. You said you wanted to talk to me about something?" He stopped.

"Housekeeping first." She continued to walk, pulling him along.

She was stalling.

She'd told Laney she would tell him about Bella, but it didn't seem like the right time between her own indecision and Conor's problems with his brother. That was a lot for a night like tonight. "I ordered the uniforms. The website is as clunky as heck. It took three tries. And I ordered the thingy that goes in his ball cap to protect his gray matter if he gets hit in the head."

"And the DNA kit for Mac? For her paper? Did that get ordered? She asked me about it yesterday."

Natalie wondered why she hadn't asked her. McKenzie knew very well that her mother was the one who did that sort of thing. Shopping. This was one of her sneaky, teenage moves. If she didn't like Mom's answer, she went to Dad. But Natalie didn't say that to Conor. The matter was between her and her daughter.

"In the cart," she told Conor, lifting her face to catch the cool air coming in off the ocean. It had been a hot day, and the breeze felt good. "But I wanted to check with you before we cough up a hundred dollars for a social studies paper. I thought she was going to write about the western migration of families in the US in the nineteenth century. That's a better topic."

"I don't know. You can ask her, but last I heard, she was going with migration to the US and wanted to be able to use examples of her own family. Which I have to admit"—he looked at her—"is a good idea. It makes the subject more real for a kid."

"Don't you think that's going to be a harder paper to write?" she asked him.

He shrugged. "I don't know, babe. But she's almost sixteen. I feel like we need to let her make that mistake on her own."

"Right," Natalie said with a sigh. "I just wish it wasn't going to cost us a hundred bucks."

"Oh, come on. We can afford it." He swung her hand in his. "We're not paupers. You said our household finances were looking good."

"They are. And they'll continue on that trajectory if we don't spend money overindulging our children too often."

He pulled a face. "I don't think buying a DNA test for a paper that's one-third of her first-semester social studies grade is indulging our daughter too much." He shrugged. "And then she'll have all of the cool ancestry information. Honestly, I think that's why she wants the DNA test. The paper is just an excuse to get us to buy it for her."

"Let me make sure she's doing that paper," Natalie said, and they continued walking. They had just passed the starfish condo, as they called it. A small, older condo of only twelve units and two stories with a big copper starfish on the front of the building.

"Great. So what did you want to talk to me about?" Conor asked.

"We can talk about it another time," she said, trying to sound casual.

"Am I in trouble?" He stopped again. "Because if I am, I'd rather know now. I'm already in a *shite* mood. It's a good time."

She laughed, but mostly to stall again. Suddenly she had a bad case of cold feet. She didn't want to turn her family upside down if she didn't have to, and she knew that if she pursued this with Bella that would happen. How could it not? So she had to be sure that was what she wanted. "It can wait," she said.

"Nope." He waggled his thumb. "Out with it. We're not going to start this. Not after being married these many years, Nat. We tell each other everything. Right? That was the agreement. When we married, we promised each other we would be better communicators than our parents were."

Now what did she say? She suffered a moment of panic and looked away, out over the outgoing tide, thankful clouds had drifted and the moonlight wasn't so bright anymore. Then it came to her. She looked at him. "I hear we're getting a Tesla."

"Laney," he said, lowering his chin to give her a look. He and Laney had always gotten along well. Conor loved her as much as Laney loved him, but that didn't mean they never argued or disagreed with each other. And while Natalie preferred to handle disagreements calmly, Laney loved a good row.

"She said something about a code we needed so we could get free charges?" Natalie narrowed her gaze. "I wasn't aware we were buying a Tesla."

"Babe, we've been talking about an electric car for years." He took her hand, and they walked again. "And your car has got to go."

"My car's fine," she argued, relieved they weren't going to talk about Bella tonight. Because . . . because she wasn't ready to commit yet and if she told Conor, she almost felt as if she would have to go through with it.

"It's leaking oil."

"We don't have money for a car payment right now," she countered. "And we won't get anything for mine, even if we repair the problem. So I may as well drive it until it doesn't drive anymore."

"But, babe, we've got that hefty down payment for a car sitting in the bank."

"I know, but I thought you wanted to save that for McKenzie."

He laughed and stopped. "I'm not buying *her* a Tesla. I want to buy you a Tesla. How about this? How about we get the Tesla, which you can drive—"

"I don't want to drive a Tesla. I want to drive my old, oil-leaking car."

"—And we'll get the Subaru fixed and McKenzie can drive your old car when she gets her license." He grabbed her hand, keeping her from walking away from him. "Then when she wrecks it, it won't be a big deal."

"When she *wrecks* it?" Natalie laughed and let him pull her into his arms. "Do you think we should let her get her license if she's just going to wreck our car?"

"Give us a kiss," he told her, looking into her eyes.

She gave him a quick peck. "No, a real kiss," he told her, his voice husky. With one hand, he tucked a lock of hair behind her ear. "I like your hair longer like this. I'm glad you're growing it long again."

"Compliments will not a Tesla get you," she teased.

"No? How about this, then?"

Conor's lips brushed hers, and she relaxed in his arms, returning his kiss. As their mouths met and she realized he was hungry for her, thoughts of Bella and the lost baby faded in her mind, and she left the hard decision for another day.

CHAPTER 13

"Conor says the burgers will be done in five," Laney told Natalie as she slid a plate of raw beef patties back into the refrigerator. "He made half of them, figuring he'd make the others for later." She closed the door with her hip, munching on a chicken wing. "Christ on a crutch, how was I ever a vegan?" she asked. "These are the best smoked wings I have ever had in my life. Ev-er."

"They are good, aren't they?" Natalie poured dressing onto the pasta salad she had made just in case her sister-in-law didn't show up with her assigned dish. Pasta salad. Beth had not brought it. Which was fine because hers would have been out of a box. Which was also fine—for Beth, but as she had pointed out many times before, Natalie was a food snob. Natalie didn't like pasta salad or anything else processed and from a box. *Except, of course, Cheez-It crackers. Which she was trying to quit.* She liked fresh vegetables, good pasta, and homemade dressing. Beth had brought corn chips and guacamole and salsa, instead, which was perfect. Natalie should have asked her to bring that to begin with.

"Good move, you and the kids getting him the smoker grill

for Father's Day." Laney leaned on the counter, still gnawing on the chicken wing

"Confession," Natalie said sheepishly. "It was on impulse to distract him from the idea of buying a new car."

Laney laughed. "Okay, I can see that. Was he surprised? By the fancy smoker grill, not the bait and switch."

"That's not a bait and switch. There was no bait. Not exactly. And he was surprised. And tickled." Natalie added a little more dressing and folded it gently to keep from crushing the delicate orecchiette pasta. "He'd already picked it out a year ago. But it wasn't cheap, and we were arranging the loan for the pub, so we held off on any big, unnecessary expenses. Luckily, they were still in stock yesterday."

"You should sell these smoked wings at the pub. You'd make a killing." Laney dropped the bone into the trash can and went to the sink to wash her hands.

"So . . . you get to talk to Bella?" Natalie asked, lowering her voice. Everyone was outside around the pool, so there was no one, to her knowledge, around to hear her, but she wanted to be careful.

"I did."

Natalie grabbed a spoon and tasted the salad, then reached for the pepper grinder. Laney had her back to her. "And?"

"And . . ." Laney shrugged, drying her hands on a dish towel. "She's . . . you know, nice."

"She is *so* nice. So sweet," Natalie went on excitedly. "And talented. She made that beautiful charcuterie board. Did I tell you that?"

"You did. *Twice.*"

Natalie ignored her sister's tone. "I don't know that McKenzie knows what a charcuterie board is."

Crossing her arms over her chest, Laney gave Natalie a look.

"What?" Natalie added more pepper and tasted the salad again.

"You can't do that."

"Do what?"

"Start comparing the two—Mac and Bella. There's a two-year difference between them, and from what you've said, they've been raised very differently. Bella can whip up a charcuterie board, so what? McKenzie reads to her great-grandmother in a nursing home and cleans shitty cages for the animal shelter."

"Bella's going to do a shift with Mac at the shelter this week," Natalie went on. "I don't know what day. Depends on their work schedule. They're so desperate for help this time of year that the volunteer coordinator said they could come in whenever they could make it. I guess people don't want to fight the traffic to get over there. Everyone is telling her they'll be back in the fall."

"And meanwhile, unspayed kitties are getting knocked up all over town," Laney griped, taking the spoon from her sister and sampling the pasta salad. "Good." She licked the spoon. "Speaking of reading to Nana, where is she? She was outside in her wheelchair guarding the beer cooler, and then she was gone."

"I brought her inside to lay down. She's on our bed, dead to the world."

Laney cringed. "You better be careful using that word. One of these days, she *is* going to be dead to the world."

"What a terrible thing to say!" Natalie added a serving spoon to the pasta salad bowl and handed it to her sister. "Can you take that out to the food table?"

Laney accepted the bowl. "Why is that terrible? She *is* going to die at some point. So are you and I."

"Could you take that outside? I'm going to check on her and then bring out the condiments." Natalie opened the refrigerator to retrieve them. "And try to talk to Bella some more. See what you can find out about the parents." Again, she had lowered her voice when she mentioned the teenager's name. "See if you can get any intel. You're good at that."

"I am not going to be your infiltrator!" Laney declared indignantly. "You really need to let this go. Take your chickening out telling Conor the other night as a sign."

"I did not chicken out," Natalie lied. "It wasn't a good time. He'd had a bad day at work." She added a bottle of ketchup and mustard to a metal serving tray. "And I don't believe in signs."

"Neither do I, but I'm telling you, Sis. I see Do Not Enter signs all over this one. You're going to create a monster here that you cannot put back in the bag."

Natalie hesitated, trying to decide if she was willing to turn this discussion into an argument, and decided she wasn't. And not on Father's Day, not with so many people there. Not when there was a risk of Conor finding out they had disagreed and asked what they were arguing over. "*Noted*," she said with a nod, and then began to dig around in the door for the mayonnaise.

Laney stood there in her cute red shorts and a white tank top that looked way too good on her for a woman of forty-one, staring at Natalie, and then she exhaled dramatically and walked out of the kitchen.

A few minutes later, having checked on Nana, Natalie stepped out into the sunshine, armed with the tray of condiments. The party was in full swing in their backyard with Jimmy Buffett music playing from a mini speaker, and paper lanterns swinging in the faint breeze coming off the bay. Earlier people had been gathered around the new smoker grill and the beer cooler, but now they were grabbing paper plates and getting into a line for the buffet table.

It was a nice-sized group: Conor's brother Shay and his wife, Beth, and Patrick; Conor's uncle Sean, and his wife, and their two sons and their wives and kids. No sign of the black sheep of the Sullivan family, Rory, yet, which was fine with Natalie. Then the older couple Lillian and Phil, who lived next door and were like family, were there, too. As well as Conor and Natalie's friends Alice and Ted Durham and their kids. And, of course, Laney. And then there was her and Natalie's cousin Lara and her family, who vacationed in Albany Beach every year. *The usual suspects.* Initially, Natalie had thought it was a shame Conor's parents couldn't be there. They were still on another cruise, somewhere in the Baltic, but then considering Rory's latest nonsense, maybe it was better.

"There you are." Conor slid a platter of burgers and cheeseburgers onto the table and took the tray from her. "I was just coming in for you. The kids were hungry, so I told them to go for it." He leaned down and kissed her.

"Sorry. Checking on Nana."

"She okay?"

"Fine. She likes our duvet. Maybe I'll get her one for her birthday. She says they keep it too cold at her place. She has a service guy coming around tomorrow."

Conor's mouth twitched into a smile. Nana was always talking about workers she was waiting on. Memories from when she had her own home, Natalie assumed.

"Just buy her the duvet. Who knows if she'll be with us by the time her birthday rolls around again."

Natalie spread open her arms. "Why is everyone talking about Nana dying?" She laid her hand on his muscular forearm. "We good on ice? I guess the ice maker is going to have to be replaced. Wouldn't you know it would die Memorial Day weekend?"

"We've got plenty. Shay brought a whole cooler full from the pub. If we need more, he said he could—"

"Can I have two burgers?" Mason interrupted his father. He and Patrick had bypassed the line and were going straight for the hot dogs and burgers.

"Just one the first time through," Natalie directed, tugging on the back of Mason's T-shirt to pull him away from the table. "Everyone gets one before you get seconds. But no butting. Get at the end of the line. You too, Patrick," she told her nephew.

"We have pickles?" Conor asked, tipping a bottle of beer.

He was wearing an apron that read *Best Dad Ever* over his shorts and T-shirt, a gift from the children the previous year. "I thought we had pickles in the fridge."

Mason groaned as he walked away from the tropical-print-covered table in full sulk. "After we eat, can we go skateboarding? Just on our street."

"Sure. Wear your helmets!" Natalie called as they walked away. "And check with Aunt Beth before you go," she added. She turned back to Conor. "We have pickles. I'll get them."

"I can do it." They stepped back to make room for their guests filling their plates.

"Oh, my goodness. What a gorgeous charcuterie board," their neighbor Lillian remarked. She was wearing a bright pink and teal Lilly Pulitzer shift dress that made her look fifty instead of seventy. The oversized sunglasses helped.

"It is, isn't it? McKenzie's friend Bella made it," Natalie said. "And where are McKenzie and Bella?" she asked, looking up at Conor.

He shrugged. "Dunno. They were in the pool a few minutes ago. Probably went inside to do whatever teenage girls do after they swim. Some kind of hair thing."

"Ready for another beer, Conor?"

Conor turned to the woman speaking, and when he moved Natalie saw that it was Margot from the pub. Where had she come from? She must have arrived while Natalie was in the house. She hadn't realized Conor had invited any employees, and it struck her as strange that a) he didn't say something to Natalie about her coming and b) he had invited her at all. They hadn't invited friends and acquaintances other than their neighbors and the Durhams, whom they had been palling around with since Mason was little. It wasn't that kind of party. It was a family thing.

"I'm still good," Conor told Margot. "Thanks. You remember Natalie." He slid his arm across Natalie's shoulders and rested it there. "On second thought, I will take it." He chugged the last of the beer he already had, and Natalie took the empty bottle from him.

"Nice to see you, Margot." Natalie lowered the bottle to her side, not positive she meant it. There was something about this young woman she didn't like. She just wasn't sure what it was. "I'll get the pickles." She flashed a smile at Margot and walked away. As she stepped into the house, she caught a glimpse of Conor and Margot chatting together and made a mental note to ask him later what had prompted him to invite her. It just seemed . . . odd.

Natalie checked on her nana in the bedroom, still asleep, and then grabbed a jar of pickles from the pantry. As she headed back out onto the patio, she heard the front door fly open and hit the wall with a bang.

"Mom! Dad!" McKenzie screamed.

The tone of her voice told Natalie something was wrong, and she set the jar down hard on the counter and took off for the front of the house. "What's wrong?"

"Mom!" McKenzie cried, reaching for her hands. "You have to come! It's Mason." She let go of her mother and whipped around and ran for the open door. "Bella is on the phone with nine-one-one!"

"Nine-one-one?" Natalie ran after her. "What happened?"

McKenzie ran out the door and across the front porch. "Someone hit him. With her car. The old lady with the purple hair down the street."

Natalie's brain went numb, but her legs didn't fail her. *Oh my God, oh my God*, she kept thinking, tears filling her eyes. The moment they hit the sidewalk and turned right, she spotted Mrs. Ranger's yellow VW Bug with eyelashes over the headlights at a strange angle in the road in the intersection. Mrs. Ranger was standing in front of her car in a floral housedress, looking down. Other people were gathered in a circle; some Natalie knew, some she didn't.

Bella ran toward them. "Someone's on their way." As she

said it, the sound of an emergency vehicle wailed in the distance. They were only half a mile from the firehouse.

"Is he conscious?" Natalie demanded, sprinting past Bella, running toward the car and the knot of people. To her son. There was a loud buzzing in her ears, but she wasn't crying. She was too scared to cry. *Please let him be all right, please let him be all right*, she prayed to God and to anyone else in the universe who would listen.

"He's conscious. He's talking," McKenzie said. "He's afraid you're going to be mad."

"The nine-one-one lady said to leave him where he was!" Bella called after them. "Don't move him until they get here!"

"Get your father!" Natalie told McKenzie as she pushed through the crowd.

The moment she saw Mason sprawled on the road, she dropped to her knees on the pavement. He was lying on his side, his eyes open, his helmet, thankfully, still on his head. "Mason," she exhaled.

"I didn't do anything wrong, Mom," he said, crying. "She was supposed to stop. She didn't stop."

Natalie inched closer to him on all fours, reaching out to smooth the hair that had fallen forward over one eye. His chin was scraped and bleeding and she used the hem of her T-shirt to brush loose gravel from the wound gently. "It's okay, sweetie. Can you tell me what hurts?" She looked over her shoulder to see McKenzie pushing her way through the crowd. "You need to go get your father," she told her sternly.

"I sent Bella."

"Nothing hurts," Mason protested, his lower lip quivering. "I want to get up."

McKenzie dropped to the ground and crawled up next to Natalie, looking down at her little brother. "You dumb *s-h-i-t*," she said, spelling the curse word the way he did. "You're supposed to stay on the skateboard and off the road." There was emotion in her voice: relief and sisterly love, but she was also calm. Remarkably calm.

"Butt wipe," Mason countered.

"The paramedics are on their way, fartknocker," McKenzie told him. "So chill. They're going to check you out."

Mason started to try to get up, and Natalie saw blood all over his hand. She wondered where else he was bleeding. What wounds she couldn't see. "Just lay there, sweetie, until they get here," she told him, fascinated that her children could be teasing each other at a moment like this. At least it meant his brain was okay, didn't it? If he could make fun of his sister, he didn't have a brain injury? "You're okay," she told him, looking him over for anything obviously wrong—broken bones, anything dislocated. She had no formal medical training, but her mom's instincts were pretty good. "You're going to be fine."

"I *am* fine," Mason fussed. "I just scraped my knee bad. And maybe my elbow."

"Oh my God, Natalie? I'm so sorry," a woman blubbered behind her.

Natalie glanced over her shoulder to see Mrs. Ranger in her bright floral housecoat and flip-flops with big plastic daisies glued on them. "I was going over to Lefty's to get takeout, and my phone rang, and I didn't see the boys and—"

Patrick. Natalie had been so intent on Mason's injuries that she hadn't even asked if Patrick was okay. Had he been hit, too? "Where's Patrick?" she asked Mason, meeting his gaze. What if Patrick was dead and her son was alive? She suddenly felt like she might be sick. "Mason, where's Patrick?" she repeated.

He craned his neck, and McKenzie laid her hand on his arm, which was also bloody. "Lay still, dude. Otherwise, if your neck's broken, they'll have to amputate your head."

Natalie blinked. "Where is he? Where's your cousin?"

"I don't know. He saw McKenzie and Bella on the front porch and went to get her when Mrs. Ranger hit me. By the time I realized she wasn't going to stop at the stop sign, it was too late to get out of her way."

"I didn't see them," Mrs. Ranger sobbed from behind Natalie.

Natalie ignored her. "So Patrick wasn't hit?"

Mason's lips were quivering again. "No, he jumped off his board, but I couldn't get out of her way soon enough."

The sirens were louder now, two distinct sounds: police and the paramedics.

"Nat!" Conor hollered from a distance.

"Here, Dad!" McKenzie jumped up and waved.

The crowd of neighbors and motorists that had gathered parted to let Conor through, and he dropped down on the other side of Mason. He met Natalie's gaze for a split second as he gently laid his hand on his son's shoulder. "What's going on here? Family meeting called, and no one told me?"

"Good one, Dad," McKenzie said.

The emergency vehicles arrived, one coming from each end of the street, and an authoritative voice urged the onlookers to step back. A moment later, Natalie spotted a female police officer she and Conor knew from the pub. They also knew one of the two paramedics approaching carrying duffel bags. Leo, an Eagle Scout, had taught Mason's general first-aid class at his Boy Scout meeting.

"Could you let us have a look?" Leo said, setting his bag down beside Natalie. When he saw Mason, he smiled. "Hey, I know you. What's going on, man?"

"Just hanging out on the road," Mason piped up. "Not going to need resuscitation, but I think you better check my vitals."

Behind them, Natalie could hear the officer speaking to a sobbing Mrs. Ranger.

"I think you're right." Leo crouched down over Mason, pulling his bag closer. "Mom and dad of this fine young man?" he asked as he reached for Mason's wrist to check his pulse.

Natalie wiped at her eyes. "Yes."

"If you don't mind giving us just a bit of room, we're going to give my friend Mason here a quick look, and then we'll probably transport him."

Natalie was suddenly shaking. "Transport him? He has to go the hospital?"

"Just so a doc can have a good look at him," the other paramedic explained.

"Come on, Nat." Conor helped her to her feet. "The paramedics need to check him out, but he's fine," he told her gently. "Come on, Mac, let's give them some room."

Natalie looked up at Conor. He had tears in his eyes, but they seemed like tears of relief more than anything else.

"He's fine," Conor repeated calmly, wrapping his arms around her.

Natalie closed her eyes and rested her forehead on his shoulder. She knew Mason was going to be fine, but all she could think was, *What if he hadn't been? What if he had died?*

At that moment, she realized she had to find out if Bella was her daughter because her children were too precious to her not to.

CHAPTER 14

That evening, after they had checked on Mason in his bed for what seemed like the one-hundredth time, Natalie and Conor sat outside in the dark in deck chairs. Conor took a sip of beer, staring into the darkness, and she wished she hadn't told him about Bella tonight. But she'd been so scared and . . . and it just came out.

His long silence was worse than if he had just lost it and raised his voice to her. Which he never did, but at this point Natalie would have welcomed it. He had never been this angry with her before, so angry that he wouldn't speak.

Natalie sat with her hands in her lap, looking at a spot of blood on the hem of her jean shorts. Mason's blood. *He's okay. He's okay.* The thought had been running through her mind nonstop for hours.

As Mason had self-diagnosed, he was fine. Just banged up. A doctor had given him a thorough exam at the emergency department, cleaned and bandaged his scraped leg. He also had his wrist X-rayed, which turned out to be sprained but not broken. Everyone Mason saw in the emergency department reiterated that he had possibly saved his own life by wearing his helmet and wearing it properly. Mason had been given a removable splint to immobilize his wrist, had been advised to take an over-the-counter pain reliever, and had been released. They'd arrived home from the hospital before seven, and he had gone straight to bed, angry that he wasn't supposed to play video games for a few days to give his wrist a rest.

Once he was in bed, Natalie and Conor had done some cleaning up, though there hadn't been much to do because Laney . . . well, Laney was Laney, and she had put all their guests to work putting away food, taking out the trash, doing dishes, and even cleaning the new grill. After McKenzie had retired to her room, Natalie and Conor went out back to sit at the pool and have a Father's Day drink together.

Halfway through Conor's second beer, Natalie had blurted out that she thought Bella was her birth daughter. Things had gone downhill from there. Conor was now finishing his third beer.

Natalie shifted her gaze to look at him. Light reflected off the pool water across his face. He looked tired. And angry. Definitely angry. She could see it in the set of his square jaw and the way his eyes crinkled at the corners.

"Are you going to say something?" she asked when she couldn't stand it anymore.

"What more is there to say?" He glanced at her as he tipped back the beer bottle and then looked away again. "It sounds like you've already made up your mind. What I think is irrelevant. *Apparently.*"

"Conor." She rested her hand on his bare knee.

"What? What do you want me to do? Say you should do this? Because I can't say that. My opposition is—" He stopped and started again. "Adamant."

She exhaled. What *did* she want from him? She wanted his support in her choice, of course, but she also wanted his blessing. Which she had suspected she wouldn't get. That was why she had put off talking to him about it. "I guess I need you to understand why I want to do it." *Have to do it.*

He leaned back in his chair, closing his eyes, the beer bottle dangling from his fingertips. "I don't think that's going to happen," he said, his tone neutral.

She gripped the arms of the lounge chair with teal and orange cushions and sat upright. "If Bella is my daughter, doesn't she have the right to—"

"See, Nat," he interrupted, his eyes flying open. "That's part of my not understanding any of this." He turned his head to look at her. "I'm not going to be able to understand because, in my mind"—he gestured to his temple with the bottle—"the baby you put up for adoption was never yours. In my mind, you carried that baby for another woman. For another couple. That baby wasn't yours, she was theirs, and she was *always* theirs. Basically, you were holding her for them."

She didn't say anything because she didn't know what to say. What he was repeating back to her were words that, if not exact, were close to what she had told him when they met.

When he realized she wasn't going to respond, he went on. "You told me yourself back then that by the end of the first trimester you'd decided to put the baby up for adoption. Your parents didn't make that decision for you. They may have nudged you in that direction, but from everything you told me, there was no pressure from them. They would have supported you no matter what your choice would have been. But you decided, *you* decided, that the best thing for the baby, and for yourself, was for her to go to people who were ready to be parents. A couple who desperately wanted a child but couldn't conceive."

Tear clouded Natalie's eyes, and she shifted her gaze to watch the automatic vacuum creep along the bottom of the pool. "I guess I can't expect you to understand," she said quietly. "What it's like to carry a life inside you."

"No. I cannot completely understand it because I haven't

experienced it." He spoke each word in staccato. "But I do know what it's like to be responsible for those two lives in the house." He hooked his thumb over his shoulder in that direction. "Have you thought about them? About what this could potentially do to them if they find out you gave away their sister?" There was anger in his voice, but he kept it under control.

The words "gave away" cut her deeply. She hadn't *given her baby away*; she had sacrificed herself for that child. Because it was the right thing to do. At least at the time, she had thought so. But that act of sacrifice had left a hole deep inside her that no matter how happy she was, how successful, could never be filled. And who knew, maybe even if she found her daughter, the void would remain. Because she would still have done what she had done.

What she would do over, had she been her twenty-year-old self.

"Of course I've thought about McKenzie and Mason!" she snapped. "All I've done is think about them and how this could potentially affect them. But does it have to be a bad thing, finding they have a half sister? If I tell them about the adoption, explain why I did it, they're smart kids. They'll understand." As she spoke the words, she thought of McKenzie's negative comment about a mother giving up her child. But when Natalie explained the situation, McKenzie would understand, wouldn't she? And Mason, he wouldn't be upset. His belief system, his emotions, were uncomplicated. When she explained what had happened, he would accept her choice to not have kept the baby with the idea that she was doing the best she could at the time. And she knew he had such a big heart that he would accept a half sister into his life without any fuss or angst.

"Okay," Conor said. "You've considered McKenzie and Mason. So what now? You want to tell them that you think Bella is the daughter you gave up for adoption?"

She looked at him, surprised he would say such a thing. Of course she wasn't going to say anything to them. Not now, at least, not when she didn't know. She'd always thought that Conor was the one person who truly understood her, who knew her better than anyone. Was she mistaken?

"I'm not going to say *anything*. Not now. Not yet, at least." She shifted her body so that she was facing him, her bare knee brushing his. She needed him so badly right now to understand her. She needed him to take her in his arms and tell her everything would be okay. That if this was what she wanted, it was what he wanted.

But that wasn't going to happen. Conor was making that clear.

So . . . she needed to either let this go—something she might have done early on in the marriage when she often acquiesced to him because she trusted his decisions better than her own—or . . . Or she could do what she wanted to do. She could find out if this teen was her daughter without his blessing.

As Natalie waited for Conor to say something, to say *anything*, she felt as if she was teeter-tottering on the edge of some great cliff in their marriage. In all these years, she had never gone against him on a decision this momentous.

He stared at the pool, not looking at her. "But if it turns out this girl was the baby you gave birth to, you'll tell them then?"

She thought for a moment. "Honestly, I don't know, Conor." She balled her hands into fists. "I guess it would depend on her. On what she wanted."

"Oh, so if you find out Bella is your daughter, you're going to tell *her*? How about her parents? They're going to be thrilled. You agreed to a closed adoption and then you tracked down their baby and opened the whole damned thing right up." He took another drink of his beer. "Do you realize how crazy this is? There's no way you could have a baby and eighteen years later she ends up becoming friends with your daughter. It's too big of a coincidence. A ridiculous possibility."

Laney had made the same argument, and Natalie considered giving him the same examples she had given her sister. But she knew it wouldn't sway him. And she knew he was right. It did seem like a crazy coincidence. But wasn't life crazy?

"Do you not think Bella resembles McKenzie?" Natalie studied his face. "Not just a little bit?"

He groaned. "Not really. I mean . . . she looks like a teenager, a pretty, Caucasian blonde. They both do. Honestly, I think that friend of hers . . . what's her name? Olivia? I think they look more alike than Mac and Bella."

"Olivia and McKenzie don't look anything alike. Olivia's not even a natural blonde. She bleaches her hair."

Conor made a fist, clenching his jaw. "Dammit, Nat."

"What?" She stared at him, trying to see the man she loved, not the man sitting beside her trying to silence the most primal need of a mother: to know her young. "Why are you so angry?"

"*Why am I angry?*" he asked, his anger turning to perplexity. "You have to ask me that?" He set his bottle down hard on the table beside him. "I'm angry because I'm afraid you're going to ruin everything. We have a really good life here, Nat. We love each other, we love our kids, and they're *good* kids. Happy, healthy kids. And we have a good life—the pub, our jobs, our friends. The community. And you want to *fecking* bust it all open?" The anger was there again, raw and so unlike him.

Tears filled her eyes, but she didn't look away from him. In the same way she couldn't look away from the fact that Bella might be hers. "I think I have to do this," she whispered. "So can we . . . agree to disagree? At least for now?"

"I'd rather you agreed to think about it a while longer before you do anything."

"But I've *been* thinking about it. I've thought of nothing else since I met Bella."

"Two weeks," he argued.

"Going on three," she murmured.

He held her gaze for what seemed like minutes and then quietly said, "At least promise me you won't tell anyone else. I know Laney knows, but no one else. Think on it a little longer before you— How are you even going to find out? It was a closed adoption."

"I don't know." She toyed with her wedding ring. "See what I can find out from the adoption agency."

"They're not going to tell you anything. It was a binding agreement you signed."

"The information might be somewhere on the Internet. Remember that friend I had when we first got married and were living in the apartment. Tiana. She lived two doors down." He didn't say anything, so she went on. "She was put up for adoption when she was like six months old, and she found her mother."

"She was an adult, and she found her. Her birth mother didn't go looking for her. Totally different." He took a deep breath. "Please don't tell anyone you're doing this. Not our family, our friends, not Bella or her parents. And for God's sake, don't say anything to McKenzie. Don't make some sort of impulsive, guilt-ridden confession."

She wanted to shoot back that she would never do anything so impulsive, but occasionally she did make imprudent decisions that she later regretted. Didn't everyone? But she never made them on big things. It was more agreeing to make a hundred cupcakes for a school event or buying a pair of expensive jeans on sale in a size smaller than she wore in the hopes of losing the ten-pound bag of flour she was carrying around her waist.

Natalie covered his hand resting on the arm of the chair with hers. "I won't say anything to anyone without talking to you first. I promise."

"I can't believe you told Laney first."

Sensing maybe there was a bit of jealousy there, Natalie chewed on her lower lip. "If it makes you feel any better, she's in your camp."

"Good for her." He ran his hand over his face and then his head, pushing his dark hair back. "I think I'm going to hit the shower and go to bed. I've had enough fun for one day." He rose, pulling his hand from hers. "You coming?"

She looked up at him. She hated doing this to him—upsetting him this way. She hated it so much that she was tempted to tell him never mind. Or at least agree to think on it a while longer. Because she was a people pleaser. And because she didn't want to make those she loved unhappy. But she was beginning to realize that, over the years, she had sacrificed herself, her own wants and needs, to do that. And maybe, just maybe, she'd sacrificed too much.

"I'm going to check the salt level in the pool, and then I'll be in," Natalie answered, looking at the moonlight dancing across the water instead of him.

He grabbed the three empty beer bottles. "I'll check on Mason."

She watched him walk into the shadows of the house and wondered if this moment was one she would look back on and realize it was the one that changed their marriage, their lives. "I love you, Conor!" she called after him.

"I love you, too," he responded.

But he didn't look back.

CHAPTER 15

Mac dropped onto her bed, pushing her earbuds into her ears. "About time you picked up," she told Bella. "Where have you been? I called and texted you like ten times."

"I went to Gunner's." She sounded like she was in her car, the windows down.

"Your parents let you?"

Bella laughed. "Of course not. They thought I was still at your house."

"Wait. So my brother gets run over by a car, practically in front of our house, and you're hooking up with some guy who makes French fries for a living?"

"He got fired."

Mac refused to even respond to that. Gunner was a Loser with a capital *L*. "Why did you leave without even saying goodbye?" She tried not to whine, but she was upset. If the same thing had happened at Bella's house, there was no way in hell she would have left until she knew her friend's little brother was going to be okay. Or, at the very least, she would have told Bella she was leaving.

"He was not run over. He got knocked off his skateboard by

an old lady going like, what? Five miles an hour? The paramedics said he was fine. And I figured you needed to be with your family and that whole thing."

Mac's eyes got watery, and she wiped at them, annoyed with herself. She felt stupid being so upset about the little butt wipe. Bella was right; he was fine. Mrs. Ranger had barely tapped him with her silly car with the eyelashes. But it had still been scary. So scary. And she was hurt that Bella didn't get that. Of course, she didn't have a brother or sister, so maybe she didn't understand how much Mac loved the little dweeb. Mac's mom was always saying you should look at things from the other person's point of view when you don't get why they said or did something.

"You should have told me you were leaving," Mac said. "I didn't even know you'd left until after they took Mason away in the ambulance. I couldn't find your car—that's the only way I knew you were gone. Mom was hollering at me to get in the car, so we could go to the hospital, and I'm standing in the street looking for you. You should have told me you were leaving," she repeated.

"Fine, Mom. I'll tell you next time your brother gets hit by a car."

Mac heard her inhale, and she guessed she was smoking. She didn't ask Bella *what* she was smoking, but she could make a good guess. She'd smelled it on her before. In her car, too. Mac didn't think smoking weed was a big deal, not any worse than drinking vodka, for sure, but Bella was only eighteen, and like the vodka, it wasn't legal. Mac had told her that she might not ever get to be a PA if she ended up with a drug arrest. She wouldn't be able to get a license to write prescriptions. Aunt Laney had told Mac all about it. Once Aunt Laney decided she wanted to be a veterinarian, she stopped smoking marijuana because she said she wanted to be a vet more than she wanted to get high.

Bella held her breath and then exhaled loudly. "How is he anyway? The little nut sack?"

"He's fine." Mac drew her leg up and picked at her lime-green toenail polish. She wasn't crazy about Bella calling Mason names. It was okay if she did it; she was his sister. But Mac didn't say anything because she really liked Bella. She was so different from her other friends that Mac didn't want to do anything that would ruin their friendship.

"Hang on," Bella said. "Pulling into the garage. I might lose you for a sec when my phone switches over from the car."

While she waited, Mac took a couple of deep breaths. Something else her mother had taught her, though she didn't remember the exact details as to how it helped. Something about the vagus nerve sending a signal to your body to tell it to chill out. It worked, and she secretly used it all the time when she was nervous or scared, like when she had a big test or when she interviewed for the Burkes job. All of her friends and the adults she knew thought she was so confident in herself, but she wasn't. She had tried it the first time she had to stand in front of a group and speak. She had been in the fourth grade and had to give a presentation on the life cycle of a monarch butterfly. As her mother had suggested, she had pretended to feel confident and fooled everyone. And it was still working.

"Can you hear me?" Bella asked.

Mac heard the automatic garage door closing. It was interesting that Bella thought her parents were mean to her, yet since she'd started driving, one of her parents always parked in the driveway, so there was room in the two-car garage for Bella's car. Mac would have to park on the street when she started driving. They didn't have a garage and there wasn't room in the driveway.

"What were we talking about?"

"My brother? Getting hit by a car? He's got a sprained wrist. A bad scrape on his leg. He'll live," she said, trying to brush off the uncomfortable fear she'd felt when it happened, an emotion that still lingered. She didn't like feeling this way. It was . . . terrifying. "How's Gunner? What did you guys do?"

"You know. We hung out at his place. Had a couple of beers. Made out on his couch for a while, but then one of his room-mates came home and plopped himself down on the couch beside us and started playing Fortnite. Without even wearing headphones. Jerk-off."

"Dipstick," Mac said. She lay back on the pillows on her bed. If she kept picking at the polish, she'd have to take it off, and she really liked the color.

"Such a dipstick," Bella agreed.

"The parents home?" Mac asked.

Bella snorted. "Of course not. But they left a to-do list for me on the kitchen counter. Let's see. I'm supposed to clean my bathroom. She even left this bucket with cleaning supplies and like big rubber gloves."

Mac hesitated. She didn't talk too much about their parents, her own or Bella's. Her parents had always been up in her busi-ness, but not really in a bad way. They were just . . . involved. It didn't seem right to talk about them when Bella hadn't had a great childhood. Not like anybody hit her or diddled her, but still . . .

"I don't know," she said hesitantly. "Don't you think that's a reasonable request? Why would the maid clean your bath-room? You made the mess."

"We have a maid who cleans every week," Bella explained as if Mac were a child. "Why wouldn't the maid clean my bath-room? That's her *job*. If people cleaned up their own messes, she'd be unemployed."

"I get what you're saying," Mac told her. "But I have to clean my bathroom. It's not that big a deal."

"Girl, you're cranky. You should come over, and we'll do something."

Mac had been to Bella's house twice now, but just for a few minutes each time. She hadn't met Bella's parents. Bella lived in a huge house in one of the bougie neighborhoods west of Route 1. It looked like a mini mansion compared to her house.

But not as lived-in. There were no shoes or cleats piled by the doors and they didn't have a dog, so it smelled different. Mac liked the house. The staircase was so wide you could probably drive a car up it. Like a Jeep Wrangler, maybe. She really liked Jeep Wranglers, but so far her parents weren't going for it. The other day, her dad told her she would probably end up with her mom's car because she was getting a new one.

"So you want to? I can come to pick you up."

The idea was tempting, but she doubted her parents would let her go. And really, she didn't want to. She wanted to be here, just to make sure her brother was okay. The doctor who took care of him said he didn't seem to have a concussion, but there were signs to keep an eye out for.

"No way my parents will let me come. Not tonight. And my mom is still saying she has to talk to your mom before I stay the night."

"So sneak out after they go to bed. I'll pick you up at the end of the block and we'll hang out at Gunner's for a while. I'll bring you home later. They'll never know."

Mac wasn't sure what to say. She really, really liked Bella, and she didn't want her to think she wasn't *Gucci*, her word meaning "cool," but the idea of sneaking out of the house . . . while she might do it sometime, tonight wasn't going to be the night. "I—"

By some miracle of God or something, there was a knock on Mac's bedroom door.

"Mac?"

"I got to go. My mom," Mac whispered.

"Text me if you want me to come for you," Bella said.

Mac dropped her phone on the bed and grabbed the summer reading book she'd started for her honors English class off the nightstand. "You can come in!" she called as she opened *Franny and Zooey*.

The door opened, and her mother peeked in. "Not sleeping?"

Mac stretched out her legs. "Reading for school." She held up the book.

Her mother walked into her room. "J. D. Salinger. I liked *Catcher in the Rye*. I think I was around your age when I read it."

"Read it last summer." Mac had actually read it twice the previous summer, but she hadn't admitted that to anyone. She knew she was a geek but didn't feel it was necessary to advertise it to the world. Reading the book, she'd found herself relating to Holden. All of a sudden, growing up, leaving being a kid behind, had seemed very real to her. She'd wanted to be older her whole life, and now that she wasn't a kid anymore, it was hard sometimes not to wish she still was. Which made no sense to her because she couldn't wait to get out into the world and do things, be things she imagined she could be.

"You like it?" Her mother walked over to her bed and sat down on the edge.

"Just started it."

Her mother looked tired. She had mascara under her eyes, like maybe she'd been crying. She'd been really great today with Mason's accident. She didn't lose her shit or anything, which impressed Mac because she knew how awful she'd felt and she was just the sister. She couldn't imagine being the parent of a kid who got hit by a car.

"I meant *Catcher in the Rye*," her mother said.

"It was okay." Mac *had* liked it, but she was noncommittal because she didn't want to get into a literary discussion with her mother tonight. Her mother had had two minors and one of them had been American literature. "Way better than *The Last of the Mohicans*."

"Yeah, that was pretty awful." Her mother laughed and stroked Mac's quilt close to Mac's leg. But she didn't touch her. Probably because a few months ago Mac had asked her to back off with the hugs and kisses and stuff. It just didn't seem appropriate now that she was about to be sixteen. None of her friends' mothers expected their daughters to kiss them hello and good-bye. And Mason never did. Her mother's excuse had been that he was a boy and boys didn't like that stuff. At the time, Mac had snapped back. "And what made you think girls do?" Now she kind of missed her mother's hugs. Sometimes.

"He asleep?" Mac asked.

"Your brother?"

She nodded.

"He's fine," her mother said. "Will be fine. These things happen." She started petting the quilt again and then said, "Mac, I wanted to tell you how proud I was of you today. How well you handled the accident."

Mac felt her cheeks get hot. Compliments made her uncomfortable. Mostly because she rarely thought she deserved them. She shrugged. "I didn't do anything."

"You did," her mother argued. "You did everything right. You got someone to call nine-one-one. You found me. And you stayed with your brother, and you kept him calm until the ambulance arrived. That's means everything in a situation like we had today."

Mac fiddled with the cover of her book. The corner was dog-eared, which kind of annoyed her. Didn't eleventh-graders know you were supposed to show a little respect for J.D.'s work? "The cops arrest Mrs. Ranger?" she asked to change the subject.

"I don't know what happened, but she didn't get arrested. It was an accident." Her mother pointed at Mac's toes. "I like the green polish."

Mac looked down at them, thinking to herself how awkward she felt in conversations like this with her mom, just the two of them. She'd had this idea in her head that by the time you reached sixteen the awkwardness she felt all the time would just like . . . disappear. It hadn't. In fact, it seemed worse sometimes now. She felt so overwhelmed. Like she had taken her training wheels off too soon. She felt like she was wobbling all the time, trying to make the right choices, trying to act older, think older. It was a lot harder than she had thought it would be. And suddenly people expected so much from her: her parents, her teachers, even her friends. And now she had a job and summer school assignments out the ass. She was trying to cover other people's hours at the animal shelter, and she had no idea when she was going to start prepping for her SATs in the fall.

"Bella let me use her polish," Mac said.

"That was generous of her. I like her. She's nice. A good friend."

A good friend who left me while my brother was lying on the road, run over by an old lady, Mac thought. Which, of course, she didn't say. Instead, she just lay there staring at her stubby toes.

"Well, I'm going to bed." Her mother stood up. "Thank you for today, Mac. I mean it."

The way her mother was looking at her made all that emotion she was trying to suppress well up. She could feel it in her throat, in her chest, in her stomach. She didn't like feeling this way.

"I know this might be hard to believe, but because you were calm, you helped me be calm."

Before Mac knew what her mother was doing, she leaned over and kissed the top of her head. Mac didn't say anything, do anything, but as her mother walked out of the room she felt this weird stillness come over her. Like she was going to be okay.

CHAPTER 16

The following morning, Natalie got up early with Conor. The elephant was still in the bedroom, but neither of them brought up the previous evening's discussion. Instead, they stayed to the typical morning topics husbands and wives shared: their schedules for the day, dinner plans, a quick recap of personal finances, and the division of tasks on their to-do list. They agreed that he would call to get the gutters cleaned and she would look into ordering a new ice maker for their refrigerator once she YouTubed how to install one to be sure she could do it herself.

In their home, she was the repairman, not Conor. Always had been. She had grown up learning from her father how to re-caulk a bathtub, repair a leaky faucet, and install a new ceiling fan. In Conor's childhood home, when things broke or needed replacing they called a professional. Natalie had never minded the reversal of typical "pink and blue jobs," as he liked to call them, and Conor was proud that his wife knew how to change a bulb in a head lamp and save them a hundred-and-fifty-dollar bill. He bragged about her skills all the time to friends and family, which she loved because, obviously, he didn't find her knack for home repairs emasculating.

That morning, Conor was headed for breakfast with a vendor, but she offered to make him a coffee to go. He walked into the kitchen, dressed, and looking as hot as ever in khaki shorts, a lavender polo, and a pair of flip-flops.

"You decide if you're still going to let Mason go with Beth and Patrick to pick strawberries at that farm?"

"I thought Beth was supposed to be taking it easy at home."

Conor shrugged as he went into a narrow cabinet near the microwave and pulled out a bottle of generic pain reliever. "Anyway, I think they were talking about seeing a movie after."

"You have a headache?" she asked.

"Probably just allergies," he said, fiddling with the child-proof cap.

"I don't know about Mason." She slid a mug under the spout of their espresso machine and hit the button for a double. Then she swished the hot water she'd poured into his travel cup to heat it up and poured the water down the sink. "What do you think?"

"I think he'll be fine. And—" The coffee machine got loud as it ground the beans to make his espresso, and he waited for it to stop. "And he'll be with Beth." He gritted his teeth, still unable to get the lid off the bottle of pills. "I'd say it's a win-win. He'll be with an adult to keep an eye on him, and he'll be away from his gaming console."

Seeing Conor still struggling with the pain reliever bottle, she took it from his hands and snapped it open. "You don't think I need to keep him here with me?" She handed him the bottle and the lid.

"How do you do that?" he asked, popping three tablets into his mouth. He took a drink of water from the water bottle he carried with him all the time. "It's like magic. You're like a Houdini. No, I don't think you have to keep him with you. The doc said he didn't think he had a concussion."

She poured Conor's espresso into his travel mug and put on the lid. "But he said to watch for signs."

"And there haven't been any. He's fine, Nat. Mason will go nuts sitting around today with you. Let him hang out with Patrick. Gotta go. Chuck will be waiting for me." He reached for his travel cup, and as he took it from her hand he kissed her lightly on the mouth.

Natalie closed her eyes, enjoying the brush of his lips against hers, and she wondered, for the briefest moment, if she should listen to Conor's advice to think on it a little longer before she pursued the adoption thing. Because what if it *was* a mistake? What if she would ruin everything they had here? She loved Conor so much. She didn't want to risk altering the relationship she had with her husband. But if he loved her as much as she loved him, they wouldn't let that happen, would they?

When she opened her eyes, he was looking into them. "I don't want to get into last night's discussion," he said, his tone even. "But we agreed you'd say nothing to anyone, not yet at least. Correct? And maybe you'll think on it some more before you start looking into it?"

She nodded. "I won't say anything to anyone. But I . . . I'm pretty sure I'm going to do this. I think I have to."

For a moment he was silent, and then he nodded and said, "Gotta go. Love you."

"Love you!" she called after him.

When Conor was gone, Natalie let the dog out, washed her face, and spent several minutes studying her pores in the 10x mirror, bemoaning the aging process. Then she slathered on vitamin C serum, a moisturizer, and her daily tinted sunscreen and went back to the kitchen. It was a cloudy day and it felt like it was going to rain, so she decided to enjoy her coffee and read her emails at the kitchen island. Ordinarily, if she didn't have to be off somewhere first thing in the morning, she would have had her first cup on the patio. She loved sitting outside in the morning, hearing the birds, smelling the ocean breeze, and enjoying a good cup of coffee.

Even though Mason and McKenzie were both home, they

were still asleep, which made Natalie feel as if she had the whole house to herself. She didn't get enough time home alone in the summer, so it felt good. She felt like she could think. Armed with her cup of coffee in a purple mug that McKenzie had made for her in the sixth grade when she went through a crafty phase, she opened her laptop to read her email. Half a dozen deleted-without-reading emails later, she switched screens to a search bar.

Maybe she would take Conor's advice and think on the adoption a bit longer, but it wouldn't hurt to figure out what she would do if she did pursue it. Her fingers flew over the keyboard. She Googled "how to find a baby you gave up for adoption at birth."

She was surprised by how many hits she got. Sadly, she wasn't the only mother who wanted to know the identity of the baby she never held in her arms. Sipping her coffee, Natalie read that there were two types of searches, the passive and the active. In passive searches, the idea was to go to as many web-sites as possible designed for such inquiries by adopted kids/adults and upload information so the child can find you. In an active search, a birth mother or father gathers as much informa-tion as they can about the birth child to initiate contact.

She read that there were support groups for those searching for babies they put up for adoption. In these groups, informa-tion was offered on ways to slog through the process of finding your child, but also to offer support with the emotional bag-gage that comes with the act of giving up your baby. Natalie discounted that idea at once, because with her luck she'd join one of these groups, either online or in person, and someone she knew would be there. Of course, she supposed online she could use an alias. It was an idea she'd have to think about, because a part of her thought she could do this alone. But an-other part of her yearned to talk with someone who had been through the trauma of an unplanned pregnancy, giving birth and then handing a newborn to a stranger.

As she reread the article a second time, she realized she would need to take notes, and went to her office and dug through a drawer of extra paper, folders, and notebooks for the kids. Toward the bottom of the stack, she found an old spiral notebook she'd used for their family budget when she and Conor were first married, before they switched to keeping everything on their computers. She'd keep it hidden, but just in case someone saw it, there wasn't much chance anyone would open it, as it read across the front of the red cover in her block handwriting in a Sharpie "HOUSEHOLD BUDGET."

With a second cup of coffee, this one black, because she'd only lost half a pound since she saw Pixie Patty, she sat down with the notebook and a pen and began to take notes. She was scrolling through a list of adoption registries for children and birth parents when the doorbell rang. Winston began to bark and bolted for the front door.

"Knock it off!" Natalie called after the dog as she got off her stool. It was probably a delivery, though why it wasn't just left on the porch she didn't know.

But in the front hall, she saw through the glass storm door that it wasn't the Amazon delivery guy . . . it was Bella.

Natalie's hand flew to her messy, slept-in ponytail. She hadn't brushed her hair this morning because she planned to take a shower. She looked down at her nightclothes—knit shorts and an oversized Eric Clapton tour T-shirt. The shirt was ratty and wrinkled, but at least she hadn't spilled coffee down the front. She tucked a stray hank of hair behind her ear, feeling self-conscious, and opened the door. "Bella." She couldn't help but smile.

Bella was wearing a pair of white shorts and an aqua tank top, her long, gorgeous hair in a knot at the nape of her neck with short tendrils framing her face. "Hey, Mrs. S."

"Hi." Natalie opened the storm door, tickled to see her. In the confusion of the day before, she'd lost track of Bella and when she'd left. She'd never gotten to thank her for her calling the paramedics. "I've got the plate you brought over yesterday washed and dried. I love that it's slate and that you can write right on it to identify the different cheeses and meats."

"Right?" Bella said, the way teenagers did, with a question mark at the end.

Natalie ran a hand over her dirty hair, wishing she'd showered first thing in the morning. She knew she had to look like heck. "Come on in. And don't you dare," she chastised Winston, catching the dog by his collar as he dove for the door. "Sorry about that," she told the teen, letting go of him when the door closed. "McKenzie's still asleep. We can get her up, though."

"Actually . . . I kind of stopped by just to ask how Mason was and see if there was anything I could do to help you clean up from the party." Bella followed Natalie into the kitchen.

When Natalie walked into the kitchen, she saw she'd left her laptop open. The screen showed a list of various adoption registries. She closed it and swept it off the countertop, trying to act casual. "That's so nice of you. Mason is going to be fine. A bunch of scrapes and bruises and a sprained wrist. He's still sleeping, too. And everything was cleaned up by the time we got home from the hospital last night. My sister took care of it."

"Laney, right? She seemed nice." Bella dropped onto one of the stools.

"Yes, Laney. My own sibling." Natalie set her laptop and the notebook facedown on the kitchen table and moved to the far side of the island. She felt nervous but also excited to have Bella to herself for a moment. "You want a cup of coffee? I think we have oat milk. You like oat milk, right?"

As Natalie spoke, she tried to study the teen without making it obvious. Conor had said he didn't think she and their daughter looked alike. Natalie disagreed. Looking at her now, she saw even more similarities than she'd seen before. Their eyebrows looked identical, thicker and bigger than her own. And McKenzie had the same patch of freckles across the bridge of her nose and her cheeks as Bella.

"I'm good on coffee. Thanks. Already had two cups."

"Okay." Natalie reached for her mug. "Um. Breakfast? I have eggs and scrapple or stuff to make açai smoothies or bowls. I bet you didn't eat breakfast," she pressed. She sounded like a mom. But was that a bad thing?

Bella turned and twisted her mouth one way and then the other. "I don't know. I *am* kind of hungry. A smoothie sounds good."

Relieved to have something to do with her hands, Natalie went to the freezer and began to pull out bags and containers. "Let's see, we have frozen bananas, strawberries, açai puree"— she began to pile the items on the counter—"spinach, kale, ah, and blueberries, too." She closed the freezer and opened the refrigerator. "Oat milk, almond milk, plain yogurt."

"Wow. Do you always have so much food in the house?" Bella asked. "My mom never buys oat milk for me."

Natalie said nothing as she set the oat milk out and crossed the kitchen to walk into the pantry. "What kind of nut butter do you like?" she called. "We've got peanut butter and almond butter." She stepped out to show her a jar in each hand.

"Either one. I like both." Bella got up and went to the sink to wash her hands. "I'll make the smoothies. You want one, right? You can finish your coffee, and I'll make them. Where's the blender?"

"Um . . ." Natalie was momentarily taken aback. No one ever made her anything to eat. "In the pantry." She set both nut butters on the counter. "I'll get it." She came back out carrying the large blender with a container of chia seeds tucked under her arm.

Bella took the blender from her and the seeds. "Sit. Relax. Yesterday must have been so stressful for you. I'm so glad Mason's okay. I can't believe that old lady just drove right through the stop sign. I bet the cops took her license. I hope they did."

Natalie sat down at the counter and took a sip of her coffee. It had gotten cold, but she didn't want to ruin the moment by getting up to reheat it or make a fresh cup. She sipped it. "I don't know what happened with Mrs. Ranger. I should call her later and let her know Mason's going to be fine. But it was an accident. I hope they didn't take her license. She made a mistake. We've all done it, though maybe not to this degree."

"Sorry. Somebody ran my kid over, I'd want them arrested," Bella said as she set up the blender.

"Well . . . I guess because of potentially dangerous mistakes I've made over the years"—Natalie pressed her hand to her chest—"I like to give people a little grace when I can. The boys weren't seriously hurt, and I don't think Mrs. Ranger will ever try to answer her phone at an intersection again."

"You're a nicer person than I am." Bella dumped pieces of frozen banana into the blender. "Anything you don't like?"

"Nope. Which is not necessarily a good thing." Natalie patted her slightly rounded middle. "I'm getting to be quite a chub. Trying to lose weight, but it's not easy. Especially when you own a pub," she added.

"I bet that is hard. Having all that good food available. That's free." Bella threw a big handful of frozen kale into the blender. Then she added frozen spinach. "But there's no way you're chubby, Mrs. S. You look great for your age."

Natalie set her mug down, cutting her eyes at the teen. "I *think* that's a compliment. Unless you think I'm like sixty."

Bella laughed and dumped an assortment of berries into the blender. "PB or AB?"

It took Natalie a minute to realize she meant peanut butter or almond butter. "Either or."

"Both, then. Seriously, Mrs. S," Bella threw over her shoulder. "No way you look old enough to have a sixteen-year-old. You're the kind of woman my mom would be jealous of."

The mention of her mother made Natalie wonder if she could use it as a segue into asking some questions about her parents, her home life. But she couldn't think of anything that she could say that wouldn't weird the teen out or make her suspicious in some way. McKenzie hated it when Natalie questioned her. She hated it more when Natalie questioned her friends. Sometimes maybe Natalie was being nosy, but usually, she was just interested in what was going on in their lives. What was wrong with that?

Natalie watched Bella flip the switch on the appliance, stopping it several times to scrape the sides of the blender jar. As Bella worked, Natalie noted how confidently she moved. There was nothing awkward about her. Unlike so many girls her age, she seemed comfortable in her own skin. Certainly more relaxed than Natalie had been at eighteen.

Bella let the blender run for another full minute and then, declaring the smoothie perfect, turned off the motor. "Glasses up here, right?" she asked, opening an upper cabinet to the right sink.

"Bella?"

The sound of McKenzie's voice behind Natalie startled her. She hadn't heard her come into the kitchen, probably because of all the racket the blender made. She spun around on the stool, feeling guilty for some reason. Why, she didn't know. "Hey, sleepyhead."

McKenzie looked at her mom and then at her friend. "What are you doing here?"

Bella was pouring the drinks. "Making smoothies. Want one? I made plenty."

McKenzie stood there in her sleep shorts and a tank top, her arms crossed over her chest. "No." She went to the coffeemaker, pulled out a mug, and made herself a cup. While the machine ground beans and strained water through them, she grabbed the oat milk Bella was putting away. "How long have you been here?"

Bella shrugged. "Few minutes. I texted you I was stopping by, but I guess you were still asleep."

McKenzie poured some of the milk into a little cream pitcher, and when the coffeemaker clicked off, she used its frother. While it ran, drowning out any chance of conversation, Natalie watched the girls, comparing them. Did they move like sisters? Was that even a thing? She wondered. She and Laney looked very different. Natalie took after her dad; Laney, their mom. But they both had their father's widow's peak and their mom's detached earlobes. She didn't know that they had many of the same mannerisms.

Satisfied with the froth, McKenzie turned off the machine and poured the milk into her coffee. She sipped it in silence, leaning her back against the counter, giving her mother the evil eye.

Bella slid a glass of smoothie across the island to Natalie and began putting the frozen fruits away.

"Straws in that drawer," Natalie said, pointing.

"I'm good." Bella took a sip of her drink.

"Delicious," Natalie said after tasting it. "The right balance of spinach to fruit."

When Bella was done putting the frozen foods away, she leaned against the counter, mimicking McKenzie's stance. She glanced at her friend as she sipped her drink. "We don't have to be at work until four. I was wondering if you wanted to go to the outlets with me. My mom says I need a decent dress. My grandmother is taking me out to eat at some fancy restaurant at the Du Pont hotel up in Wilmington. Have you been there?"

When McKenzie didn't respond right away, Natalie said, "You've been there. Right, Mac? Your cousin's wedding."

McKenzie made a face. "What wedding? What cousin?"

"Tom's wedding to Alicia. Your great-uncle Sean's son Tom."

"Mom." Her daughter shook her head. "How old was I?"

"I don't know." Natalie shrugged. "Nine? Maybe eight?"

McKenzie exhaled impatiently and looked at Bella. "*Anyway*, so you have to go out to eat with your grandmother."

"I don't want to, but my mom says I have to. Grandmother wants to give me a big check for graduation and I'm supposed to act surprised when she does. And I have to have a dress. A suitable dress. So I have to go shopping." Bella sipped her smoothie. "I don't even know what that means. *Suitable.*"

"It's adult-speak for you can't have your ass cheeks hanging out," McKenzie said. "Or your ti—"

"We get the idea," Natalie interrupted, embarrassed by her daughter's frank language, even though her assessment was accurate. "Your mom's not going with you to buy a dress?" she asked Bella.

The teen pressed her lips together and shook her head. "I wish. She just gave me her credit card and told me to go buy one at the outlets. But I don't know what I'm supposed to get. I don't know what my grandmother would think is appropriate or what people wear to a place like that."

Before Natalie could think it through, she blurted, "I could go with you. I've been to the Green Room at the Du Pont. We went last year to an anniversary party there."

"No, Mom!" McKenzie snapped. "Bella doesn't need your help."

"I don't know." Bella shrugged, looking to McKenzie. "It might be fun."

McKenzie stared hard at her friend.

"Okay, so maybe not fun," Bella conceded. "But at least I won't have to return whatever I buy because it's not right. Come on, Mac." She moved closer to her friend. "We'll go get a dress for me, and then we can go to the bathing suit store. They had crocheted bikinis in the window the other day. You said you wanted one. We could buy matching bikinis."

Natalie held her breath. She didn't know exactly why, but she wanted to take Bella shopping for a dress. Maybe because McKenzie didn't want Natalie involved in any of her clothing purchases and hadn't since she left middle school? Or maybe just because Bella had asked her. Because Bella did want her opinion.

McKenzie took a sip of coffee. "Fine," she finally said. "But we're taking your car," she told Bella. "And you have to drive yourself, Mom." Again, she exhaled impatiently. "What about Mason? Is he coming, too?"

Natalie got off her stool and grabbed her phone, notebook, and laptop from the kitchen table. "He's going strawberry picking with Aunt Beth and Patrick." She looked to Bella. "I need to get Mason moving and grab a quick shower. I can drop him off on the way."

Bella threw up her hand. "Plenty of time, Mrs. S. Don't rush."

As Natalie walked out of the kitchen, she heard McKenzie say in a harsh whisper, "I can't believe you invited her to go shopping with us."

As she walked back to her office to put the computer and notebook away, Natalie felt a sense of guilt for agreeing to go shopping with Bella when obviously McKenzie didn't want her to join them.

But not guilty enough not to go.

CHAPTER 17

Running late, Natalie wheeled into the nursing home parking lot, grabbed her keys, and hurried to the front door. Inside, she approached the reception desk, pushing her sunglasses back on her head. "Hey, Ruby," she greeted the attractive sixty-something woman with a rich, dark skin tone she would have given her right arm for. *Or at least her pinky finger.*

Ruby looked up. She was wearing orange cat-eye glasses that looked amazing on her. No one would guess she was a grandmother to seven in those glasses. "Back to get your daughter, are you?"

Natalie had dropped McKenzie off an hour ago to visit with her grandmother. Meanwhile, she'd run over to the home improvement store to return the ice maker she'd ordered online. The day before, she'd wasted two hours watching YouTube videos, trying to hook it up, only to eventually realize that while she'd ordered the correct replacement, they had sent the wrong one. She'd been online at midnight the night before, placing another order.

"Mom's taxi service," Natalie responded, sounding cheerful, though she wasn't feeling it. That morning she'd stepped on the scale to discover that despite walking an hour most days and watching what she ate, she'd gained half a pound. Then, while she was trying to get ready to go, she'd received a call from the vice principal asking her to serve on some sort of advisory board, and she hadn't been able to get off the phone with her. Which had forced her to leave the house later than she wanted . . . later than McKenzie expected. That had resulted in her starting the excursion in a bad mood. McKenzie hadn't said a word to her all the way to the nursing home. And to top it all off, Natalie had left her phone at home, which made her feel as if she were missing the limb she was willing to sacrifice for better skin.

"But she'll be driving herself soon, won't she?" Ruby asked. "She told me she did well in driver's ed class."

Natalie jangled her car keys in her hand. "She tells you more than she tells me, then. I never saw her last report record. She thinks that a young woman of her advanced age doesn't need to share her grades with her parents. Even though she's never gotten anything less than an A since preschool. Of course, she's willing to share the cost of her car insurance with us."

Ruby laughed. "Well, enjoy her while you can. Once teenagers can drive, they're gone. You never see them. I remember when my oldest got his license. He had been a bit of a mama's boy before that, but once he had that car, I never saw him." She smiled nostalgically, a little sadness in her voice. "It wasn't until he was gone—school, job, girlfriend—that I realized how much I'd liked having him around. Even if he was a pain in the neck most of the time."

As grumpy as McKenzie had been all week, the idea of her being out of Natalie's hair wasn't all that distasteful. Since their trip shopping with Bella on Monday, McKenzie had been particularly critical and moody. Natalie had only shopped with them for an hour, and Bella had found the perfect dress—one she liked, but that was appropriate for the occasion. And Natalie had bought both girls the crocheted bikinis they wanted, but

150 / Colleen French

that wasn't enough for McKenzie. Nothing was ever enough, never good enough, when it came to Natalie.

"Gotta run," Natalie said as she walked away. "Mac has to be at work shortly. Her first job," she added, feeling a bit of pride.

"Good to see you!" Ruby called over the sound of the phone ringing on her desk. She picked up as Natalie walked away. "Good morning, Bayside, how can I help you?"

Just past Reception, Natalie made a right-hand turn, then a left, and at the double closed doors she punched numbers into a keypad. The family's passcode. Now that her grandmother was in a memory care unit, there was more security for the protection of the patients. On the other side of the doors that closed and locked automatically, she followed another hallway to her grandmother's room.

From the doorway, Natalie saw McKenzie sitting on a straight-backed chair in front of her great-grandmother in a recliner. Nana looked small and shriveled in the big chair. As Natalie walked into the room, she sighed. Despite the air freshener plug-ins, the place always smelled of disinfectant and urine. *The smell of aging.*

"I called you to see where you were." McKenzie got up from the chair as she closed the paperback book in her hand. "I'm going to be late for work."

"You're not going to be late, and I told you on the way over here I didn't have my phone." Natalie pressed her hand to her forehead. "I could have sworn I left it on the counter. I bet Mason had it, playing one of his games. I hope he didn't take it with him."

"*Mother*, he didn't take your phone to Patrick's."

That was new, calling her Mother, the tone heavy with disdain

"So maybe it's in his room, or on the deck or . . . I don't know." Natalie looked to her grandmother and raised her voice. Nana was hard of hearing but refused to wear her hearing aids anymore. She'd told Laney that mice talked to her through them and all she could hear was their squeak, squeak, squeaks. "I'm back, Nana. To pick up McKenzie."

Nana squinted until her pale blue eyes were nothing more than slits. "Henry? That you?"

Natalie understood maybe confusing Laney with their mother. Laney looked something like her, at least. But there was little resemblance between Natalie and her mother. "No, it's Natalie. Henry's daughter. Your granddaughter."

"I thought she was my granddaughter." Chomping loudly on her gum, Nana pointed a wizened finger at McKenzie. Nana was proud to still have all of her own teeth and she loved gum. "You pulling my leg? People are always pulling my leg around here."

"No, no, McKenzie is *my* daughter," Natalie explained patiently. "She's your great-granddaughter."

"What's that?" Nana demanded, leaning forward to hear better, cupping her hand around her ear.

"She's your great-granddaughter," Natalie said louder.

"What?" Nana shouted.

"Mom, it doesn't matter," McKenzie muttered under her breath. "None of this matters." She leaned over and kissed her great-grandmother's leathery cheek and Natalie noticed that Nana was wearing blush. She had two big circles of it on the apples of her cheeks. Natalie wondered where she had gotten the makeup. Laney had tossed Nana's entire cosmetics bag after she caught her using a mascara wand to brush her teeth.

"It doesn't matter, Nana," McKenzie said, peering into her face at eye level. "I know who you are. You don't have to remember me."

Nana nodded. Chewed. She was a two-pack-of-gum-a-day girl. Laney and Natalie bought it for her by the case, but doled it out. Otherwise, she'd chew through three hundred pieces in less than a week. And when she accidentally swallowed too much, that created digestive issues.

"You going to bring that book back, right?" Nana asked. "Good story, the one about Franny. Now I want to hear about Zooey."

Natalie cut her eyes at her daughter, as surprised by her grandmother's lucidness as by the fact that McKenzie was entertaining her great-grandmother with her eleventh-grade summer reading list. "You're reading a school assignment to her?"

McKenzie shrugged. "Why not? She likes literature." She raised her voice. "You like Salinger, don't you, Nana?"

"Good-looking man in his day," Nana remarked. "Did you bring chips?" she directed to Natalie. "Henry brings me potato chips. I like the kind in the can with the green sprinkles."

It was Laney who brought her chips all the time, not their mother. Not that it mattered. Henry didn't know her stepmother the way her girls did. They'd never had a good relationship. Their mother had never been able to get past the fact that her father had married the woman from his church so quickly after her mother's death. Lucky for Natalie and Laney, their mother hadn't ever kept them from her stepmother, and over the years grandmother and granddaughters had formed a close bond.

"I'll wait in the car." McKenzie opened her hand, her mouth in a pucker. "Can I have the keys?"

Natalie dropped them into her hand. "I'll be right there."

McKenzie walked away. "I'm going to be late for work. Later, gator!" she called, waving a hand as she left the room.

"Afterwhile, crocodile!" Nana hollered after her.

Natalie couldn't resist a smile at the exchange. She leaned down to straighten her grandmother's lap blanket. Nana was always cold, even keeping the room at a sweltering eighty degrees. Anytime Natalie planned to stay, she dressed in layers. She and Laney joked all the time about stripping down to their underwear to visit.

"She's a good girl, that one," Nana observed, watching McKenzie walk out the door.

"She's a lot of things, that one." Natalie searched the small end table next to the chair her grandmother spent most of the hours of each day in. "I'll turn your TV on for you. I bet I can find an old Western. Maybe even John Wayne if we're lucky."

One of the hard things about moving her grandmother to this facility was the fact that the room was smaller than she'd had before, so she hadn't able to bring the furniture she'd had from her home. Most of Nana's furniture had been sold, given away, or thrown out when Natalie's mother had put her in the home. But the matriarch had been attached to the bedroom suite, bookcase, knickknack cabinet, and the few end tables she'd managed to squeeze into her room in the first nursing home. They had made it look homier and less institutional. Here, she was sleeping in a hospital bed and the only furniture she'd been able to keep were the recliner, the end table, and a single straight-backed chair for guests to sit on.

Nana had cried the day she had been transferred to Bayside after her third wander, as Laney liked to call it, from the previous nursing home. Nana went missing for four hours that day after she walked out the front door. She was found eating chicken and dumplings at Cracker Barrel. How she managed to walk the mile there no one had ever figured out.

"Did you lose the TV remote again, Nana?" Natalie asked, moving her tissue box, some magazines that hadn't been touched since the last time she was there, and a pile of gum wrappers. She picked up all the wrappers and dropped them into the nearby waste can. "You have to keep track of the remote, right? If you're going to watch TV." Two had already been lost and Laney had joked that they should put replacements on auto-ship.

Nana reached for her pack of gum. "Where's the wrapper, daggone it? I need a wrapper to spit out my gum. Tastes like it's been on my shoe." She opened and closed her mouth, flashing remarkably nice teeth for a woman born in 1923. "Need a freshy."

Natalie reached down into the chair cushion along her grandmother's side. If the remote wasn't there, she'd be digging through the trash, which was where she'd found it earlier in the week. Her fingers brushed smooth, hard plastic and came up with the remote. "Aha! Here it is." She fished one wrapper out of the trash. "And here you go."

As Natalie turned to channel-surf on the TV mounted to the wall, her nana got rid of her old gum and plucked a fresh piece from the pack. She chomped loudly with great, wet gusto.

"You ever wish you hadn't done something, Nana?" Natalie asked as she zipped past infomercials and twenty-four-hours-a-day news channels. She kept thinking about her twenty-year-old self giving her baby up for adoption. She kept telling herself that she'd done the right thing, but the more time she spent with Bella, the more she wondered if she *had* made a mistake. "Something you can't undo? Something you can't decide if you had it over to do, if you would have done it differently?"

Nana smacked her lips. "Wish I hadn't put on this blue housecoat." She plucked at the cotton flowered dress she wore. She had a big stack of them in her dresser. "I like this yellow one, but I don't like those kinds of pockets."

Natalie smiled, pleased her grandmother was so clear-headed today. When Natalie arrived, she never knew what state Nana would be in. Sometimes she talked as if she were the woman she had been twenty years ago, but sometimes she made no sense. The worst times were when she seemed to be lost in her thoughts and wouldn't speak at all. "I mean something big in your life."

"Wished I married Elon when he proposed when he came home on leave. If I'd married him, maybe I'd have had a son." She chewed thoughtfully. "But then he got blown up by the Japs, and that was that. So if I'd married him, I'd have been alone with a baby." Nana had never been able to have children of her own. And she had never gotten over losing her first love. And while she and Natalie's grandfather had always seemed to get along, it had been clear theirs had never been a love match. He had married the woman from his Sunday school class shortly after his first wife died because he thought his daughters needed a mother. There had been two girls in the first marriage: Natalie and Laney's mother, Henrietta, and then her younger sister, Jane, who died in a car accident when she was a teenager.

Natalie studied her grandmother. "But at the time, you thought it was the right thing to do, didn't you? You said you were too young to marry. That you wanted to go to college and become a teacher."

"Too long ago to remember what I was thinking. Elon was a good catch. I should have married him and had his baby. Did you bring chips?"

Natalie smiled as she found the channel that showed old westerns like *Winchester '73, The Gunfighter,* and one of Natalie's favorites, *The Treasure of the Sierra Madre.* "I didn't bring chips today, but I'll bring some next time." She set the remote by the tissue box. "I have to go. My daughter needs me to take her to work."

"Mac," Nana said. "She's a good girl. I like her. Got a good head on her shoulders."

Natalie held her tongue, gave her grandmother a quick kiss, and hurried out of the building and into the sunshine. She found McKenzie sitting in the passenger's seat of the car, engine running, the air conditioner and the radio blasting. Natalie could hear it from across the parking lot. She got into the car and turned it down before closing the door.

"I have to be there in half an hour." McKenzie reached into the back to grab her work T-shirt off the back seat. Today it was lime green.

"We've got time. Traffic's not bad. You'll be early." As Natalie put the car in reverse, McKenzie whipped off her shirt, flashing a pink, lacy bra.

"Mac!" Natalie looked around to see who was watching the teen do her striptease.

McKenzie made a face. "What?"

"Really? You're changing in a parking lot?"

McKenzie pulled the clean shirt over her head. "Technically, in a car," she said drolly. "In a parking lot." She made a sound of derision. "What is it with adults getting so wound up about their bodies? You think everything is about sex."

Natalie gripped the steering wheel. She had had just about enough of her daughter's lousy behavior. It hadn't seemed possible, but she had been worse since the other day when Natalie had met her and Bella at the outlets. For heaven's sake, Natalie had only gone into three stores with them. She hadn't been with them more than an hour. She didn't understand why McKenzie had been so upset about her going. Why she was still upset.

It crossed Natalie's mind as she pulled out of the parking lot that maybe she should just ask McKenzie what was going on. Why was she angry with her? But Natalie didn't know if she had it in her today.

She'd begun her initial inquiry into the closed adoption by reading everything she could about how to do it. She signed up on all the registries in case Bella was looking for her. As a legal adult, she could register as well. Natalie had learned that the adoption agency they had used had merged with another shortly after she'd given birth. She'd also found out that it wasn't going to be easy to find her child—to find out if Bella was her—because the records were sealed.

So she had that stress. And then there was the ice maker, her weight, her missing phone, and Conor's no-shows for dinner all week. She understood that their business had to be his priority right now, but his emotional distance since she'd told him about her suspicions concerning Bella had left her feeling lonely and a little concerned about their relationship. The night before, she'd asked him if he was avoiding her, but he'd insisted he wasn't. Knowing when to push him into talking and when not to, she'd let it go.

On Route 1, Natalie slowly made her way over into the

correct lane to shoot off downtown. At a light, she glanced at McKenzie. "You never told me if you needed me to order that DNA kit. If you want to get the results back—"

"I don't need it." The teen stared out the window.

"Okay." Natalie signaled and eased over into the turn lane. Out of the corner of her eye, she saw the oil light flashing on the dashboard again, and she was tempted to curse. "Your dad said that you needed it for that paper."

"I'm not writing that paper. The teacher didn't like my idea, so he didn't approve it." She didn't look at Natalie. "He liked the one you and Dad came up with better. So I guess I'll do that."

"So—" Natalie wanted to tell her that if she didn't like their idea, she should just come up with another. That the possibilities in such a broad subject were endless. But then she let it go, thinking Conor might better initiate the discussion.

Instead, forcing a cheerfulness she didn't feel, Natalie changed the subject. "Have you thought about what you wanted to do for your birthday next month? It's coming up fast. Sixteen is a big one. You want to go to a water park? Have a pool party?"

McKenzie glanced at her. "I want a party at the pub."

Natalie looked at her daughter as the light turned green and she hit the gas. "You want your sweet sixteen party at a bar?"

"Sweet sixteen? Is that like from *Happy Days*?"

Natalie gritted her teeth. Why did everything have to be so hard with this kid? She bet Bella didn't talk to her mother this way. Even if she wasn't what she should have been to her adopted daughter. "I don't know where it came from. It's just something people say."

"And it's not a bar. The license is for a restaurant that serves alcohol. I'm not asking you to serve beer. We can use the back room people rent for family dinners and parties. I asked Dad. He said the room wasn't reserved for the weekend of my birthday."

"Your dad said you could have the party there?"

McKenzie looked at her mother. "He said the room wasn't reserved and that he was fine with it, but I had to ask you." Every word she spoke was with attitude.

Natalie took the traffic circle onto Albany Avenue. "I'm not saying no; it's just that I—" She tapped the brake as the car in front of her slowed, looking for a parking space. "You're not going to find one here, buddy." She glanced at McKenzie. "Why do you want to have it at the pub?"

"I don't know. Because I've done the pool parties, the mini-golf parties. We went to Kings Dominion last year. I want to do something different. Something people will want to come to."

"Okay."

"I mean . . ." McKenzie looked out her window again. "It might be nice just to have dinner together for the party. Not a big group. Not any more than will fit around the table that's usually up. We could have dinner and play some music and just talk. I want my friends to meet Bella. I don't think this is an unreasonable request, Mom."

Natalie made two lights in a row and eased over into the right-hand lane so she could let McKenzie off near the board-walk. Ten minutes before she had to clock in. "Mac, I said okay."

"You did?" She whipped around to look at her mother.

"Let me talk to your dad. But it sounds like he'll be fine with it."

"Really?" She grinned. "Thanks, Mom."

Natalie pulled up to the curb.

"Be okay if I spend the night at Bella's tonight?" Mac asked as she opened the car door.

Natalie put the car in park and looked at her. "Good try slipping that in. Bella says it's fine if I speak with her mother about you coming over. You're the only one with an issue with it."

"But I'm sixteen," she argued, though for once there was no ugliness in her voice. She sounded as if she was genuinely trying to understand. "Almost sixteen. You're going to trust me to drive your car in three weeks. Don't you think if I'm mature enough to drive a car, I'm mature enough to decide where I'm safe? Who I'm safe with? You know Bella. You know what kind of person she is, Mom."

Natalie gripped the wheel, wondering if eleven in the morning was too early to stop for a beer at the pub. "Let me think about it."

"Yeah?" McKenzie asked.

Someone behind them lay on the horn, and Natalie looked up in the rearview mirror and then back at her daughter. "I've got to go." The horn sounded behind her again. "This lady is going to have an apoplectic seizure if I don't move and I don't want to be responsible for that. Get out." She tilted her head in the direction of her door. "We'll talk about it tonight."

McKenzie stared at her for a minute and then startled Natalie when she leaned over and gave her a peck on the cheek. "Thanks, Mom!"

Certain her mouth was hanging open, Natalie watched her daughter get out of the car and stroll toward the boardwalk, not sure what had just taken place. Had McKenzie just thanked her? Shown appreciation? Kissed her? It felt a bit like an out-of-body experience or maybe a dream.

The lady behind her hit her horn and held it down, and Natalie rolled her eyes. "Fine, I'm going, I'm going!" she hollered as she pulled away from the curb. "Gosh darn it!"

CHAPTER 18

Laney pumped her arms as she walked in the wet sand. "Okay, I'm going to ask, even though I feel like I shouldn't encourage you. How's the search going?" This morning she was wearing all pink: pink yoga shorts, pink strappy tank, pink ball cap, and sneakers. And looking amazing for seven in the morning, which Natalie hated and adored her for all at the same time.

But Natalie had stepped up her game, too. She had worn her new navy gym shorts and a tank top, her hair piled on top of her head the way every teenager in Albany Beach wore theirs. "How is asking me encouragement?" Natalie took a double step to catch up with her big sister. She glanced at her watch. *Had they only walked three-quarters of a mile? It felt like a mile, at least.* They were walking north on the beach, into the wind, adding to what seemed like a death march—especially since Natalie hadn't had any coffee yet for fear of needing a bathroom at an inopportune time.

Laney glanced at her. *"How?"*

Natalie watched her sister's eyebrows arch and thought she

looked just like their mother for a split second. Something she chose to keep to herself so early in the morning. Laney hadn't had any coffee yet, either, and she could be cranky without her morning hit of caffeine.

Laney opened her arms wide. "Because it might give you the impression that I'm in some way giving you my approval." She stuck her face in Natalie's while keeping up her unrelenting pace. "And I'm not."

"That's already been noted," Natalie quipped. "But thanks for asking." Her sunglasses slid down on her sweaty, sunscreen-covered nose and she pushed them up. They were her old, beat-up beach glasses. She couldn't find her new ones. "You'll be happy to know it's not going anywhere. I've spent hours and hours signing up on registries, reading about various ways to work around sealed records. If Bella's registered, I can't find her."

Something caught Laney's eyes in the wet sand, and she leaned over and scooped it up. A seashell. She studied it for a moment and then sailed it into the air, watching it make a satisfying splash in the water. "You call the adoption agency yet?"

"No," Natalie admitted sheepishly. "Not yet. Didn't I tell you? The agency we used doesn't exist anymore. Another agency absorbed it."

"They'd still have the records, wouldn't they?"

"I would assume so. There's got to be regulations." Natalie nodded to a couple walking hand in hand past them, going south. Seeing how they exchanged looks, the way the young men smiled at each other, made her wistful. She wanted Conor to look at her that way again. He certainly hadn't since their conversation about Bella. But even before that, how long had it been? She was beginning to worry that their marriage wasn't what it had once been, that maybe Conor's love for her had faded. It wasn't a big worry, but more and more often it was popping up in her head. Maybe him seeming distant *was* just because he was working long hours. But what if it was something else?

Looking at Laney, Natalie pushed those thoughts aside for the time being. "The whole process of a closed adoption is fascinating. Did you know that when I put her up for adoption, her original birth certificate was filed somewhere, never to be seen again? The state of Delaware created a new birth certificate saying my baby was born to her adoptive parents, as if the adoptive mother was the one in that delivery room. Why would they do that?"

Laney tilted her head as if Natalie were daft. Natalie couldn't see her sister's eyes behind her Ray-Bans, but she knew she was looking at her wide-eyed. "It was a closed adoption. They did it so no one would know who the birth parents were. That's the point of a *closed* adoption, Nat."

"I didn't put Sébastien's name on the birth certificate," Natalie said, as much to herself as to Laney. "Just mine. I don't know why. I guess because he never knew. Because we never contacted each other again."

Laney squeezed her hand. "You should have absolutely no regrets. You did the right thing. For the baby, for you, for everyone who loves you. And loves her. I'll believe that until the day I die." She hesitated. "I was so proud of you when you were brave enough to do it. I still am."

Natalie kept walking, saying nothing, unsure how she felt about her sister being proud of her for giving her baby away. She picked up her pace as she got a second wind. She was down half a pound this morning and feeling good about it. She wasn't going to show up at her appointment with Pixie Patty in September looking like she'd been eating Thrasher's French fries and drinking beer for the last three months. Though she was having a few beers a week. . . . And a couple of fries.

"Let's circle back," Laney said.

Natalie wasn't going to argue with her. She had a full agenda for the day, taxiing children, going over the payroll, and putting a report together for Conor and his brothers on alcohol sales. She stopped to turn around, but Laney grabbed her arm and tugged.

"I didn't mean circle back home. We've still got a little more than a quarter of a mile to go. That way, we hit two and a half by the time we're back at your place," she explained, releasing Natalie. "I meant back to my question. I get why you don't want to ask what Bella's birth date is. Mac's pretty astute. She might get suspicious. People don't give teenagers enough credit. They're not stupid. They just have fewer life experiences. Why haven't you called the agency?"

Natalie chewed on her lower lip. She'd been asking herself the same question all week. But she knew the answer. "Because what if they won't tell me anything?"

"Then you'll—"

"But what if they do give me the information?" Natalie continued. "What if she's Bella?" She felt a lump rise in her throat that was becoming all too familiar. Every time she thought about what she would do if she found out Bella was her daughter, she choked up.

Laney sighed. "Aw, sweetie. She's not. It's not her. And even if it was, no one is going to tell you she is. That's not how the system works. It's set up this way, so women facing the fact that they will no longer be able to have children don't start tracking down their long-lost babies."

"Then why do you think I should call?"

"To *end* this."

Tears stung Natalie's eyes, and she was glad she'd been able to find her old sunglasses because she didn't want Laney to see her crying. Even knowing what her sister was saying was true, it was still painful. "Can we talk about something else? How much farther? Let's talk about something else."

"The blue house with the sailfish flag." Laney pointed into

the distance. "We turn around at the sailfish. Okay, we'll talk about something else." She thought for a second and grinned. "Guess what? I had another date with Clancy."

"Tom Clancy the writer? Isn't he dead?"

Laney gave her a push. "Very funny. No, Clancy, from Bethany Beach. I told you about him the other day. At least I think I did," she added.

"Is this the guy who showed you a bunch of photos of his mother while you were having coffee?"

Laney groaned. "That was Joey. No, not him. I didn't go out with him again. Ew. Why would you think I'd go out with a guy who had fifty-six photos of his mother on his phone? In an album, arranged chronologically."

"Clancy," Natalie repeated. The sun was getting higher by the minute, and hotter. "Not the writer."

"Not the writer. Clancy owns a construction business. *Widowed.*" She said the word as if it was somehow sexy.

"How'd you meet him?"

"Tinder."

Natalie looked at her sister. "Isn't that a hookup site? One of those places you swipe yes, I want to have sex with you, or no, I don't?"

Laney shrugged. "Can be a hookup site. Doesn't have to be."

Natalie stopped, unable to hide her shock. "Are you telling me you use it to hook up with guys for sex?"

Laney laughed. "Would you think any less of me if I did?"

As Natalie paused to think about the answer, her cell phone began to vibrate. She pulled it out of her pocket and looked at the screen. Bella? Bella was calling her? At seven-something in the morning.

"Come on," Laney urged, walking again. "Another fifty yards, and we can turn around."

Natalie began to walk again as she answered the phone. "Hello?"

"Mrs. S. Thanks for picking up," Bella said, sounding upset.

"I was afraid you wouldn't. I'm sorry it's so early. I know you don't get up early, but I didn't know what to do."

"No, no, it's fine. I'm out walking."

"I knew you'd say that," the teen said, sounding calmer. "I didn't know who else to ask, and you've been so nice to me."

"What's up?" Natalie asked, trying to sound normal. She couldn't fathom why Bella would be calling her. At the same time, she wondered what McKenzie would think about her friend calling her mom. There wasn't a chance in heck she'd be pleased.

"I lost my driver's license, and I don't know how to get a new one," Bella said. "My mom will kill me if she finds out I lost it again."

"Who are you talking to?" Laney asked, looking at Natalie.

Natalie waved her off as they reached their destination point—the swordfish house—and turned around. "It's easy," she said into her phone. "You go to the DMV and get a new one. They print it out right there while you wait. There's probably a charge of ten dollars, maybe, for a replacement."

"That's it?" Bella asked, sounding relieved.

"That's it," Natalie said. "You can go as soon as they open. I don't even think you need another ID to replace a license because your photo is on file."

"Thank you so much," Bella gushed. "I'm already in trouble with my mom over curfew. I'm eighteen years old. I'll be leaving at the end of the summer. Why would I still have a curfew?" She laughed. "Anyway. Thank you again. I'll see you this weekend. I think I'm staying over Saturday night. Mac and I are going to a concert in the park in Ocean City."

"You're welcome, Bella. See you Saturday." Natalie disconnected, smiling.

"Bella?" Laney demanded. "Bella is calling you at seven o'clock in the morning?"

Natalie looked at her watch. "Seven-thirty-five."

"What did she want?"

Natalie explained.

"And exactly *why* did she call you?" Laney asked.

Natalie walked faster, feeling good, now. It was going to be a good day. "I told you. She's already in trouble with her mother. She wanted to get a replacement without her mother knowing. Which she can legally do."

"No." Laney waved her away. "I mean, why was she calling *you* about it? Why didn't she just Google it?"

Natalie thought for a moment. "I don't know. Maybe she didn't think of it. She sounded a little panicked."

Laney frowned but said nothing and swung her arms faster as she walked.

"What?" Natalie asked when she couldn't stand it anymore.

"Bad idea. Getting chummy with her."

"Why would you say that?"

"You know why. Your relationship, friendship, whatever the hell you want to call it, is getting weird."

Natalie stared at her sister, annoyed. *"Weird?"*

"Okay, inappropriate. And weird. Eighteen-year-old girls don't become friends with women our age." She shook her head. "I don't get it. What's she up to?"

"She's not *up* to anything," Natalie said, annoyed. "She needed some advice."

"The girl has a mother, Nat. And a father. You are not one of her parents, and you should not be acting like you are."

"What am I supposed to do?" Natalie snapped back. "She called me asking for help."

"What was she doing when she lost her license? Where was she?"

"I don't know." Natalie wished now that she hadn't told her sister what the phone call was about. She should have just made something up, but that wouldn't have worked. Laney heard her end of the conversation. Besides, Natalie had always been completely honest with Laney. About anything and everything, and, to her knowledge, Laney was the same.

Adjusting her sunglasses, Natalie looked at her sister. "Her mother is never home. Her father, either. She's at a crucial place in her life. She needs guidance."

"Oh, bullshit. She's playing you. I just can't figure out why." The beach was beginning to fill up now with tourists setting out their blankets and chairs. Two college students who worked an umbrella stand were setting up shop in the sand near the boardwalk. "Playing me how? I told her to go to DMV," Natalie said.

"I'm not going to argue with you about this," Laney grumbled. "But I'll tell you something, you're moving into dangerous territory here. She's not your daughter. And even if she was, this would be wrong. I'm telling you, Nat"—she shook her finger at Natalie as if she were a naughty child—"you're going to end up making a mess of your family. And that girl's, too, if you continue to pursue this relationship."

Natalie clamped her jaw tightly and pumped her arms the way her sister was doing. "But what if it is her?" she said softly. "What if Bella is my daughter, Lane?" She stopped to look at her sister, pulling her sunglasses off to wipe her sweaty face with the back of her hand. Overhead, seagulls circled. "If Bella is my daughter, that means McKenzie has a sister. I know Conor and I agreed no more children after Mason was born, but I always regretted not giving McKenzie a sister. I regretted it because of the relationship I have with you. Wouldn't it be wonderful if McKenzie had her own Laney?"

"Bullshit, squared," Laney muttered, and took off.

Natalie hurried to catch up with her. "Please don't say anything about the call to Mac. She'd be upset."

"As she should be."

"Or Conor," Natalie added, feeling guilty as she said it. She never kept things from Conor.

Laney didn't respond, and the sisters power-walked side by side along the shore in silence for half a mile. They'd soon reach the point where they would cross the beach to go up on the street to walk back to Natalie's house, where Laney had parked her "summer" car, a Miata convertible. She drove her Tesla during the rest of the year.

Not able to stand the silence anymore, Natalie said, "You started to tell me about Clancy. If you're having a second date, I guess you like him. You never go on second dates."

Laney was quiet for a moment, probably debating whether or not to go to round two of the Bella conversation. But then she said, "I do like him. A lot. Which means it's going to end in disaster. You know my track record. Nice guys never like me. Just the losers. I know I've always said I'm not interested in marriage, but . . . I don't know. It might be nice to have a partner."

Natalie looked at her sister and shrugged. "So maybe your luck has changed. Tell me all about him. And don't leave out any juicy details."

CHAPTER 19

Natalie relaxed in the chaise lounge on the deck while Mason and Patrick swam in the pool. The sun had set and the air had cooled, but it was still eighty degrees outside and humid. So many people complained about the humidity in Delaware, but she liked it. Maybe because she had been born and raised there, but she didn't think so. Every time she went to Arizona to visit her parents, she thought about how people said that the heat out west was so much more comfortable than the East because it was a dry heat. She begged to differ. Every time she stepped out of the Phoenix airport, she felt as if she were walking into a human-sized oven. She'd take humid heat over dry anytime.

Natalie sipped a glass of flavored seltzer water and looked down at the notepad on her lap. Her to-do list included grocery items she needed to pick up and online orders she needed to place. They were going to a family crab feast at Beth and Shay's house on Saturday and then to watch the fireworks Albany Beach sponsored for the Fourth of July every year. Shay was getting a bushel of crabs and Natalie had offered to provide fried chicken that she would buy and a couple of homemade sides. The following weekend, they would celebrate McKenzie's sixteenth birthday, so she had to get the orders in for the teenager's gifts. Right now, she had too many gifts in her cart and needed to decide what not to buy.

Natalie had given in and agreed to let Mac have her party in the private dining room at the pub. She still wasn't certain it was an appropriate venue for a sweet sixteen, but she'd given in or, more accurately, given up, when Conor had told her she was acting like an old fart. That there was nothing wrong with a teenage girl having her party at her family's restaurant, which happened to be a pub. His silly name-calling had hurt Natalie's feelings. But she'd gotten his point. If there was no alcohol being served to minors, how was this any different from having the party at any place in town? It just irked her that Conor always got to be the cool parent and she was . . . the old fart.

Natalie felt water dripping on her feet, and she glanced up. Mason and Patrick were both standing in front of her, towels wrapped around their shoulders, dripping on her. She drew up her knees. "Done swimming?"

Mason nodded. The week before, he'd had a follow-up appointment with an orthopedist, been deemed healed, and had ditched his splint, no worse for wear after his encounter with the VW Bug with eyelashes. Given the okay for playing sports again, he had a swim meet on Friday evening and a baseball game in Rehoboth Beach Saturday morning. Which was another reason why she needed to get herself organized and get things done before the weekend.

"Starting to shrivel." Mason held one hand to show her the wrinkles on his palm and fingers.

Patrick, standing beside him, demonstrated with the opposite hand, which made Natalie smile. The two boys were becoming inseparable. They'd been friends since they were toddlers, but at ten, they were discovering how much they had in common, besides being Sullivan boys, and their bond was even stronger. Of course, the fact that Mason hadn't abandoned Patrick when he was dealing with his cancer and had treated him the same as he always did likely had something to do with their closeness.

"You move in here, Patrick?" she teased her nephew. He'd stayed the night before and was apparently staying again, as it was just after nine and Beth's bedtime these days was eight-thirty at the latest.

Mason shook his shaggy, wet head of hair like a dog. "I told you at dinner that he was staying, Mom."

"Dad said I could stay another night," Patrick told her. "As long you guys didn't care." He frowned. "My mom's crabby."

Natalie smiled. "Well, it's hard work carrying a baby around in your belly." Beth, an insurance adjuster, had dropped to part-time and was working at home, as per her obstetrician's recommendation. The baby was due in September.

Mason wrinkled his nose. "Mom, babies develop in a woman's uterus, not her belly."

Natalie raised an eyebrow. "Oh, yeah? How do you know that?"

The ten-year-old rolled his eyes. "YouTube."

Natalie drew back. It was hard enough having McKenzie maturing in front of her eyes. She wasn't sure she was ready for her baby to do the same. "What are you watching on YouTube?"

Patrick raised his towel, draping it over his head "My mom made me watch this gross video about babies being born and stuff so I would know about how my baby sister was getting out. I showed it to Mason."

Natalie nodded. "Okay. Well . . ." She looked to Mason. They'd had the birds and the bees talk when Beth announced her pregnancy because she and Conor had agreed it was timely. But the discussion had been brief, and he hadn't seemed all that interested. "Cool. If you have any questions or are confused about something," she told both boys, "you can always ask Aunt Beth or me. When she's not feeling crabby," she added.

"We're going in to play video games." Mason walked away.

Natalie looked at her watch. "Your sister should be home

anytime. Could you send her out here when she does? Before she disappears into her room for the night."

"We'll tell her," Patrick said, trudging off behind his cousin.

Natalie picked up her to-do list again, wondering if Conor would be home soon. He'd promised he'd try to get away by ten so they could spend some time together before bed. She'd showered, put on a little makeup, and even spritzed herself with a little perfume he'd bought for her on her last birthday. If he was in a good mood and wasn't too tired, she was hoping he'd want to make love. They'd always had an active sex life and she felt it was an important part of their relationship, a way to re-connect. She felt like the physical intimacy brought emotional intimacy to their marriage.

The French doors from the house to the deck opened and closed. "You wanted me?" McKenzie muttered.

Natalie looked up to see her daughter walking toward her. More accurately, slouching toward her. McKenzie had always had good posture, but lately it seemed as if she was going through life with hunched shoulders. Natalie suppressed the urge to tell her to stand up straight.

"You alone?" Natalie swung her legs around and planted her bare feet on the deck. "I thought Bella was coming to spend the night."

"She was supposed to." She shrugged, her disappointment evident. "She changed her mind. She wanted to go to some party."

"And she didn't invite you to go with her?"

McKenzie was still wearing her work T-shirt, but she was barefoot. "She did, but I didn't want to go."

Natalie studied her daughter's face by the glow of the security lamps on the house and the reflection of the light off the surface of the pool. "Why not? You could have gone for a while, and then you both could have come home. I made those blueberry muffins Bella likes so you guys could have them for breakfast."

McKenzie did not make eye contact. "It wasn't my kind of party."

"What's that supposed to mean?"

"It doesn't matter," McKenzie huffed. "It doesn't even start until ten, and I'm not supposed to be out later than eleven. What would be the point?"

"But if you and Bella were going together, I wouldn't have minded if you—"

"*Mother*," McKenzie interrupted. "I didn't want to go to the stupid party. I worked all day, and I need to get up in the morning and work on that stupid social studies paper."

"Could Bella have helped you with the paper? She said she graduated in the top ten in the class."

McKenzie rested both of her hands on her hips. "Why do you have to do that all the time?"

"Do what?" Natalie asked, genuinely not understanding.

"Automatically assume that I need help with schoolwork, Bella's help. I'm in the top five percent of my class!"

"I know, but Bella's older, and I just thought, I don't know. She's written more papers. And . . . and she said the other day that the curriculum hadn't changed since she had the class as a junior. She had the same teacher. She knows what he's looking for."

"Why do you like her so much better than me?" McKenzie blurted.

"What?" Natalie got to her feet. "What are you talking about? I don't like her *better* than you. You're my daughter." She pressed her hand to her heart. "I love you."

"She told me about calling you about her driver's license last week." McKenzie's tone was accusatory.

"Why are you angry at that?" Natalie was beginning to get irritated. Why was everything she did wrong in the teen's eyes? "Bella called *me*. I didn't call her. She wanted to know how to replace her license. I told her. That was it."

McKenzie narrowed her gaze. "You know, she's not the goody-goody you think she is."

Natalie had no idea what was going on with McKenzie, but she didn't like it. Her tone was bordering on being disrespectful. "I never said she was a goody-goody. Whatever that means."

"You know what it means. You think she's perfect, and she's not."

"I never said—" Natalie stopped midsentence, staring at her daughter. "What is Bella doing that she shouldn't be?"

McKenzie's pretty face twisted sourly. "I'm not tattling on her. She's still my friend, even if you do like her better than me," she flung.

"Aw, Mac—" Natalie started to reach out to hug her daughter, but McKenzie stepped back.

"Can I go?" she asked. "I feel gross. I had to change the stupid hermit crab cages today. I want to take a shower and go to bed."

Natalie hesitated. A part of her wanted to stand there and spar with her daughter who was now taller than she was. But a part of her, a tiny part of her, feared that maybe there was some truth in McKenzie's accusation. Maybe she was giving McKenzie the impression she liked Bella better than her. But that was only because McKenzie was so difficult this summer. And Bella . . . Bella was easy to get along with. And Bella helped Natalie when she came to visit and asked her how her day was and other adult-like things.

Natalie sighed, massaging her temples. Suddenly she had a headache. "You can go." She watched McKenzie walk back to the house and felt terrible. "I don't like Bella better than you," she called after her. "I love you, Mac."

"I love you," Natalie repeated in a whisper as the teen walked into the house.

CHAPTER 20

Natalie sat on a barstool in the pub and sipped her pint of beer as she checked her watch. It was after ten. Twenty minutes ago, Conor had said he was ready to go, but then he'd retreated to the office to do *just one more thing* before walking home with her. A part of her was so annoyed that she considered leaving. He'd not come home to spend time with her the night he had promised earlier in the week, nor any night since. But her desire to be alone with him, even just the twenty minutes it would take to walk home, was more significant than her exasperation with him. So she continued to wait, nurse her beer, and listen to his brother talk.

"Are you hearing anything I say?" Rory asked.

Natalie looked up at her brother-in-law, mopping the bar top. "Nope," she answered. "Because nothing you're saying matters, Rory. Getting out of hot water with the state, with your ex and your brothers, is incredibly simple. *Pay your child support.*" She emphasized each word. "And maybe start using condoms?" Meeting his gaze, she raised an eyebrow. The fact that he had fathered children he never intended to raise was something she had a hard time forgiving him for. Even if she did love him because Conor loved him.

He drew back dramatically as if offended. But Natalie knew he wasn't. It was all a part of his charm—pretending to experience emotions he didn't have.

Rory, fourteen months younger than Conor, could have been her husband's twin. In looks, at least. He had the same thick dark hair, chiseled chin, and come-hither smile. Which, maybe, explained the trail of broken hearts and fatherless children he left in his wake.

He brought his fist down on the dark, stained bar top that he and his father had purchased many years ago. They'd ripped the bar out of an old pub that had gone out of business in Boston's South End and reassembled it in Albany Beach. A proper Irish bar top, their father had said. And it was gorgeous after Rory had refinished it, bringing it back to its glory days from the 1940s. "Nat, this is more complicated than you seem to understand. Elaine—"

"Elaine is the mother of your son and always will be," she interrupted. "And Drew is your son. Period. It's your responsibility to financially support him, especially since you never even see him."

"I see Drew all the time. Last week I took him overnight so Elaine could go on a date," he argued.

"That was not last week. That was two months ago. I remember because you called us at least a dozen times asking for advice in the twelve hours you had him." She held up her finger to silence him when he opened his mouth to dispute the facts again. "And we're done talking about this. I don't have the patience tonight."

"Being a little hard on me, aren't you?" Now she was getting puppy eyes.

"'Going easy on you' is more like it," she responded. "Are you coming to Shay and Beth's tomorrow for crabs?"

"I don't know." He tossed the wet bar mop into the sink

behind him. "The way everyone is ganging up on me, maybe I should just stay here and work."

She sighed and sipped her beer. "Maybe you should. But you were missed at the get-together at our house on Father's Day. You never even said why you didn't come."

A customer on the far end of the bar raised his hand for another drink, and Rory signaled he'd be there in a moment. "I didn't come because Shay and Conor were mad as hornets with me." He opened his arms wide. "Over something I couldn't control."

She looked at him, making her disbelief so apparent that there was no need for words.

"What?" Rory demanded. "I didn't ask to be served court papers at my place of business."

"No, but you chose to look like a butthole in front of your customers."

Rory walked away from her, shaking his head. "You're as bad as they are. But I still love you, Nat the Brat," he threw over his shoulder with a handsome smile. "I'll always love you."

"*Why* does my brother love you?" Conor asked, walking up behind Natalie. He pressed a kiss to the nape of her neck beneath her ponytail. "I told you before. Keep your filthy hands off my wife, Rory!" he shouted, his tone playful.

Natalie looked up at him and smiled. He was in a good mood. She was glad she hadn't walked.

Conor pressed his hand to the small of her back. "Ready to roll?"

She felt a familiar shiver of pleasure at his touch and vowed not to get into any arguments with him tonight. She was determined not to say or do anything that might ruin his mood or hers and nix any chance there was of them making love when they got home.

"Done with that?" Conor asked, pointing to her pint as she got off the barstool.

She nodded. In her effort to lose weight, she was practicing leaving the last sip or two of beer in her glass, the last bite or two on her plate. Breaking old habits was hard when you grew up in a family where you were forced to stay at the table until bedtime if you didn't eat all your canned spinach, and then the spinach was served cold for breakfast the following day. But her habit of always finishing everything whether she wanted it or not, she had realized, was probably contributing to her weight issues.

Conor grabbed her beer and finished the last swallow. "You have the con, Mr. Sullivan; you have the con. Batten down the hatches and lock 'er down," he told his brother, meaning Rory was in charge of closing that night.

"Aye, aye, Cap'n." Rory slid the pint of beer to the customer at the far end of the bar and then stood at attention and saluted Conor.

Conor laughed, shaking his head. "You're a mess. See you tomorrow."

"See you tomorrow. Who's opening?" Rory called after them as they headed for the door.

"Margot," Conor answered. Then they walked out of the pub and into the humid sea air and the caramel smell of Fisher's popcorn.

"Margot is opening for you now?" Natalie asked.

One way they had all agreed they would run a tight business financially was only to allow a few carefully chosen employees to open and close. The beginning and the end of the day were when booze and cash could most easily find their way out the door.

"She is. She opened and closed with me a couple of times last week and did a super job."

Conor led Natalie around a gaggle of twentysomething women in cutoff white shorts, wearing plastic crowns on their heads. In the group's center was a very drunk young lady wearing a white sash that read *BRIDE*. Natalie saw that the other girls were all wearing skimpy, torn tank tops that read *Patty's*

Crew. She hoped that Patty wasn't getting married the following day, as she looked as if she would need some recovery time after tonight.

"You didn't tell me she was opening and closing," Natalie said, returning to the conversation about Margot.

"I told you," he defended.

She looked at him.

"I told you," he repeated. Then he added, "At least I thought I did. Meant to."

"I didn't realize we had decided to let newly hired waitresses open and close."

"Margot's been helping me out in the office, too. When we don't need her to wait tables. She's super smart."

"So you said."

Conor looked down at her. She knew the look on his face. He was trying to decide whether he wanted to continue this conversation or drop it.

She wanted him to drop it, so she said, "Before I forget, the mechanic called. There *is* an oil leak in my car, but they haven't found it yet." She hesitated. "So . . . maybe we need to think about that new car. *I* need to think about it," she corrected. She already knew Conor was ready to place the order. They couldn't legally buy a Tesla in Delaware due to some crazy law, no doubt supported by local car dealers, so they would have to pick it up out of state. Which wouldn't be a big deal because it was only a two-hour ride to the Philadelphia area, where she *could* buy one.

"Really?" Conor asked, his eyes lighting up the way Mason's did when a new version of Fortnite was released. "I thought you said we couldn't afford it."

"It's not that we can't afford it, per se," she told him. "I'm just trying to be careful with our money." After they married, they had agreed that even though they were both pretty good with money, it would be easier if only one managed their household budget and finances. With Natalie pregnant with McKenzie, they had played rock, paper, scissors for the job and Natalie had lost. She has been doing their home finances ever since.

They reached the boardwalk steps, and Conor stopped to lean down and kiss her on the lips. "I know you are. And I appreciate it."

She smiled up at him. "So, go ahead and place the order." She raised a finger. But we're getting the Model Three."

"No gullwing doors?" he teased. "Mason is going to be incredibly disappointed. He's been sending me photos of Model Xs for weeks. No message, just photos. He's fond of the black models with the white leather interior. Can you imagine him with white leather?"

They laughed together, and she raised her arms and hugged him tightly. "I miss you, Conor. I feel like we never get to talk anymore. Just be together." She leaned back and looked into his eyes. Light from a streetlamp made it possible to see the features of his face. "You're never home."

He took her hand and they walked down the steps. When they reached the bottom, they both kicked off their sandals and picked them up. Conor didn't speak the distance to the water's edge and Natalie wondered if she'd just wrecked her chances for a romantic evening.

"Nat, we talked about this," Conor said, his tone neutral. "We discussed it for months before we agreed to buy the place from Daidí. That the only way to make buying the pub and building up the business financially feasible was for me—for Shay and me—to manage it. Even at the rate we're going now, and our profits are better than we had hoped, it's going to be this summer and the next before we can even consider hiring a full-time manager for the summer."

Cold water lapped at Natalie's bare feet as they began the walk south along the shoreline toward home. "I know we talked about it. And . . . and I thought I was prepared," she told him. "But . . . I'm lonely, Conor. I *really* miss you. I hate going to bed alone at night. And . . . and even when you are home, you're . . . distracted." Saying how she was feeling brought tears to her eyes, but at least it wasn't turning into a full-blown crying jag. Which she'd had the week before when he didn't come home until two-thirty in the morning, well after the bar had closed for the night. "I don't feel like we're connecting the way we always have."

"I don't know what to say," he told her. "I don't know what you want me to do. We're in this now. We'd lose everything if we tried to sell the place."

He continued to hold her hand, but she could feel the closeness to him she'd experienced back at the bar fading. And she needed that connection with him right now. She *desperately* needed it. "I don't want you to sell your pub. Our pub," she said. "And I don't want to fight with you."

"Who's talking about fighting, Nat? We're having a conversation here. The kind of conversation husbands and wives have."

Natalie breathed deeply, the salty air tingling in her nose. She loved this place so much. She loved the sound of the waves crashing onto the beach, the foam that tickled her toes, the vastness of the ocean that stretched beyond their shore. "I don't mean to complain. You're right. I knew what I—*we* were getting into when we bought the place. And you're doing an amazing job running it; I'm just . . . I guess I'm feeling overwhelmed at home alone every day. I'm trying so hard to lose weight and it's going so slowly."

He squeezed her hand as they walked, water splashing against their ankles. "I told you, I think you're perfect just as you are. I love your curves, Nat."

She smiled in the darkness and swung her flip-flops in her free hand. "I know you do. But the doctor says I need to lose weight. And there's the hysterectomy in September or October." She groaned. Just thinking about everything going on in her life made her temples throb. "And Nana. She hates the new place. I think she's worse since we moved her."

"I thought she was better. On Father's Day, she and I had

a twenty-minute conversation about Roosevelt's reluctance to enter the war before Pearl Harbor." Conor had always been a World War II buff, and before Nana's memory had begun slipping they had often discussed various topics about the war.

"She has her moments, but they're getting further apart," Natalie told him. "And then Mason's accident. And Mac . . . I'm not going to sugarcoat it. Mac is driving me crazy. Everything has to be hard with her these days. She can never just let the dog out. Pick her wet towels up off the bedroom floor. Take out the trash. Speak civilly to me. *Everything* has to turn into a verbal brawl."

"Babe, we encouraged her to be independent, to think independently. When she does, we can't get upset with her."

"Smart-mouthing me isn't being independent. It's being disrespectful. I was so annoyed with her tonight that I told her she could spend the night with Bella. I just wanted her out of the house."

He tilted his head, looking at her. "And . . ." He drew out the word. "You didn't speak with Bella's mother first?"

"I did not, because your daughter refuses to get me the phone number and I didn't want to ask Bella."

"Smart move."

"I told her she had to stay with Mason until we got home, but then she could go. When I left, Bella was on her way over to hang out until Mac could leave."

"So maybe now that you've agreed to let her stay with her friend, she'll go a little easier on you."

Natalie cut her eyes at him even though he probably couldn't tell in the dark. "Not a chance in heck of that."

He tilted his head back and laughed.

"And then there are the books for the pub," Natalie went on. "And I'm supposed to be on this board at Mason's school and . . . and I feel like I'm spinning a dozen plates in the air. And I keep waiting for one of them . . . *all of them* to come crashing down around me."

Conor pulled his hand from hers. "I hear what you're saying, but . . . do you think you might be bringing part of this stress on yourself?" He hesitated. "With this whole thing about the baby? Looking for her. Thinking Mac's friends could be her."

Natalie took a moment to think through her response before she said anything. Because a part of her wanted to tear into him. But a part of her just wanted him to hold her in his arms. She wanted to make love and fall asleep with her head on his chest. She made her decision quickly. "Not all of her friends," she said. "Just Bella. And on that front, you'll be happy to know I have found out absolutely nothing with Internet searches. Zilch. I don't know that I'm going to, either. When the adoption agency explained to me before the baby was born that it would be a closed adoption, I guess I didn't fully understand. This door isn't just closed, it's locked. With chains and padlocks."

"Don't do that, Nat."

"Do what?"

"Make me seem like the bad guy in this." He stopped and wrapped his arms around her, flip-flops dangling from his hand. "I'm not happy to know that you're not finding what you think you want. I don't want you to be sad. Upset." He hesitated and then went on. "But I think it might be for the best. There are so many ways this could go wrong. I think we'd all be better off if you don't find out."

She looked up at him. "Can we just go home, Conor? Climb into bed and snuggle?"

"Naked?"

His tone was teasing, and she met his gaze. "Is there any other way to snuggle in bed together, *except* naked?"

CHAPTER 21

Mac walked beside Bella on the sidewalk, headed toward Bella's car. "I wish you'd stop doing that," she said.

"Stop doing what?" Bella looked at her. She was wearing a cool Blacktop Mojo band T-shirt that she had cut the sleeves off and opened up the neckline by cutting through the crew collar. Bella had seen the band the year before with her mom. Which Mac thought was cool—even if Bella's mother did wear earplugs and was on her phone the whole time.

Bella hit her key fob and her car beeped and unlocked. She walked around to the driver's side and looked at Mac over the roof of the car. A streetlight illuminated her friend's face. Bella was wearing a thin headband, 1960s-style, and Mac wondered if she'd look good in one, too.

Mac opened the car door, threw her backpack onto the rear seat, and got in. She waited until Bella was in the car to answer. "Hitting on my mom."

Bella laughed and fastened her seat belt. "I'm not *hitting on your mom*." She cut her eyes at Mac, and then the interior lights went off. "Now your dad, I might hit on him, because *he* is hot."

Mac buckled in. "You know what I mean. You're supposed to be my friend, not hers."

"But I like your mom." Bella started the engine. "She's GOAT."

"My mom's a goat?" Mac asked as they pulled away from the curb.

"Not a goat. GOAT. What kind of school do you go to?"

Not a fancy private one like you, Mac thought, but she didn't say it.

Bella opened her eyes wide as if the answer were obvious. *"Greatest Of All Time?"*

That's a dumb one, Mac thought. But again, she didn't say it. She didn't have the energy for Bella tonight. Bella took a lot of energy. Mac had planned to go to bed and watch episodes of *Buffy the Vampire Slayer*. She knew the show that ended before she was even born wasn't the *GOAT*. Bella would think it was dumb. But it was what Mac's mom called a guilty pleasure—something you would be embarrassed for anyone to know you watched. Her guilty pleasure was *The L Word*. Bella probably wouldn't think Mac's mother was *GOAT* or *Gucci* if she knew she streamed an old series about lesbians in L.A.

Mac didn't really want to spend the night with Bella tonight. She was on her period and felt gross and bloated. She'd only asked to go out of habit and to remind her mother of how ridiculous she was being. Mac would have her license in a week. In six months, she'd be driving on her own and she could go anywhere she wanted, do anything she wanted. It also kind of hurt Mac's feelings that her mother didn't have more confidence in her. That she didn't know who Mac really was.

When her mother said she could go to Bella's, Mac had been so shocked that for a moment she hadn't known what to say. Then she'd pretended to be excited. Because how could she not be after weeks of being such a bitch about wanting to go? So she was stuck. She had to text Bella and tell her tonight was the night. Their first sleepover.

186 / Colleen French

Mac put down her window and let the warm, humid breeze hit her face. "I'm serious. She's not your friend. She's my mom."

"Easy for you to say. You know who your mom is."

"What do you mean? You know who your mom is."

"Not my real mom."

Mac made a face. "She's been your mom since you were two days old."

"Not my birth mom." Bella hesitated and then went on. "Can you keep a secret?"

Mac looked at her friend, refusing to dignify the question with an answer.

"I'm thinking about trying to find my birth mother."

"Wow," Mac said. She looked out the window, watching the beach houses fly by. A group of guys standing on a corner hooted as they passed, and she waved. "You sure you want to know?" she asked Bella.

"Why wouldn't I?"

"I don't know. There had to be something wrong with her. Why else would she put you up for adoption? What if she's a . . . a drug addict or something? A heroin addict living on the streets prostituting herself? Or . . . in jail for committing a murder. What if she killed your birth dad and that's why she had to give you away? Because she's doing forty to fifty in a maximum-security prison."

"That's not a very nice thing to say." There was an undertone of hurt feelings in Bella's words.

"Or I guess maybe—" She thought about what her mother had said about women giving up babies if they couldn't take care of them. "Maybe she got pregnant young, like fifteen, and she couldn't keep you. Maybe her parents were going to kick her out of the house, so she decided to give you up for adoption so she could finish high school, go to college, and become a physician and save lives."

"If that were true, she'd have come looking for me by now, wouldn't she?"

"I don't know." Mac shrugged and stared out the window, watching a cute little old man walking a great big, hairy dog. She couldn't tell if it was a Bernese mountain dog or a New-foundland. When Mac had a house of her own, she was getting a Bernie. Winston was okay, but she'd always wanted a big dog. Which her mother had nixed because they pooped too much.

"What's wrong with you tonight?" Bella asked. At a stop sign, she signaled and turned.

"Nothing. I'm hormonal. Got my period. Cramps."

"Sounds like we need frozen yogurt, then." Bella looked at her, a smile on her pretty face. "Feel like frozen yogurt? We'll put every topping on it they have: Oreo cookies, gummy bears, Reese's cups, Sour Patch, hot fudge, and hot butterscotch. With like a cup of rainbow sprinkles. We'll put so much delicious-ness on it that we'll feel sick the rest of the night."

Mac smiled at her friend, thinking she needed to adjust her attitude and enjoy the little bit of freedom her mother had given her. And she should be relieved. At work, earlier in the day, Bella had said something about going to her boyfriend's place tonight, and Mac wasn't interested in that. His place was filthy and stank of old pizza boxes and cigarettes, and his roommates were creepers.

"I think we should get a large," Mac said.

"Extra-large," Bella came back, laughing. And then she turned off Albany Avenue onto the highway and headed south toward their favorite frozen yogurt place.

The windows open, a hot breeze blowing on their faces, Mac felt her mood improving as she cranked up the music and together she and Bella sang off-key to their favorite Blacktop Mojo song.

CHAPTER 22

The sun had set when Natalie rolled up the last of the make-shift newspaper tablecloth covered in blue claw crab shells. Fireworks would begin downtown in an hour, and she wanted to get Beth's backyard cleaned up so she wouldn't have to come back afterward.

Laney walked past her with a recycling bin full of empty beer bottles. The family had scattered and they were the only two left in Natalie's in-laws' backyard. "Need help?"

Natalie held the big roll of wet, heavy paper in her arms, in front of her, looking at the black garbage bag at her feet. "I would love some." Her nose was itchy, but there was no way she could scratch it. It was all she could do to hold the big roll of wet paper and shells out in front of her to keep from getting it on her T-shirt. Which probably already had crab goo on it.

Laney set down the can and opened the black trash bag, holding it under the newspaper in Natalie's arms.

"Got it?" Natalie asked. Her nose was so itchy, she couldn't stand it.

"Got it," Laney told her.

Natale dropped the trash into the bag and scratched her nose with the back of her hand. She'd washed her hands multiple times, but she still smelled like crabs and Old Bay Seasoning. She loved family crab feasts where everyone sat around picking crabs and talking for hours, only rising occasionally to grab an ear of corn or a grilled burger. It had been an exceptionally nice afternoon: good weather; fat, meaty crabs steamed to perfection; and the sweetest local corn to be had. And better yet, the Sullivan boys had all behaved themselves. There had been no arguments, and Rory had been on his best behavior, practically genuflecting to get back into his brothers' good graces again. Natalie had eavesdropped on one of the brothers' conversations and heard that Rory had come to an agreement with his ex and the matter had been settled outside of court.

Laney tied up the heavy trash bag and lifted it. "Dumpster?" she asked.

"Dumpster," Natalie echoed. "Trash pickup is Monday." She followed Laney across the backyard. "Let me get the gate and the lid."

The sisters disposed of the trash and returned to the fenced-in backyard that Beth had decorated with US flags, red, white, and blue balloons, and a big banner that read *Happy Fourth*! Beth loved the Fourth of July because she was a first-generation American. Her parents, as newlyweds, had fled Castro's Cuba and come to the United States to make a better life for themselves and their children. Beth's paternal grandfather, a journalist, had been imprisoned by Castro, never to be heard from again, a story she told anyone who would listen.

"Where is everyone?" Laney asked as they began to clean up the food table. They had already taken anything perishable inside, but there were chip bags to roll up, more trash to be tossed, and extra plastic cutlery to be collected. Everything was red, white, and blue on the tables, even the disposable cups. "Just like this bunch to disappear when it's time to clean up."

"Let's see. Beth is lying down before we head to the beach for the fireworks. Her ankles are swollen again. And the boys are in the garage playing darts," Natalie said, referring to Conor and his brothers. She had learned when she first started dating Conor that competitive darts was big with the Irish.

Natalie rolled up a bag of honey barbeque potato chips and closed it with a clip. "And . . . McKenzie walked the boys to the boardwalk to get frozen custard. Then they were going to stake out a place on the beach where we can watch the fireworks from. She took towels with her, and she's going to text me where we should meet them."

"That's nice of her to take her brother and cousin downtown." Laney eyed Natalie as she scooped up a pile of napkins that were wet from a questionable substance and tossed them into a trash can with a fresh liner.

"Um-hm," Natalie agreed.

"Nat." Laney stopped what she was doing. "I'm going to cross over into 'it's probably none of my business territory' here."

"What else is new?" Natalie teased. Her sister did butt into her business sometimes, but that had never been an issue with Natalie. She wanted to hear Laney's opinion. And, to be fair, Natalie had no problem commenting on Laney's doings. They had always had that sort of relationship.

Laney hesitated and then said, "I feel like you're not giving Mac credit where credit is due."

"What do you mean?" Natalie dropped extra forks and knives into a box Beth had stored under the table for easy access.

"I feel like you only see the negatives and not the positives. Mac is an amazing young woman. What sixteen-year-old girl wants to drag her little brother around town? And his sidekick." Laney stuffed more trash into the bag. "But she offered. You didn't even ask her to do it."

"You grabbed one of Beth's star bowls." Natalie pointed to the trash can. "She counts them. One is missing, she'll have us all dumpster diving."

"Damn it," Laney muttered, and reached into the trash. "Ew. This is disgusting. And did you see Mac with Nana?" she went on. "She sat with her for hours picking crabs for her. Sixteen-year-olds don't do that, either. Not typical ones. And then she rode back to the nursing home with me and got Nana settled. She undressed her and put her in her nightgown." Laney pulled out the missing bowl and threw it on the table. "I don't even like to dress her. It weirds me out." She held up her palm. "I know that's what will happen to my body if I'm lucky enough to live to be old, but I prefer to ignore my saggy, baggy future as long as absolutely possible."

Natalie stopped what she was doing and looked at her sister. She saw Laney's point. Concerning the inevitable changes in a woman's body . . . and her daughter. McKenzie *had* been terrific today. Natalie had noticed, but she hadn't said a word to her daughter about it. She wondered why. It wasn't like her not to give credit due. Maybe because she was holding a grudge because of the teen's recent behavior. With her. Natalie didn't see it with anyone else. McKenzie was sweet and mature with her father and nice to her brother, if you didn't count the potty-words name-calling. Which was their thing and Natalie got that. Sort of, because, as McKenzie often pointed out, boys are gross.

"You complain about her immature behavior," Laney continued. "And I agree that she shouldn't be mouthing back to her mother. But if you're going to point out every little misstep she takes, I think it's important that you also recognize when she does something good."

"Misstep?" Natalie asked. "Yesterday she told me that when she goes to college, far away, she's never coming home again. Ever. And she was mean about it."

"Again, the tone is not excusable, but don't all kids say things like that? I know I did. Hell, I wanted to go to school in *London*."

Slowly turning over her sister's words in her head, Natalie

put the items they needed to carry into the house into a laundry basket. After a moment, she said, "You're right. Conor, more or less, said the same thing to me last night." She stopped what she was doing, pushed her sunglasses up on her head, and ran her stinky hand over her face. She felt like she had a little sunburn, though how she didn't know, because she had applied sunscreen and reapplied. The impending hysterectomy was enough to fret over; she didn't need the threat of melanoma on top of it. "I just, I don't understand her. I don't understand her frustration with me." A lump rose in her throat. "She and I used to be so close. Or at least I thought we were." She wiped her eyes and lowered her sunglasses, feeling foolish that she would let a teen-age girl make her cry.

"Aw, sweetie." Laney gave her a quick hug. "I think her be-havior is perfectly normal for a girl her age. I was the same way with Mom. That summer I worked at Dunkin' Donuts, do you remember me bringing home your and Dad's favorite donuts and bringing a coconut one for her?"

Natalie managed a chuckle. "And she *hated* coconut."

"Was *allergic* to coconut. I was such a brat. But I thought I was a grown-ass woman, and I thought Mom and Dad, but particularly Mom, were getting in my way of that." She met Natalie's gaze. "When I look back, I realize that was all about me creating a separation between us. We were talking about college, about me moving hundreds of miles away. It was like I needed to practice living without their help, their advice, their . . . their love, I think." She shook her head. "And I knew they would always love me, but I needed to be loved as an adult, not their child. Does that make any sense? At least framing it with a sixteen-year-old's logic?"

"It does," Natalie agreed.

"Being Mac's age, there's a lot to deal with." Laney tilted her head one way and then the other. "So maybe cut her a break once in a while? Throw her an occasional bone?"

Natalie wanted to say that she was wrestling with a lot, too.

That being thirty-eight with two kids, a business, a grand-mother with dementia, and a child she'd never known out there somewhere in the world was hard, too. But she knew this conversation was about McKenzie and not her. And besides, if she brought up the baby, Laney might go off on her, and it had been too nice a day to get into a tiff with her sister. Instead, she patted the back pockets of her jean shorts. "Seen my phone?"

Laney shook her head. "Not recently. You had it at the table when we were eating crabs. I remember because you said Dad texted you about flying in for Mom's birthday in October."

Natalie patted all her pockets again, as if that would make her phone appear, then glanced at the two picnic tables pushed together under a pop-up canopy. They were clean of the crab debris and just needed to be washed down. "I hope I didn't wrap it up in the crab shells."

"Use your locator on your watch." Laney tapped hers on her wrist.

"Right. I keep forgetting that." The watch had been a Christmas gift from Conor. She'd been insisting for years that she didn't need one, didn't want one. So he'd bought it as a gift so she couldn't turn it down. And he was right; she did like it. She just wasn't used to using it yet. "Okay, listen for the ding," she told her sister. She tapped the button and listened. Nothing.

"Maybe you left it in the house?" Laney asked after a moment when they both stood still, listening for a sound they couldn't hear.

"Maybe the kitchen? Bathroom?" Natalie thought aloud.

"What do you need it for? Want my phone?" Laney pulled it out of her pocket.

"Need mine. I've had McKenzie's birthday gifts sitting in my cart for two weeks. Trying to decide what to get and what not to. I think I'll just get it all. As a peace offering," she declared, tapping her watch again as she walked toward the house. "She'll return half of it anyway."

"That's the giving spirit," Laney quipped.

"Wait. I think I heard it." Natalie paused to listen.

"I hear it. It's over by the grill next to the house." Laney strode across the grass. "I swear, you're still like a third-grader, losing things." She laughed as she picked up the phone.

Natalie reached for it, and Laney pulled it just out of reach. And then they were laughing like they were girls again.

CHAPTER 23

"A kids' party in a bar!" Laney shouted in Natalie's ear. Hip-hop music blasted from speakers in the far corners of the room. "Great idea! Can I have my next birthday here?"

Natalie sipped water from a glass. She'd already had her allotment of beer for the day and the following day. "You'll have to talk to the party animal," she answered, loudly. She nodded in the direction of Conor, who was standing between two of McKenzie's friends from school trying to learn some crazy dance move that looked like the Electric Slide Meets Startled Dad.

Laney danced in place enthusiastically as she watched Conor stumble his way through the moves. "What is he doing?" she asked, laughing.

Bella, carrying a plate of wings, walked behind them. "That? That's a pop and lock, your basic hip-hop move."

"But they're all doing it differently," Laney said, indicating the teen girls gathering around him to join in the impromptu dance lesson. She watched, trying to copy their motions.

"It's a move everyone does, but you're supposed to add your own thing," Bella explained, showing off her pop and lock while balancing the plate of chicken in one hand.

She was wearing a short white denim skirt and white tank and her suntanned skin looked gorgeous. However, Natalie wondered again if Bella's mother had educated her on the dangers of long-term sun exposure without SPF or if she ought to try to work it into a conversation the next time the teen came over. Even though Natalie had given in and let McKenzie stay the night at Bella's when she wanted to, the girls seemed to end up at their house usually. In the last week, Bella had spent three nights with them and intended to stay that night after the party.

"Are they girl break-dancing, now?" Laney asked, laughing as the teenagers began showing off a new move.

"I guess so, only we call it breaking or B-girling. B-boying if you're a guy," Bella explained.

Natalie watched her carry the food to the long table where teens who weren't dancing sat. McKenzie was there, drinking a soda and talking. There were mostly girls in attendance, but a few boys. At a smaller table behind them, adults sat—family members and two parents of teens who she guessed hadn't been crazy about the idea of their fifteen- or sixteen-year-old daughter going to a birthday party at a pub.

"Bella's been so much help today," Natalie said, watching her replace an empty wings platter with the fresh batch. "She asked to get off work early so that she could help us set up. And she's the one who took Mac to the party store to get decorations—which I'd been asking her to pick out for at least two weeks." She raised her hands as if being robbed. "Heaven knows I wouldn't pick the right things."

Laney eyed her sister and took a sip from her pint. "You call them?"

"What?" The song from McKenzie's party playlist she and Bella had created had changed and this one seemed even louder than the last.

Laney grabbed her sister's arm and dragged her farther from the Praxis ring of sound. "The adoption agency. Did you call them?" she demanded.

Natalie set her water glass down at a table near the door that led from the private party room out into the main pub. Through the window in the door, she could see that the place was packed, which was great. Their receipts were turning out to be higher than they had even hoped. She didn't know if it was the money they were spending on advertising or just word of mouth, but it was getting to the point where they couldn't serve everyone who wanted to come in and eat. The previous night, Conor said they'd had to turn people away at the door.

"I did not contact the agency," Natalie admitted. "But last night, I was on this interesting site that gave suggestions on how to work around the whole double birth certificate thing. I don't think it's going to work, though. Delaware is serious about its sealed records. Unlike some states where the electronic gates are not as well protected."

"Just call the agency, Nat."

"I know. I'll get to it this week."

"Call the agency," Laney repeated, obviously annoyed.

Natalie shook her head. "Why are you bugging me about this? You want me to drop the whole thing."

"Because you're making me *fecking* crazy, Nat." She used Conor's favorite Irish curse word. She also loved the Irish word *fag*, meaning "cigarette," and used it whenever she could fit it into a conversation.

"How am I making you crazy?" Natalie asked indignantly. "I haven't said a word about the adoption to you in days!" she whisper-shouted.

"No, but you've ramped up on the Bella the wonderful, Bella the great comments. It's no wonder Mac's upset with you."

Natalie stood there for a moment, watching the girls dance. Conor had given up on his pop and lock lesson and walked over to the adult table, where he poured beer from a pitcher into pint glasses. "You know, if I had done that," she said, pointing at the dance floor, "Mac would have had a conniption. She'd have had a full-blown temper tantrum and not cared what anyone thought." She gestured toward Conor, who was laughing and goofing around with Nana. She didn't like to come out in the evenings but had insisted she wouldn't miss her great-granddaughter's sixteenth birthday for the world. Even though she hadn't remembered why she was even there when Laney brought her into the pub.

"Her father does it," Natalie went on, "and she doesn't even notice."

"It's the bitterness that's going to make you an old lady." Laney took a drink of her beer. "Not the hysterectomy."

Natalie stuck her tongue out at her sister. Then laughed at her own ridiculous behavior. Luckily, Laney laughed with her.

"See that boy?" Natalie asked, trying gracefully to move away from the subject of Bella. "The one in the teal shirt with the surfboard."

"Not bad looking, for a sixteen-year-old boy." Laney squinted. "Do we know him? He looks familiar."

Natalie reached for her water glass, wondering if she needed to turn up the air conditioning. It seemed hot in this back room, hotter than in the main dining area. She said a silent prayer of hope that their system wasn't about to go kaput. Of course, it could just be her hormones raging as they did every month. And she was bleeding like a stuck pig again. "That's Matthew Landon, the boy standing next to McKenzie in the prom photos. And he's seventeen. Will be a senior this year."

Laney stared at him for a moment and then grimaced. "The one with the nose hair?"

Natalie laughed. "Yup. Though I can't say I saw it, but then I didn't get all that close to him."

Laney continued to stare, not even trying to be stealthy about it. "I thought she didn't like him."

Natalie shrugged. "Your guess is as good—" The music stopped, and Natalie felt as if she was talking loud enough for all twenty-five people in the room to hear. She lowered her voice. "Your guess is as good as mine. I didn't know she invited him."

"Maybe she didn't. Maybe he crashed the party and she was too nice to tell him to get lost."

"I don't think so," Natalie said slowly, watching as Matthew leaned across the table to say something to her daughter. McKenzie laughed in response to his comment. As if she *did* like him. "See that?" Natalie raised her chin in the direction of the teens' table. "That's as close to flirting as I've ever seen her."

Laney watched them. "Hm . . . so maybe he bought one of those nose hair trimmers. Certainly be worth it for a girl like Mac." She looked at the empty glass in her hand. "I'm going to get Rory to pull me another pint. Want anything?"

"Conor just brought a pitcher in."

"Yeah, but I have to tinkle. And you know me. Not a drop of Irish in my blood. I like my beer icy cold. No pitcher beer if I can avoid it." Laney started for the door and then turned back. "Hey, any way you can get Conor to take Nana home later? I know I said I would be in charge of transportation tonight, but I have a date. And I'd like to meet him a little earlier than I said I could."

Natalie raised an eyebrow. "Same guy you were telling me about?"

"Same guy," she sang. "Clancy. He had a family thing to go to, but we're meeting at the Tiki Bar for a drink later."

Laney did a Grouch Marx thing with her eyebrows. Which Natalie realized she must have had waxed that morning. Which meant she definitely liked him. If Natalie got wind of a bikini wax, there was no telling how far the relationship might go.

"I was considering following it up with a romantic walk on the beach," Laney mused. "If he continues to be as smart, engaging, and deliciously handsome as he's been."

Natalie smiled because her sister was smiling. Laney had always claimed she didn't want to be married, but in the last year or two Natalie had gotten the impression that while Laney maintained that she didn't want marriage and babies, maybe, just maybe, she was beginning to hope for a long-term relationship. Which made Natalie happy. She worried about Laney being so untethered. What was she going to do when she got too old for dates every Friday and Saturday night, for Tinder and flirting at vet conferences? Who, besides her family, would love her when she was as wrinkly as their mother and as crazy as their nana?

"No problem. Conor or I can run her home," Natalie said, keeping her tone casual. If she made a fuss, Laney wouldn't be happy. "Or Beth. She wouldn't mind and it might give her an excuse to sneak out early."

After Laney left the room, Natalie went to the gift table to pick up the torn wrapping paper and load the gifts into a couple of large gift bags. As she stuffed purple and white elephant paper into the garbage bag, McKenzie came over to her.

"Sorry. I should have done that. Everyone was talking to me at once and—" She lifted her hand and let it fall. "I guess I squirreled."

"It's fine," Natalie said. And she meant it. She liked having something to do. She wasn't as good about sitting around and socializing as Conor was. "It's this or break dancing."

To Natalie's surprise, her daughter laughed at her joke. Something she never did, even when it was good.

"I know. Dad looked pretty silly, didn't he? But my friends thought it was funny." She shrugged. "So whatev."

"It was pretty funny from where I was standing," Natalie agreed, picking up the DNA kit and a hot-pink designer handbag that she and Conor had given McKenzie. Along with a whole pile of other stuff. For months, their daughter had been drooling over the bag that wasn't much bigger than her cell. Natalie had told her she would have to save her own money to buy such an extravagance. Then when her guilt gland had kicked in, she'd decided, what the heck? She could afford to spoil her children occasionally. And it had also occurred to her, albeit shamefully, that Mac might be nice to her for a while, if she gave her such a spendy gift.

"I can do that." McKenzie took the gifts from her mother's hands and slid them into a cardboard box under the table. "It was nice of you to get me the DNA thing." She scrunched up her nose. "But . . . you know I'm not writing that social studies paper now. Right?"

"I know." Natalie added more wrapping paper to the trash bag. "Want this bow?" She held it up.

The teen shook her head no.

"But I thought you might like to have it anyway," Natalie went on. "Maybe you'll find some skeletons in the Sullivan/Thompson closet?"

McKenzie laughed. "I am kind of curious. This girl I know from the animal shelter said her father always said they were Cherokee Indian and then he did a test and found out they weren't Native American at all. They're Romas. Like Travelers or Gypsies or whatever you call them. How dope is that?"

"Pretty dope," Natalie agreed.

"Anyway, thanks," McKenzie said. "I know you're the one who got all the gifts. I love, love, *l-o-v-e*," she spelled out, "the bag. My friends are already asking me if they can borrow it."

Natalie glanced up to see McKenzie looking at her, which was a nice change. So often, she stared at her feet, or the dog, or her own hands just to avoid eye contact. "You're welcome. And if any of those clothes don't fit or you don't like them, you can exchange them. I tried to get exactly what you asked for, but sizes aren't always the same across brands." She scanned the room, her gaze settling on the larger table where the teens sat. "I was surprised to see Matthew here. I thought you were on the outs with him."

"Not exactly. We've kind of been talking." McKenzie's tone was noncommittal.

Someone called McKenzie's name and she looked up. One

of the girls was waving her toward them. "Here comes your song!" someone else yelled as a whole gaggle of girls got to their feet to dance.

McKenzie hesitated, looking at her mother.

"Go," Natalie said. "It's your sixteenth birthday party. You'll never have another," she said, feeling a tenderness for her daughter that she didn't quite know what to do with. She'd been so angry with her for so long that the emotion swelling in her chest felt foreign. "Have fun with your friends."

"Thanks, Mom." McKenzie threw her arms around Natalie and gave her a hug.

It was so quick that Mac was gone before it registered in Natalie's mind what had just happened. Natalie was still standing there, stunned, when Laney walked back into the room, right behind Margot, who was bringing in another huge pepperoni pizza. It wasn't usually on the menu. Too many other places in Albany Beach did pizza. But the chef, who had worked there for years, had made them for McKenzie because she had a soft spot in her heart for her. She still remembered McKenzie as a little tyke riding her tricycle around in her grandfather's pub.

Natalie must have had a strange look on her face, because Laney halted at the gift table. "You okay?"

"I . . . I think so." Natalie returned to straightening up the table. She added a pile of small gifts like earrings, gummy bears, and a plastic My Little Pony with pink hair keychain into a bag. "Mac just came over, as in left her friends, to offer to help me clean up here. And then, when she had me completely off-balance, she thanked me for the gifts Conor and I gave her. And hugged me." She looked at her sister, wide-eyed. "Laney, I don't know what to do. Do I call the police?"

Laney looked at her quizzically. "I'm confused."

"I'm afraid someone has kidnapped my daughter and swapped her out with an imposter. I imagine the responsible thing to do is contact the authorities. But what if I want to keep the imposter?"

Laney laughed. "Never happy, are you?"

The gifts bagged up and the paper in the trash, Natalie turned around to watch a group of girls lined up, dancing in synchronized steps. She took her sister's full glass from her hand and drank from it.

Laney watched her. "I thought you were out of your allotted beer calories for the day."

"I am. But if I drink from your beer," Natalie said, taking another sip before she passed the pint back, "then the calories don't count." She poked her sister in the arm with her finger, feeling better at that moment than she could remember having felt in a long time. "Because then, they're . . . *your* calories."

"I don't think that's how it works, Nat."

"You sure?" Natalie crossed her arms over her chest, her gaze shifting to Conor, who took the pizza from Margot and put it on the adult table. He and Margot were now standing close together, talking. She watched carefully for a moment. Something wasn't quite right with what she was seeing, but what it was she couldn't put her finger on. Something about the way they were interacting. The way Margot was looking at him. "Does something seem off to you there?"

"What?" Laney asked, looking around the room. "Where?"

"Conor. And Margot."

Laney settled her gaze on the two of them. They had moved a couple of steps away from the table. "I don't know. They're just talking. But," she said slowly as she continued to watch, "I think you need to keep an eye on her. Conor's a damned fine catch."

Natalie watched a moment longer. "But Conor would never—" She didn't finish her sentence because she wasn't even sure what she wanted to say. Conor would never cheat on her? Of course he wouldn't. Wouldn't flirt with another woman? She would hope not. But he hadn't been himself lately. Even after their talk the week before, he was still distant. He was still working late hours. Coming home well after he had said he'd be there. And he hadn't been talking to her about the day-to-day goings-on of the pub as much as usual. Was he sharing that with someone else? *With Margot?*

"Look, Nat." Laney faced her. "We've talked about this. Everyone's under a lot of stress right now, trying to find their way running this place. You've said yourself how hard it is, looking at the numbers every day. And Conor . . . I'm not saying he'd ever do anything inappropriate, but guys, they're not always aware of what's going on around them. She might have a thing for him, and he wouldn't know it until she bit him on the ass."

Her sister had such a unique use of the English language. Natalie tipped her head back and groaned. "Great. One more thing for me to worry about." Then she snatched her sister's pint from her hand and helped herself again.

CHAPTER 24

Mac walked out of the bathroom stall in the pub's ladies' room to find Bella washing her hands. Mac went to the sink. She had been afraid it might be weird to have Bella there with her friends because they were all younger, but it seemed to be going fine, which was a relief. Mixing groups of friends was always a little awkward for her. Like she didn't usually hang out with friends from school and friends from the animal shelter at the same time.

"*Gucci* party," Bella said over her shoulder. "My parents would never, in a million years, have let me have my birthday party in a pub. I bet when I turn twenty-one they wouldn't even go for it."

"It's just a restaurant with a bar." Mac pumped soap into her hand as she looked at a large road sign on the wall stating the distance from Cork to various cities in Ireland.

They'd renovated the bathrooms themselves over spring break after her parents and uncles bought it from her grandfather, because her dad said they were outdated and *manky*. He used all kinds of silly Irish words. *Manky* just meant "gross," but she liked the sound of the word. When they'd done the renovation, he'd let her use a sledgehammer to break up the old tile and shown her how to lay new tile. She'd painted walls with him, too, and then he'd said she could do the decorating. It wasn't like she would become an interior designer, but she had to admit she did a *Gucci* job. She'd given an old European look, or at least one that Americans would think was old European. The road sign that she found on eBay wasn't authentic, but it looked real enough. The faucets were her best find. They were copper and came right out of the wall. But they had a sensor that detected movement, so they were touchless. Her goofy brother had liked them so much from an epidemiology perspective that he'd asked if they could put the same ones in the house. Their dad had told him to get lost.

"Right," Bella said, sticking her hand in the fancy air dryer. Those had been Mac's idea, too. They were expensive, but they eliminated the need to put a big trash can in each bathroom and empty them every night, and of course they kept paper out of the landfill.

"So dickweed texted me and he wants me to come over. Instead of me going to your house. You care?" Bella asked.

Mac pretended not to hear her over the sound of the hand dryer because she wasn't sure what to say. She knew it was silly, but her feelings were kind of hurt. It was her birthday. Weeks ago, they had planned to have a sleepover and stay up all night watching movies.

On the other hand, Gunner was Bella's boyfriend. Mac's other friends would have ditched her in a second to see their boyfriends. Especially if their parents had forbidden them to see them, but this felt different. Maybe because it was happening more often. The other night when they were supposed to have a sleepover, Bella had sneaked out after Mac's parents went to bed, hung out with the creeper, and then sneaked back in at three in the morning. Which was not *dope*, *GOAT*, or cool as far as Mac was concerned. But she hadn't said anything to Bella because . . .

Because why? she asked herself. Usually she was good at speaking up for herself.

She didn't know why she couldn't do it with Bella. She guessed she didn't want her to be upset with her. They were having such a fun summer together and it made Mac feel good that a girl older than she was wanted to be friends with her. Plus, Bella was just fun. She said and did things Mac would never dare and it was kind of exciting to live vicariously through her.

"You hear what I said? I think I'll go to Gunner's after this."

"You coming to my house after that? Or are you going home?"

"Are you *mangry* at me?" Bella watched her in the mirror. "Why are you *mangry* at me?"

It took Mac a second to realize what the word meant—it was a combo of mad and angry. Bella used a lot of slang, words Mac had a hard time translating, but she didn't want to seem like the total dork that she was and ask.

Mac went to the hand dryer. "I'm not angry at you," she said, choosing not to use the word "mangry." "I just want to know if you're going home with me and then sneak out the window, or if I'm supposed to tell my parents you went home to your house. Whatev. We just need to get our stories straight. You said your mom threatened to call mine the other day." She thrust her hands into the dryer, forcing a pause in the conversation.

"And that cannot happen." Bella wiped her hands on her white jean shorts, which looked amazing against her tanned, toned legs. Mac didn't see herself as a jealous person, but if she was, she'd be jealous of Bella's legs.

"They compare notes and I'll be on Mom's shit list for the next decade."

"But you're eighteen," Mac argued. "You can kind of do what you want."

"Not if I want her to keep paying my credit card bill." Bella glanced in the mirror and smoothed her perfect hair. "Did your mom plan something for breakfast tomorrow morning?"

"Um . . ." Mac thought for a moment. "French toast casserole, sausage patties, and . . . fruit salad, maybe?"

"I love that French toast casserole. I'll go to your house with you guys and then go out after the 'rents go to bed. Or maybe I'll tell dickweed I'm not coming at all." Bella hopped up to sit on the sink, her long, tanned legs dangling. "That casserole sounds better than anything Gunner has to offer."

Mac laughed with her, though she wasn't positive if Bella meant it in general or if she was referring to sex with him. That eating French toast casserole was better than having sex with him. Mac assumed they were doing it, but Bella had never said so outright, so she didn't know for sure. It wasn't her business and thinking about it grossed her out, so she didn't think about it. "Whatev," she murmured.

Bella jumped down from the sink, and in Mac's head she sighed with relief. When Bella had been sitting there, she'd been worried the sink might come out of the wall and ruin the pretty backsplash she'd put in herself.

"You got some dope presents," Bella said, headed for the door.

Mac nodded, following her. Matthew said he was leaving soon, and she wanted to tell him good-bye. They'd been texting back and forth for about a week. At first it was just about the stupid honor society officers' nominations, but then he'd said something about maybe playing Skee-Ball on the boardwalk some night after she got off work. On impulse, she'd invited him to her party, and was shocked he showed up. She'd had a good time talking to him and was thinking maybe she *would* play Skee-Ball with him sometime.

"I know. Right?" Mac said. "I can't believe Mom got me the purse. She doesn't even buy stuff like that for herself."

Bella put her hand on the door pull but then turned to Mac. "Can I have the DNA test she gave you?"

Mac was so surprised by the request that she didn't know

how to respond. How awkward was that, a friend asking for one of your birthday presents? From your parents.

"I was thinking it might be an easy way to find my birth mom," Bella went on. "You know, if she's registered on the site, we'll match. I'd buy one myself, but my mom would see the charge. She goes over the credit card bill like a freak every month. And she and Dad are totally against me looking for her."

"I don't know. I don't really want it," Mac lied, though not sure why. "But you know, it was a gift."

Bella walked out of the bathroom with a shrug. "It's probably a dumb idea to take one of those tests anyway. If my mother gave me up, she didn't want me."

"Or she's a serial killer and you don't want her," Mac said brightly.

Bella laughed and then the awkwardness was gone, and they were best friends again.

CHAPTER 25

Natalie stood outside her grandmother's door and took a couple of deep breaths to calm herself. She had always been good at handling stress, but over the last few weeks she'd begun to feel anxious. She found herself overwhelmed by simple tasks and every little unexpected blip in her day irritated her.

That morning, she snapped at Mason when he accidentally spilled trash on the kitchen floor while trying to take it out. She'd apologized and hugged him, but she still felt guilty. What was wrong with her? It was so unlike her to get worked up over such an insignificant occurrence. Kids, especially boys his age, spilled things, dropped things. She was also having a hard time falling asleep at night, and when she did sleep she was restless. And she was fixating on details that, in the scheme of life, she knew were insignificant. Like not being able to find her favorite eyelash curler.

Sweating profusely from the late July heat, she glanced up and down the hall. Seeing no one but Mrs. Anderson, who was slumped over, asleep in her wheelchair, Natalie pulled a Mason and used the sleeve of her T-shirt to wipe her face. Feeling a blast of frigid air from a register in the ceiling, she looked up.

She felt bad for the nurses and CNAs who had to deal with the heat in the patients' rooms because, like her nana, the nursing home occupants were always cold. To counterbalance the heat their patients required, the air conditioning was kept frigid in the halls. Ruby, at the front desk, said it was the only way to keep the staff from walking out on days like today when the temperature outside hovered in the nineties.

Natalie exhaled with pleasure, enjoying the feel of the cold air on her sticky face. The last few days, she'd been having what seemed like hot flashes, except that she was too young for hormonal hot flashes; at least she would be until she had the hysterectomy.

When she'd Googled her symptoms, one of the diagnoses had been anxiety disorder. Just thinking about it made her more anxious. She talked briefly with Laney about it, but her sister hadn't been all that helpful. She told Natalie, without so much as a dusting of sugarcoating, that she was causing the anxiety by doing something she knew was wrong. Meaning looking into her "lost" baby. That and the fact that she was running herself ragged between work, the house, and the kids.

Natalie had almost skipped today's visit to the nursing home. Her sister had reminded her that an hour after she left, Nana wouldn't remember she'd been there anyway. Which was a fair point, but in the end, Natalie decided to come because Nana was the one person she felt was on her side these days. Next to Mason, maybe, but he was a ten-year-old boy setting his sights on playing first base for the Orioles after high school, so he wasn't exactly her go-to for support in the rationality department.

Today had been a lousy day, in a string of lousy days. After the birthday party, Mac's congeniality had lasted three whole days. The teen had then become as mad as a hornet with Natalie when she refused to allow her to go with Bella for a weekend in Virginia Beach. Natalie hadn't gotten the impression McKenzie even wanted to go all that badly. It had been Bella who had asked Natalie if Mac could go with her and her friends. Natalie had made it clear to both girls that it wasn't appropriate for a sixteen-year-old to spend a weekend with girls so much older than she was.

Bella had tried to sweet-talk Natalie into letting Mac go, making promises there was no way she could keep. As much as Natalie wanted to say yes to Bella, she instinctively knew it had to be a hard no.

Natalie still remembered the week she spent with her friends in Dewey Beach after graduation from high school. There had been plenty of underage drinking, drug use, and more inappropriate hookups than she could remember now. Not that Natalie had been all that badly behaved or that she thought McKenzie would be. She knew McKenzie had a good head on her shoulders. But Natalie had remembered how uncomfortable it had been when she had said no when her friends were saying yes. That was partially why Natalie wasn't allowing McKenzie to go—because she didn't want her daughter to suffer the way she had.

The fact that Conor had wholeheartedly agreed with Natalie on the decision didn't seem to matter to McKenzie. As usual, Natalie was the one taking the blame for the nixed vacay and everything and anything else that her daughter perceived wasn't going right in her life. She'd even blamed Natalie for the fact that she couldn't have Natalie's old car yet because the Tesla Conor had ordered wouldn't be ready until September. The fact that McKenzie wasn't legally allowed to drive alone on her graduated driver's license didn't seem to matter. It was as if McKenzie thought she had a right to have her own car.

And it wasn't just Mac who was stressing her out. It was work, too. A huge bill had come in for food they hadn't ordered. Food she eventually discovered had been accepted, then picked back up, when the chef discovered the mistake. However, because Natalie wasn't informed of the error, she hadn't been able to follow up to be sure they weren't billed for it. Which they had been, and they were now being sent bills with late payment penalties tacked on. There was also an issue with her last unemployment payment for the employees at the pub that had wound up in someone else's account after a state employee had fat-fingered her employer identification number. Everyone agreed a mistake had been made, but, so far, it hadn't been fixed.

And then, the cherry on her sundae for the day had been the return phone call she had finally received from the adoption agency that maintained the records of the baby she'd given up. Granted, it had taken Natalie a week after Bella's party to get up the nerve to make the call. But then it had taken another week for someone to get back to her. That morning on the phone, Mrs. Guthrie, the director, had been pleasant but firm.

"I'm sorry, Mrs. Sullivan. I completely understand how you must feel about not knowing where your birth daughter is. Mothers often hit this wall when their babies reach adulthood, but the agreement you signed is still in place."

Natalie had griped her cell so tightly that her hand was still sore hours later.

"The adoption records are sealed," Mrs. Guthrie had continued. "And we cannot, nor can the courts, provide the information you're requesting. I can, however, give you the contact information for a couple of support groups where parents meet to work through dealing with what you must be dealing with now. They meet online or in person, depending on what you're comfortable with, and many parents have told us that groups like these helped them heal."

When Mrs. Guthrie had finished her spiel, which Natalie was sure she had memorized, all Natalie had wanted to do was shout, *I don't want to heal! I want to know who my daughter is!* Instead, she had asked the agency director if she had any other recourse. Mrs. Guthrie's only suggestion had been to register on the available sites online so that if her daughter ever tried to find her mother she would be able to contact Natalie.

Natalie had managed not to cry until after she had thanked

Mrs. Guthrie and disconnected. The tears that had followed had not just been her frustration, but because she couldn't even think of anyone to call to tell how sad and discouraged she was. Because she had no one to tell, because right now it seemed like her only buddies were a ten-year-old boy and an escape artist dog that continued to foil her attempts to keep him safely in the house and yard. And neither was an appropriate confidant.

Ordinarily, she would have called Laney the minute she got off the phone with Mrs. Guthrie, but her sister was losing her patience with Natalie's quest to determine if Bella was her child. And Laney had less time for her these days, anyway. Her casual dating of the construction guy had turned more serious, and they saw a lot of each other. And of course, there was no way Natalie was going to tell Conor about the call, at least not until she was feeling less emotional, because he had made it clear that while he supported *her*, he did not support her quest. She wasn't even sure how that was possible for a spouse, but it hadn't been up for negotiation.

Natalie sniffed, knocked on the slightly ajar door, and walked into her grandmother's room. "Nana?" The lights were off and the room-darkening shades on the windows pulled down. "Nana, are you here?"

"Close the door!" came Nana's crackly voice. "Where else would I be? No way to get in and out of Oahu, even if I had the money. Talked to Elon's mother today. She's waiting for the telegram to tell her he's gone." The near centenarian sighed. "Not that it matters much. Bellows Field was hit hard. Heard it on the wireless. I know he's gone. I can feel it here." She motioned to her heart.

Natalie did as she was told. When her eyes adjusted to the dim light in the room, she saw her grandmother seated in the recliner. She was wrapped up in a lavender afghan she knitted herself years ago. One she now thought her mother had made for her. Nana's hand rested on her chest over her heart.

"Don't think I'll ever get over that boy," Nana murmured.

Tears welled in Natalie's eyes. It broke her heart to see her grandmother sad, particularly over an event that had happened eighty years ago. Especially when, in Nana's mental state, the news sometimes seemed brand-new.

"I'm so sorry," Natalie murmured, not sure what else to say. She pulled up at a chair and sat down across from her grandmother. She took one of Nana's hands between hers. "I'm so sorry."

"I loved him, you know," Nana said wistfully.

Natalie smoothed the fragile, blue-veined hand in hers. "I know."

Nana exhaled and pulled her hand away. "But it is what it is. How are you today, dear?" She squinted. "You don't look so good."

Without warning, Natalie began to cry.

Nana took her hand. "There, there." She patted Natalie rhythmically. "It's going to be okay. In the end, it's always okay." She hesitated. "You're my granddaughter. I know that. But what's your name again?"

Natalie smiled through her tears. "I'm Natalie. Henrietta's daughter."

"Henrietta." Nana frowned, still holding Natalie's hand. "A cold one, that girl. Never liked me much. I was good to her anyway, though."

"You were," Natalie said, sniffling. "She's told me that. Here." Nana picked up a white handkerchief from the small table next to her recliner. "Blow your nose. It's clean."

Natalie chuckled and accepted the handkerchief with tiny violets embroidered in one corner. Nana had made them herself years ago. Natalie and Laney each had one nestled safely in a dresser drawer.

"There you go," Nana said. "Now tell your nana what's wrong."

"Nothing." Natalie shook her head, wiping her nose with the hanky. When she left, she'd take her grandmother's dirty clothing and the handkerchief home to wash. The care facility offered laundry services, but she preferred that Natalie do it. Her grandmother said she liked the smell of Natalie's soap better. "I'm fine."

"Horse hockey." Nana leaned over and reached in what seemed like slow motion for the small lamp on the table. It took so long that Natalie wanted to do it for her, but early on, when she had still been able to discuss her dementia, she'd made her granddaughters promise to let her do things on her own as long as possible.

Natalie had to literally sit on her hand to keep from overriding the agreement.

At last, Nana reached the switch and the lamp came on, casting a golden circle of light around them. "Tell me what's wrong, Natalie." She met her gaze with her blue eyes that were so pale now that they seemed gray. "While I can still listen."

Natalie understood what she meant, and tears welled in her eyes again. Even though her grandmother's mind came and went, she was still able to find her way back to the present. Soon, she wouldn't be able to.

Suddenly Natalie felt an overwhelming desire to tell her grandmother about her magical time in Paris and about the baby. About Bella.

And so she did.

Nana listened patiently, asking the occasional question. But mostly, she just listened.

As Natalie talked, she began to feel better. Maybe just because she knew Nana was on her side. Because she knew Nana would understand and support her because her grandmother had always supported her.

"And so now . . . now I'm trying to find out if it is her," Natalie finished. "Only Laney and Conor are completely against it and—" She sniffed, using the balled-up hanky to wipe her nose again. "And I feel so alone, Nana. No one understands what it feels like to have given your baby away." Without thinking, she moved her hand to her abdomen as if she could still feel her daughter's kicking in utero.

Nana turned her head to look away and was quiet for a long time, so long that Natalie began to wonder if she was all right. Just when Natalie was about to lay her hand on her grandmother's bony knee, Nana looked back.

"Sad tale," Nana said. "But at least you had a choice."

Nana's response was not anywhere close to what Natalie had thought her grandmother would say. She'd expected words of comfort, maybe even a few harsh words for Natalie's sister and husband who were not being supportive.

"My mother didn't have a choice."

"What?" Natalie asked

"Everybody thinks the modern world is complicated," Nana continued. "That the old days were easier. Better. Maybe some things were easier, but not everything. People didn't talk like they do now. People kept secrets." The old woman sighed. "So many secrets."

Natalie stared at her grandmother, realizing the older woman was about to tell her a secret of her own. Which seemed incredible because she thought she knew everything there was to know about Nana.

"You know, growing up, I always thought I was different. Different than my parents, than my sisters and brother. Grew up in a little town outside of Baltimore. Small town of good folks, good *Christian* folks." Her voice grew stronger but also sharper.

"I always suspected something wasn't right but didn't know for sure. There was a little girl a year older than me in my fourth-grade class. Got held back. They did that in those days. Kept kids back when they didn't do well or missed too many days. Her name was Millie. And she looked so much like me that the teachers used to get us confused."

Nana met Natalie's gaze with watery eyes. But there was something in her pale blue eyes that made Natalie think that what her grandmother was saying was true. Not like the other day when she had insisted the Roosevelt had come to her room to express his condolences for the loss of her fiancé.

"Millie was your friend?" Natalie asked.

"Not really. But then I saw her big brother. I looked like him, too. And Millie's mother? She had the same birthmark I have." She touched the kidney-shaped port wine spot at her temple that Natalie gave no thought to because it had always been there.

Natalie cocked her head. "A woman in town had the same birthmark as you?"

"Lillian was her name." Nana worked her jaw. "She was the town floozy. That's what my mother and father, *good Christians*, called her. *The town floozy*. My father was less generous when he was drinking. We were told to stay away from her. Cross the street if we saw her. I wasn't friends with Millie because my mother said I couldn't be."

"I don't understand." Natalie shook her head. She'd never heard any of this. Why had she never heard about Lillian the floozy or Millie? "Why did . . . why did Lillian have the same birthmark as you?"

Nana sat back in her recliner, but she didn't take her eyes from Natalie's. "I asked my mother the same thing. She told me to never speak of it again. When I was twelve, I did ask again." Nana hesitated. "I was that age when I was getting a smart mouth on me. One day we argued, my mother and me. Don't remember what it was about. But I was angry, and I asked her outright. I said, 'Is Lillian my mother?'" She laid her hand on her cheek. "Mother slapped me so hard that I can still feel the sting of it. The shame that came with it."

Nana's mouth quivered and Natalie waited.

Nana took a breath and went on. "She told me to never, *ever* speak of it again." She shrugged. "So I didn't. I saw Lillian almost every school day of my life on one street corner or another. She looked at me, I looked at her, but I never asked again, and my mother never spoke of it again. But I knew. And Lillian knew I knew. But she never tried to speak to me."

Nana grew quiet for a moment as if lost in the memory. Then she went on. "At Mother's funeral—Daddy had been dead for years by then. At the funeral home, the organist came up to me and told me the craziest story. Turns out, Millie *was* my sister. Half sister, and so was the organist. Her name was Angeline. Her mother, *our* mother, was Lillian. Angeline told me a story so terrible that I knew it was true. Turns out, I was born at home. The midwife was a member of my parents' church. Nobody knew who my papa was. Don't know if Lillian knew. She was a drinker and she got her booze the way women did in those days. By giving something in return to the men who brought it to her."

A lump rose in Natalie's throat and she wanted to say something but sensed she needed to listen. How many more opportunities would her grandmother get to tell the story before it was gone from her mind the way so many other memories were?

"Midwife took it on herself to decide that the baby, me, would be better off with another family. That Lillian wasn't a fit mother. She took me that day and left me at the house where I grew up. Everyone in the whole town had to have known, but no one ever thought I had the right to know. Things like that happened back in those days. Secrets a whole church, a whole town, could keep."

"Oh, Nana," Natalie breathed. "I'm so sorry."

Nana brushed her fingertips over her birthmark. "My parents were decent enough folks, but how could they do such a thing? I still think about Lillian. Maybe she couldn't take care of me. But Lillian wasn't given a choice whether she wanted to put me up for adoption. How could my parents have done such a thing to her?"

"Did you . . . were you able to meet her? Lillian?" Natalie asked.

Nana shook her head no. "She died long ago." Her unfocused gaze became attentive again. "The point of telling you this isn't to make you feel sorry for me. The point is—" She hesitated. "The point is that Lillian never had a choice in the matter. She wasn't given the opportunity to decide if she wanted to keep me." She pointed a rheumatism-gnarled finger. "You had a choice to keep that baby or give her a different life. My mother didn't have that choice. Who knows, maybe I was better off. But that doesn't make what that midwife, what my parents, what the whole town, did to her right. I was kidnapped from her. And there was nothing she could do about it, Henrietta."

CHAPTER 26

Mac sat on the front step of her house and watched the water sprinklers come on across the street. Their neighbor, Mr. Loren, was really into his lawn, into growing perfect grass. He ran his sprinklers practically twenty-four hours a day. She guessed that his grass was more important to him than the planet Earth or kids in Qatar who were dying of thirst.

She checked her phone in case a text from Bella had come in since the last time she checked five minutes ago. Maybe three.

Nothing.

Mac usually liked going to work, but today had been boring without Bella. Not that she needed her there. There was nothing Mac couldn't do anymore. In fact, she could put out the rafts in the morning faster than Bella, and the same in the evening. Bella was making it way more complicated than she had to, and her way took too long. And Mac could run the cash register and box a hermit crab in her sleep now, something she hadn't realized until Bella left on her trip to Virginia Beach with her friends.

Bella had invited her to go with them, but Mac's mom had said no. No surprise there. Mac had known there was no way

in hell she'd let her go. But she tried. She had even gotten Bella
to ask her. Her mom was obsessed with Bella, so obsessed that
it was bordering on weird. She was constantly telling Mac to
invite Bella over for dinner or to spend the night and the questions were endless. Did Bella have extended family other than
her grandmother in Wilmington? Did she play an instrument?
Sports? Did she like pork chops?

To be fair, it wasn't all her mother's fault. Bella played a part
in it because she acted like she and Mac's mother were friends.
And Bella had weird relationships with lots of adults, like Mr.
Burke. The Burkes, the old one and the young one. They both
fawned over her like she was some kind of TikTok star or something.

Mac smiled to herself when she realized her analogy made
no sense. She doubted either of the Burke men had ever heard
of TikTok. And it wasn't just the Burkes. It was the guy who
worked the day shift at the nearby Wawa convenience store, the
older lady who was a hostess at Grotto's Pizza on the boardwalk . . . and the list went on. Adults loved Bella.

Mac glanced up to see a guy walking by with a Pembroke
corgi that looked just like Winston, only this pup was a chub.
Aunt Laney said that corgis tended to get fat, and Mac wouldn't
let that happen to Winston. He was on a strict diet of dog food
and the only human food he was allowed was carrot or sweet
potato they cut up for him.

Mac watched the guy and the dog.

The guy had come by last night about the same time—right
after she got home from work. With Bella out of town, Mac
came straight home after work. But she liked to sit on the front
step and chill for a little while before she went inside because
she never knew what kind of hell she'd walk into. Her mother
was acting so nutty these days—losing stuff like her keys, her
phone, putting the jelly in the freezer instead of the pantry,
stacking Mac's laundry on Mason's bed and vice versa. The previous night, her mother was walking around with her T-shirt

on inside out. Dad told Mac to keep it to herself as long as her mother wasn't leaving the house, saying that she was under a lot of stress right now.

"Nice evening," the guy walking his dog said to Mac. He was wearing a floppy hat and floral shirt. This one had surfboards all over it. Last night it had been tacos. The surfboards were nice, but she liked the tacos better.

"It is. Not too hot," Mac said. She smiled as he passed on the sidewalk. "Have a good walk."

The guy who was forty, maybe—she wasn't good at the ages of adults—nodded. "Thanks. You have a nice evening."

"Thanks," Mac echoed as she rechecked her phone.

She hadn't heard from Bella all day, but she pretty much knew what she'd been doing minute by minute because she was posting on Instagram hourly. At noon, Bella and her friends had a massive breakfast of greasy food at a diner to beat their hangovers down, probably. Then they'd gone to the beach. There were lots of posts of Bella posing in a white string bikini—under a striped umbrella, stretched out on her hot-pink beach towel, standing in the surf. She was so gorgeous that Mac got tired of looking at the posts. Bella knew she was hot, but Mac was beginning to realize that it was super important to her that everyone around her acknowledge it. Like constantly. And it was getting irritating.

But Mac knew she probably did things that irritated Bella, and Bella didn't let those things get in the way of their friendship. So Mac always made a point to tell Bella how cute her outfit was or how much she liked her nail polish. And she religiously liked all Bella's Instagram posts, even when there were six bikini ones in a row. Bella paid attention to who liked her posts and how many likes she had and would say something if Mac missed even one.

Mac's phone vibrated and she glanced at the screen. No text from Bella, but another Instagram post. In this one, Bella was wearing short white denim shorts and a crocheted tank top.

She was posed in front of an array of blow-up rafts hanging in a storefront the way they hung them at Burke's. Because Mac hadn't responded except with likes all day, she commented on the post.

Gucci, she keyed. Mac didn't use the word often, but Bella said it all the time.

Mac set her phone on the step beside her and stretched out her legs. She knew she should go inside. See if her mom needed her to do anything. Mac had always done chores around the house, but it seemed like the daily list was getting longer and longer. And sometimes she had to even do some of Mason's jobs, like clean up the dog doo in the backyard. She didn't know why she had to do it. She'd worked forty-two hours in the last six days. Why couldn't the little dweeb do the pooper scooping?

Mac's phone vibrated again, and she picked it up. Bella was supposed to be home the following day and Mac had purposely switched evening shifts with someone so she and Bella could hang out. Maybe she'd spend the night with Bella and they'd binge on junk food and dumb Netflix shows.

The text wasn't from Bella. It was Matthew:

Whatcha doin'?

Mac smiled and texted back:

Paddling down the Nile. You?

It was this stupid thing they did. Checking in with each other once or twice a day, making up something ridiculous they were doing. The day before, when he was at work at Grotto's Pizza where he was a server, he'd told her he was in a hot-air balloon over Chernobyl. It had made her laugh. And she appreciated that he knew about the nuclear accident at Chernobyl before they'd ever been born and what the danger of flying over it would be.

Picking wild mushrooms in Norway, he responded.

Mac smiled again. He was paying homage to the fact that she loved mushrooms on pizza. Turned out he did, too. The other night, they'd each grabbed a slice after they got off work and sat on a bench on the boardwalk and eaten, sharing a lemonade. She hadn't told anyone she was meeting him places. If she did, her mom would pump her nonstop for information and probably start planning a wedding. Bella wouldn't like it for some reason and would pressure her to tell him to *feck off*. But Bella didn't know him.

Come to find out, Mac hadn't, either. Even though Mac had gone to his junior prom with him, she hadn't really gotten to know him. They'd just gone to prom and hung out with a bunch of other people and barely talked to each other. And now she kind of liked him. Especially since his nose hair had mysteriously disappeared. Maybe his mom or his sister had told him there was no need for nose hair nowadays when there were shaver things you could buy to get rid of it.

Mac thought for a moment what to say and then texted back: **Bring some home. We'll make pizza.** She used a pizza emoji instead of the word.

He responded with a thumbs-up.

Mac stared at the screen, waiting to see if he would say anything else. Sometimes they talked. Sometimes they didn't. He was home from work by now and probably hanging out with his grandfather.

His grandfather, who was dying of lung cancer, lived with them, and Matthew liked to play cards with him after work. They played poker for actual money, which Matthew's mother said they shouldn't be doing, but his grandfather insisted, saying he couldn't take his money with him. Matthew was pretty sure his grandfather was letting him win the way he did when they used to play Go Fish when he was little, but he said that was okay because it made his grandfather happy. Mac and Matthew talked a lot about his grandfather and her great-grandmother and how much they would miss them when they were dead.

Bubbles appeared in the message box. **I'm thinking about fries I want fries.**

Thrasher's? she texted back.

Is there anything else? he responded.

Feeling bold, she asked: And Skee-Ball?

If you're buying.

He was teasing her, because the first time they met for fries on the boardwalk right after her birthday party he'd tried to buy them for her like it was 1950. She'd told him she had her own money and could buy her own. He'd shrugged and said he was cool with that. So, at first, they'd each paid for themselves, but now they kind of took turns, which she liked because she liked it when it was her turn. It made her feel very grown-up and independent.

Tonight? she asked.

He texted a sad emoji face. Can't. Grampa sitting. Mom had a work thing. Tomorrow night????

Mac hesitated. She was supposed to do something with Bella the next night. Spend the night with her, maybe. But Bella still hadn't told her when she would get home or even if she was coming home tomorrow for sure. It seemed dumb not to make plans with Matthew, but Bella would be upset and she'd start the whole "you don't like me anymore" bullshit.

Another text from Matthew popped up: C'mon, know you want to.

Mac nibbled on her lower lip, thinking about how to respond. Liking a boy was stressful. When she watched other girls flirt, they made it look so easy. Bella had a boyfriend, but she flirted with guys all the time and Mac swore she could see them drooling over her. Guys didn't look at Mac the way they looked at Bella.

The front door opened behind Mac, startling her, and she dropped her phone into her lap, screen down.

"Hey, I didn't know you were home."

Mac looked up to see her mother dressed in gym shorts, a tank top that showed her bra, and sneakers. "Um . . . just got home. It's nice out. Not so hot after the rain this afternoon." She shrugged. "I was just sitting here reading emails." Not a complete lie. She had read an email from her social studies teacher about the stupid paper she was working on. Everyone had to turn in an outline, which the teacher had made notes all over and returned.

Her mom walked down the steps and turned to look at her, hand on her hip as if Mac were already in trouble. "I'm going for a walk with Aunt Laney. Want to go with us?"

Mac felt herself stiffen. Her mother was always angry with her. And Mac didn't care what her dad said; whatever was going on with her mother, it did have something to do with her. She could feel it. Mac's response was to overcompensate sometimes, by like not just cleaning her own bathroom but all the bathrooms in the house. Or skimming the pool without being asked. But other times, she got angry and she purposely didn't do what her mother asked her to do—told her to do.

"Nah," Mac said. "I'm waiting for Bella."

Her mother pursed her lips. "I thought she wasn't coming home until tomorrow."

"Waiting for her to call." *Or text*, she thought silently. She didn't really expect Bella to call. She was obviously having more fun with her friends who were her own age. Which was interesting to Mac because all Bella did was complain about the girl she'd gone with. But whatever.

"You'll have your phone with you," her mother said.

"Mom, I don't want to go anywhere with you," Mac blurted, the words coming out meaner than she intended. Her mother just made her so damn mad. She was always talking about how Mac needed to be responsible if she wanted greater responsibility. More independence. How was Mac supposed to do that when her mother treated her like a child?

Her mother crossed her arms over her chest and set her jaw, a stance Mac was all too familiar with. She was pissed. "I guess you're still upset about not getting to go to Virginia Beach. I'm sorry, but there was no way in heck you were going. I'm surprised Bella's mom let her go."

Bella's parents didn't know she'd gone to Virginia Beach with her friends. They thought she'd gone with Mac. And the family. But of course, *her* parents didn't know that had been Bella's story. "Mom . . ." Mac drew out the word. "Bella's old enough to do what she wants."

"Well, I can tell you one thing. Eighteen or not, if I'm providing you with a car, and car insurance, and a *college education*," her mother said, obviously ticked off, "you won't be going on vacations getting drunk every night with your friends."

Her mother's words made Mac so angry that she got to her feet. She wasn't so much angry about what her mother was saying as the fact that her mother didn't know her any better than that. Had she been allowed to go, Mac wouldn't have drunk anything more than a wine cooler. She didn't like alcohol. And she didn't like weed, either. Her mother's angel Bella, on the other hand, liked getting drunk and high at the same time.

But of course, Mac couldn't say that because she didn't betray her friends. Instead, she said in as ugly a voice as she could manage, "You know, I really hate you sometimes."

Mac expected her mother to yell at her, maybe to ground her or take away her phone. Instead, she lowered her arms to her sides, a really hurt look on her face, and said quietly, "I know."

And then she just walked away, and Mac felt so bad that she thought she might cry. She loved her mother and she missed her. She missed the relationship they'd had when she was younger. She knew it was her own fault, because her mother hadn't changed. She had. And she didn't know how to fix it.

CHAPTER 27

Natalie took a shortcut off Albany Avenue, one few tourists knew, and immediately there was less traffic. She picked up her travel mug of black coffee, which she was trying to get used to drinking. Laney and Conor had suggested she might be getting unnoticed calories in her multiple cups of coffee by adding sweeteners, half-and-half, or nondairy creamers. That might be one of the changes she could make in her diet to speed up her weight loss, her sister had told her less gently, but Natalie was struggling. Even though she knew her morning coffee shouldn't be a dessert, it was hard to break old habits and darned hard to fight her sweet tooth.

She took a big swallow of the coffee and grimaced at its bitterness. Then she took another because she needed the caffeine. It was the only way she would stay awake today because she hadn't gotten much sleep the night before. While waiting for Conor to get home from the pub, she'd decided to go through emails she was behind on and found one that was two days old from an adoption registry to whom she'd provided information. The email said she had a hit on her name and that she just needed to click the link that would take her to her long-lost relative.

However, Natalie noticed that the word "relative" had been misspelled, and even though she'd been excited, she had resisted the impulse to click the link. She was suspicious of any email or text that had multiple misspellings or was poorly worded, knowing it could be someone phishing for secure information. Instead, she had nervously gone directly to the website where she found that she did, indeed, have a message. At which point she'd been so anxious that it had taken her twenty minutes to get up the nerve to open it. Staring at the computer screen, she'd been bombarded by an assortment of emotions.

What if Bella had found her? Then what? Did she tell Conor or Laney before she talked to Bella? Because what if Bella didn't want anyone to know? What if Bella didn't want any kind of mother/daughter relationship? Did it make sense to let her tell her parents before Natalie shared the information with anyone else? What would Natalie do if Bella didn't want her parents to know?

When Conor hadn't come home at the expected time of eleven-thirty, Natalie had poured herself a glass of wine, gritted her teeth, and opened the message on the site. It turned out that the suspicious email had nothing to do with the site. Her message was just one welcoming her to the registry, a copy of the one she'd received in her email account weeks ago. And suddenly she'd felt so deflated that she had struggled not to cry. Which made no sense to her. First she'd been afraid to go to the site for fear Bella was trying to contact her, then she was upset because that wasn't the case?

Natalie had deleted the phishing email, chugged the last of her wine, and gone to bed. But she hadn't been able to fall asleep, and when Conor had finally made it home and into bed she'd been grouchy with him. When he'd fallen asleep in five minutes, as he always did, she'd lain there semi-awake, asking herself what the heck she was doing on those registries to begin with. It didn't make sense for so many reasons

Conor was against it. Laney was against it. And Natalie

was so sure her parents would be as well that she hadn't told them anything about Bella or even that she was thinking about contacting the girl she had put up for adoption. Her thoughts had jumped from one to another, the kind of thoughts that she knew would make sense in the daylight, until she had herself nearly in a frenzy.

And then it was 7:00 a.m. and Conor's alarm was going off. She'd apologized to him for her crankiness the night before and he'd accepted her apology, but she'd felt a detachment from him that worried her. Made her feel lonely.

Despite her bad evening and lack of sleep, as her mother always said, the show still had to go on. Natalie had dragged herself out of bed, paid bills online, made several phone calls scheduling and rescheduling various appointments for the family, and called their pest control company to find out why they hadn't shown up the day before. Midmorning, she had waited impatiently in the car with Mason for McKenzie. It had irritated her that her daughter refused to get out of bed until the absolute latest possible moment to still make it to work on time. McKenzie was working the middle shift, as she called it, which meant she didn't have to open or close the store. After work, she was going home with Bella to spend the night with her, which was just fine with Natalie.

With McKenzie now dropped off, Natalie and Mason were going to run errands and then stop by to see Nana. With baseball camp and the summer swim team over, Mason would be her buddy for the day. He had begged to be allowed to go to Patrick's and skip time in the car, but because he'd been there all day the day before she felt they needed to give her pregnant sister-in-law a break. And selfishly, Natalie wanted Mason with her today because he always had a way of cheering her up. He was such an easygoing, sweet kid. He reminded her that not everything she did in life was a mistake. Which was one of the self-accusations she'd wrestled with in the middle of the night.

Natalie glanced in the rearview mirror as she set the coffee in the holder in the console. "So first the pet store and dry cleaners, and then we'll stop for the socks your dad wants. Then maybe Nana's before we go grocery shopping? Sound good?" she asked.

Mason was playing with his Switch, a handheld game console. Natalie could hear him tapping it.

"Sounds good," the ten-year-old echoed. "Can we stop at Wawa for an Icee?" Before she could answer, he said, "Oh, crap."

"That's it," Natalie said, unable to comply with the agreement between her and Conor to just ignore her children's *colorful* language. "I'm starting a swear jar. Fifty cents a swear. And I'm keeping the money for myself," she threatened.

"But 'crap' isn't a bad word. 'Shit' is a bad word. I didn't say 'shit.'"

She struggled not to smile. Otherwise, he would say it ten more times in the next two hours. "What were you going to say?" she asked him instead.

"About what?"

She glanced in the rearview mirror at him again and then focused on the road as she merged onto Route 1. "You said 'oh, crap,' as if there was a problem?"

"Oh. Yeah. Mac's backpack."

Natalie looked in the rearview mirror again to see him holding up his sister's purple backpack that also served as her overnight bag.

"She left her bag," he said. "Should we take it to her at work?"

Natalie only hesitated for a moment before she said, "Nah. We're already on One. We'll just drop it off at Bella's."

Her wise-beyond-his-years ten-year-old hesitated. "Ahh . . . I don't think Mac's going to like that," he said from the back seat.

"She'll like it less if she doesn't have her toothbrush and clean underwear."

"Ew, Mom. Ga-ross."

Natalie heard him start his video game again, and she

gripped the steering wheel tightly, hoping she wouldn't regret this decision.

Fifteen minutes later, she pulled into a circular drive in front of a traditionally styled two-story home that wasn't the biggest house in the exclusive neighborhood, but it wasn't the smallest, either. She gazed up at the pretty gray cedar shake siding and dark, granite-colored shutters. "Can you hand me the back-pack?" she asked, slipping her hand into the back seat, still looking up at the house.

"She is gonna be so pissed," Mason muttered as he dropped the weight of the bag into her hand.

"Fifty cents."

"Mom, that's not even a bad word!"

"I'll be right back." She opened the windows, front and back, and got out of the car. The flower beds that bordered the sidewalk and flanked both sides of the front stoop were simple but well maintained. But they'd used black mulch, which looked harsh, she thought, feeling a sense of superiority. She always ordered the brown. Everyone knew brown was classier.

"Stay here," she said over her shoulder.

"Not a chance in hell I'm getting out of this car here," Mason muttered as she walked away.

"I heard that," she said, not looking back. "Now you owe a dollar."

As Natalie approached the colonial-style front door, which was painted the same color as the shutters, she wondered what she would do if no one was home. Did she just leave the bag on the front stoop? It certainly didn't look like a neighborhood where a teenager's backpack would be stolen from a yard. Or did she just take it to Mac at work as Mason had suggested and never say a word about driving to Bella's house?

The bigger question was, what was she going to do if one of Bella's parents answered the door? Bella was at work with Mac, so that wasn't a concern. But what would Natalie say to the mother or father?

234 / *Colleen French*

Reaching the door, she began to rethink her impulsive decision to come, but it was too late to retreat now.

She rang the doorbell.

Waited.

When no one answered, she pushed her sunglasses up on the bridge of her nose. The car had been nice and cool, but it was hot and muggy outside, and she could feel her armpits sweating despite the extra layer of antiperspirant she used that morning.

Natalie stood there in indecision. What did she do now? Ring again? Leave the backpack? Just get back in the car with the bag and pretend she'd never come? What if they had a camera with a motion detector on the front door? A lot of people did. Did Bella's parents get an alert on their phone that someone was at the door? Were they watching her at this very moment?

She was just about to go back down the steps when she heard a dead bolt turn. She whipped around just in time to see the door opening.

And there she was, the woman who was possibly the adopted mother of her daughter.

"Good morning." She was petite with dark hair and dark eyes. Of Asian descent, Natalie quickly surmised. How did she not know Bella's adoptive mother was Asian?

Which was a stupid thought because how *would* she know? Bella had never shown Natalie any photos of her family, and it wasn't something teenagers would think was important to disclose. Fortunately for the world, fewer and fewer kids their age cared about such things.

"Um, good morning." Flustered, Natalie pushed her glasses up on her head. "I'm Natalie. McKenzie Sullivan's mother," she added quickly. Cool air from inside the house felt good on her sweaty face. "She, uh . . . she said she was spending the night with Bella."

"First I've heard about it." The woman rolled her eyes. She was pretty with high cheekbones and cute, red-framed eyeglasses. She was barefoot, wearing denim shorts and a tank top. "But that's nothing new. I'm Ara." She smiled warmly.

"Nice to meet you. Natalie," Natalie said. She tried to laugh, but it sounded stiff. "Already said that, didn't I?" She was so nervous. Why was she so nervous? "Anyway, if you're sure it's okay if she comes over." She hung on tightly to the purple backpack. "She forgot her bag this morning."

"Of course it's fine. McKenzie is such a nice girl. Jeff—my husband, Bella's dad—he and I were just saying last night that we think McKenzie's been a good influence on her. There's been a lot less trouble in the house lately."

"Trouble?" Natalie asked.

"Do you want to come in?" Ara stepped back, opening the door farther.

Natalie could see into the foyer now. It was painted yellow with white trim. A flowery, Asian-influenced canvas hung on the wall, and she could hear running water, not from a faucet but some sort of fountain or something. For some reason, she was dying to see what the house looked like. The house and property were nothing like the impression she'd gotten from Bella, who hinted that she didn't live in a lovely house. Natalie was familiar with the neighborhood, so she should have realized it had to be a nice place.

"I . . . I'd love to come in, but my son is waiting in the car. Grocery shopping." Natalie was still flustered but trying to hide it. Ara was so open and friendly. She didn't seem anything like the bitch Bella described her as. She held up the backpack again. "I figured I'd be in trouble if I took it to her at work. If I showed my face there."

Ara laughed. "I hear you. I'd never go to the store, not even if I needed a raft and a hermit crab. Bella would have a fit. I'm afraid even to go in when she's *not* working."

The two women laughed together and Ara took the backpack. "I'll be sure she gets it."

Natalie knew this was the time for her to say thank you and return to her car, but she wasn't ready to go. Instead, she looked up and then back at Ara. "Gorgeous house. Have you lived here long?"

"Thank you. We've been in the area five years, but we bought this house last Christmas."

"And you're a nurse at the hospital?"

"Respiratory therapist. Jeff's the nurse. He's an R.N., but he's in administration now. He manages the nursing staff in day surgery at the hospital."

"He like it?"

She tilted her head one way and then the other. "He misses patients, but he likes the regular hours. No more on-call shifts. It gives him more time with us and for the Tay Foundation."

"Tay Foundation?" Natalie asked, trying to wipe the sweat from above her upper lip without making it too obvious.

"Bella never said anything to you about it?" Ara frowned, setting Mac's purple backpack on the hardwood floor just inside the door. She exhaled. "Not surprising, I suppose. We're very active in an organization created for families with children with Tay-Sachs disease, and Jeff runs the mid-Atlantic region. We offer support groups online and in person, but the big thing we do is connect families and promote awareness of the disease, supporting funding for research into treatment and maybe someday a cure." She shrugged. "You never know."

Natalie had very little knowledge of Tay-Sachs disease, except that it was fatal. Children diagnosed with it rarely lived beyond babyhood. "So you, ah . . . how did you get involved in that?"

Ara pursed her lips and glanced away. Another sigh. "I guess our daughter wouldn't have mentioned that, either. Even though she's spent more time with you this summer than she's spent with us. Also, not a surprise." She met Natalie's gaze. "Jeff and I are very committed to the organization because our son died of Tay-Sachs when he was seventeen months old."

Natalie felt a flush of heat across her face. "I'm so sorry." Just thinking about losing a child to a disease made her heart ache for Ara and her husband. And a tiny piece of her heart ached for her own loss of the baby she had never held in her arms. "I didn't know. I'm so sorry. I didn't mean to pry."

"You're not prying. Part of the foundation's purpose is to prompt discussion in our communities. The more people who know about the disease, the more it's in the spotlight, the better chance of more funding for research."

"May I ask his name?" Natalie asked, her heart breaking for this woman she'd known less than five minutes.

Ara's smile was bittersweet. "Elijah. Had he lived, he would have been three years older than Bella. In college," she added, her voice breaking.

Natalie didn't know what to say, but she sensed that was okay.

Ara took off her glasses and wiped one eye and then the other. "You wouldn't think that after all these years, it would still make me so emotional." She took a deep breath, exhaled, and put her glasses back on. "I think it's Bella's lack of interest that upsets me. I know she never knew him, but . . ."

But she's old enough to have some understanding of how great a loss it must have been for her parents, Natalie thought.

Ara paused and then went on. "The foundation was what kept us going after Elijah's diagnosis. He was such a perfect baby when he was born. We had no idea that something was wrong, not until we realized he wasn't progressing like other babies. At first, we kept making excuses. We said it was his laid-back personality, that he took after his uncle Reuben, Jeff's brother who was a free spirit. But then it began to become obvious something was wrong, and—" Ara stopped suddenly. "I'm sorry. You don't want to hear all of this. You came to drop off your daughter's backpack, not hear all this."

"It's fine," Natalie insisted.

Ara nodded, taking a deep breath. Exhaling slowly. "I

just . . . it hurts that Bella is jealous of Elijah. A dead boy. Her dead brother. It's as if no matter what we do for her, what we give her, it's never enough. I love my daughter. We wanted her so much and we went with adoption instead of having another birth baby because of the genetics of Tay-Sachs, but she . . . Well, let's just say that Bella can be difficult. You know?" Ara met Natalie's gaze again.

Natalie understood difficult daughters for sure, but it was interesting seeing Bella from her mother's perspective.

Ara hesitated and then went on. "I can't tell you how much we appreciate McKenzie. She is such an amazing young woman. It's hard to believe she's younger than Bella. She's so mature for her age."

"You wouldn't think so," Natalie said with a chuckle, "if you heard the names she called her brother."

Ara smiled. "Having never had two children at the same time—we adopted Bella after Elijah died—I wouldn't know from personal experience, but I wouldn't think that's too uncommon. I grew up with three sisters, and I think we spent most of my childhood calling each other buttheads."

Natalie laughed.

"Anyway," Ara continued. "We appreciate McKenzie's friendship with Bella. I know it can't always be easy. And we appreciate you welcoming Bella into your home. I can tell your family is very generous. And kind."

"Thank you. I'd like to think we are," Natalie responded.

"I just hope Bella doesn't—" Ara hesitated and then went on. "I hope she doesn't take advantage of that generosity. She can . . . She likes to ingratiate herself to others. Other people's families. Her girlfriends' mothers."

Ara's words made Natalie stiffen. *Ingratiate herself to others?* What was that supposed to mean?

"Mom, are we going? It's hot in the car."

Natalie glanced over her shoulder. Mason was standing beside the car, his door open. She looked back at Ara as she backed down the steps. "Thank you again for having Mac over."

Ara raised her hand in a good-bye. "You're welcome. It was nice to meet you."

"You too."

As Natalie walked toward the car, she wondered what Ara had meant when she said that Bella particularly liked ingratiating herself to her friends' mothers. Was she trying to tell Natalie that Bella might somehow be playing her?

At the car, she looked at Mason. "I asked you to stay in the car. Get in." She fumbled in her shorts pockets, looking for her keys. "What did I do with my keys?" she asked, more flustered now than she had been when she went to the door. She looked through the open passenger side window. "Did I leave them in the car?"

"Mom." Mason was looking at her strangely. "What's wrong with you? They're in the ignition."

"What?" Natalie said.

He pointed to the dashboard. "They're in the ignition."

Natalie blinked. "Of course. Right. Get in the car," she ordered, walking around to get in. Inside, with Mason buckled in, she put the windows up and blasted the air conditioning. As she rolled past the front door in the circular driveway, she lifted a hand to wave good-bye to Ara again.

She knew there were two sides to every story, but seeing Bella's house, meeting her mother, learning about Elijah, made Natalie wonder if she had been seeing Bella through rose-colored glasses. And if she had, did it change anything?

CHAPTER 28

Mac stood in Gunner's crappy little kitchen that smelled of cigarettes and greasy fries and sipped from the warm can of beer Bella had given her. Outside, she could hear Bella's boyfriend's *band* warming up in the lame shed they called a garage.

The beer tasted gross. She hadn't really had beer, except for the few sips from her uncle Rory's pint when her parents weren't looking. The beer on tap at the pub tasted way different from PBR in a can. It was cold and not watery like this stuff. She didn't love her uncle's Irish beer, but it didn't suck like this.

An off-key guitar riff drifted through the open window; the air conditioning wasn't working. The last note made Mac cringe. Gunner's guitar-playing skills sucked more than his warm beer. She set the can on the counter covered in beer cans, McDonald's bags and cups, and other assorted trash, including a broken bong. She sighed, looking around, half tempted to find a trash bag and clean the crap up. But this wasn't her house, and Gunner wasn't her boyfriend. He'd clean it up himself. Or not.

Mac glanced out the window. Thankfully, Gunner had stopped playing. She now fully understood the meaning of the phrase "nails on a chalkboard." She could see him tuning his guitar—as if that were going to improve the sound. She couldn't figure out why Bella was dating him except that he was an older guy. He wasn't that cute, and his personal hygiene was awful. He always smelled like stinky armpits to her.

She didn't know why she'd agreed to come over. She wasn't in the mood for Gunner or his creepy friends who acted like she was a middle schooler but then would hit on her. But Bella had asked her the other night when she'd stayed over, and Mac hadn't been able to come up with an excuse fast enough to get out of it. Besides, Bella was her friend. Supporting Bella's boyfriend was a way to support her, but after hearing the band warming up for twenty minutes she was seriously regretting her choice. The idea of being at her desk in her bedroom, working on her social studies paper, was way more appealing.

"There you are." Bella walked into the kitchen, a beer in a K-Coast koozie in her hand. She was wearing ripped jean shorts that Nat's mother referred to as Daisy Dukes and a pink crop tank top that Mac wished she could wear. But there was no way she could pull it off. She'd be too self-conscious.

"You said you were going to the bathroom, and you never came back," Bella said, kind of whiny.

Mac wasn't sure how to respond, but luckily, her friend kept talking, not waiting for an answer. Something she did a lot. Sometimes the habit annoyed Mac, but times like this it worked out just fine.

"Done with your beer?" Bella raised hers as if in a toast and took a slug. "Want another? There's a coffee mug around here somewhere; you can't miss it: it has tits on it. We're supposed to put a dollar in every time we take a beer out of the fridge." She sipped hers and shrugged her thin, suntanned shoulders. "But I never do."

The sound of Gunner torturing his guitar came through the window again. His buddy Tadpole began to beat on his drums. Was it possible for drums to be out of tune? Mac didn't know much about percussion instruments, but she was pretty sure something didn't sound right.

"Guess they'll start playing once they warm up," Mac said.

Bella rolled her eyes. "Maybe. Sometimes this can go on for hours. They might not even get to actually playing, maybe because they can only play a couple of songs. Gunner's all about booking gigs and crap." She frowned. "I keep telling him they suck and no one's going to book the Three-Headed Spiders, but he says I don't know music."

Mac laughed. "Three-Headed Spiders? That's the name of their band?"

"It is this week. Last week it was the Spitting Spiteful Spiders."

"Good alliteration." Mac laughed again because it was just too funny. She couldn't believe these guys were adults; they acted like they were the middle schoolers.

Bella took another sip of her beer. "I keep forgetting to tell you that I sent off my spit in the tube last week. Thanks for giving the kit to me."

"How long is it supposed to take?" Mac backed up to lean on the counter and accidentally knocked a couple of beer and Mountain Dew cans to the linoleum floor.

"I don't know. A couple of weeks."

Mac picked up the cans, trying to strategically place them on the counter in a way they wouldn't fall again. "And then what?"

Bella shrugged. "I see if anyone's a match on the ancestry site. It might be as easy as that. If there's no match, I guess I can put the info into online databases that help kids find their birth parents."

Mac leaned against the counter again. It was oppressively hot in the kitchen, and it reeked of old beer, weed, and something nasty in the sink she couldn't identify. She thought about suggesting they go outside, but she couldn't decide what was worse, the heat and stench inside or the sound of Three-Headed

Spiders outside. She looked at Bella. "You sure you want to do this?"

Bella frowned. "Do what?" She finished her beer, pulled it out of the koozie, and tossed the can on the counter. The pile of cans rattled.

Mac hesitated. She'd sort of tried to talk about this before when Bella had asked for the third or fourth time if she could have Mac's DNA kit. Mac still felt guilty about giving away a birthday gift from her parents. Bella rationalized that it was just regifting, which people did all the time when they didn't want a gift. She insisted it was like recycling, only better. Mac didn't see how it was regifting since she wanted the gift, but she'd given it to Bella, mostly to make her stop asking. She hadn't told her parents yet. Luckily, they hadn't mentioned the kit since her birthday.

Mac made herself meet Bella's gaze. "Do you really want to find your birth mother?"

"Why wouldn't I?" Bella gestured with the empty koozie and opened the fridge covered with menus from local restaurants. "Those people are not my parents. *Ara and Jeff Townsend.*" She spoke their names in a mean tone. "What if I have really cool parents out there somewhere? But how would you get that? You live in your *perfect family* with a mom who makes dinner every night, a hot dad, and an adorable little brother. And a dog," she threw in as she shoved a full beer into the koozie.

Mac chewed on her lower lip, trying to decide if she wanted to continue the conversation or drop it. She hated confrontation, but her mother said that everyone hates it and everyone needs to learn how to handle it. Her mother also said that not all conflict was bad, that often both parties got something out of it in the end. Mac searched for the right words to express what she was thinking. "But, Bella, Ara and Jeff *are* your parents," she said, purposely ignoring the whole thing about her having a perfect family.

Mac knew how fortunate she was to have a nice house,

plenty of food to eat, health insurance, and stuff like that. She also knew that she did have a good family and, even though her parents and her little brother made her crazy sometimes, they loved her and she loved them. And she'd do anything for them. She'd step in front of a train to save one of their lives, without even having to think about it. But this wasn't about her; it was about Bella.

"They're not my parents," Bella retorted. "They adopted me."

Mac shrugged. "Okay, so what's a parent? I don't think a parent is a sperm or an egg. I think a parent is a person who, I don't know . . ." She hesitated again, thinking maybe this was a big fat mistake. Maybe it was a waste of time trying to talk to Bella because she would do this thing no matter what Mac said. But she needed to say it anyway. She took a breath and went on. "I think a parent is a person who carries you into the waves on her shoulders when you're too little to swim. A parent's the guy who cuts up your waffles into teeny tiny squares and fills each square with maple syrup because that's the only way you'll eat them. A parent wipes your snotty nose with the hem of her shirt, holds your hair when you barf, and listens to you, even when you're talking bullshit."

Mac thought for a moment, trying to come up with an example of a non-conventional family. "Think about Latoya at work? Her grandmother raised her. She calls her Mom even though she's not her birth parent and Latoya loves her more than anyone on earth. She says the first tattoo she's getting when she's old enough is her grandmother's name on her arm."

Bella just stared at Mac as she chugged the beer, making Mac feel stupid. But also better, because Mac was saying what she felt like she needed to say. What kind of friend would she be if she didn't? "What are you going to do if you find your mother or father?" Mac pressed. "Who will they be to you? Maybe they'd be worse parents than Ara and Jeff. What if they're idiots or in jail?"

"I don't think people in jail have the money to do genetic

testing," Bella quipped. "And I don't care that much about finding my dad. I just want to find my mom."

"You know what I mean," Mac said. "What if your mom is a drug addict or, I don't know, a hooker?"

Bella shrugged. "Girl's gotta do what a girl's gotta do."

Now Mac was annoyed; no, she was angry. She didn't feel like Bella was thinking this thing through and she didn't like how Bella was talking to her. Like she was dumb or something.

"And you were the one who told me that sometimes women gave their babies up for adoption so they could have a better life," Bella said. "Drug addicts don't do that. Drug addicts keep their kids so they can collect big bucks on welfare."

Mac frowned, thinking about a girl she knew in her Algebra 2 class who lived in public housing. Maisie only had a mom, no dad, and a little brother who had some kind of serious cognitive disability. She worked at McDonald's until midnight some school nights to help her mom pay for stuff. "Nobody on welfare is making big bucks." She softened her tone. "Think about it, Bella. What if you find her and she's not someone you want to be your mother? What if she's someone you want nothing to do with?"

"Then I won't have anything to do with her." Bella's tone was flat.

"But she'll already know your name. Where you live, maybe. Stuff like that." Mac crossed her arms, realizing this conversation was pretty much over. Bella was going to do it and Mac's opinion didn't really matter. Most of the time, Mac thought Bella treated her like an equal, but occasionally she acted like Mac was just a kid who didn't know anything. She was getting that vibe now.

As a second guitarist joined Gunner's noise in the shed, Mac realized she didn't want to be here tonight. She had known she wasn't in the mood, and she shouldn't have come.

And she didn't have to stay.

Mac pulled her phone from the back pocket of her shorts

and pretended she had just gotten a text. The last text she'd received had been from Matthew an hour ago asking if she wanted to play mini-golf at the little course on the roof of a hotel on the boardwalk. He said someone at work had given him coupons for two free games, but they couldn't play until after seven. She'd texted back saying she already made plans with Bella. Now she responded again:

Still have the golf coupons???

"Sorry. My mom's texting me," she said to Bella as bubbles appeared on her screen. She felt bad lying to Bella, but not bad enough not to do it. Matthew was answering her:

I don't want to beat anyone but u.

Ha-ha, she texted back. Meet u there 8?

I'll be there, he answered immediately, only he used a bee emoji instead of typing the word. Which was geeky, she knew, but she didn't care; she thought it was cute.

Mac looked up at Bella. "I gotta go."

"Why? The guys didn't even start playing yet."

Because I've heard enough, Mac thought, but she didn't say it. She walked out of the kitchen toward the rickety front door. The house was on the edge of town on a street that didn't look all that great. It needed serious work: cracked windows, sagging roof, a bathroom door that wouldn't close. Gunner was supposed to be fixing it up for his uncle, who owned it, in exchange for cheap rent. Which was funny because Bella said he couldn't fix things. He'd had a flat tire on his bicycle the other day, and she'd had to change it for him so he wouldn't be late for work and get fired again. According to Bella, the twenty-five-year-old was *between cars right now.*

"Maybe another time," Mac told Bella. At the front door, she had to yank it hard to open it.

Bella followed her. "Why's your mom want you to come home?"

"She didn't say exactly. You know how she is." Mac stepped out onto the front porch that you had to walk on carefully because some of the decking was rotted through. It was probably still eighty out, but it felt better outside than inside. And it didn't stink. "Something about my great-grandmother," she said vaguely, hoping she wouldn't jinx Nana by claiming she was sick or something when she wasn't.

Bella stood on the porch, her arm around one of the fake pillars, her beer still in her hand. "How are you going to get home?"

"Walk. It's only like twelve blocks." Mac stopped on the sidewalk that had grass growing up between cracks in the cement and turned around. "I think you need to be sure about this, Bella. About finding your birth parents. I'm serious." She hesitated because she'd learned that she had to be careful about sharing too much personal stuff with Bella, stuff about who she was, what she thought about deep stuff, because Bella could be pretty judgy. Worse, dismissive. "If I was adopted, I don't think I would want to know. At least not now, not at my age. Not before I thought I could handle it."

"Yeah, well, that's because you're a chickenshit." Bella raised her hand. "See you tomorrow. Hope Nana's okay."

Bella's accusation stung, but Mac chose not to get upset about it. That was just how Bella was; she called people names when she didn't like what they said or did. "See you at work tomorrow." Then Mac walked to the street, turned right, and headed to the boardwalk, thinking the evening was going to turn out all right after all.

CHAPTER 29

Natalie strode down the lamplit sidewalk, enjoying the quiet evening. Albany Beach bars and restaurants only stayed open until nine on Sunday nights and it was just after ten, so tourists and townies alike were tucked in for the evening. It was a mild night with a breeze coming off the bay that had the slightest hint of the scent of the mud flats. Some thought the air stank when the wind turned and came from the bay rather than the ocean, but Natalie liked the earthy smell. There were still a few folks out for an evening stroll, but it was a nice change from the bustle of most August evenings.

She'd been restless all day, not being able to concentrate on one thing for long, and it felt good to stretch her legs even though she and Laney had walked that morning. Because it was Sunday, she hadn't done any of her accounting work. Instead, she'd paid Nana an extra-long visit, taking her for a ride to Cape Henlopen State Park. Nana hadn't wanted to get out of the car even though they'd brought a wheelchair with them, but she had enjoyed seeing the gentle lapping waves on the protected beach from an accessible parking space. She had savored the salty smell of the ocean and the caw of the seagulls and chattered about how she and her sweetheart were going to go to the beach as soon as he came home from the war.

Conor had spent the day at the pub—nothing new or unexpected there. But he had said that morning that he was going to have Rory close and be home around eight. When he wasn't home by nine-thirty, Natalie texted but got no answer. She guessed he'd ended up closing instead of Rory and decided to go help him, so they could walk home together. The dog was accounted for when she left the house, and Mason and McKenzie were playing a board game. Both unusual but welcome events.

After Natalie had dropped off Mac's backpack at Bella's the previous weekend, she'd expected World War III when her daughter realized how it had gotten there. Natalie had braced herself for Lady Voldemort's wrath, but it had never come. Teenagers were certainly full of surprises. Instead, McKenzie had, in passing, thanked her for dropping the bag off but said nothing more. Natalie didn't know if McKenzie knew she had spoken with Bella's mother, but she wasn't going to bring it up if her daughter didn't. No one stepped into a snake pit voluntarily.

Natalie strode across a street at a crosswalk. Realizing she'd better text Conor to be sure they didn't miss each other, she slid her hand into her shorts pocket for her phone.

And came up with nothing.

She checked the other back pocket, then both at the same time—as if it were going to materialize suddenly. No cell.

No cell? How had she forgotten her phone? She never left the house without her phone. *Except when she couldn't find it.* It was practically an extension of her hand. She could have sworn she remembered picking it up off the kitchen counter and slipping it into her pocket.

But maybe that had been earlier in the day when she'd walked with Laney. Thinking back, she wasn't sure now.

She stood for a moment in the middle of the sidewalk trying to decide if she should go back for it. What if the kids needed her? Or Nana.

But she was only two blocks from the pub. And her sandal was rubbing the blister on the back of her heel from her new sneaker. She groaned aloud. She was tired and worried about a hundred different things and all she wanted was a few minutes alone with her husband.

Rather than standing there any longer, stressing, she made a decision. One Conor or Laney would have made without a second thought. She would not walk all the way back to the house. If the kids needed something, they could call their dad. And if there was a problem with her grandmother and the nursing home couldn't get ahold of her, they'd call Laney. Then Conor, then Natalie's mother, in that order. And Natalie would be home in less than an hour.

Choosing not to feel guilty, she started walking again, circumnavigating an older man approaching her. He was trying to control two big Golden Labs on leashes and losing the battle. "Hi," she said as she passed him, stepping off the curb so as not to get tangled in the nylon leashes.

"Nice night," he responded, lurching past her behind his pooches.

Alone again on the sidewalk, Natalie took a slow inhalation and then exhaled, then did it again, trying to calm her parasympathetic nervous system. That was a thing. She'd read an article about it that morning. *Pranayama* breathing could apparently improve circulation, promote oxygenation of the blood, and even help improve memory.

She could sure use a boost with her memory. How could she have forgotten her phone? The same way she had forgotten the cheddar cheese she'd gone to the grocery store for the day before. The same way she'd forgotten the homemade chocolate chip cookies for Nana in the car earlier in the week and had returned for them to find them a single cookie of melted mush in a plastic bag.

Natalie had been even more scatterbrained than normal since she met Bella's mother. She was so confused. Bella had painted her parents as over-restrictive, unreasonable, uncaring people. But the teen had made statements about her home and her parents that didn't seem to be accurate now that Natalie had seen the house and met the mother. While Natalie knew that Ara's behavior might not exactly reflect her relationship with her daughter, the woman was not the ogre Bella wanted Natalie to believe she was. And how, when Bella had complained about her parents not having time for her, had the teenager failed to mention their devotion to an organization that supported parents with children with a fatal disease? How had Bella never mentioned that her parents' first child, technically her big brother, had died as a baby from the disease? Bella ate dinner with the Sullivans two or three times a week and spent at least one night a week with them. They swam in the pool together and played the board game Catan for hours and made ice cream. Natalie had talked more this summer with Bella than with McKenzie. Why would Bella want Natalie to believe her homelife was something it clearly wasn't?

And what had Ara meant when she had said that she hoped her daughter wasn't taking advantage of Natalie? The part about Bella ingratiating herself with other girls' mothers worried her even more. Natalie thought Bella was friendly with her because she liked her. Because they had connected. And now she felt foolish. She had believed everything Bella had said was true and told herself the teen needed a good role model.

But if she was truthful with herself, she had seen cracks in Bella's portrait of herself even before she met Ara. McKenzie had certainly made comments saying as much. Now Natalie wondered if, in her need for the teen to be her long-lost child, she had ignored all the signs. Of course, if Bella *was* her daughter, the untruths wouldn't matter. Bella would still be her child. However, the fact that Natalie had misjudged Bella worried her to the point that she wondered if she should be questioning her conclusions on other issues.

Reaching the pub, Natalie slipped her hand into her front

pocket and pulled out the two keys to the door. A *Closed* sign hung behind the glass and all the neon beer lights were off, but she knew Conor was still inside because there was a dim glow of light from the bar's main room. The last person to leave every night turned off that light. Suddenly she was excited to see Conor and enjoy the walk home with him along the beach. They'd both been so busy all summer that the connection between the two of them felt frayed.

She needed to hold his hand, to converse about something other than accounting or whether to replace the garbage disposal. She wanted to see how he was doing and holding up under the stress of their first summer running the pub. She wanted to talk about Mac and Mason and what a crappy mother she felt like right now. She wasn't giving Mason the time he wanted with her and she didn't seem to be able to talk to McKenzie. She really wanted to discuss Bella with him, too. She wanted to tell him about meeting Ara and how she was feeling about it. She'd been careful not to mention Bella or her Internet search for her baby over the last few weeks because she knew he didn't want to hear it. But he was still her husband, and she knew if she needed him, he could be there for her, even if he didn't understand her choice right now.

Natalie slipped the key into the dead-bolt lock, turned it, and heard the mechanism click. She gave the door a push to see if the second lock had been engaged. It had not—confirmation that Conor was still inside. They didn't set the second lock until they walked out the door, turning on the security system.

She pushed open the door and stepped inside, enjoying the cool air pumping through their new HVAC system. It had been worth every penny; thank goodness Conor hadn't let her be cheap on it. She'd wanted to go with the lowest bid, but he'd overridden her and chosen the higher-end unit. Thank goodness. She'd have to remember to tell him that he'd been right and she'd been wrong.

Tucking the key into her shorts pocket and locking the door

behind her, she walked from the vestibule where the hostess station was into the pub's main room. She started to call out Conor's name so as not to startle him. She'd been here alone at night a couple of times, and she would have wanted him to warn her if he'd come in unexpectedly. But as she came around the corner, she lost her voice. The room was mostly dark, with only a few dim pendant lamps over the bar. She saw Conor first, seated on a barstool, a pint of beer in his hand. Then she saw the waitress Margot, also with a beer. They were sitting side by side, turned toward each other, their knees practically touching.

Natalie felt like she was going to throw up. There was no mistaking the body language. Conor and Margot had a relationship that went beyond employer and employee.

Because of the way they were sitting, Margot spotted Natalie first. They must have been so engaged in conversation that they hadn't heard her enter the pub. The younger woman instantly leaned back from Conor, swinging her legs away from his. "Natalie."

Conor swung around, his surprise obvious. "Hey," he said, getting off the barstool. He brushed his hair off his forehead. "I didn't know you were coming."

Obviously not, Natalie thought, her gaze flitting from Conor to Margot and back to Conor again. "I forgot my phone," she said, fighting the instinct to scream at the pretty, young, has-her-crap-together Margot, *"What are you doing with my husband?"*

Of course, technically, all the waitress was doing was having a beer with him. It's what people did in pubs. It's what employees in pubs did together at the end of the day. In the early days when they'd been preparing for the grand opening, Natalie had sat alone at the same bar with Rory, with Shay, with their chef, and had a pint.

But this situation was different from a pint with a fellow employee after hours. She saw it in their body language.

"Damn," Margot said, hopping down from her stool as she made an event of looking at her Apple watch. "I didn't realize it was this late." She chugged the last of her beer and started to walk around behind the bar to put the glass in the sink.

"I'll take care of it," Conor told Margot. "Go home. Get some sleep."

Margot set the glass down. "Okay. Um . . . see you tomorrow." She flashed him a quick smile and walked past Natalie. "Have a good evening, Natalie."

Natalie couldn't tell if Conor realized he'd done something wrong, but Margot certainly had. As their gazes met for a split second, Natalie saw it in the younger woman's eyes. Margot knew she'd crossed an invisible line between Natalie and Conor's marriage and herself. Natalie didn't know what had happened here, but she knew she didn't like what she'd seen. And Margot knew it.

With Margot gone, Natalie just stood there in the semi-darkness as Conor walked behind the bar with the two glasses.

"Your timing's perfect. We were just getting ready to walk out the door," he said.

Not trusting herself to speak yet, Natalie didn't. But her mind was running a thousand miles a second. And coming in first and foremost was, *Is Conor having an affair with their employee?*

She didn't think so.

She'd have known if her husband was having sex with someone else. She was sure she would. Besides, he would never do that. It wasn't in his DNA. He wasn't Rory. He'd never looked at another woman since the day they met all those years ago in college. He wasn't even a flirt. He didn't say inappropriate things to women, even when he'd had one too many pints. Natalie had never, *ever* had to worry about him cheating on her.

Was that still true? If she was wrong about who Bella was, could she also be wrong about Conor?

But Conor and Margot had just been having a pint, she told

herself. They hadn't even been touching when she'd walked into the room, unseen.

But still, a tiny piece of her heart chipped off. She couldn't quite catch her breath and she practiced the breathing exercise she'd done on the way over. She couldn't jump to crazy conclusions, she warned herself. She couldn't make accusations. This was too important to handle poorly. She loved Conor; she loved their marriage too much for that.

So she remained quiet and tried to calm her nervous system. She wasn't going to pretend she hadn't seen what she saw or what it looked like, but she needed to wait for her light-headedness to pass before she said anything.

Conor set both clean glasses on the drying rack and walked in front of the bar. "Walk home along the beach?" he asked. "I'll leave my bicycle. Shay can give me a ride over in the morning."

She nodded.

It wasn't until they walked the two blocks to the board-walk and went down the steps to the beach that Natalie finally spoke. By then, she'd had time to think about what she wanted to say and how she needed to say it. She kicked off her flip-flops and picked them up. "You said you were going to be home early tonight." She took care to keep her tone neutral.

He picked up his leather flip-flops from the sand and they began the trek across the beach to the water's edge. "Rory had something come up, so I closed. Margot stayed to help."

"It looked to me like Margot stayed to have a pint with you," Natalie observed.

He exhaled, shaking his head. Not getting the implication. "She's been dating this new guy. Suddenly, he's getting posses-sive. Wanting to know where she is all the time, who she's with. Texting nonstop. She wanted some advice."

The moon was just rising, so it was dark on the beach. She couldn't see his face.

"You need to be careful, Conor. I'm not saying this is the

case," she told him, her voice wavering slightly, "but sometimes younger women develop a thing for older men. For their bosses. She . . . The two of you looked pretty cozy."

Conor stopped in the soft sand and turned to look at her. Her eyes had adjusted to the darkness and she could see his face now that he stood close. He looked shocked.

"Nat, y . . . you don't think—" he stammered. "Nat, you know me. You know I would never—" He drew his hand across his mouth. She could tell he was thinking, trying to recall what Margot had said, what she'd done. And maybe not just tonight, but other nights. He was trying to remember if Margot had indicated interest in him. "Margot and I are not—" He groaned, struggling for words. "I am not having an affair with Margot, if that's what you're suggesting."

He looked into her eyes when he said it, and Natalie saw, with relief, that he was telling the truth. To her knowledge, he had never lied to her, not even about if he was the one who had eaten the last piece of mushroom pizza. She knew him as well as she knew herself. Better. He wasn't lying. He had not had sex with Margot, which was what he was saying. But sex wasn't even the thing Natalie was worried about. It was his emotional relationship with her. And thank goodness it didn't seem to have progressed to that.

"I know you're not having sex with her," she said softly, continuing to gaze into his eyes. "But you can't stay out late drinking with her, Conor. It's not appropriate."

He gestured with his flip-flops. "But she wanted my advice. Was I supposed to say, 'No, I won't have a beer with you'?" Now he sounded a bit defensive.

"Yes," she told him, surprised by how well she was dealing with this. "Because sitting on a barstool listening to a pretty, young woman's problems is how a man married for nearly twenty years to the same woman ends up having sex with someone not his wife."

He knitted his brows, opening his mouth to disagree, and

then closed it. He exhaled loudly and looked down at their bare feet.

"I know she's a nice girl and a great employee, but it's not a good idea. Margot needs to find someone her own age to talk about her problems with. And someone she doesn't work with, work for," Natalie added.

Conor just stood there. "I wasn't flirting with her, Nat. I was just trying to be a good listener. Trying to be a good friend."

"You can't be her friend, Conor. She works for us." Natalie hesitated, gazing over his shoulder at the waves breaking on the beach in frothy turmoil. The cleaning machines had already been by, picking trash and debris and leaving neat lines on the beach. The sand beneath her bare feet was soft and warm. "And while you may not have had an ulterior motive for having a pint with her—quite a few pints over the last month, I would suspect—you don't know what her motives were."

He drew back. "Nat, you don't really think she'd be interested in a guy my age with a wife and kids and a beer belly?" He ran his hand over his abdomen, which, while it might have been a little soft, was by no means a beer belly.

"I don't know, Conor," she said pointedly. "And neither do you."

He was silent for a long moment, thinking, and then murmured, "I feel like an arsehole, now. I'm sorry, Nat." He reached out to her and she stepped into his arms. "I would never do that to you. To us," he whispered in her ear. "You have to believe me when I say I was just nice to her."

"I know." Natalie rested her cheek against his shoulder, closed her eyes, and breathed in the scent of him.

"I love you, Nat. You know that, too, right?" He hugged her, his voice cracking. "I would never, *ever* knowingly do something to hurt you. I'd never have sex with another woman. I couldn't. You're my girl," he whispered in her ear. "You'll always be my girl. My life. My love."

She took another breath, exhaled. "I know," she murmured.

"But no more late nights with the help, okay? If you want to talk about work, come home and talk about work with me, okay?"

"Okay," he whispered.

She stepped back and took his hand. "Come on. Let's go home to the kids."

They walked in silence to the water's edge and turned south toward home. They didn't speak for half a block and then Natalie said, "I'm not angry at you, Conor. I know what kind of stress you're under."

"We're *both* under." He squeezed her hand. "I feel like you've got more on your shoulders than I do. With Nana, your surgery is coming up, having the kids home for the summer. This thing with the baby."

"*Right.*" Natalie pressed her lips together, trying not to be annoyed with how he had referred to her firstborn. She understood what he was saying. And what he wasn't. "Bella," she said simply.

"Bella," he agreed. "*There's that.*"

His tone made her say, "There's what?"

Conor held her hand tightly. "Nat, I don't want to fight with you. I screwed up. That's on me. But, if we're honest with each other here—" He hesitated. "I don't want to fight."

"We're not fighting. We're not arguing. We're not even disagreeing. We're having a conversation. We're supposed to always be honest with each other, right?" she asked.

He nodded but then faltered, as if he wasn't sure if he wanted to say what he was going to say.

"Tell me," she said. "Because I don't know when we're going to get twenty minutes alone again."

He exhaled as if getting up the nerve to say what he wanted to say, which upset her. Because she never ever wanted him not to tell her what he was going on in his head.

"The thing with Bella," he finally said. "You think she might be your daughter. You're obsessed with her, with the idea of it. I think it's made you a little . . . nutty. "

She laughed, though why she didn't know. Maybe because he was spot-on. She might argue that the word "obsessed" was a bit heavy-handed, but she *had* been acting a bit nutty. Had been all summer. And it had started when McKenzie got into the car, telling her about her new friend.

"And if we're totally honest right now, throwing it all out there on the table," he said slowly.

"We are."

"This isn't an excuse. You're right about Margot. I shouldn't be drinking after hours with her. I should be home with you and the kids, but . . . she's a good listener, Nat. And, she's willing to hear about my day and, I don't know. I feel like she's listening to me, not waiting for her turn to talk so she can tell me about stalking her daughter's best friend."

"Ouch," Natalie said as she winced. The funny thing was, he was too accurate for her to disagree with. Or, honestly, even be hurt by his words. She hadn't been asking about how he was, or if she did, it was only so she could get past the superficial question to move on to her own problems.

"I'm sorry," Conor said, and stopped again. They had almost reached the spot on the shore where they needed to cut across the beach to reach the street. "I'm not saying that's a good excuse, but I have worries, too. I have *shite* things happen to me, too."

Natalie stopped, too, and looked up at him, then down at her bare feet. She wiggled her toes in the cool, wet sand. "I can't explain to you what it's like for me. Thinking Bella might be my daughter."

"And I guess there's no way that I can understand it. Because . . ." He looked out at the wide expanse of the ocean. "Let's face it, I'm a guy. I've never carried a human being in my body. I don't have the instincts so many women seem to be born with. From the beginning, from the day you told me about the baby, I attacked the whole thing logically." He returned his gaze to her. "But I know love for a child isn't always logical." He gave a little laugh. "My love for Mac and Mason certainly isn't always logical. That pool we couldn't afford at the time is proof of that."

Natalie looked up at him, not sure what to say, mostly because she didn't know how she felt. He was probably right in saying she'd been obsessed with Bella. And she knew her behavior had probably been over-the-top at times. But that didn't mean she was just going to drop the whole thing. She still didn't know if Bella was her child.

But not giving up trying to find out didn't mean she couldn't take it down a notch, not just for her family but for herself. Because she was driving not just her family crazy, but herself as well.

"You're right, me acting nutty isn't a good reason to start palling around with your waitstaff," she said. "But." She looked up at him. "I've not been there for you the way I should be. And I'm sorry, Conor. And I'm going to try to do better."

He smiled down at her. "Thank you for saying that. It's all right, Nat. This isn't easy. None of it is. But I love you. And I know you love me. And maybe we can both do a little better together. *Aye?*"

And then he leaned down and pressed his mouth to hers, and Natalie felt better than she had in ages.

CHAPTER 30

Natalie tucked the homemade quilt under her sleeping grandmother's chin, kissed her forehead, and whispered, "I love you a bushel and a peck." *And a hug around the neck.* That was the way Nana always finished the saying. She'd been repeating it since Nat was a little girl. Her grandmother had told her that it was a phrase used long before Doris Day ever sang it in a song.

Dimming the bedside light, Natalie let herself out of the room, closing the door quietly behind her. She checked her watch as she walked toward the front lobby. It was just after 9:00 p.m. She didn't usually stay at the nursing home so late. The nurses usually put her grandmother to bed after she watched one of the hours of recorded Lawrence Welk shows. But after her talk with Conor the previous weekend and several subsequent talks poolside in the evening, Natalie had been making a concerted effort to care for her family and herself and control what she could rather than what she couldn't.

Natalie had not asked McKenzie a single time this week if Bella was coming over, and she hadn't even asked what Bella was up to. Interestingly enough, McKenzie hadn't spent the night with Bella all week, though she had gone out several times to *meet friends*. Natalie didn't ask who she was meeting, trying to give her a little privacy. And independence. After all, she was old enough to drive now. In the spring, she'd be driving completely on her own. Natalie wouldn't know where she was every minute of the day or what she was doing.

Taking a break from Bella was feeling pretty good. As the days passed, she felt like a tightly wrapped ball of string that was ever so slowly unwinding. She felt like she could breathe. She had still checked the registers this week to be sure there had been no hits, but she hadn't obsessed, checking multiple times a day as she had the previous week. In fact, she'd only looked once.

Natalie passed the front desk on her way out. "Good night," she told Richard, who worked the night shift. A phone to his ear, he waved.

As she stepped out into the hot, humid night, she looked up into the sky at black clouds gathering. It smelled like rain, which might bring some relief to the heat. It had been in the nineties every day for nearly a week and was beginning to feel oppressive.

She used her key fob to unlock her car door and was getting in when her phone vibrated in her shorts pocket. She looked at the screen with one hand as she started the car with the other.

Bella? Bella was calling her? She answered at once.

"Hey," she said, wondering if Bella had locked herself out of the car again. She'd done it a couple of weeks ago and texted Natalie about what to do. It had somehow never occurred to the teen that she had a spare set at home, and the problem had been quickly resolved by her father bringing them to her at work.

"Natalie," Bella said, obviously upset. "I . . . I don't know what to do. My period is late and I think I need to get a pregnancy test, but—" She began to cry.

Natalie felt a tightness in her chest as she was transported back to her dorm room. She clearly remembered sitting on her bed trying to get up the nerve to walk down the street to buy a home pregnancy test. And suddenly her heart was breaking not just for Bella but for the girl she had been at the time.

"Bella, Bella," Natalie said calmly. "How late are you?"

"I don't know." The teen took a shuddering breath. "A week maybe. Ten days?"

Natalie took a deep breath. "Okay, well, if you take a test and you are pregnant, that should be enough time for your hormone levels to have increased." She didn't ask the teen when she'd last had sex. That question seemed too private. And what did it matter? Bella would have the answer quick enough. "So you should go get one and take it. Because the sooner you know, the sooner you'll—" She exhaled, unable or unwilling to finish the sentence. "You'll feel better after you know. One way or the other."

"So . . . so I just go to the dollar store and get one? And pee on it?" she asked, sniffling.

"Yup. It's that easy." Natalie turned up the air conditioning, moving a vent to blast directly on her face. "But no, forget the dollar store. I don't know how reliable they are. You need to go to a drugstore."

"Is anything open?" Bella sounded so pitiful that Natalie wished the teen was there so she could hug her. So she could tell her everything was going to be all right. No matter what. Natalie was proof of that.

"Where are you?" Natalie asked.

"Sitting in my car. Off the avenue."

"Okay, so the Pill Box won't be open, but any of the chains on the highway will be. Just go there. The pregnancy tests will be with tampons and such. They're like twenty or twenty-five dollars. Do you have money?"

"I cashed my paycheck. I have cash," she sniffled. "But I'm scared."

"I know you are, sweetie." Natalie stared at the puddle of light cast across the hood of her car. "But you have to find out. And the sooner, the better. Trust me."

"Would you go with me?" Bella asked. "Please. I don't want to go in alone."

Natalie exhaled. She understood not wanting to go alone because she had felt the same way all those years ago. "Do you think you'd better go home and tell your mom?" she asked.

"No. No, no, I can't do that. She'll kill me. And what if I'm not? It'll be a whole thing." She began to cry again in earnest.

Natalie wanted to ask her if she had a friend who could go with her, but would she call McKenzie? McKenzie was only sixteen. If the test came up positive, would Mac know how to help her friend? Natalie hated to put that burden on her daughter. "Okay, sure," she heard herself say. "I'm at my grandmother's nursing home. Want to meet me?"

They made arrangements to meet at a drugstore Natalie knew was open twenty-four hours a day, and twenty minutes later Natalie was standing with Bella in a parking lot. The teen was clutching a small brown paper bag to her chest. She wasn't crying anymore, but her face was red and splotchy.

Natalie hugged her. "You're going to be okay, Bella. No matter what the test results, you're going to get through this." She leaned back to look into Bella's beautiful face. "But if it's positive, you need to tell your parents. Your mom at least."

Bella started to protest, but Natalie stopped her. "I know it doesn't seem like it right now, but if you are pregnant, your parents need to know so they can help you." She wanted to tell Bella that she knew this from experience, but she held back because it seemed like an inappropriate truth to share. Though why, she didn't know. Was it because Bella might still turn out to be her child? Or was it because it seemed like something she shouldn't share with Bella when her own children didn't know?

Natalie stepped back, a little teary eyed herself now. "You okay to drive?"

Bella nodded.

"So go home and take the test."

Bella got into her car and Natalie walked toward hers. "And text me!" she called. "Let me know one way or the other, just so I don't worry. I won't tell anyone. I promise. Not even Mac."

Bella waved good-bye and pulled out of the parking space and Natalie went home to wait for the text.

CHAPTER 31

But the text never came that night. Nor the following day. And Natalie was worried to death about the kid, but she didn't know what to do.

Finally, after twenty-four hours and an impending second sleepless night, she texted Bella. *And got no response.* Not right away, not even the following day. Natalie couldn't tell if she had read the text or not because she knew, like McKenzie, she had turned off the notification allowing others to know if their texts had been read. Half a dozen times over the weekend, Natalie picked up her phone to call Bella, but each time she decided not to because she was trying to establish better boundaries.

By day three, she was angry with Bella. Why would the teen ask for her help and then not tell her what the test results had been? It was insensitive. It occurred to Natalie that maybe Bella had been too afraid to take it, or maybe she had, and found she was pregnant, and at this very moment she and her parents were talking about her options. Much the same way Natalie had sat down with her parents when she'd accidentally gotten pregnant. But no matter what was happening, Bella should have had the courtesy to say so and not left Nat hanging.

On the afternoon of the third day after Natalie met Bella at the drugstore, she was cleaning up the mess she and Mason had made baking whoopie pies for his baseball team and decided to see if she could get any information out of McKenzie. She'd have to do so carefully because she had promised that she wouldn't say anything to anyone. That included McKenzie.

Natalie was standing at the kitchen sink when McKenzie walked in to say good-bye.

"I'm going," McKenzie said.

Natalie turned around, grabbing a dish towel to dry her hands. "Have a good time. Who's going bowling with you? Bella?"

"Nope." McKenzie took a water bottle from a cabinet and carried it to the refrigerator. Ice clink, clinked into the bottle.

Natalie continued to dry her hands. "She doing okay?"

McKenzie shrugged. She was wearing a cute denim skirt and tank top and Natalie noticed she was wearing a little mascara. The teen rarely wore any makeup.

"She's fine. I worked with her yesterday, and we're both on the schedule tomorrow. She's rethinking the whole gap year thing. I think she might end up going. I guess she never notified them that she wasn't."

"I imagine her parents are happy with that."

McKenzie didn't respond.

Natalie listened to the water falling into the bottle, wondering if her daughter knew about Bella taking the pregnancy test or not. Wondering if she knew the results. "And she's okay?" She hesitated. "You two haven't had a fight or anything, have you? She hasn't been here in more than a week."

"Mom!" McKenzie whipped around. "Do you know how weird it is for you to be asking me about her constantly? Back off. She's my friend; she's not yours."

Her daughter's outburst startled her. McKenzie had no problem expressing anger with her mother, but she rarely raised her voice to her.

"I'm sorry," Natalie said. "I just—"

"You just what? Mom, this isn't normal, you being so involved with my friends. You asked me who I was going bowling with; I'm going with Matthew." She set her water bottle down hard on the countertop. "On a date. I've been dating Matthew since my birthday and I didn't tell you because I was afraid if I did, you'd be inviting him over for breakfast and stopping by his house to talk to his mom."

McKenzie's words stung Natalie and it took a moment for her to recover. "You . . . you're dating Matthew?" She hesitated, upset that her daughter hadn't told her. But happy for her at the same time. "That's wonderful." She pressed her lips together, watching her daughter screw the lid on her water bottle. "I'm sorry you didn't feel like you could tell me. I like Matthew."

"I know." McKenzie snatched up the water bottle and walked out of the kitchen. "That's why I didn't tell you!"

Natalie stood in the kitchen listening to her daughter's footsteps, then the front door open and close. She was close to tears. She was hurt by what McKenzie had said. She was also upset that McKenzie thought it was okay to speak with her that way. Why didn't Natalie say that to her?

Maybe because McKenzie was right.

Natalie wasn't supposed to be friends with her teenage daughter's friends. And maybe she did need to back off from her relationship with Bella. There was no way she could have told Bella she wouldn't help her with the pregnancy test. Because Natalie had been that girl once and she knew how scared and alone she had felt. But had Natalie not become friends with her, maybe she would have gone to her mother or a friend. When Natalie had discovered she was pregnant that first time, it was Laney she had told, and Laney had helped her tell their parents. Going to a friend would have been more appropriate for Bella.

With a sigh, Natalie picked up the damp dish towel and hung it on the dishwasher handle to dry. Since her talk with

Conor the night she found him with Margot, she'd been rethinking her boundaries with Bella. If Bella did turn out to be
her daughter, when she found out, if she ever found out, she
could decide then what relationship they would have.

They would decide together.

CHAPTER 32

Matthew slid into the booth beside Mac at Grotto Pizza. "I can't believe you beat me both games," he said, almost sounding like he was proud of the fact that she could whip his ass bowling.

After two games, they'd decided to go out for something to eat but chose the Route 1 location instead of the one on the boardwalk in Albany Beach where he worked. He could drive now because he was a year older and had an unrestricted driver's license, so they weren't limited to going out to places they could walk. And this way, they could talk while they ate without people they knew stopping to say hi. And eating their pizza. She was glad because then she didn't have to worry about Bella seeing them, either. It wasn't a complete secret that she was seeing Matthew, but Mac didn't want to get into another conversation about him with her because all she would say was that Mac could do better. Which was a dumb thing for her to keep repeating because she didn't even know him. And he was a hell of a lot nicer and smarter than Gunner.

"Second game was close. You almost beat me," Mac told him, picking up the menu on the table. She liked that he wanted to sit next to her instead of across from her. She'd never really dated anyone before, so she didn't know if kids her age did that, but she had decided she didn't care. Her mom and dad always sat next to each other when they ate, whether it was at home or in a restaurant. Her dad said it was so he could fondle her mother under the table, which Mac always thought was gross, but now she was beginning to think it was cute in an old-married-couple kind of way.

"Right. I almost beat you." Matthew laughed.

He looked good today in a pair of board shorts and a teal T-shirt. He'd gotten his braces off the week before and now he smiled all the time. He had a nice smile. And no sign of any nose hair.

"Until that second strike," he added.

She shrugged, glancing at the menu. "What can I say? You got beat by a girl. *Again*," she teased.

He leaned closer and she didn't move away from him. It was weird, but when they'd gone out a couple of times in the spring before the prom, she hadn't even liked holding his hand. He'd only tried to kiss her once then and she'd turned her head away, making for an awkward moment for them both when he kissed her cheek. Looking back, she guessed it hadn't been so much about him as how she was feeling about herself. She hadn't felt like she was pretty enough or smart enough or skinny enough for a guy to like her. She didn't know exactly how or when her mind-set had changed, but she didn't think those things were true anymore. And now she liked holding his hand. And she liked his kisses. He wasn't pushy like a lot of her friends' boy-friends. He hadn't even tried to touch her boobs or anything else. And she liked that. She liked that he was able to read her and respect her choices.

"Yup, I got beat by a girl," he said in her ear. "But *my* girl. So that makes it okay."

She turned her head to look into his eyes that were green with little specks of brown. "I didn't say I was your girl."

"I know." He kissed her on the lips, a quick kiss. "But I'd like it if you said you were."

"You asking?" she teased, drawing back to look at him.

"I guess I am. Again."

"You want *me* to be *your* girlfriend?" she went on, acting like she was a badass.

"I do," he said, but he sounded less sure of himself, and suddenly she felt bad.

She shrugged. "Okay." Then she looked at the menu again. "Let's order. I'm hungry."

Mathew's gaze narrowed. "Okay as in okay we're officially dating, or okay you want to order?"

"Both." She smiled behind her menu.

He was still grinning when they ordered pizza and a large soda with refills to share. While they waited, they talked about school starting up soon and whether she would play field hockey again. He told her about the family vacation to Maine he was leaving for the next day and that he would miss her. That made her feel good.

Good enough that halfway through her first piece of pizza she said, "I need your opinion on something."

He groaned. "Not about Bella again. That girl's cray-cray, if you ask me."

"I didn't ask you," Mac quipped. "And it's about her, but not really. It's more about my mom." She licked her fingers and reached for a napkin. "You have to promise not to say anything to anyone."

He made a face. "You know I wouldn't do that."

Mac reached for their soda, stalling because now she was having second thoughts about asking him. But she couldn't think of anyone else to talk to about it. She'd considered talking to Aunt Laney; she was a good person to talk to because she never treated Mac like she was a kid. But in this case, it didn't seem right to ask her. And if she did, Aunt Laney would be all pissed at Mac's mom, and that wasn't what Mac wanted.

"So . . ." Mac took a breath and suddenly a lump rose in her throat, and she couldn't speak.

"Hey, it's okay," Matthew told her, covering her hand with his. "Tell me if you want. But you don't have to."

"No, no, I want to." She hesitated and then went on. "So last week, Bella decided she might be pregnant. Now, I think this is the third month in row she's said she might be pregnant, but anyway. Instead of getting me to go into the drugstore and buying the pregnancy test like she did last month, she texts my mom."

"*Your* mom?" He made a face. "*Your* mom, not hers."

"I told you she's trying to steal my mom. Anyway, she tells my mom the situation and I'm sure how she could never talk to her mom, blah, blah, blah, and so my mom goes with her to get the test. But Mom never said anything to me." Mac reached for a second piece of pepperoni and mushroom pizza. "Because—"

"Bella asked her not to," Matthew finished for her.

"I'm sure. And now I'm pissed. At Bella but mostly at Mom. That's not appropriate. She should not be taking my friends for pregnancy tests. Especially when Bella's eighteen years old and supposed to be an adult. And if she's adult enough to be doin' it, she ought to be adult enough to go buy her own *feckin'* pregnancy test."

Mac must have said the last words too loud, because two guys in their twenties in the booth across the aisle both looked at her.

"I get what you're saying." His eyes scrunched at the corners. "But as an adult, Bella has the right to ask anyone she wants."

"A)" Mac said, holding up her index finger, "she's more like a middle schooler than an adult most of the time, and b)"—she added her middle finger—"it doesn't matter! She's my friend. Mom can't be friends with my friends. Moms shouldn't be friends with anyone our age. Or close. So now I can't decide, do I say something to Mom? Because she doesn't know I know she went with Bella. Or do I tell my dad? Because Mom's not going to get what a big deal this is."

"But is she?" Matthew asked.

Mac looked at him like he was the cray-cray one. "Is who what?"

"Is Bella pregnant?"

Mac rolled her eyes. "No. She's not. I'm not even sure she's actually having sex with Gunner or any other guy. I thought she was, but seeing them together, I get the idea he's more into video games than her." She took a bite of pizza. "But who cares. We're talking about me. Do I say something to my dad?"

"To get your mom in trouble?"

As she thought about that, she reached for the red pepper flakes, adding some to her piece of pizza and then Matthew's. "Not to get her in trouble. So we can talk about the situation. I've tried before to talk to her about Bella over and over again and she doesn't get it. And when I try, I just get pissed and I say the wrong thing. I'm pissed all the time with her." She hesitated, emotion welling up. "One day, I told her I hated her." She waited for him to react, but he didn't, which was good. She went on. "And that was mean. And I don't want to be mean to people. Not even my mom. My dad knows how to talk to her. Maybe he can make her understand."

Matthew grabbed a napkin. "Sounds like you already decided. What's the question?"

Mac sat back. "I didn't *decide*. That's why I'm asking you what you think. She's going to be mad at me, and I don't want her to be. I just want her to stop."

"And you don't want her going to the drugstore with me for a pregnancy test," he quipped.

She laughed, thinking he sounded like her dad with his dumb jokes. Then she wondered if that was creepy, her dating a guy who reminded her of her father. "Do I say something to Dad, or do I just let it go?" she asked. "I mean, hopefully, Bella will go to college in Maryland in three weeks and maybe the problem will be solved. She won't be around for Mom to be best friends with."

"I don't know." Matthew wiped his mouth thoughtfully with the napkin. "I can't tell you what to do because I'm not in your situation. And my mom and dad are different. I don't think I could have that kind of conversation with my mom or my dad. But you have a better relationship with your parents. They seem pretty cool."

Mac sat there for a minute, thinking. "What you're saying is you're not going to be any help here."

"Not necessarily. Doesn't it help to talk things out sometimes with someone who's got no skin in the game?"

"I have no idea what that means," she told him, deciding she was done with her pizza, even though she hadn't finished the second piece. It didn't matter. He'd eat it. And he'd take what was left on the table home to eat for breakfast the next day. "'No skin in the game'?"

"It's this weird horse-racing term my dad uses all the time. He grew up in horse racing in Kentucky. It means I'm a good person to talk about this because I don't have anything to win or lose in this situation." He took the half-eaten slice of pizza off her plate and bit a piece. "What's it going to be? Are you going to tell your dad?"

Mac watched a waitress try to explain the bill to a table of old people. "I'll let you know," she said finally. "As soon as I do."

CHAPTER 33

"Nat? You here?"

"In the laundry room!" Natalie called, pleasantly surprised to hear Conor's voice.

She was doing laundry and pretreating Mason's filthy baseball pants, hoping to get the stains out before she put them away for the season.

Conor walked in from the hall.

She looked up at him, smiling. "This is a nice surprise. I wasn't expecting you until later."

"Shay's closing." He didn't smile. He looked tired, and she realized that he hadn't shaved that morning. Maybe not for a couple of mornings, by the look of his scruffy face.

Natalie tossed the pants into the washer with the other whites and began to hit buttons, choosing cycles. "Want something to eat? We had Cobb salad for dinner. I saved some in case you were sick of fish and chips."

"We need to talk."

The tone of his voice made her look at him as she started the washing machine. There was something wrong. She could hear it in his voice, see it on his face. "You okay?"

He sighed and ran his hand across his mouth. "I feel like I could sleep for a couple of days. I cannot wait for school to start and people to go the hell home. Let's go outside. Out of earshot." He tilted his head in the general direction of the living room. "Mason and Patrick are playing video games on the TV."

"Sure." She studied him, trying to figure out what was going on. "Want a beer?"

"No." He walked out of the laundry room, through the house, and into the backyard.

Natalie followed, wondering what on earth was going on. Probably something with Rory. It always was. She just hoped he hadn't emptied their business account and taken off for a country with which the United States didn't have an extradition treaty. But it couldn't be that because her phone was set to message her anytime money moved in or out of the account. Outside by the pool, she stood in front of Conor. The pool pump hummed, and she heard the whoosh of Mr. Loren's sprinklers coming on next door. "Is this an I-better-sit-down kind of conversation?" she asked, trying to lighten his mood.

Again, he didn't smile. "I don't think it's going to take long enough to sit down. I've got a killer headache. I'm going to shower and go to bed."

Now he was scaring her. "What's going on?"

"Mac came by this evening to talk to me." Now he sounded angry.

Natalie drew back. "When? She had dinner with us. She's in her room working on her paper."

"Does it matter when, Nat?" he asked impatiently. "I saw her after she got off work. Before she came home."

"Okay. . . ." Natalie drew out the word the way her kids did. "What did she say?"

He looked down at her. "She's really upset. And I have to tell you, I am, too."

"About *what*? And why didn't she come to me if she had a problem with me?" she asked, becoming defensive. "She shouldn't be bothering you at work."

"She wasn't bothering me. I'm glad she came. As to why she came to me and not you, I think she feels like she's tried." His hands were on his hips now, as if he was preparing for a fight. "Been trying. All summer."

"*All summer?*" she echoed.

Conor stared at the pool for a moment, and when he returned his gaze to Natalie his tone was less angry. "Bella told her about the pregnancy test. That you bought one for her." He opened his arms wide. "Nat, what were you thinking?"

"I did not buy the test for her," she argued. "I met her at the drugstore and showed her what she needed to get."

"It doesn't matter. It wasn't your place," he told her. "She's someone else's daughter."

The accusation in his voice, no, worse, the disappointment, brought tears to her eyes. It took her a moment to respond. It had never occurred to her that Bella would tell McKenzie, which in hindsight was ridiculous. They were best friends; of course Bella told Mac.

"I was just trying to help, Conor," Natalie explained. "The kid was scared. And she didn't feel like she could tell her mother, and I know what it feels like to be where she was that night, and—" Tears began to run down her cheeks. "I was just trying to help," she repeated.

Conor sighed, seeming to release the last of his anger in one long exhalation, and reached out to hug her. "I know. I get it. But, Nat, that was crossing the line."

Natalie clung to him, feeling betrayed by both Bella and McKenzie. If Bella didn't care if Mac knew, why hadn't she told Mac in the first place and kept Natalie out of it? And McKenzie knew very well that her father would be angry.

"This whole thing with Bella has gotten out of hand," Conor continued. "Mac feels like you're trying to steal her friend. Like you've stolen her. And she's not completely blaming you. She says she knows that Bella was the one who started texting you and whatever has been going on between the two of you, but that doesn't mean it's okay. I don't care if she's eighteen. You're the adult here."

Natalie looked up at him, suddenly afraid. "You didn't— you didn't tell her about the baby?" she asked, unable to voice the bigger question. "My baby?"

He frowned and let go of her, taking a step back. "Of course not. That's not my thing to tell. We agreed on that a long time ago, Nat."

"I know." She sniffed. "I'm sorry. You're right. Mac's right. I wouldn't have wanted Bella's mother to go with Mac to buy a pregnancy test. I should have respected that. I'm sorry," she repeated. "I don't know what else to say."

"It's not me you need to say anything to. It's your daughter. I was angry when she told me, especially knowing you're look- ing for your first daughter, that you think she might even be Bella, but as we've discussed, I understand you're under a lot of stress. Some I can't begin to understand. I'm not angry now. You know me. I say what I have to say, and then I'm over it."

And that was true about Conor. Always had been. It took Natalie a bit of time to get over a disagreement, especially with him. But with Conor, all was forgiven and forgotten quickly. It was a trait she'd always admired in him. And been a little jealous of.

Natalie stared at the pool and the reflection of the moon across the smooth surface. Even two blocks off the ocean, she could hear the crash of the waves. She could smell the spray on the evening air. "I feel bad that Mac couldn't talk to me about this," she said at last.

"I think it snowballed. She was upset with you, and then she got more upset. I also get the feeling that Mac and Bella aren't quite as good friends as they were at first. Maybe she thinks that's somehow your fault. And I don't know that that's true." He shrugged. "It happens in friendships, especially when you're a teenager. And with Bella going to college, or to work or whatever, they're not going to have as much in common soon anyway. I don't know Bella very well, but maybe she's just outgrowing Mac." He exhaled. "Anyway, I'm going to jump in the shower. You going to talk to Mac now or tomorrow?"

Natalie wiped at the tears on her face. "I won't be able to sleep tonight if I don't do it now."

He moved toward her. "Kiss?"

She tilted her head to receive his kiss. "I'm sorry for putting you in the middle of this," she told him, looking into his blue eyes. "For . . . for being a shitty mother."

He laughed. "I don't think you're a shitty mother. A shitty mother would never admit to making a mistake." He turned to head back into the house. "You probably owe the curse jar a buck, though," he said over his shoulder.

"Why a dollar?" she called after him, relieved his mood had lightened. "The kids only pay fifty cents a curse." After the incident in the car with Mason the day they dropped off Mac's backpack, she'd put a Harry Potter mug on the counter and she was making Mac and Mason put their fines in it.

He opened the patio door. "Exactly. But you're the adult and you know better."

After Conor had gone inside, Natalie stood by the pool for a couple of minutes thinking. In retrospect, she probably shouldn't have met Bella at the drugstore. But in her defense, if any other of McKenzie's friends had texted her telling her they needed help, she'd probably have gone. She was trying to do the right thing when she met Bella, wasn't she?

But maybe a part of her, a tiny part of her, *had* wanted to do it because she wanted to be the person in Bella's life who she came to when she needed advice. When she needed help. Whether she was Bella's birth mother or not, she didn't really have that right, though, did she? Because no matter what, Ara was her mother. Ara would always be Bella's mother.

That thought heavy on her heart, Natalie walked into the house. She stuck her head through the living room doorway to see Mason and Patrick side by side on the couch. They had shut down the video game and started a movie, one they were so engrossed in that they didn't see her. She left it that way.

At McKenzie's door, Natalie knocked. "Mac?" she said softly. "Can I come in?" Through the door, she heard McKenzie's voice. She was talking on the phone.

A full minute passed before McKenzie called, "Come in!"

Natalie walked into the bedroom they had painted lemon yellow together the summer before. The walls were covered with McKenzie's artwork: fairies and giants and mythical beasts. And posters: a professional surfer she liked, the life cycle of a butterfly in brilliant colors, and a red Tesla, which Natalie had never seen. It had to be new. They had not ordered Mac's choice—a red one—though. Natalie had chosen white—mainly because there was no upcharge for that color. Her daughter's desk was piled with paperwork, a couple of books, and a basket of brightly colored nail polish. There were clothes everywhere: draped on the closet doorknobs, over the desk chair, and strewn on the floor.

Natalie pushed the door closed behind her. She loved Patrick, but her nephew was a snitch. Whenever he spent the night, he relayed to his mother how many times Winston had escaped, what flavor ice cream Natalie had sneaked from the freezer when she thought no one was looking, and how many beer bottles were in the recycling bin. She certainly didn't want him going home to her in-laws to tell this little tale.

She took a deep breath. McKenzie was sitting in bed, against a pile of pillows, her laptop on one side of her, her phone in her hand. She was wearing a tank top and cotton sleep shorts, pimple patches stuck all over her face, her hair in a bird's nest on top of her head. Ready for bed.

"Talking to Matthew?" Natalie asked. McKenzie looked a little pale.

"Yeah. He's in Maine for a week visiting his grandparents. They're going kayaking in Acadia tomorrow."

"Nice." Ordinarily, when Natalie came into her daughter's room, she would start picking up clothes and lecture Mac about taking better care of them. Tonight she ignored them and went to sit on the edge of the bed. "Your dad told me about your conversation with him today."

McKenzie looked away and Natalie couldn't see her expression because a scarf hung from the bedside lamp, casting shadows across her face.

"The first thing I want to say—" Natalie's voice caught in her throat, and she cleared it before she went on. "Is I'm sorry that you didn't feel like you could come to me and tell me you were upset about me meeting Bella at the drugstore."

McKenzie didn't make eye contact. Nor did she speak. She just lay there, her arms crossed over her abdomen.

Natalie went on. "At the time, I thought I was doing the right thing, Mac. Helping her because she said she couldn't tell her mother. In retrospect, I can see that I shouldn't have done it. If she needed someone and couldn't ask her mother or father, she should have asked one of her friends." She gestured lamely. "She could have asked you."

"I doubt she would have." McKenzie looked at Natalie, her tone sour. "Because I would have told her to stop being a dumb ass and start carrying condoms. Or get on the pill. She ought to do both. Birth control pills don't prevent STIs. If she'd been paying attention in health class, she'd know that."

McKenzie's irritation at Bella surprised Natalie and she wondered what was going on between them. They had seemed like such good friends at the beginning of the summer. Was it just the natural cycle of some friendships, as Conor had suggested, or was part of this her fault?

"Anyway," Natalie said, studying the veiled lamp. "I'm sorry for interfering that way. You asked me to back off and I was trying, but then Bella called, and she was so upset and—" She returned her gaze to McKenzie. "And I met her, and I helped her get what she needed. The weird thing is that she said she'd text me after taking the test, but I never heard from her. I know it's not my business, but is she—"

"No, it's not your business, Mom," McKenzie interrupted. "But she's not pregnant. She was just late. And her not telling you that after she got you roped into the whole thing, that's classic Bella."

This discussion wasn't how Natalie had thought it was going to go. She thought she'd apologize and McKenzie would accept her apology and then maybe they'd talk about things, not just about Bella, but maybe the new boyfriend, her social studies paper, just things—the way they used to. But she could tell by McKenzie's tone that that wasn't happening tonight. She rose from the bed, looking at her daughter. "You feeling okay?"

The teen shrugged. "Stomach hurts."

"Cramps?" Natalie asked.

McKenzie rolled her eyes. "Not menstrual cramps. If it was cramps, I'd say so." She removed her hands from her abdomen and pressed them to the bed. "I'm going to sleep. I have to open tomorrow."

Natalie hesitated, thinking McKenzie looked a little flushed. *Was she running a fever?* But maybe that was just her anger.

"Anyway," Natalie said. "I'm sorry that you couldn't tell me you were upset with me and that you had to go to your dad. I don't want you to feel that way and I promise I'll try to be a better listener when you come to me. Okay?" Natalie made it all the way to the door before McKenzie responded.

"Okay," McKenzie said, her tone begrudging.

"I love you, Mac," Natalie said as she went out the door.

If her daughter responded, Natalie didn't hear her.

CHAPTER 34

Natalie leaned back in a plastic Adirondack chair and reached for her drink. She and Laney were sitting inside a gazebo on the nursing home grounds watching ducks paddle in a man-made pond. A light summer rain fell softly. Nana had resisted coming outside, insisting it was going to rain, with Natalie and Laney telling her there was no rain in the forecast. Nana had eventually given in and allowed them to wheel her out of the building to get some fresh air.

It had started raining halfway to the gazebo.

"Thanks for the iced coffee," Natalie told her sister, savoring the flavor. "Please tell me it's decaf."

Laney sipped from her plastic cup. "I ordered decaf. Guess we'll know about eleven tonight when you try to go to sleep if the guy got it right."

"Hahaha." Natalie stuck her tongue out at her sister and tucked the blanket tighter around their grandmother.

Nana was sound asleep, her head thrown back so that Natalie could see all the little hairs on her chin. Taking another sip of the creamy coffee with two full pumps of vanilla syrup in it, Natalie made a mental note to bring tweezers with her the next time she came. Nana's hands weren't steady enough for plucking any longer. But she insisted she wasn't old enough for chin hairs and had made Natalie promise that even when she couldn't remember that any longer, her granddaughters would remember for her.

"She's sleeping a lot these days," Laney murmured, plucking a Goldfish cracker from the bag she'd brought along. Ordinarily, Nana loved the cheesy crackers, but today she hadn't wanted any. She glanced at Natalie. "Have you noticed that?"

Natalie nodded. "Yesterday morning she was still asleep at nine-thirty, even though she'd gone to sleep the night before by nine."

Laney pressed her lips together. Natalie knew what she was thinking—the same thing Natalie was thinking. That their grandmother was slowly slipping away from them. Nana still had moments of complete lucidity, but they were coming further and further apart. She was also beginning to become confused over simple tasks like choosing what utensil to use to cut her food or working a button through a buttonhole. Even though she was almost one hundred years old and they knew what was coming, knew this disease would take her life, it was still hard to watch.

"You bring it up when you took her to see her primary care the other day?" Laney asked.

"I did." Natalie kicked off her flip-flops and tucked her feet under her, watching several *teenage* mallards paddle in a circle in the pond. She wondered if mother ducks had as many problems with their teenagers as humans. Despite her apology to McKenzie the night before, her daughter was not speaking to her.

That morning Natalie had made her favorite breakfast sandwiches and wrapped one in foil for her and Bella, but Mac refused them. The teen had grabbed a cup of iced coffee from the refrigerator and headed off to work with little more than a grunt in Natalie's direction. She'd looked tired and still a little flushed, but Natalie had decided she'd better not ask if she was all right for fear she would snap at her. Instead, she'd watched in silence as McKenzie walked out of the kitchen and out the door.

"Nat?" Laney waved her hand in front of Natalie's face. "Hello? Hello? Is anyone there?"

Natalie pushed her sister's hand out of her face, glanced at the bag of crackers and then away. She was trying to resist them; she wasn't supposed to be eating snacks. She'd lost a little weight and her clothes were fitting better, but she had a feeling Pixie Patty was going to give her heck when Natalie had her pre-op appointment after Labor Day. Conor said she was more muscular and that would account for the fact that she was smaller, but the scale didn't reflect that. She was also feeling better physically, but she doubted Pixie Patty would care. Pixie Patty loved her BMI chart and didn't seem interested in the history of the chart or its original purpose, which was not to tell women how much they were supposed to weigh. "Dr. Murphy said the sleeping isn't uncommon. Nor the confusion about how to do everyday things. As the disease progresses," she added.

Laney looked away and watched the ducks, lost in her thoughts. Rain pattered rhythmically on the gazebo roof and Natalie wondered what she would make for dinner that night. Conor had said he'd be home for dinner and would, in fact, be home three or four nights a week from now on because Rory and Shay would both be closing at least twice a week. She didn't know if Conor was doing it for her or to protect the children from her. She didn't really care which it was; it would be nice having him home more often.

"How about a more uplifting subject?" Natalie asked at last. Neither of them was in denial about Nana's diagnosis and how it would slowly take her from them, but they didn't need to fix-ate on it. She was still here with them and at least parts of her personality were still with them. They had to be content with that. "How's the love life going?" She picked up her giant iced coffee again. The gazebo was nice, especially on a day when it wasn't so stinking hot. She needed to bring Nana out here more often, even if she groused about coming.

Laney smiled almost shyly, which tickled Natalie because her big sister didn't have a shy bone in her body. "That good?" Natalie teased, giving in and scooping up a couple of crackers from the bag on her sister's lap. "Don't tell me you've found a good one after all these years of insisting they didn't exist."

"I never said they didn't exist." Thunder rumbled in the distance. "I said you already married him."

"Tell me all the dirty details," Natalie begged, putting a single cracker into her mouth and savoring it.

"Nope. I want to know what's going on with you. I heard Conor had to come home from the pub last night and give you hell about something."

Natalie drew back, wondering who on earth could have told Laney about it. And so quickly. Certainly not Conor. He loved Laney like a sister, but he would never ever tell her about a private conversation between him and Natalie. She shifted forward in the chair that was a soothing green. "Did McK—"

"It wasn't McKenzie," Laney interrupted.

Natalie thought for a moment and then realized who it had to have been. "That little creep Patrick. I didn't even drop him off at home until ten this morning."

"I talked to Beth about ten-thirty."

Natalie shook her head, wagging her finger at her sister because she couldn't wag it at her nephew. "The next time Patrick spends the night, I'm serving escargot for dinner."

Laney wrinkled her nose. "You can't blame him. I think Beth pays him for the family gossip she's been missing while she's stuck in bed with that beach ball." A week ago her OB had put her on bed rest at home, and their sister-in-law was none too happy about it.

Natalie threw one of the crackers at Laney, hitting her in

the elbow before it bounced to pavers in front of their grandmother's wheelchair. "Don't call my niece a beach ball." She
threw another. "What a terrible thing to say."

"I'm saying I don't think the kid deserves snails for dinner.
He didn't have any details. He just knew Conor was worked
up about something. And that after you two talked outside,
you went into Mac's room. Beth wanted to know if I knew
anything that was going on."

"What did you tell her?"

"The truth. I didn't know anything."

Saying nothing, Natalie made a little bowl with the Dolle's
popcorn T-shirt she was wearing and dropped the crackers into
it. She hated the idea that she was providing juicy gossip for her
in-laws. And she felt bad for Conor because Beth would tell
Shay and Shay would ask Conor what was going on so he could
relay the information back to Beth.

"Let me guess what the argument—"

"We didn't argue," Natalie interrupted.

"What the *discussion* was about," Laney said. "You did or
said something crazy with Bella, about Bella, *for* Bella?"

Her accuracy stung. "What makes you immediately jump to
that conclusion?"

"Let's see, maybe because you've decided some kid who
works at the boardwalk and kind of, sort of, maybe looks like
your daughter is your daughter, too. Even though you don't
even know her birthday."

"I told you I did ask McKenzie the other day when I was
feeling brave and she told me it was none of my business. She
would lose it with me if I asked again."

"You could have asked Bella, as cozy as you are," Laney
pointed out. "You know, I think you haven't asked Bella because if it's not the baby's birth date, then you'd have a definitive answer."

"That's not true. Even if I knew her birthday, even if it

wasn't the same, that wouldn't be the definitive answer. Mistakes are made on birth certificates. And adopted children have new ones made. Typos happen."

Laney frowned, crossing her arms over her chest.

Natalie raised her hands, palms out. "I'm trying to back off. That's what McKenzie said she wanted. For me to back off."

"And she's right."

Natalie looked away. The rain was beginning to lighten up. She wondered if they ought to make a run for it and get Nana back to the unit.

"You have any luck with the adoption registry?" Laney probed, softening her tone.

Natalie shook her head. "It could take years. I've been reading a lot about adopted kids. Often, it's not until they have their own children or are at least thinking about it that they look for their parents. If they look at all. I read this article the other night. I don't know how old it was, but anyway, according to some research, about sixty-six percent of all adopted females look for their birth parents and only thirty-four percent of men."

"Interesting." Laney popped a cracker into her mouth. "I wonder why."

Natalie shrugged. "I guess males are just less interested in their biological origins."

"You know," Laney said gently, "it wouldn't be the end of the world if you don't find her." She raised her hand when Natalie started to react. "Just let me say this," her sister went on. "You know, you've never said anything to me about wanting to find the baby. It wasn't until Bella showed up and you got it in your head that she might be your little girl."

"Lane, she really does look like McKenzie!"

"You're right." Her sister continued to speak gently. "They do have some similar characteristics, but so do a lot of girls their age. They dress like clones, for God's sake."

Natalie took the last two Goldfish crackers on her lap and threw them in the direction of the duck pond. They hadn't tasted as good as she remembered.

"All I'm saying is that even if you don't find her, you've got a damned good life here," Laney said. "You have more than most people can ever even hope for. No, you're not wealthy, but you're financially secure. You have a home and food and health insurance. And you have an amazing husband, sweet kids. And you have me," she added.

"You're right." Natalie closed her eyes for a moment. "I know you're right. That all of you are, but this isn't just about logic. It's about . . ." She hesitated. What *was* it about? "It's about how I feel." Choking up, she pressed her hand to her heart. "Here. You can't imagine the physical ache I feel, not knowing where one of my children is."

"You're right. I can't." Laney reached over and squeezed Natalie's arm. Then she said, "So you want a little dirt on Clancy?"

Natalie took another sip of coffee and looked to her sister. "Of course."

Laney got a mischievous look on her face. "I think he said the *l* word the other night."

Natalie opened her eyes wide. "Lust? He said he lusted for you?"

They both laughed.

"No." Laney shook her head. "See. This is why I don't tell you anything."

Natalie's phone vibrated in the back pocket of her shorts and she pulled it out. "What other *l* word is there?" she teased. "I hope he didn't say he loathed you." She looked down at her phone. The text was from Bella. *Bella?*

"He said he loved me." Laney giggled nervously. "We were in the middle of, you know, so I don't know if it's something I bring up outside the bedroom or—Nat, I'm dishing out the tea here and you're looking at your phone. This is serious. No one has told me they loved me since Billy Trap in the tenth grade."

Natalie stared at the phone in her hand. All the text said was: U there?

"Who is it?" Laney asked.

Natalie hesitated. "Bella," she said finally.

"What's she want?"

"I don't know." Natalie hovered her thumbs over the keyboard.

"Don't do it. Texting with your teenage daughter's best friend is not appropriate, Nat."

Natalie looked up at her sister. "But what if she needs something?"

"Then she can text her own damned mother!"

The bubbles appeared again, and another message popped up: Natalie?

Before Natalie could decide whether to answer, the phone rang. It was Bella. Natalie looked up at her sister.

"Don't answer. This is not stepping back."

Natalie didn't know what to do.

"Nat, do not—"

Natalie couldn't stand it. "Hello?" she said into the phone.

"They took her to the emergency room."

"Who?" Natalie asked, getting out of her chair.

Bella sounded breathless. "Mac. The pain got so bad that she fainted. Mr. Burke called nine-one-one. The old one."

"What pain?" Natalie asked, confused.

"Her stomach. She got all sweaty and dizzy and said it hurt. I guess it started yesterday or the day before. She was saying she didn't feel good, and then she just fell over."

"Are you with her?" Natalie asked, grabbing her handbag.

"They wouldn't let me go in the ambulance. I'm going to my car now."

"I'm on my way," Natalie said numbly. Lowering the phone,

292 / *Colleen French*

she said to Laney., "I have to go. Mac was taken from work to the emergency department."

Laney came out of her chair. "What's wrong?"

"I don't know. Mac's been taken to the ED." Natalie took a deep breath and walked out of the gazebo. "You can get Nana back to her room?" she asked.

"Of course. Go, go, and text me as soon as you find out what's going on!" Laney called after her. "I'll be there as soon as I can get there."

Natalie didn't respond as she autodialed Conor and took off across the wet grass at a run.

CHAPTER 35

"How can this be happening?" Natalie murmured, pacing the tiny exam room in the emergency department of the hospital. "A kid taken to the hospital by ambulance twice in one summer?" She pressed her hand to her forehead. She'd never had a panic attack before, but she felt like she was fighting one. She took a deep, slow breath and then another. "Before this summer, the last time we were in here was when Mason cut his forehead jumping out of his bunk bed when he was six."

"It happens, Nat," Conor said calmly. Because he was always the calm one. He was sitting in the only chair in the room. He'd offered it to Natalie several times, but she refused to sit, so he did. "She's going to be fine. You heard the doc. Pain in the lower abdomen, a temp, nausea, and vomiting. It's a classic case of appendicitis."

"Then why does she need a CT scan?" Natalie worried.

"To confirm the diagnosis," he answered patiently. "So the doc doesn't open her up for an appendectomy when she doesn't need it. It's an easy, definitive way to diagnose appendicitis. You don't want them cutting her open if that's not what's wrong."

"But what else could it be?" Natalie reached the wall where

294 / Colleen French

various monitors were mounted, turned, then went back toward the privacy curtain between them and the open corridor. "Ovarian cysts? Something worse." The word *cancer* floated in her head, but she didn't say it. The possibility was too awful to speak aloud.

He leaned back in the chair. He was wearing cargo shorts and a pale blue polo with *O'Sullivan's* embroidered on it. Looking at him, she realized he'd lost weight. When had that happened? He didn't look bad, just different.

Conor pulled out his phone and thumbed the screen. "I say we go with appendicitis until that's not the diagnosis."

"Right. You're right." She glanced at the large institutional clock on the wall. "But what's taking so long? Shouldn't she be back by now? I feel like she should be back."

McKenzie had been gone half an hour. The tech who had taken her had said no one else was allowed in the scan room, so it was better that Natalie and Conor stay where they were. Mac would be brought back to the exam room. Natalie hadn't liked the idea of being separated from her daughter when she was in so much pain, but she had understood the logic of just staying here. Now she was beginning to regret the decision. She should have at least walked with McKenzie to Radiology.

Natalie and Conor had arrived in the emergency department at the same time and immediately been escorted back to where McKenzie was lying in a hospital bed, sweaty and barely coherent. The nurse with her had explained her symptoms and told them she'd been given pain medication. Natalie had stood at her daughter's bedside and held her hand. She hadn't been able to tell if Mac was in too much pain to acknowledge her or if she was ignoring her. It didn't matter which it was. The moment Natalie had seen Mac's flushed face, her deepest maternal instincts had kicked in and she'd been overwhelmed by the need to care for her child. When the tech had wheeled McKenzie out of the room for her scan, Natalie had felt as if Mac was being ripped from her arms.

"Do you think they decided not to bring her back down?" Natalie asked Conor as she walked past him again. "Did they take her right to the operating room?"

"She'll be back soon." He grabbed her hand and rose from the chair. "Come on, Nat. You're making *me* nervous now. Sit down and stop fretting. She's going to be fine."

"But she's my little girl." Natalie choked on her words. All she could think about was the conversation she'd had with McKenzie the night before. McKenzie had been so angry with her about Bella and the pregnancy test. Had still been angry when she'd left for work that morning. "She's my baby," she said, her voice cracking as tears ran down her cheeks.

"I know, I know." He pulled her into a bear hug. "And she's going to be fine," he soothed. "Your baby is going to be fine."

"But she could die. People die having an appendectomy. Something goes wrong with the anesthesia, and . . . and, anything could happen."

"She's not going to die, Nat," Conor insisted, still holding her. "Surgeons do appendectomies every day. I had one when I was seventeen and I'm fine. Shay had one, too. He's fine. We're both fine."

Natalie slid her arms around Conor's neck and held on tightly, thinking to herself about what a mess she'd made of their summer. In the spring, she'd been so looking forward to spending time with her children, with McKenzie in particular. Because she began driving on her own this school year, Natalie knew McKenzie wouldn't be home anymore. She'd done the same thing at sixteen, but these summer months should have been ones to savor. Instead, Natalie had made their home into a war zone.

"She's so angry with me, Conor."

"Shhh," he hushed, rubbing her back. "Of course she is. She's a teenage girl. It's in their DNA."

"No, this is my fault. I did this." Her tears were making his shirt damp. "I dug this divide between us."

"Nat, it's okay." He leaned back and gazed into her eyes. "They don't come with service manuals. Kids. You're doing your best, just like the rest of us."

There was a sound of footsteps on the other side of the curtain and a woman in her mid-fifties in scrubs walked in. She was wearing a batik-print scrub cap and blue eyeglasses. "Mr. and Mrs. Sullivan?"

Natalie let go of Conor and wiped at her eyes. "Yes?" she and Conor said in unison.

"I'm Dr. Naomi Kimothi, McKenzie's surgeon." She shook their hands. "I consulted with Dr. Martin, who saw your daughter first, and we've got our confirmation. It's that pesky appendix, all right." The tall, thin woman seemed quite pleased with the diagnosis. "She'll be back down here in the few next minutes, we'll get her prepped, and I'll remove the appendix laparoscopically. I will tell you that I'm a little concerned that it's ruptured. From what McKenzie could tell me, the pain started at least two days ago, and the CT does show signs of a possible rupture, but I want be sure until I have a look."

"Two days ago?" Natalie murmured in disbelief. She had thought McKenzie didn't look right the night before, but she hadn't pushed it. Why hadn't she asked her to be more specific about her pain when Mac told her she didn't feel well?

"But you'll be able to take it out, even if it's ruptured?" Conor asked, sounding more concerned now than he'd been before.

"I will. But whether it's ruptured will dictate the treatment. Not ruptured, she'll be out of here in the morning. If it has ruptured, there will have been spill into the abdominal cavity. Bacteria and other disgusting stuff. I'll clean it out, possibly leave a drain in for a few days, and she'll be on IV antibiotics."

"She'll have to stay in the hospital?" Natalie asked, feeling light-headed. How could her child have been sick and she didn't know it? She felt terrible. Like a terrible mother. The terrible mother she was.

"IV antibiotics are the way we go in these cases. At least initially," Dr. Kimothi explained. "Let's see what we've got first, and then we'll go from there."

"Can I stay with her in the hospital?" Natalie asked, not sure she could leave McKenzie tonight even if they said she had to.

The doctor smiled as if she understood what was going through Natalie's head. "I imagine we can arrange that."

Conor rested his hand on Natalie's shoulder, maybe because he could see her shaking. "You said someone will bring her back here before you take her to the OR?"

"Sure will. You'll have time for kisses and good-byes while all the paperwork is prepared." She gestured. "We'll need signatures and such. And then I'll be back in to explain the procedure to everyone and see if there are any questions." She clapped her hands together. "And then we'll roll. Don't worry, I've done three of these in the last week. She'll be fine. If it's ruptured, that makes things a little more complicated, which is why we're doing the surgery now. But I've got a good team." The smile again. "We're going to take good care of her."

She walked out through the part in the curtain wall and then stepped back in again. "Almost forgot. The radiologist confirmed the arm is fractured. McKenzie's got an Aircast on it right now, but someone from Ortho will be in in the morning to get a better look and decide if it needs a full cast."

Natalie stared at the doctor in confusion. "Her *arm*?" She'd been covered with a sheet, so Natalie hadn't seen anything but her flushed face.

Dr. Kimothi frowned. "No one told you? She broke her arm when she fainted and fell. She said she fell into the hermit crabs? I have no idea what that means." She gave a wave. "See you shortly."

The following two hours were a whirlwind, and Natalie couldn't tell if two minutes had passed or two days. McKenzie was barely back in the ER exam room before being whisked off for surgery. Conor and Natalie both talked to her, but she only acknowledged her father, which set Natalie off pacing again once they were in the surgery waiting room. While Conor returned to the ER waiting area to let Laney and Bella and Beth, Patrick, and Mason know what was going on and send them home, Natalie had the chance to work herself into a frenzy.

She didn't pray often, but as she paced, she thought about how foolish she had been to take so much for granted in her life—especially McKenzie. Laney had been right; Mac was such a good kid and Natalie had lost sight of that.

Natalie alternated between praying for her daughter's safety and making promises to God in exchange for saving McKenzie's life. Natalie promised to be a better wife, a better mother, a better business partner. She vowed to spend more time listening and less talking. The one subject she didn't broach with God was Bella. Because she just couldn't go there right now. She didn't think she had the strength.

An hour and thirty-five minutes after Natalie and Conor kissed McKenzie good-bye, Dr. Kimothi entered the surgical waiting room, which was thankfully empty. Probably because it was evening and all of the scheduled surgeries had been over hours ago. The surgeon reported that McKenzie's appendix *had* ruptured but that she'd done a nice *cleanup* and she expected a full recovery.

"I'm going to go home to my sixteen-year-old and give her a hug," Dr. Kimothi told them from the doorway, "and someone will come for you in a few minutes to take you into Recovery, where yours should be coming around soon. Unfortunately, only one of you can go, but I imagine she'll be in her room in an hour, hour and a half, tops."

Natalie and Conor thanked the doctor repeatedly, and the minute she walked out of the room Natalie said, "I'll go. I need to go." She looked up at him. "I know she doesn't want me there, but I need to be there when she wakes up."

Conor put his arm around her and kissed the top of her head. "Of course you can go. I'll run home and get your toothbrush and sweats and stuff and grab something for us to eat. I haven't eaten since lunch."

Natalie pressed her hand to her queasy stomach. "I can't eat."

"So I'll bring you some crackers in case you get hungry later."

A young man dressed in blue scrubs walked in. "Mrs. Sullivan?" He smiled. "I'm here to take you to Recovery."

Five minutes later, Natalie stood beside a hospital gurney brushing hair from McKenzie's face. The teen was no longer flushed but now pale and cool to the touch. Her right arm was wrapped in an Aircast, an IV inserted in the left.

Natalie watched as McKenzie's eyelashes fluttered.

"Hey, sleepyhead," Natalie murmured.

McKenzie rolled her head slowly back and forth, her eyes closing again. "Mom?" Her voice was gravelly.

"I'm right here," Natalie said, taking her hand and squeezing it. As their hands touched, she felt a closeness with her daughter that she hadn't felt in a very long time. And she realized that the teen still needed her, even if it was in a different capacity than she'd needed her when she was younger. The connection was still there, and maybe it had been all along. It was just different. "The surgery's over and the doctor says you're going to be just fine. A couple of days of antibiotics and you'll be out of here. Good as new."

McKenzie nodded and then murmured, "Mom?"

"Still here," Natalie told her, wishing she could hold her daughter in her arms the way she had when McKenzie was a baby.

"Don't leave, Mom," she said, her eyes remaining closed.

Tears slid down Natalie's cheeks. "I won't, sweetie."

CHAPTER 36

Mac held out her hand, making sure not to kink her IV line as she admired her freshly painted fingernails. Bella had done them for her, alternating between robin's-egg blue and grass green. "Thanks. I love it."

Bella dropped the bottles of polish into her crocheted shoulder bag hanging off her chair. "I knew you would. The blue's nice with your skin tone." She sat back in the chair that Mac's mother had vacated.

To Mac's surprise, when Bella had shown up her mother had said hi and then excused herself to go to the car to get her laptop. She'd spoken to Bella but not acted any different than she did with any of Mac's other friends. Which was a relief because while Mac was feeling a hell of a lot better than she had when she'd come in by ambulance two days ago, she wasn't up to dealing with any weirdness from her mother.

The even odder thing about her behavior was that she hadn't been acting crazy at all since Mac got to the hospital. About anything. She hadn't been overly emotional about Mac's appendicitis, and she hadn't bitched her out about not telling anyone how much pain she'd been in sooner. Having her mom act like a normal person had made everything that had happened in the last two days seen not quite so awful. The night of her surgery Mac had been too beat to care that her mother was spending the night, but the previous night she'd been glad she was there. Not that Mac couldn't spend a night somewhere without her mommy, but she felt like she hurt everywhere and just getting to the bathroom had been hard.

Mac was uncomfortable telling a nurse she had to pee, even though she had the little button to call them for anything she needed. But she didn't mind getting her mom to help her to the bathroom. They had a system going where Mac walked like an old lady, bent over with a pillow against her stomach, to the bathroom, while her mother pushed the IV pole. Mac hadn't even had to ask her to give her some privacy in the bathroom. Her mother had just stepped outside, closed the door, and told Mac to let her know when she was ready to get back in bed. She'd even assured Mac that she didn't look like an old lady in her hospital gown because of the bike shorts she was wearing. Bike shorts her mother had had the forethought to pack when she'd brought Mac's underwear and a toothbrush and stuff.

"So what's going on at work?" Mac asked, lying back on the pillows her mother had piled up for her. She had no idea where she'd gotten the extra pillows; she'd just walked into the room carrying them. It was some kind of magic mom thing she did. She could make an extra blanket or a Coke appear out of nowhere. Whatever Mac wanted, her mother found it.

"Let's see." Bella slipped her feet out of her flip-flops and propped them on the edge of Mac's hospital bed. Her toenails were painted the same alternating shades as Mac's fingernails. "Yesterday was Darren's last day and we had one of those big cookie things to celebrate. He goes back to Clemson Sunday. Oh, and Mr. Burke the Younger has a black eye. He says he got hit with a ball playing tennis, but we're wondering if Mrs. Burke clobbered him." She popped her gum. "Oh, and the security cameras captured your dive into the hermit crab cage—"

"I did not *dive* into the cage," Mac protested, laughing, even though she was embarrassed. Especially now, knowing she'd been captured on film. "I fainted. Probably when my appendix burst. Nobody has control of where they fall when they faint."

"We all watched it like ten times in the office," Bella went on, laughing, too. "Before Mr. Burke the Older bitched us out and erased it."

Mac closed her eyes, covering them with her palm while being careful not to smudge her wet polish. "I'll never live this down. I'm glad I can't go back to work."

"I thought you were going to work weekends through the fall."

"That was when you were going to still be here. And I didn't have a broken arm." Mac took the emery board Bella had given her and scratched her itchy wrist just under the edge of the Air-cast. Because her arm had a hairline fracture, the doctor had told her he would give her a removable cast so she could shower and stuff. But only if she promised to wear the cast, except when showering.

Mac looked up at Bella. "I'm glad you decided to go to college this year. I didn't think your plan to go to Tahiti was all that good."

Bella laughed, tucking her hair behind her ear. She'd bleached it so blond that it almost looked white. It didn't look as pretty as her natural color with the highlights, but Mac hadn't told her that because what would be the point? It would take years to grow out now.

"That's just because you're a chicken and don't understand the fun of an unplanned adventure," Bella said.

"You tell Gunner you're leaving?"

"No, but I don't think he cares. He got that job at the motel out on One and he's been talking about this girl he met there who's from Russia. Luda." She made a face. "What kind of a name is Loo-da?" she asked, drawing out the first syllable. "Loo-da can have him. He's a douche."

Mac closed one eye. "Ouch, that's harsh. You were kind of going out with him all summer."

"Not really." Bella nudged Mac's leg, covered with a white sheet, with her bare foot. "And you didn't like him to begin with."

"Still don't." Mac shifted uncomfortably in the bed. Her whole abdomen still hurt. Not like when she passed out at work. It had hurt so bad then that she'd been sick to her stomach. This was more of a dull ache everywhere that hurt when she moved. "You can do better," she told her friend, using the exact phrase Bella had used talking about Matthew. Luckily, he wasn't coming by to see her until later, after Bella was due at work. Mac had arranged it purposely that way.

"So you still haven't asked me," Bella said.

"Asked you about what?

Bella rolled her suntanned shoulders. "My surprise. I told you I had a surprise."

"You did?" Mac frowned. "When?"

"Last night, when I was texting you." Bella sounded hurt. "Remember? I told you something had been going on, but I was keeping it to myself until I knew for sure?"

"Sorry. I was kind of drugged up still." Mac picked up her cell phone but didn't look for the messages Bella had sent. "And you texted a lot last night."

"So it worked." Bella scooted forward in the chair, getting closer to the bed. "I found her," she said, smiling.

Mac had no idea what she was talking about. "You found who?"

"My birth mother." Bella rolled her eyes. "Who else would I be talking about?"

Mac sat up in bed, then cringed because she moved too fast. She pressed her hand to where her stitches were from her surgery. "Oh my God. You did? *How?*"

"The DNA test." Bella grinned. "She was already registered. I found her and I did what you told me I should do. I told my

304 / Colleen French

mom and you're not going to believe this, but she isn't even pissed. She said she'd take me to see her."

"Your birth mother wants to meet you?" Mac grabbed Bella's hands, not caring if she messed up her nails. "Oh my God, when? Where?"

"She lives in Wisconsin now. Even though I was born in Delaware. I don't know the story yet." Bella pulled her hands away. "But my mom is flying with me to meet her."

Mac opened her eyes wide, shaking her head. She was so happy for Bella. Maybe knowing where she came from would help her figure out where she wanted to go in life. Maybe it would help her make better choices than Gunner. "That is crazy."

"I kind of wanted to go by myself. In case she's a complete bust—her name is Cynthia. But Mom said she'd fly there with me and we could decide later if I wanted her there when I actually meet her." She shrugged. "Whatever."

"Bella, that is so amazing," Mac said, genuinely happy for her. "Because even if your birth mother is a bust, at least then you'll know."

"I guess." Bella chewed on her lower lip. "Except now I'm worried. What if she doesn't like me? She's really pretty. But older than I thought she would be. I always assumed she was a teenage mom. She wasn't. She was thirty-five when she had me."

"Wow," Mac breathed. "And . . . do you have a brother? A sister?"

"I don't know. We just emailed each other. I didn't talk on the phone to her yet. Anyway, so that's my news." Bella looked at her Apple watch. "And if I don't go now, I'm going to be late for work. I had to park like in Dover and walk all the way here. I told Mr. Burke I'd work through Sunday, but then I'm outta here. We leave Monday and—"

"Wait," Mac interrupted. "You're going to see your birth mom *this* week?"

"I told you I was going to go meet her."

"I know," Mac said. "But I thought you meant like some-time. Like in the future."

"Nope. We leave Monday morning, fly back Tuesday night, and I check into my dorm on Friday. Some kind of freshman orientation bullshit." She got out of the chair. "But Mom said we could go shopping Thursday in D.C. I'm getting all new bedding and towels and those expensive jeans I really wanted."

Mac smiled up at her. The last couple of weeks, she'd been half hoping Bella would go to college and leave Albany Beach, because she realized that her friend wasn't exactly everything she'd thought she was and the friendship was kind of getting lame. In some ways, Bella seemed younger than Mac. She just kept making bad choices. And she could be kind of mean, and it was beginning to become a problem between them. But Mac wasn't mad with her anymore for all her crap, even that stunt she'd pulled calling her mom to get the stupid pregnancy test.

"Am I going to see you before you go?" Mac asked, suddenly feeling sad that Bella was moving away.

"I'll be back tomorrow. You'll be here another day, right?"

"At least until tomorrow. Hopefully, I can go home at din-nertime, after I have my last dose of antibiotic."

"*Gucci*," Bella said, slinging her bag over her shoulder. "And I'll be back Labor Day weekend. I have to go for this freshman bullshit, but classes don't start until the Tuesday after Labor Day. Maybe we can go out for Thrasher's fries one more time."

Mac nodded. "Sounds good." She flung off the sheet. She needed to go to the bathroom again. Because of the IV, probably. But the bathroom looked so far away. "Hey, if my mom's out there, can you tell her I need her?"

CHAPTER 37

Natalie rested her hand against the wall outside McKenzie's room, feeling as if someone had just kicked her in the stomach. She hadn't meant to eavesdrop. She tried not to do that with her kids—with anyone. She'd just stopped at the doorway to listen to see if Bella was still there. If she was, Natalie had decided she would go to the waiting room around the corner from Mac's room and do a little work on her laptop until the visit was over.

She hadn't meant to overhear their conversation.

McKenzie had given Bella the DNA test Natalie and Conor had gifted Mac for her birthday.

And Bella had used it to find her birth mother.

And it wasn't Natalie.

Bella wasn't her daughter.

She wasn't her baby.

Natalie closed her eyes for a moment, feeling dizzy. Upended. Feeling like . . . like she'd lost that little baby she'd never held all over again. It felt like someone had ripped a Band-Aid off a wound. No, like someone had ripped one of her limbs off.

For a moment, it felt like a big, gaping wound that would kill her.

But it wasn't. Didn't.

She took several deep breaths until she felt like she wouldn't make a fool of herself and collapse in the hall; then she opened her eyes.

Bella wasn't her baby. She wasn't her child. She had never been her child and Natalie had been wrong. She'd been wrong and she'd made herself crazy, made a mess of her family life based on that mistake.

Bella isn't my daughter.

The thought kept running through her head like a ticker tape.

Bella wasn't her daughter. She hadn't found her lost daughter.

As if conjured by the thought of her, Bella walked out of McKenzie's hospital room. "Oh, there you are." The teenager, who was not Natalie's child, smiled at her. "Mac's looking for you." She tilted her head in the direction of the open door, her long, freshly bleached blond hair rippling over her shoulder.

"Mom?" McKenzie called from the room. "Could you help me? I kinda really have to go."

Natalie watched Bella walk away and then rushed into the room to her daughter. To the daughter she knew. And loved.

CHAPTER 38

Natalie stared at her reflection in the bathroom mirror as she brushed her teeth. Her face looked a little thinner, but she wasn't sure if it was her imagination. Or wishful thinking. She would be down three pounds when she went to her pre-op appointment with Pixie Patty tomorrow, but she felt no sense of guilt for not losing more weight. She'd let that go along with so many other worries she'd had that summer.

Natalie was trying to give herself some grace. Maybe she hadn't lost as much weight as her gynecologist wanted, but she'd made healthy improvements in her lifestyle. *While keeping a few less-than-healthy habits like a beer at the pub.* She could now keep up with her sister walking, and when Laney had to miss one of their daily walks because of work or plans with her new boyfriend, Natalie walked the three miles alone. And didn't mind. She was now eating more green stuff and far less sugar and keeping an eye on her carbs. Nothing crazy, but she was trying to make her diet more balanced. The changes seemed to be helping. While she hadn't dropped a clothes size, everything in her closet fit better. More importantly, she felt better.

She rinsed her mouth out and blotted with a hand towel, meeting her own gaze again.

That afternoon, Labor Day, Bella had stopped by to say good-bye. She'd brought McKenzie a University of Maryland sweatshirt and told the whole family about her trip to Wisconsin to meet her birth mother. Bella had seemed emotionally disconnected as she told them about how her birth mother had given her up for adoption because she'd been unemployed, recently divorced with three kids to care for, and could not afford to care for another child. She talked as if her birth mother had been some stranger she'd bumped into at a restaurant. Bella had spent more time during her visit talking about her new roommate and a guy in her co-ed dorm who was hot.

As the teenager rattled on, Natalie had continued to prepare dinner for the family. A part of her had wanted to speak to Bella privately and ask her why she had misrepresented her home life, why she had *ingratiated* herself with Natalie's family, with Natalie in particular. But somewhere between adding the cilantro to the rice and grating cheese, Natalie realized it didn't matter. More importantly, she didn't care all that much.

Once McKenzie was safely home from the hospital and it was apparent that she would be fine, Natalie had felt herself relax with a massive sigh of relief. Mac was going to be okay. They were all going to be okay. And while Natalie had occasional pangs of guilt for putting her family through so much in one summer, she found that giving herself grace was the greatest gift she could give them. And give herself. Because a guilt-ridden mother, wife, sister, granddaughter couldn't be everything she needed to be for those she loved.

At this point, Natalie was almost thankful that Bella had come into their lives for this short time because Natalie realized now how much she had taken for granted. Mac was such an amazing kid—*young woman*—and she had somehow lost sight of that. But she was seeing Mac as she was now and trying to appreciate all her good traits and not fixate on the ones she didn't care for.

As Laney had told her over and over again, Natalie had so much to be thankful for. She was so blessed. Yes, she'd suffered from getting pregnant and putting her baby up for adoption, but as her nana had pointed out, at least Natalie had had a choice. Unlike Nana's birth mother.

"Hey, you coming to bed?" Conor called from their bedroom.

"Almost done." Natalie dropped her toothbrush into its holder. Tucking a lock of hair behind her ear, she walked into the bedroom to find the room dim with battery-lit candles on every surface in the room. "What's all this?" she asked with a smile of surprise.

Conor must have gathered every candle she had in the house and placed them around the room when she'd gone into the bathroom to shower and get ready for bed. Soft music played from a mini speaker. He was lying in bed, shirtless, the sheet pulled up to his waist.

"My awkward attempt to romance my wife?" he asked, sounding uncharacteristically unsure of himself.

"Wish I'd known," Natalie teased. "I'd have dressed for a date." She indicated the oversized O'Sullivan's T-shirt she was wearing.

"I think you're a bit overdressed." He lifted the corner of the sheet for her.

Natalie slid into the cool, fresh sheets and rolled onto her side to face him. "Thank you," she said, smiling, gazing into his handsome face.

He stroked her cheek with the back of his hand. "For what?"

She shrugged. "For not divorcing me and running off with a perfectly good waitress. For putting up with my neurotic behavior."

"I knew when we married that I'd never get bored with you."

She laughed. "You're more gracious than I deserve."

"Not more than you deserve, Nat. Come here." He opened his arm to her.

She snuggled into his embrace, resting her hand on his bare chest. "I'm glad Bella stopped by to say good-bye to Mac. I don't know if we'll see her again."

"Yeah, she's a bit of wild card, isn't she?" he said, stroking Natalie's arm.

She chuckled. "That's a kind way of putting it." She sighed and closed her eyes, enjoying the warmth of her husband's embrace and the security of it.

"I haven't said this to you," Conor said quietly, "but I'm sorry it wasn't her."

"I don't know that I am," Natalie admitted. "I mean, how awkward would that have been? If she had been my birth child. With the girls being friends first, and Mac not knowing I had a baby before her."

"Pretty awkward," he agreed.

They were both quiet for a moment, and then he asked, "Are you going to keep looking? For your daughter?"

"I don't know," she said, looking into his blue eyes, remembering all the reasons why she'd fallen in love with him so long ago. "Maybe I should leave it up to her. Let her find me if she wants to, someday."

Conor drew his thumb across Natalie's cheek. "If she's even half the woman you are, she will."

THE SUMMER DAUGHTER

ABOUT THIS GUIDE

The suggested questions are included to enhance your group's
reading of Colleen French's *The Summer Daughter*!

DISCUSSION QUESTIONS

1. Why do you think Natalie jumped so quickly to the conclusion that Bella might be her daughter? What were the underlying reasons?

2. If you had been in Natalie's situation in college, would you have considered adoption? Why or why not? Did she make the wrong choice?

3. Do you think Conor reacted appropriately when Natalie told him she thought Bella might be her daughter? Could he have handled his response better? How do you feel about his stand on the adoption?

4. Do you think Natalie's role as McKenzie and Mason's mother was affected by the fact that she put her first baby up for adoption? How and why?

5. Why do you think Bella became so friendly with Natalie? Was their relationship appropriate? Who was responsible for how it developed?

6. Do you think that Natalie could have handled her relationship with McKenzie differently? How did the loss of her first daughter affect her relationship with Mac?

7. Do you think Laney was as supportive of her sister as she could have been? How do you think her own life affected her advice?

8. Do you think Natalie and Conor had a strong marriage? Do you think the events of the summer, over time, would strengthen or weaken their relationship?

9. If you had been Natalie, would you have wanted to know if Bella was your daughter? Why or why not?

10. What are your experiences with adoption, and how have they shaped your beliefs on the subject?

Visit us online at
KensingtonBooks.com
to read more from your favorite authors,
see books by series, view reading
group guides, and more!

BOOK **CLUB**

BETWEEN THE CHAPTERS

Visit us online for sneak peeks, exclusive
giveaways, special discounts, author content,
and engaging discussions with your fellow readers.

Betweenthechapters.net

Sign up for our newsletters and be the first
to get exciting news and announcements about
your favorite authors!
Kensingtonbooks.com/newsletter